P9-DEI-462

CRIME THROUGH TIME III

Steven Saylor tells a tale of adultery and political intrigue in ancient Rome in "The Consul's Wife" ... Master of science fiction *Harry Turtledove* offers his first mystery story, "Farmer's Law" ... *Maureen Jennings*'s "The Weeping Time" relates events following the execution of Sir Thomas More ... *Elizabeth Foxwell* presents a mystery in Theodore Roosevelt's White House in "Come Flit by Me" ... and many more stories featuring a fascinating array of periods, people, and places throughout history ...

MORE MYSTERIES FROM THE
BERKLEY PUBLISHING GROUP...

SISTER FREVISSE MYSTERIES: Medieval mystery in the tradition of
Ellis Peters...

by Margaret Frazer

THE NOVICE'S TALE	THE SERVANT'S TALE	THE BOY'S TALE
THE OUTLAW'S TALE	THE BISHOP'S TALE	THE MURDERER'S TALE
THE PRIORESS' TALE	THE MAIDEN'S TALE	THE REEVE'S TALE

PENNYFOOT HOTEL MYSTERIES: In Edwardian England, death takes
a seaside holiday...

by Kate Kingsbury

ROOM WITH A CLUE	DO NOT DISTURB	PAY THE PIPER
SERVICE FOR TWO	EAT, DRINK, AND BE BURIED	CHIVALRY IS DEAD
CHECK-OUT TIME	GROUNDS FOR MURDER	RING FOR TOMB SERVICE
DEATH WITH RESERVATIONS	DYING ROOM ONLY	MAID TO MURDER

GLYNIS TRYON MYSTERIES: The highly acclaimed series set in the
early days of the women's rights movement... "Historically accurate and
telling."—Sara Paretsky

by Miriam Grace Monfredo

SENECA FALLS INHERITANCE	NORTH STAR CONSPIRACY	THE STALKING-HORSE
BLACKWATER SPIRITS	THROUGH A GOLD EAGLE	MUST THE MAIDEN DIE

MARK TWAIN MYSTERIES: "Adventurous... Replete with genuine
tall tales from the great man himself."—*Mostly Murder*

by Peter J. Heck

DEATH ON THE MISSISSIPPI
A CONNECTICUT YANKEE IN CRIMINAL COURT
THE PRINCE AND THE PROSECUTOR

MAGGIE MAGUIRE MYSTERIES: A thrilling new series...

by Kate Bryan

MURDER AT BENT ELBOW	MURDER ON THE BARBARY COAST
A RECORD OF DEATH	

CRIME THROUGH TIME III

EDITED BY
Sharan Newman

INTRODUCTION BY
Anne Perry

BERKLEY PRIME CRIME, NEW YORK

If you purchased this book without a cover, you should be aware that this book is stolen property. It was reported as "unsold and destroyed" to the publisher and neither the author nor the publisher has received any payment for this "stripped book."

This is a work of fiction. Names, characters, places, and incidents are either the product of the author's imagination or are used fictitiously, and any resemblance to actual persons, living or dead, business establishments, events, or locales is entirely coincidental.

CRIME THROUGH TIME III

A Berkley Prime Crime Book / published by arrangement with the editor

PRINTING HISTORY
Berkley Prime Crime edition / June 2000

All rights reserved.
Copyright © 2000 by Sharan Newman.
This book may not be reproduced in whole or in part, by mimeograph or any other means, without permission. For information address: The Berkley Publishing Group, A division of Penguin Putnam Inc., 375 Hudson Street, New York, New York 10014.

The Penguin Putnam Inc. World Wide Web site address is http://www.penguinputnam.com

ISBN: 0-425-17509-X

Berkley Prime Crime Books are published by The Berkley Publishing Group, a division of Penguin Putnam Inc., 375 Hudson Street, New York, New York 10014. The name BERKLEY PRIME CRIME and the BERKLEY PRIME CRIME design are trademarks belonging to Penguin Putnam Inc.

PRINTED IN THE UNITED STATES OF AMERICA

10 9 8 7 6 5 4 3 2 1

"The Consul's Wife" © 2000 by Steven Saylor

"Merchants of Discord" © 2000 by Laura Frankos

"Farmer's Law" © 2000 by Harry Turtledove

"The Case of the Murdered Pope" © 2000 by Andrew Greeley

"Lark in the Morning" © 2000 by Sharyn McCrumb

"The Weeping Time" © 2000 by Maureen Jennings

"The Irish Widower" © 2000 by Leonard Tourney

"Smoke" © 2000 by William Sanders

"The Episode of the Water Closet" © 2000 by Bruce Alexander

"Suspicion" © 2000 by Michael Coney

"Murder in Utopia" © 2000 by Peter Robinson

"Dr. Death" © 2000 by Peter Lovesey

"Dinner with H.P.B." © 2000 by Eileen Kernaghan

"The Haunting of Carrick Hollow" © 2000 by Jan Burke and Paul Sledzik

"Howard" © 2000 by H.R.F. Keating

"Come Flit By Me" © 2000 by Elizabeth Foxwell

"Murder on the Denver Express" © 2000 by Margaret Coel

"A Single Spy" © 2000 by Miriam Grace Monfredo

CONTENTS

VIII · CONTENTS

Introduction

We categorize stories by genres to help us find what we want on the bookshelves. I suppose it serves a purpose, although many of the best defy labels. "Historical crime" does promise certain things, and for me at least, it is a very definite lure.

But the recorded past stretches behind us for six hundred years, and one could always guess and invent beyond that! "Crime Through Time" could touch on tragedy and evil in any of our rich, wild, and varied yesterdays, anywhere over the earth, the passions and sins of civilizations long buried where grass grows now, and the owl and the lizard keep watch.

This collection of stories ranges from the violent and the macabre of our near past, as in Peter Lovesey's "Dr. Death," to Steven Saylor's humorous realism in the teeming, sophisticated ancient Rome of "The Consul's Wife." We have the subtle and delicate conscience of H.R.F. Keating's "Howard," in a more recent India. I always find his explorations of right and wrong immeasurably pleasing.

We have the fierce, intimate grief of a war widow, past and present meeting in true understanding, a seamless fabric of our common humanity in Miriam Grace Monfredo's "A Single Spy." Perhaps that is the great gift of the best historical writing, not only to bring the past and its people to life, but to make us urgently aware of all we have in common with others, regardless of time, place, and culture. Love and hate are the same, the sense of fear and guilt, the need to know the truth, the burdens of living with it when we do, the seeking for justice and a measure of mercy.

Daily life may be very different, and yet in "Farmer's Law" set in the Byzantine Empire, as one who lives in the country, I saw excellent sense in their rules. How like us they were!

In "The Case of the Murdered Pope," how unlike us! I hope! And yet the shadows of our political corruption are there only too clearly. And how fascinating the history was! What intrigue . . . what people! The story's postscript has lit a whole new fire of hunger for knowledge in me. Now I *have* to read more about the entire dynasty. Who else could possibly make the Borgias pale into sorry innocence by comparison? Don't you have to find out, too?

What a contrast is the anchorite in Sharyn McCrumb's "Lark in the Morning," alone in her sunken cell with its one eye-level window to the green outside world. And yet she knows the world and its sins as only the observant can, who has time to watch, to listen, and to think. And she has ways of bringing justice to pass.

Another man with a subtle conscience is Peter Robinson's hero in "Murder in Utopia," also a man with sudden insights of compassion. Here is produced a world, idealistic and complex, showing that little is as simple as it appears. Why do we learn so little from the past, and treat its lessons with such contempt? Its people are as real as we are and their trials and their victories as sharp.

But in case you think this sounds a trifle heavy, relax and go to a party with Teddy Roosevelt and his highly individual daughter Alice in "Come Flit by Me" and enjoy a little wit and glamour. Or join the "unsinkable" Molly Brown in the "Denver Express."

In fact, pick your time and place, choose your company, real or imaginary, and in the comfort of your best armchair, travel the ages and join in the adventures, discover the solutions, and enjoy yourself! If you learn something new as well, and whet an appetite for more, so much the better!

ANNE PERRY

Preface

When Miriam Grace Monfredo and I conceived the idea of an anthology of original historical mystery stories some six years ago, we had no idea how popular it would be, not only with readers interested in the fascinating and diverse work being done in this field, but also with writers. We were astonished at how many of our friends who wrote either contemporary mysteries or in other genres were really closet historians.

For *Crime Through Time III* several authors known for their historical mysteries have contributed stories. Steven Saylor gives us a new Gordianus the Finder tale. Leonard Tourney and Bruce Alexander have also shared adventures featuring their series characters, Joan and Matthew Stock and Sir John Fielding respectively. I know readers will be delighted with the added insights into the lives of their old friends.

Other historical mystery authors have decided to explore new territory. Peter Lovesey's "Dr. Death" is a far cry from jovial Prince Bertie, and Maureen Jennings has left her native Canada for a story set in England at the time of Henry VIII's break with Rome.

Peter Robinson's confession that he had a degree in history long before he began writing about Inspector Banks was the reason I asked him for a story, and the result, "Murder in Utopia," shows that he still has the knack for solid research along with his writing talent. Another history major, Jan Burke, has left her protagonist, Irene, in Long Beach to team up with forensic specialist, Paul

Sledzik, for a chilling New England tale.

Elizabeth Foxwell and Laura Frankos are both students of history who have only in the past few years begun to translate their knowledge into fiction, but I hope they do it much more, as will the readers of their stories, "Come Flit by Me" and "Merchants of Discord."

Andrew Greeley's novels usually deal with the Irish in America, but in his story "The Case of the Murdered Pope," he reminds us that the Irish were wanderers long before they emigrated to the New World. Sharyn McCrumb writes lyrically about Appalachia and how the past there mingles with the present. But for this collection, she has gone back much further, to the world in which many of the Appalachian ballads were born.

Margaret Coel and H.R.F. Keating both write about modern relationships between very different cultures. In Margaret Coel's books, Vicky Holden is torn between Arapaho tradition and her training as a lawyer. H.R.F. Keating's Inspector Ghote has the same problem in Bombay, treading between Indian custom and a British legal system. They have both given us stories that reflect their interests in a light different from that seen in their series.

Several of the authors in this anthology are primarily known for fantasy and science fiction. Harry Turtledove, however, has written a number of books of "alternate history," a genre he has almost invented, and Michael Coney, especially in his "Gods of the Greataway" books, has created a history of the universe of which we are merely a part. In the last two volumes in this series, he tackles the legend of King Arthur from an entirely new perspective. So I had no qualms about asking these writers to contribute.

In the same vein, Eileen Kernaghan uses both history and mythology in her fantasy work, and the remarkable Madame Blavatsky certainly embodies both.

William Sanders has written in so many genres that one needn't worry about anything he decides to do. I was particularly pleased with his story "Smoke" not just because it's a compelling mystery, but also because he gives us a look at Cherokee society from the inside, with almost no connection to the European invaders.

Finally, I am so grateful to my friend and collaborator (even cohort) Miriam Grace Monfredo. Compiling the first two *Crime Through Time* anthologies was much easier for me with her to share the editing duties. While her schedule made it impossible to work on the present volume, she still contributed a beautiful story, "A Single Spy," that rounds out the book by demonstrating poignantly how the past never really leaves us and how a small incident in history can still change a life today.

Beyond the entertainment that all of these stories gives the reader, the historical mystery reminds us that the past is not just kings, battles, and dates, but people and, as the variety of this collection shows, people not unlike ourselves.

CRIME
THROUGH
TIME III

*S*teven Saylor is the author of the Roma Sub Rosa series of mysteries, set in the age of Julius Caesar and featuring the sleuth Gordianus the Finder, the most recent of which is Rubicon, *in which Gordianus becomes involved in the struggle between Caesar and Pompey and needs all his skill at detection to discover a murderer as well as to keep his own family from being destroyed. Steven has also written an epic novel,* Honor the Dead, *set in his home state of Texas in 1885 and inspired by real-life serial murders that predated Jack the Ripper.*

"The Consul's Wife" is a blend of political intrigue, marital deception, and that most Roman of entertainments, the races at the Circus Maximus. In it Gordianus must once again balance the discovery of the truth with the reality of Roman politics, a feat as difficult as any performed in the ring.

THE CONSUL'S WIFE

Steven Saylor

"Honestly," muttered Lucius Claudius, his nose buried in a scroll, "if you go by these accounts in the *Daily Acts,* you'd think Sertorius was a naughty schoolboy, and his rebellion in Spain a harmless prank. When will the consuls realize the gravity of the situation? When will they take action?"

I cleared my throat.

Lucius Claudius lowered the little scroll and raised his bushy red eyebrows. "Gordianus! By Hercules, you got here in a hurry! Take a seat."

I looked about for a chair, then remembered where I was. In the garden of Lucius Claudius, visitors did not fetch furniture. Visitors sat, and a chair would be slipped beneath them. I stepped into the spot of sunlight where Lucius sat basking and folded my knees. Sure enough, a chair caught my weight. I never even saw the attendant slave.

"Something to drink, Gordianus? I myself am enjoying a cup of hot broth. Too early in the day for wine, even watered."

"Noon is hardly early, Lucius. Not for those of us who've been up since dawn."

"Since dawn?" Lucius grimaced at such a distasteful notion. "A cup of wine for you, then? And some nibbles?"

I raised my hand to wave away the offer, and found it filled with a silver cup into which a pretty slave girl poured a stream of Falernian wine. A little tripod table appeared at my left hand, bearing a silver platter embossed with images of dancing nymphs and strewn with olives, dates, and almonds.

"Care for a bit of the *Daily*? I'm finished with the sporting news." Lucius nodded toward a clutter of little scrolls on the table beside him. "They say the Whites have finally got their act together this season. New chariots, new horses. Should give the Reds a run for the prizes in tomorrow's races."

I laughed out loud. "What a life you lead, Lucius Claudius. Up at noon, then lolling about your garden reading your own private copy of the *Daily Acts*."

Lucius raised an eyebrow. "Merely sensible, if you ask me. Who wants to elbow through a crowd in the Forum, squinting and peering past strangers to read the *Daily* on the posting boards? Or worse, listen to some clown read the items out loud, inserting his own witty comments."

"But that's the whole point of the *Daily*," I argued. "It's a social activity. People take a break from the hustle and bustle of the Forum, gather 'round the posting boards, and discuss whatever items interest them most—war news, marriages and births, chariot races, curious omens. It's the highlight of many a man's day, perusing the *Daily* and arguing politics or horses with fellow citizens. One of the cosmopolitan pleasures of city life."

Lucius shuddered. "No, thank you! My way is better. I send a couple of slaves down to the Forum an hour before posting time. As soon as the *Daily* goes up, one of them reads it aloud from beginning to end, and the other takes dictation with a stylus on wax tablets. Then they hurry home, transcribe the words to parchment, and by the time I'm up and about, my private copy of the *Daily* is here waiting for me in the garden, the ink still drying in the sun. A comfy chair, a sunny spot, a hearty cup of broth, and my own copy of the *Daily Acts*. I tell you, Gordianus, there's no more civilized way to start the day."

I popped an almond into my mouth. "It all seems rather antisocial to me, not to mention extravagant. The cost of parchment alone!"

"Squinting at wax tablets gives me eyestrain." Lucius sipped his broth. "Anyway, I didn't ask you here to critique my personal pleasures, Gordianus. There's something in the *Daily* that I want you to see."

"What, the news about that rebellious Roman general terrorizing Spain?"

"Quintus Sertorius!" Lucius shifted his considerable bulk. "He'll soon have the whole Iberian peninsula under his control. The natives there hate Rome, but they adore Sertorius. What can our two consuls be thinking, failing to bring military assistance to the provincial government? Decimus Brutus, much as I love the old bookworm, is no fighter, I'll grant you; hard to imagine him leading an expedition. But his fellow consul Lepidus is a military veteran; fought for Sulla in the Civil War. How can those two sit idly on their behinds while Sertorius creates a private kingdom for himself in Spain?"

"All that's in the *Daily Acts*?" I asked.

"Of course not!" Lucius snorted. "Nothing but the official government line: situation under control, no cause for alarm. You'll find more details about the obscene earnings of charioteers than you'll find about Spain. What else can you expect? The *Daily* is a state organ put out by the government. Deci probably dictates every word of the war news himself."

"Deci?"

"Decimus Brutus, of course; the consul." With his ancient patrician connections, Lucius tended to be on a first-name—sometimes on a pet-name—basis, with just about everybody in power. "But you distract me, Gordianus. I didn't ask you here to talk about Sertorius. Decimus Brutus, yes; Sertorius, no. Here, have a look at this." His bejeweled hand flitted over the pile and plucked a scroll for me to read.

"Society gossip?" I scanned the items. "A's son engaged to B's daughter. C plays host to D at his country villa. E shares her famous family recipe for egg custard dating back to the days when Romulus was suckled by the she-wolf." I grunted. "All very interesting, but I don't see—"

"Read that part. Aloud." Lucius leaned forward and tapped at the scroll.

" 'The bookworm pokes his head outside tomorrow. Easy prey for the sparrow, but partridges go hungry. Bright-eyed Sappho says: Be suspicious! A dagger strikes faster than lightning. Better yet: an arrow. Let Venus conquer all!' "

Lucius sat back and crossed his fleshy arms. "What do you make of it?"

"I believe it's called a blind item; a bit of gossip conveyed in code. No proper names, only clues that are meaningless to the uninitiated. Given the mention of Venus, I imagine this particular item is about some illicit love affair. I doubt I'd know the names involved even if they were clearly spelled out. You'd be more likely than I to know what all this means, Lucius."

"Indeed. I'm afraid I do know, at least in part. That's why I called you here today, Gordianus. I have a dear friend who needs your help."

I raised an eyebrow. Lucius's rich and powerful connections had yielded me lucrative work before; they had also put me in great danger. "What friend would that be, Lucius?"

He raised a finger. The slaves around us silently withdrew into the house. "Discretion, Gordianus. Discretion! Read the item again."

" 'The bookworm.' "

"And whom did I call a bookworm only a moment ago?"

I blinked. "Decimus Brutus, the consul."

Lucius nodded. "Read on."

" 'The bookworm pokes his head outside tomorrow.' "

"Deci will venture to the Circus Maximus tomorrow, to watch the races from the consular box."

" 'Easy prey for the sparrow.' "

"Draw your own conclusion from that, especially with the mention of daggers and arrows later on!"

I raised an eyebrow. "You think there's a plot against the consul's life, based on a blind item in the *Daily Acts*? It seems farfetched, Lucius."

"It's not what I think. It's what Deci himself thinks. The poor fellow's in a state; came to my house and roused me out of bed an hour ago, desperate for advice. He needs someone to get to the bottom of this, quietly and quickly. I told him I knew just the man: Gordianus the Finder."

"Me?" I scowled at an olive pit between my forefinger and thumb. "Since the *Daily* is a state organ, surely Decimus Brutus himself, as consul, is in the best position to determine where this item came from and what it really means. To start, who wrote it?"

"That's precisely the problem."

"I don't understand."

"Do you see the part about 'Sappho' and her advice?"

"Yes."

"Gordianus, who do you think writes and edits the *Daily Acts*?"

I shrugged. "I never thought about it."

"Then I shall tell you. The consuls themselves dictate the items about politics and foreign policy, giving their own official viewpoint. The drier parts—trade figures, livestock counts, and such—are compiled by clerks in the censor's office. Sporting news comes from the magistrates in charge of the Circus Maximus. Augurs edit the stories that come in about weird lightning flashes, comets, curiously shaped vegetables, and other omens. But who do you think oversees the society news, weddings and birth announcements, social engagements—'blind items,' as you call them?"

"A woman named Sappho?"

"A reference to the poet of ancient Lesbos. The consul's wife is something of a poet herself."

"The wife of Decimus Brutus?"

"She wrote that item." Lucius leaned forward and low-

ered his voice. "Deci thinks she means to kill him, Gordianus."

"My wife." The consul cleared his throat noisily. He
brushed a hand nervously through his silvery hair and paced
back and forth across the large study, from one pigeonhole
bookcase to another, his fingers idly brushing the little title
tags that hung from the scrolls. Outside the library at Al-
exandria, I had never seen so many books in one place, not
even in Cicero's house.

The consul's house was near the Forum, only a short
walk from that of Lucius Claudius. I had been admitted at
once; thanks to Lucius, my visit was expected. Decimus
Brutus dismissed a cadre of secretaries and ushered me into
his private study. He dispensed with formalities. His agi-
tation was obvious.

"My wife." He cleared his throat again. Decimus Brutus,
highest magistrate in the land, used to giving campaign
speeches in the Forum and orations in the courts, seemed
unable to begin.

"She's certainly beautiful," I said, gazing at the portrait
that graced one of the few spaces on the wall not covered
by bookcases. It was a small picture, done in encaustic wax
on wood, yet it dominated the room. A young woman of
remarkable beauty gazed out from the picture. Strings of
pearls adorned the masses of auburn hair done up with
pearl-capped pins atop her head. More pearls hung from
her ears and around her throat. The chaste simplicity of her
jewelry contrasted with a glint in her green eyes that was
challenging, aloof, almost predatory.

Decimus Brutus stepped closer to the painting. He lifted
his chin and squinted, drawing so close that his nose practically brushed the wax.

"Beautiful, yes," he murmured. "The artist didn't capture
even a fraction of her beauty. I married her for it; for that,
and to have a son. Sempronia gave me both, her beauty
and a baby boy. And do you know why she married me?"
The consul stepped disconcertingly close and peered at me.
With another man, I would have taken such proximate scru-

tiny as an effort at intimidation, but the myopic consul was merely straining to read my expression.

He sighed. "Sempronia married me for my books. I know, it sounds absurd, a woman who reads! But there it is: she didn't assent to the marriage until she saw this room, and that made up her mind. She's read every volume here, more than I have! She even writes a bit herself, poetry and such. Her verses are too passionate for my taste."

He cleared his throat again. "Sempronia, you see, is not like other women. Sometimes I think the gods gave her the soul of a man. She reads like a man. She converses like a man. She has her own motley circle of friends—poets, playwrights, women of dubious reputation. When Sempronia has them over, the witticisms roll off her tongue. She even appears to think. She has opinions, anyway. Opinions on everything—art, racing, architecture, even politics! And she has no shame. In the company of her little circle, she plays the lute, better than our best trained slave, I have to admit. And she dances for them." He grimaced. "I told her such behavior was indecent, completely unsuitable for a consul's wife. She says that when she dances, the gods and goddesses speak through her body, and her friends understand what they see, even if I don't. We've had so many rows, I've almost given up rowing about it."

He sighed. "I'll give her this: She's not a bad mother. Sempronia has done a good job raising little Decimus. And despite her youth, her performance of official duties as consul's wife has been impeccable. Nor has she shamed me publicly. She's confined her eccentricities to this house. But . . ."

He seemed to run dry. His chin dropped to his chest.

"One of her duties," I prompted him, "is to oversee society news in the *Daily Acts,* is it not?"

He nodded. He squinted for a moment at Sempronia's portrait, then turned his back to it. "Lucius explained to you the cause for my concern?"

"Only in the most discreet fashion."

"Then I shall be explicit. Understand, Finder, the subject is acutely embarrassing. Lucius tells me you can keep your mouth shut. If I'm wrong, if my suspicions are unfounded, I can't have news of my foolishness spread all over the Forum. And if I'm right, if what I suspect is true, I can afford the scandal even less."

"I understand, Consul."

He stepped very close, peered at my face, and seemed satisfied. "Well, then, where to begin? With that damned charioteer, I suppose."

"A charioteer?"

"Diocles. You've heard of him?"

I nodded. "He races for the Reds."

"I wouldn't know. I don't follow the sport. But I'm told that Diocles is quite famous. And rich, richer even than Roscius the actor. Scandalous, that racers and actors should be wealthier than senators nowadays. Our ancestors would be appalled!"

I doubted that my own ancestors would be quite as upset as those of Decimus Brutus, but I nodded and tried to bring him back to the subject. "This Diocles."

"One of the men in my wife's circle of friends. Only closer than a friend."

"A suspicion, Consul? Or do you have sure knowledge?"

"I have eyes in my head!" He seemed to realize the absurdity of claiming his feeble eyesight as reliable witness, and sighed. "I never caught them in the act, if that's what you mean. I have no proof. But every time she had her circle in this house, lolling about on couches and reciting to each other, the two of them seemed always to end up in a corner by themselves. Whispering, laughing." He ground his jaw. "I won't be made a fool of, allowing my wife to sport with her lover under my own roof! I grew so furious the last time he was here, I . . . I made a scene. I chased them all out, and I told Sempronia that Diocles was never again to enter this house. When she protested, I commanded her never to speak with him again. I'm her husband. It's my right to say with whom she can and cannot consort! Sempronia knows that. Why could she not simply defer to my will? Instead she had to argue. She badgered me like a harpy. I never heard such language from a woman! All the more evidence, if I needed any, that her relationship with that man was beyond decency. In the end, I banned her entire circle of friends, and I ordered Sempronia not to leave the house, even for official obligations. When her duties call, she simply has to say, 'The consul's wife regrets that illness prevents her.' It's been like that for almost a month now. The tension in this house . . ."

"But she does have one official duty left."

"Yes, her dictation of society items for the *Daily Acts.* She needn't leave the house for that. Senators' wives come calling, respectable visitors are still welcome, and they give her all the tidbits she needs. If you ask me, the society section is terribly tedious, even more so than the sporting news. I give it no more than a quick glance to see if family are mentioned and their names spelled correctly. Sempronia knows that. That's why she thought she could send her little message to Diocles through the *Daily Acts,* undetected."

He glanced at the portrait and worked his jaw back and forth. "It was the word *bookworm* that caught my eye. When we were first married, that was the pet name she gave me: 'my old bookworm.' I suppose she calls me that behind my back now, laughing and joking and with the likes of that charioteer!"

"And 'Sappho'?"

"Her friends call her that sometimes."

"Why do you assume the blind item is addressed to Diocles?"

"Despite my disinterest in racing, I do know a thing or two about that particular charioteer, more than I care to! The name of his lead horse is Sparrow. How does the message start? 'The bookworm pokes his head outside tomorrow. Easy prey for the sparrow.' Tomorrow I'll be at the Circus Maximus, to make a public appearance at the races."

"And your wife?"

"Sempronia will remain confined to this house. I have no intention of allowing her to publicly ogle Diocles in his chariot!"

"Won't you be surrounded by bodyguards?"

"In the midst of such a throng, who knows what oppor-

tunities might arise for some accident to befall me? In the
Forum or the Senate House I feel safe, but the Circus Maximus is Diocles' territory. He must know every blind corner, every hiding place. And there's the matter of my
eyesight. I'm more vulnerable than other men, and I know
it. So does Sempronia. So must Diocles."

"Let me be sure I understand, Consul. You take this item
to be a communication between your wife and Diocles, and
the subject is a plot on your life; but you have no other
evidence, and you want me to determine the truth of the
matter?"

"I'll make it worth your while."

"Why turn to me, Consul? Surely a man like yourself
has agents of his own, a finder he trusts to ferret out the
truth about his allies and enemies."

Decimus Brutus nodded haltingly.

"Then why not give this mission to your own finder?"

"I had such a fellow, yes. Called Scorpus. Not long after
I banned Diocles from the house, I set Scorpus to find the
truth about the charioteer and my wife."

"What did he discover?"

"I don't know. Some days ago Scorpus went missing."

"Missing?"

"Until yesterday. His body was fished out of the Tiber,
downriver from Rome. Not a mark on him. They say he
must have fallen in and drowned. Very strange."

"How so?"

"Scorpus was an excellent swimmer."

I left the consul's house with a list of everyone Decimus
Brutus could name from his wife's inner circle, and a pouch
full of silver. The pouch contained half my fee, the re-
mainder to be paid upon the consul's satisfaction. If his
suspicions were correct, and if I failed him, I would never
collect. Dead men pay no debts.

For the rest of the day and long into the night, I learned
all I could about the consul's wife and the charioteer. My
friend Lucius Claudius might move among the rich and
powerful, but I had contacts of my own. The best infor-

mants on Sempronia's circle of intimates, I decided, would be found at the Senian Baths. Such a close-knit group would visit the baths socially, in couples or groups, the men going to their facility and the women to theirs. Massage and a hot soak loosen the tongue; the absence of the opposite gender engenders even greater candor. What masseurs, masseuses, water bearers, and towel boys fail to overhear is hardly worth knowing.

Were Diocles and Sempronia lovers? Maybe, maybe not. According to my informants at the baths, reporting secondhand the gossip of Sempronia's circle, Diocles was notorious for his sharp tongue and Sempronia had an ear for cutting remarks; there might be nothing more to their relationship than whispering and laughing in corners. Sempronia chose her friends, male and female alike, because they amused her or pleased her eye or stimulated her intellect. No one considered her a slave to passion; the abandon with which she danced or declaimed her verses was only part of her persona, one small facet of the steel-willed girl who had made herself a consul's wife and had read every volume in that consul's study.

Regarding a plot against the consul, I heard not a whisper. Sempronia's circle resented her confinement and their banishment from the consul's house, but the impression passed on by the bathing attendants was more one of bemusement than of outrage. Sempronia's friends considered Decimus Brutus a doddering, harmless fool. They playfully wagered among themselves how long it would take Sempronia to bend the old bookworm to her will and resume her social life.

One discovery surprised me. If I were to believe the bathing attendants, Sertorius, the renegade general in Spain, was a far hotter topic of conversation among Sempronia's circle than was the consul, his wife, and the charioteer. Like my friend Lucius Claudius, they believed that Sertorius intended to wrest the Spanish provinces from Rome and make himself a king. Unlike Lucius, Sempronia's friends, within the whispered hush of their own circle, applauded Sertorius and his rebellion.

Decimus Brutus had dismissed his wife's friends as frivolous people, careless of appearances, naive about politics. I tried to imagine the appeal a rebel like Sertorius might hold for such dilettantes. Were they merely infatuated with the bittersweet glamour that emanates from such a desperate cause?

From the baths I moved on to the Circus Maximus, or more precisely, to the several taverns, brothels, and gambling dens in the vicinity of the racetrack. I paid bribes when I had to, but often I had only to drop the name of Diocles to get an earful. The consensus among the circus crowd was that the charioteer's tastes ran to young athletes, and always had. His current fascination was a Nubian acrobat who performed publicly during the intervals between races, and was thought to perform privately, after the races, in Diocles's bedchamber. Of course, the Nubian might have been only a cover for another, more illicit affair; or Diocles, when it came to his lovers, might have been something of a juggler himself.

If Sempronia's circle was abuzz about Sertorius, the circus crowd, disdainful of politics, was abuzz about the next day's races. I had a nagging sense that some of my informants were hiding something. Amid the horse talk and the rattle of dice, the raucous laughter and the cries of "Venus!" for luck, I sensed an edge of uneasiness, even foreboding. Perhaps it was only a general outbreak of nerves on the night before a racing day. Or perhaps by then I had shared too much wine with too many wagging tongues to see things clearly. Still, it seemed to me that something untoward was afoot at the Circus Maximus.

Cocks were crowing when I left the neighborhood of the circus, trudged across Rome, and dragged myself up the Esquiline Hill. Bethesda was waiting up for me. Her eyes lit up at the sight of the pouch of silver, somewhat depleted by expenditures, which she eagerly snatched from my hands and deposited in the empty household coffer.

A few hours later, my head aching from too much wine and too little sleep, I found myself back in the consul's study. I had agreed to arrive at his house an hour before the first race to deliver my report, such as it was.

I told him all I had learned. The secondhand gossip of bathing attendants and tavern drunks seemed trivial as I recounted it, but Decimus Brutus listened in silence and nodded gravely when I was done. He squinted at the portrait of his wife.

"Nothing, then! Scorpus is drowned, and the Finder finds nothing. Have you outsmarted me after all, Sempronia?"

The portrait made no reply.

"I'm not done yet, Consul," I told him. "I shall attend the races today. I'll keep my eyes and ears open. I may yet—"

"Yes, yes, as you wish." Decimus Brutus vaguely waved his hand to dismiss me, never taking his furiously squinting eyes from the image of Sempronia.

A slave escorted me from the consul's study. In the atrium, a small group of women crossed our path. We paused as they flitted past, the servants escorting their mistress from one part of the house to another. I peered into their midst and glimpsed a wealth of auburn hair set with pearls. Green eyes met mine and stared back. Hands clapped, and the retinue came to a halt.

Sempronia stepped forward. Decimus Brutus had been correct: the picture did not do her beauty justice. She was taller than I expected. Even through the bulky drapery of her stola, her figure suggested a lissome elegance that carried through to the delicacy of her long hands and graceful neck. She flashed the aloof, challenging smile that her portraitist had captured so well.

"You're new. One of my husband's men?" she said.

"I had business with the consul," I said.

She looked me up and down. "There are circles under your eyes. You look as if you were out all night. Sometimes men get into trouble, staying up late poking their noses where they shouldn't."

There was a glint in her eye. Was she baiting me? I should have kept my mouth shut, but I didn't. "Like Scorpus? I hear he got into trouble."

She pretended to look puzzled. "Scorpus? Oh yes, my husband's all-purpose sneak. Scorpus drowned."

"I know."

"Odd. He could swim like a dolphin."

"So I heard."

"It could happen to anyone." She sighed. Her smile faded. I saw a glimmer of sympathy in her eyes and a look that chilled my blood. Such a pleasant fellow, her look seemed to say. What a pity if one had to kill you!

Sempronia rejoined her retinue, and I was shown to the door.

By the time I reached the Circus Maximus, all Rome seemed to have poured into the long, narrow valley between the Palatine and Aventine hills. I pushed through the crowds lined up at the food-and-beverage shops tucked under the stands, stepping on toes and dodging elbows until I came to the entrance I was looking for. Inside the stadium, the seats were already filled with spectators. Many wore red or white or waved little red or white banners to show their affiliation. I swept my eyes over the elongated inner oval of the stadium, dazzled by the crazy patchwork of red and white, like blood spattered on snow.

Restless and eager for the races to begin, spectators clapped, stamped their feet, and took up chants and ditties. Cries of "Diocles in red! Quicker done than said!" competed with "White! White! Fast as spite!"

A high-pitched voice pierced the din—"Gordianus! Over here!"—and I located Lucius Claudius. He sat by the aisle, patting an empty cushion beside him. "Here, Gordianus! I received your message this morning and dutifully saved you a seat. Better than last time, don't you think? Not too high, not too low, with a splendid view of the finish line."

More important, I noted, the consular box was nearby, a little below us and to our right. As I took my seat I saw a silvery head emerge from the box's private entrance. Decimus Brutus and his fellow consul Lepidus were arriving along with their entourages. He had made it safely to the circus, at least. Partisan chants were drowned out by cheers.

The two consuls turned and waved to the crowd.

"Poor Deci," said Lucius. "He thinks they're cheering him. The fact is, they're cheering his arrival, because now the races can begin!"

There was a blare of trumpets and then more cheering as the grand procession commenced. Statues of the gods and goddesses were paraded around the racetrack on carts, led by Victory with wings outspread. As Venus passed, favorite of gamblers as well as lovers, coins showered down from the crowd and were scooped up by her priests. The procession of gods ended with an enormous gilded statue of Jupiter on his throne, borne upon a cart so large it took twenty men to pull it.

Next came the charioteers who would be racing that day, slowly circling the track in chariots festooned with the color of their team, red or white. To many in the stands, they were heroes, larger than life. There was a chant for every racer and chants for the lead horses as well. The noise of all the competing chants ringing out at once was deafening.

Never having been a gambler or a racing aficionado, I recognized few of the charioteers, but even I knew Diocles, the most renowned of the Reds. He was easy to spot by the extraordinary width of his shoulders, his bristling beard, and flowing mane of jet-black hair. As he passed before us, grinning and waving to the crowd, I tried to see the reaction of Decimus Brutus, but I was able to see only the back of the consul's head. Did Diocles's smile turn sarcastic as he passed the consular box, or did I only imagine it?

The procession ended. The track was cleared. The first four chariots took their places in the starting traps at the north end of the circus. Two White chariots, a principal along with a second-stringer to regulate the pace and run interference, would race against two Red chariots.

"Did you get a racing card?" Lucius held up a wooden tablet. Many in the stands were using them to fan themselves; all around the red-and-white-checkered stadium I saw the flutter of racing cards.

"No?" said Lucius. "Never mind, you can refer to mine. Let's see, first race of the day." The cards listed each charioteer, his color, and the name of the lead horse in his team of four. "Principal Red: Musclosus, racing Ajax, a hero of a horse, to be sure! Second-string Red: Epaphroditus, racing a five-year-old called Spots, a new horse to me. For the Whites: Thallus, racing Suspicion, and his colleague Teres racing Snowy. Now, there's a silly name for a horse, don't you think, even if it is pure white. More suitable for a puppy, I should think. By Hercules, is that the starting trumpet?"

The four chariots leaped out of their traps and onto the track. Once past the white line, they furiously vied for the inner position alongside the spine that ran down the middle. Clouds of dust billowed behind them. Whips slithered and cracked as they made the first tight turn around the post at the end of the spine and headed back. The Reds were in the lead, with Epaphroditus the second-stringer successfully blocking the principal White to give his colleague a clear field, while the second-string White trailed badly, unable to assist. But in seven laps, a great deal could happen.

Lucius jumped up and down on his pillow. All around us, spectators began to place wagers with one another on the outcome.

"I'm for Snowy!" shouted the man across the aisle from Lucius.

A man several rows down turned and shouted back, "The second-string White? Are you mad? I'll wager you ten to one against Snowy winning. How much?"

Such is the Roman way of gambling at the races: inspired by a flash of intuition and done on the spur of the moment, usually with a stranger sitting nearby. I smiled at Lucius, whose susceptibility to such spontaneous wagering was a running joke between us. "Care to join that wager, Lucius?"

"Uh, no," he answered, peering down at the track. Under his breath I heard him mutter, "Come on, Ajax! Come on!"

But Ajax did not win. Nor did the long shot Snowy. By the final lap, it was Suspicion, the principal White, who had pulled into the lead, with no help from the second-string White, who remained far in the rear. It was a stunning upset. Even the Red partisans in the crowd cheered such a marvelous display of Fortune's favor.

"A good thing you didn't bet on Ajax," I said to Lucius. He only grunted in reply and peered at his racing card.

As race followed race, it seemed to me that I had never seen Lucius so horse-mad, jumping up in excitement at each starting trumpet, cheering jubilantly when his favored horse won, but more often sulking when his horse lost, and yet never once placing a bet with anyone around us. He repeatedly turned his race card over and scribbled figures on the back with a piece of chalk, muttering and shaking his head.

I was distracted by my friend's fidgeting, and even more by the statuelike demeanor of Decimus Brutus, who sat stiffly beside his colleague in the consular box. He was so still that I wondered if he had gone to sleep; with such poor eyesight, it was no wonder he had no interest in watching the races. Surely, I thought, no assassin would be so bold as to make an attempt on the life of a consul in broad daylight, with dozens of bodyguards and thousands of witnesses all around. Still, I was uneasy, and kept scanning the crowd for any signs of something untoward.

With so much on my mind, along with a persistent headache from the previous night's wine, I paid only passing attention to the races. As each winner was announced, the names of the horses barely registered in my ears: Lightning, Straight Arrow, Bright Eyes.

At last it was time for the final race, in which Diocles would compete. A cheer went up as he drove his chariot toward the starting traps.

His horses were arrayed in splendid red trappings. A gold-plumed crest atop her head marked his lead horse, Sparrow, a tawny beauty with magnificent flanks. Diocles himself was outfitted entirely in red, except for a necklace of white. I squinted. "Lucius, why should Diocles be wearing a scrap of anything white?"

"Is he?"

"Look, around his neck. Your eyes are as sharp as mine"

"Pearls," declared Lucius. "Looks like a string of pearls. Rather precious for a charioteer."

I nodded. Diocles had not been wearing them in the opening procession. It was the sort of thing a charioteer might put on for luck just before his race, a token from his lover.

Down in his box, Decimus Brutus sat as stiffly as ever, displaying no reaction. With his eyesight, there was little chance that he had noticed the necklace.

The trumpet blared. The chariots sprang forward. Diocles took the lead at once. The crowd roared. Diocles was their favorite; even the Whites loved him. I could see why. He was magnificent to watch. He never once used his whip, which stayed tucked into his belt the whole time, alongside his emergency dagger. There was magic in Diocles that day. Man and horses seemed to share a single will; his chariot was not a contraption but a creature, a synthesis of human control and equine speed. As he held and lengthened his lead lap after lap, the crowd's excitement grew to an almost intolerable pitch. When he thundered across the finish line, there was not a spectator sitting. Women wept. Men screamed without sound, hoarse from so much shouting.

"Extraordinary!" declared Lucius.

"Yes," I said, and felt a sudden flash of intuition, a moment of god-sent insight such as gamblers crave. "Diocles is a magnificent racer. What a pity he should have fallen in with such a scheme."

"What? What's that you say?" Lucius cupped his ear against the roar of the crowd.

"Diocles has everything—skill, riches, the love of the crowd. He has no need to cheat." I shook my head. "Only love could have drawn him into such a plot."

"A plot? What are you saying, Gordianus? What is it you see?"

"I see the pearls around his neck. Look, he reaches up to touch them while he makes his victory lap. How he must love her. What man can blame him for that! But to be used by her in such a way."

"The plot? Deci! Is Deci in danger?" Lucius peered down at the consular box. Even Decimus Brutus, ever the ingratiating politician, had risen to his feet to applaud Diocles along with the rest of the crowd.

"I think your friend Decimus Brutus need not fear for his life. Unless the humiliation might kill him."

"Gordianus, what are you talking about?"

"Tell me, Lucius, why have you not wagered even once today? And what are those numbers you keep figuring on the back of your race card?"

His florid face blushed even redder. "Well, if you must know, Gordianus, I . . . I'm afraid I . . . I've lost rather a lot of money today."

"How?"

"Something . . . something new. A betting circle set up by perfectly respectable people."

"You wagered ahead of time?"

"I put a little something on each race. Well, it makes sense, doesn't it? If you know the horses and you place your bet on the best team ahead of time, with a cool head, rather than during the heat of the race."

"Yet you've lost over and over today, far more often than you've won."

"Fortune is fickle."

I shook my head. "How many others are in this 'betting circle'?"

He shrugged. "Everyone I know. Well, everyone who is anyone. Only the best people. You know what I mean."

"Only the richest people. How much money did the organizers of this betting scheme take in today? I wonder. And how much will they actually have to pay out?"

"Gordianus, what are you getting at?"

"Lucius, consult your race card. You've noted all the winners with a chalk mark. Read them off to me, not the color or the driver, just the horses' names."

"Suspicion, that was the first race. Then Lightning, Straight Arrow, Bright Eyes, Golden Dagger, Partridge. Oh! By Hercules! Gordianus, you don't think that item in the *Daily*—"

I quoted from memory. " 'The bookworm pokes his head outside tomorrow. Easy prey for the sparrow, but partridges go hungry. Bright-eyed Sappho says: Be suspicious! A dagger strikes faster than lightning. Better yet: an arrow. Let Venus conquer all!' From 'Sappho' to 'Sparrow,' a list of horses, and every one a winner."

"But how could that be?"

"I know this much: Fortune had nothing to do with it."

I left the crowded stadium and hurried through the empty streets. Decimus Brutus would be detained by the closing ceremonies. I had perhaps an hour before he would arrive home.

The slave at the door recognized me. He frowned. "The master—"

"Is still at the Circus Maximus. I'll wait for him. In the meantime, please tell your mistress she has a visitor."

The slave raised an eyebrow but showed me into a reception room off the central garden. Lowering sunlight on the fountain splashing in the courtyard outside sent reflected lozenges of light dancing across the ceiling.

I did not have long to wait. Sempronia stepped into the room alone, without even a handmaiden. She was not smiling.

"The door slave announced you as Gordianus the Finder."

"Yes. We met—briefly—this morning."

"I remember. You're the fellow who went snooping for Deci last night, poking about at the Senian Baths and those awful places around the circus. Oh yes, word got back to me. I have my own informants. What are you doing here?"

"I'm trying to decide what I should tell your husband."

She gave me an appraising look. "What is it, exactly, that you think you know?"

"Decimus Brutus thinks that you and the charioteer Diocles are lovers."

"And what do you think, Finder?"

"I think he's right. But I have no proof."

She nodded. "Is that all?"

"Your husband thinks you and Diocles were plotting to kill him today."

Sempronia laughed out loud. "Dear old bookworm!" She

sighed. "Marrying Deci was the best thing that ever happened to me. I'm the consul's wife! Why in Hades would I want to kill him?"

I shrugged. "He misunderstood that blind item you put into the *Daily Acts*."

"Which blind item?"

"There's been more than one? Of course. That makes sense. What better way to communicate with Diocles, since you've been confined here and he's been banned from your house. What I don't understand is how you ever convinced Diocles to fix today's races."

She crossed her arms and gave me a long, calculating look.

"Diocles loves me—more than I love him, I'm afraid, but when was Venus ever fair? He did it for love, I suppose; and for money. Diocles stands to make a tremendous amount of money today, as do all the racers who took part in the fix. You can't imagine how much money. Millions. We worked on the scheme for a month. Setting up the betting circle, bribing the racers."

" 'We'? Do you mean your whole circle was in on it?"

"Some of them. But mostly it was Diocles and myself." She frowned. "And then Deci had to throw his jealous fit. It couldn't have happened at a worse time, with the races less than a month away. I had to have some way to communicate with Diocles. The *Daily* was the answer."

"You must have extraordinary powers of—"

"Persuasion?"

"Organization, I was going to say."

"Like a man?" She laughed.

"One thing puzzles me still. What will you do with millions of sesterces, Sempronia? You can't possibly hide that much money from your husband. He'd want to know where such a windfall came from."

She peered at me keenly. "What do you think I intend to do with the money?"

"I think you intend to get rid of it."

"How?"

"I think you mean to send it abroad."

"Where?"

"To Spain. To Quintus Sertorius, the rebel general."

Her face became as pale as the pearls in her hair. "How much do you want, Gordianus?"

I shook my head. "I didn't come here to blackmail you."

"No? That's what Scorpus wanted."

"Your husband's man? Did he discover the truth?"

"Only about the racing scheme. He seemed to think that entitled him to a portion of the takings."

"There must be plenty to go around."

She shook her head. "Scorpus would never have stopped wanting more."

"So he was drowned."

"Diocles arranged it. There are men around the circus who'll do that sort of job for next to nothing, especially for a fellow like Diocles. Blackmailers deserve nothing better."

"Is that a threat, Sempronia?"

"That depends. What do you want, Finder?"

I shrugged. "The truth. It's the only thing that ever seems to satisfy me. Why Sertorius? Why risk so much—everything—to help his rebellion in Spain? Do you have a family tie? A loved one who's thrown his lot in with the rebels? Or is it that you and Sertorius are . . ."

"Lovers?" She laughed without mirth. "Is that all you can think, that being a woman, I must be driven by passion? Can you not imagine that a woman might have her own politics, her own convictions, her own agenda, quite separate from a husband or a lover? I don't have to justify myself to you, Gordianus."

I nodded. Feeling her eyes on me, I paced the room. The sun was sinking. Flashes of warm sunlight reflected from the fountain outside caressed my face. Decimus Brutus would return home at any moment. What would I tell him?

I made up my mind. "You asked me what I want from you, Sempronia. Actually, there is the matter of a refund, which I think you must admit is only proper, given the circumstances."

* * *

At noon the next day, I sat beside Lucius Claudius in his garden, sharing the sunlight and a cup of wine. His interest in that morning's *Daily Acts* had been eclipsed by the bags of coins I brought with me. Scooping the little scrolls off the table, he emptied the bags and piled the sesterces into tall, precarious columns, gleefully counting and recounting them.

"All here!" he announced, clapping his hands. "Every single sesterce I lost yesterday on the races. But, Gordianus, how did you get my money back?"

"That, Lucius, must forever remain a secret."

"If you insist. But this has something to do with Sempronia and that charioteer, doesn't it?"

"A secret is a secret, Lucius."

He sighed. "Your discretion is exasperating, Gordianus. But I've learned my lesson. I shall never again be drawn into a betting scheme like that!"

"I only wish I could have arranged for every person who was cheated yesterday to get his money back," I said. "Alas, their lessons shall be more costly than yours. I don't think this particular set of plotters will attempt to pull off such a scheme a second time. I hope Roman racing can return to its pristine innocence."

Lucius nodded. "The important thing is, Deci is safe and out of danger."

"He was always safe; never in danger."

"Rude of him, though, not to pay you the balance of your fee."

I shrugged. "When I saw him at his house yesterday evening, after the races, I had nothing more to report to him. He hired me to uncover a plot against his life. I failed to do so."

And what, I thought, if I had reported everything to the consul—Sempronia's adultery, the racing fix, the betting scheme, Scorpus's attempted blackmail and his murder, his wife's seditious support of Sertorius? Terrified of scandal, Decimus Brutus would merely have hushed it all up. Sempronia would have been no more faithful to him than before, and no one's wagers would have been returned. No,

I had been hired to save the consul's life, discreetly, and as far as I was concerned, my duty to Decimus Brutus ended when I discovered there was no plot against his life after all. My discretion would continue.

"Still, Gordianus, it was niggardly of Deci not to pay you.' "

Discretion forbade me from telling Lucius that the other half of my fee had indeed been paid—by Sempronia. It was the only way I could see to save my own neck. I had convinced her that by paying the fee for my investigation, she purchased my discretion. Thus I avoided the same fate as Scorpus.

At the same time I had requested a refund of Lucius's wagers, which seemed only fair.

Lucius cupped his hands around a stack of coins, as if they emitted a warming glow. He smiled ruefully. "I tell you what, Gordianus, as commission for recouping my gambling losses, what if I give you five percent of the total?"

I sucked in a breath and eyed the stacks of coins on the table. Bethesda would be greatly pleased to see the household coffers filled to overflowing. I smiled at Lucius and raised an eyebrow.

"Gordianus, don't give me that look!"

"What look?"

"Oh, very well! I shall give you ten percent. But not a sesterce more!"

Laura Frankos earned a degree in medieval history at UCLA and used her experiences in academia for her mystery St. Oswald's Niche, *which takes place on a research trip to York. She has also published a number of short stories in fantasy anthologies and science-fiction magazines. Although Laura is a serious scholar, as the following story proves, she has a wicked talent for puns, as illustrated by one of her titles: "Hadrian's Awl."*

"Merchants of Discord" is a vivid tale of daily life at Hadrian's Wall in the first century—a small slice of life, with murder.

MERCHANTS OF DISCORD

Laura Frankos

D ecurion Quintus Vestinus Corvus was repairing his horse's tack when a watchtower guard spotted travelers from the east. Corvus decided to meet them at the gate. Brocolitia's prefect, Claudius Appelinus, was awaiting word from headquarters concerning replacements for the men their cohort had lost to winter illnesses. With Fortuna's favor, this might be a courier.

He waited under the huge stone arches, glad for shelter from the rain. Soldiers passed in and out, as did numerous *vicani,* the Britons who lived in the small settlement outside Brocolitia. The open gates indicated better than any troop reports how quiet the frontier was—for now.

By the Bull, let's keep it that way, thought Corvus. Peaceful or not, I hope we get those recruits soon. But he soon realized these travelers weren't military couriers. Four heavily laden wagons escorted by cavalrymen was a sure sign of spring—the first merchants of the season.

The decurion in charge, his horsehair plume glistening with rain, spoke to the drivers. The wagons rumbled down the track south of the fort, heading for the *vicus*. The troopers rode to the gate where Corvus greeted them. "*Ave*. Where are you from?"

"Cilurnum," the decurion answered as he dismounted, "riding herd on those merchants so the nasty barbarians won't eat them. Huh! The Brigantes are welcome to them! I'm Cammius Maximus. Got a note for your prefect."

"I'm Vestinus Corvus. You're welcome to stay the night."

Maximus shook his head. "I'll deliver this, and we'll head back."

"I'll take you to the prefecture. Can't have been a pleasant ride in this weather."

"The ride wasn't so bad. The worst part was listening to those merchants bicker." Maximus spat.

"Really? I'd have imagined a group like that, traveling across the frontier, would want to help each other. It can't be an easy life."

"No, why else would they have to suck up to every prefect of every fort on the Wall, begging for an armed escort to their next market?" Maximus snorted. "As for helping each other, they hate each other! Secundinius the Gaul screwed Tertullus, the fellow from Africa, out of some business down in Eboracum. Then there's the Briton, Brocco. He's a piece of work!"

Corvus laughed. "He's nicknamed 'Badger'?"

"Looks like one, with a temper to match. Beats his slave constantly. He's on the outs with Tertullus: says he cheated at gambling back in Arbeia," said Maximus. "They never stop arguing. The only ones who don't quarrel are the Greek and his son."

Corvus jerked a thumb at Brocolitia's hospital. "We've two Greek doctors, and all they *ever* do is argue. About the weather, history, who used the latrine last . . ."

Maximus nodded. "I know the type. But Flavius Antigonus Papias is definitely an odd duck. None of the others like him much. Anyway, they're your headache now! Is this your prefecture?"

"Yes, Appelinus is in his office. I'll find out what plans your merchants have."

Maximus rolled his eyes. "Believe me, the only plans you'll hope for will be ones for their departure!"

Corvus walked down the muddy sloping path into the *vicus*, wishing he had time to visit his wife, Tancorix. Perhaps he'd have a chance to see her at the market tomorrow . . . Harsh voices broke in on his daydreams: Two men in the local inn were shouting so loudly Corvus could hear them yards away. Cammius Maximus wasn't joking when he said the merchants liked to quarrel.

Corvus stepped through the doorway, his sword bared. "What's this row?" he shouted in his best parade-ground bellow.

The innkeeper, a retired veteran named Gaius Julius Decuminus, was trying to separate two scuffling men. One, with jutting chin and black hair streaked with white at the temples, was undoubtedly the Briton, Brocco. The other was a heavy man with a scar under one eye. The participants stepped away from each other at Corvus's entrance.

"Who are you?" said the scarred man. A trickle of blood oozed from his thick lips.

"This is Vestinus Corvus," Decuminus said with considerable relief. "First decurion, first *turma*, at Brocolitia. The prefect's right-hand man. He could pitch you out of here for causing a disturbance."

"Maybe that's not a bad idea," Corvus said. "This is a peaceful settlement. A lot of us have families here. We like it that way. Now—what's the fuss?"

"This inn has but one private room," said the Briton in excellent, though slightly accented, Latin. "I am tired of listening to Secundinius snoring. It is time *I* was treated decently. You Romans—always giving me the worst bed, the worst food, the rude names—because I am of this province. For once, I demand the private room!"

"Oh, you're *so* put-upon, Brocco," said a dark-complexioned man seated on a bench. "As if the rest of us have it any easier."

"You stay out of this, you lousy cheat," Brocco said. "This is between me and Secundinius."

The dark man chuckled. "Lousy, is it? I'm not the one who's forever scratching."

"Decuminus." Corvus addressed the innkeeper. "Who should get the room?"

"Perhaps the Greeks?" Decuminus said, gesturing at a short pair almost hidden in the back of the room. "To teach the others the advantages of holding one's tongue."

The fat merchant, Secundinius, laughed harshly. "That's the worst solution yet! Who knows what nasty things our little friends will do, given privacy?"

The Greek—Corvus remembered his name was Antigonus Papias—stepped out of the shadows. He was older than the others, with a lined face and a silvery beard. He held out his hands. "Please. That's not necessary. The common room is adequate for my son and me."

Secundinius's gibe troubled Corvus. He wondered if Papias liked boys; he'd known one Greek who did, back in his hometown in northern Italia. Still, Papias seemed innocuous enough, and his son was his living image. "We don't want any trouble," Corvus warned.

"You'll not get any from me," the Greek said. "Give Secundinius the room." Brocco squawked, but Papias continued smoothly, "If Brocco's complaint is that Secundinius snores—and he does—giving him the private room provides relief to everyone."

"Well reasoned," Corvus said. Secundinius nodded happily; Brocco muttered about favoritism. Corvus sheathed his sword. "Welcome to Brocolitia. How long will you stay?"

"Three days," said Secundinius. "And we *must* have an armed escort to the next fort. These barbaric Britons, you know." He sniffed. Brocco glared.

"Certainly," Corvus said, wondering what Cilurnum had charged them. "If you stay until the Nones, a holiday, the market will be better attended by our men. The *vicani*, I'm afraid, haven't much money to spend on imported goods."

"Four days, then," said the dark man. "Hope to see you

at the market, Decurion. I'm Titus Minthonius Tertullus of
Caesarea. I deal in wine, mostly. Also oils, scents, and
spices."

"After six months of *acetum,* my wife and my father-in-
law would be pleased if I bought some decent wine," Corvus said.

"I've wine, too," Secundinius said, "from my hometown,
Trevera. Better than *his* stuff. In fact, I'm going to unbox
my goods now. Would a local boy help me in exchange
for a piece of chipped plateware? No sense wasting my
good merchandise on *vicani.*"

"No, of course not," Brocco said bitterly. "They are only
frontier barbarians. Who'd believe they could enjoy the
finer things in life? Or that they might want to dine off
something better than a cracked dish?"

"Not I," Secundinius said blithely as he left.

Vestinus Corvus clapped Julius Decuminus on the shoulder. "I don't envy you these guests. Send to the fort if
things get too hairy."

The next morning, Corvus was in his barracks, pondering
potential troop reassignments when Calpurnius Firmus, the
fort's standard-bearer, interrupted him. "Quit working so
hard. Let's buy some wine for our mess before they sell
out."

Corvus grabbed his cloak. "You don't need to ask me
twice. Let's go."

The market in the *vicus* could have been tucked into a
side street in Roma or even Londinium, with room to spare.
Still, the local merchants had their usual stalls and shops.
There were also unfamiliar faces: Britons living on farms
farther from the fort who had brought livestock or carts
loaded with early vegetables. The four travelers displayed
their wares on their wagons. Not surprisingly, they had the
biggest crowds.

Calpurnius Firmus whistled. "Must have good stuff."

"It doesn't have to be good," Corvus said. "It's *different*.
That's reason enough to gawk after seeing the same things

all winter. Hoi, Aufidius Bonus! Aren't you on guard duty now?"

Bonus jerked guiltily and stepped away from the Greek's wagon. Corvus squeezed into the space he'd vacated. Consternation crossed the Pannonian's broad face. "Sir! You know I'm not on duty today! That's a fine trick, making a man jump just to take his place in the queue." He paused, realizing the futility of arguing with a superior. "A fine trick," he repeated. "Have to remember it. You're welcome to the Greek's goods, though. Too pricey for me."

Corvus peered into Antigonus Papias' wagon, which was filled with many flat, hinged boxes. The lids were open, displaying rows of gleaming knives, chisels, adze heads, awls, hammers, saws, and other tools. Some boxes contained handsomely enameled brooches. Corvus gestured toward them. "May I?"

"Go ahead," the old Greek said, turning back to dicker with another customer.

The brooches were superb. "Belgic work," Corvus said to Calpurnius Firmus. "Perhaps your relatives?"

"My relatives are all dairymen," Firmus said. "Why do you think I joined the army? To escape the cowshit."

Corvus laughed so hard he nearly dropped the box. As he tightened his grip, his fingernail found a groove along one side, barely visible to the eye. He tugged gently, and a hidden drawer pulled out, revealing a ring of lustrous gold.

"Father!" Papias' son cried out in alarm.

"It's all right, son," Corvus said. "I'm not stealing it."

The merchant hurried over, his face pale. "Decurion," he said, "that is not for sale. A family treasure."

"Interesting design—intertwined Greek letters," Corvus said. "Sorry I popped it open. My wife will tell you I'm always sticking my big nose where I shouldn't. Perhaps this brooch? And the bone-handled knife?"

They haggled while Calpurnius Firmus fidgeted. "Hurry, the Gaul may sell out. Look, there's Publius Rubrius; *he* can put it away."

"And there's my wife!" Corvus grinned.

They elbowed their way toward Secundinius's wagon. The Gaulish merchant took payment from an auxiliary and shouted, "Who's next?"

"I am," Corvus's wife, Tancorix, said. "I was here before your last three customers, too. Six bottles of your best wine, please."

Secundinius's eyes flicked over Tancorix, who resembled her mother, a Briton. "Wait some more while I tend to your betters, such as this fine officer," he said, turning to Publius Rubrius.

Corvus flushed with anger, but Rubrius acted first. The beefy centurion grabbed Secundinius's tunic and said, "Take this lady's order. You should've done it before. But if you're real nice to her, I might forget about that."

"But, sir! She's just a Briton!"

"She's the wife of our first decurion, too," Rubrius said. "That 'fine officer' who's just joined us. *Ave,* Corvus. This boor's been ignoring your lady wife. Considering how pretty she is, that's damn foolish."

Brocco's wagon stood nearby. Though busy with his own customers, he had observed the scene. "I wish I had wine for you, my lady," he called. "But if you need cheeses or nuts, beans or pork fat, come to me. *I* do not mistreat those of my country."

Tancorix graciously inclined her head toward Brocco. Secundinius practically dived into his wagon, pulling out *amphorae* and reading the names on the necks.

"Here," he said, "six of the best, and a jug of beer with my compliments."

Corvus didn't want to give Secundinius any business, but his wife was already putting the *amphorae* into her sack. He bought some more wine and a portion of *muria,* a pungent fish sauce Tancorix loathed, for the officers' mess. He then asked her, "Shall we settle the bill?"

Tancorix ran a finger over some of Secundinius's pottery. He did have fine merchandise: two crates of the beautiful bright red-and-orange glazed ware from central Gaul, all of it elaborately incised or rouletted. "These are splendid," she said, "but let's see the other wagons."

Secundinius shook his head. "I assure you my goods are better than my companions'. The Briton is a lout and you don't want to know what's in his cheeses; Tertullus waters his wine and isn't man enough to admit he's been fairly beaten in a business deal; while the Greek, I believe, traffics in stolen gems and practices unnatural vices. I tell you this in only the finest spirit of public interest, since I know you, as first decurion, are responsible for keeping the peace in this fort and *vicus*."

Corvus nodded. "Is that so? Well, as far as I see, things *are* peaceful here. As long as they stay that way, I'm not going to fret over wild rumors. Understand?"

Clearly, Secundinius had hoped for a better response. He turned to Publius Rubrius. "Some wine, sir? Fine pottery?"

As Corvus and Tancorix walked away, she nudged his arm. "Look there! I'd wager *he* has a different opinion of Secundinius's pottery."

Matugenus, the local potter, was surveying the fancy imports with undisguised loathing. He shouted something pungent in his native tongue that Corvus couldn't understand, but Brocco and the *vicani* did. They roared with laughter. Brocco called Matugenus over and pressed some nuts into the potter's stained palm.

"What did Matugenus say?" Corvus asked.

Tancorix smiled. "Something about not wanting cursed imported pottery here, and that Secundinius, whose ancestors were hounds, should stick his head in one of his cursed imported pots and never come out."

"I agree," Corvus said. "The obnoxious yappy kind. Let's see Tertullus's wares."

They bought a jar of peppercorns and some sweet Aminean wine from the Caesarean. The merchant seemed pleased, but noticed the goods they'd bought from Secundinius. "You got some of the *muria*, I see. That, along with the woven baskets, should have been mine to sell." The bitterness in his voice was plain. "The scoundrel undercut a deal I had established—and paid a deposit on!—with a merchant in Eboracum. This fellow had to return to Ostia because of a family tragedy and was willing to sell at a loss. I had everything planned. Then the day I was to meet the man to close the deal, he disappeared like a rainbow after a storm. Next thing I know, Secundinius is carting around twenty-five jugs of oil and three barrels of *muria* he didn't have before. *And* those miserable baskets."

"Couldn't he have gotten them from elsewhere?" Tancorix asked.

Tertullus laughed ruefully. "Good lady, there are only so many barrels of first-quality *muria* available in a town the size of Eboracum. It was the Ostian's merchandise, no doubt. But how the Gaul got it and what happened to the Ostian, I don't like to think about. My lost deposit is another matter. That I shall dwell upon for ages."

"Not a cheery quartet," Corvus observed as they walked home with their purchases. "They all loathe each other."

"I hope nothing serious happens," Tancorix said.

Vestinus Corvus stopped at the inn the next morning. Decuminus was sporting a lump over one eye. Corvus asked, "Lively night?"

"Just so," Decuminus grunted. "Secundinius kept bragging how well his *muria* had been selling. Tertullus got miffed, and they argued a bit, then Tertullus went to mope in a corner with a bottle. So then the Gaul started maligning Britons. Brocco went after him, and they started wrestling. Then Tertullus handed Brocco a plate, which he broke over Secundinius's head. I put a stop to things, but nobody was very happy, not then and not now."

"Where was the Greek?"

"Out in the stable, supposedly talking to Brocco's poor slave." The innkeeper clucked his tongue. "Brocco was still fighting mad. He couldn't take it out on Secundinius anymore, so he went to the stable and yelled at Papias to stay away from his slave. Then he beat the stuffing out of the slave."

"Cheer up. In two more days they'll leave."

"Not soon enough." Decuminus scowled.

Corvus wandered over to the market. The merchants were busy as ever, with Secundinius and Brocco both showing signs of the tussle. Brocco's slave, a dark thin Briton from a southern clan, had more bruises than both.

Tertullus greeted Corvus. "*Ave,* decurion. Can I serve you? No? Then perhaps you can help me. Where can I find some soft lead? I have a cookpot to mend."

"Cistomucus will have some. Third shop on the left."

Tertullus jotted the name on a wax tablet. "Thank you."

"Heard things got rowdy last night. Don't let it happen again."

"I apologize. But Secundinius is . . . provoking."

"I'll warn the others, too," Corvus said. He hoped that would end the quarreling, at least until they left Brocolitia. What happened to them farther along the Wall wasn't his problem.

Corvus was eating breakfast before dawn when an auxiliary entered the barracks. "Decuminus's grandson is at the western gate, sir. Says Secundinius's been murdered at Belatucadrus's shrine."

"Bugger those merchants," Corvus muttered. "Firmus, come with me." They hurried out the gate. "Who found him?" Corvus asked the youth.

"Audugus. He recognized the Gaul and fetched Grandpa. He's waiting for us."

The erect figure of the veteran became visible in the morning gloom, a stark contrast to the sprawling lump at his feet. "Fine way to start the day, huh?" Decuminus said.

Corvus glanced around the small shrine. "Why was he here? Belatucadrus is a local god."

"The Bright Shining One's followers will have to purify the site," Firmus said.

"Do the other merchants know?" Corvus asked the innkeeper.

"They're still asleep," said Decuminus. "My son's on guard; he won't let anyone leave."

"Good," Corvus said. "Let's see what we've got here. Knifed in the gut. But no weapon."

"The Greek sells knives," Firmus said.

"Just because a man sells knives doesn't mean he uses

them for murder," Corvus said. "The other merchants hated Secundinius, too."

Decuminus said, "There was another nasty argument last night. It started when Secundinius was pestering the Greek. My guess is he knew something Papias wanted kept secret."

"I even think I know what," Corvus said.

"He'd been making cracks their whole stay," Decuminus said. "Usually, Papias ignored him, but last night, he said, 'We must discuss this later. In private.' Then he and his son finished their meal quickly and went to the stable to talk to Brocco's slave. Peculiar how much time Papias spends with that wretch."

"What about Brocco?" Corvus asked. "Twice now he's scuffled with Secundinius. Where was he here?"

"After the Greek left, Secundinius began running down Britons; said he liked dealing here because they were so easy to dupe. Brocco wanted to start the fisticuffs again, but I'd started carrying my sword." He patted the hilt. "So he sat back down, with a face like a thundercloud. He said, 'You'll regret that, Gaul.' Sounded like idle threats at the time . . ."

"But he might have been deciding to kill Secundinius right then," said Calpurnius Firmus. "What about Tertullus?"

"He'd been watching everything in silence. After Brocco's comment, he held up his hand to Secundinius. He said, 'Save your breath, Secundinius. I don't want to hear how well you've done selling *my* merchandise. I, too, promise that you will be sorry for what you've done.' But Secundinius laughed and said they were both jealous."

"What happened then?" Corvus asked.

Decuminus shrugged. "Brocco left, heading north. Tertullus went to his wagon and spent perhaps a quarter hour there, hunched over his wares. Then he left, too; don't know where he went. Secundinius finished his wine and went out, also north. I closed up early and went to bed."

"You've been helpful," Corvus said. "Let's take the body to our hospital, then we'll talk to everyone."

*   *   *

"Who cares if some thieving *vicanus* killed Secundinius?" asked Tertullus. "Our business is selling our goods."

"He's right," Papias said. "Can't you let us go to the market? We won't leave without our escort."

"Nobody's going anywhere until I get some answers," Corvus said. "You've all had run-ins with Secundinius. The *vicani* never saw him before now."

"And yet," Papias mused, "didn't one of them shout something rude at Secundinius our first day?"

Brocco had been sullenly sitting in the corner of the room. He leaned forward and clapped the Greek on the shoulder, a false, hearty smile on his face. "Those were words of welcome. Why else did we Britons laugh?"

Corvus pointed a finger at Brocco. "You're lying. Matugenus cursed Secundinius for bringing imported pottery here." He nodded to Papias. "Thanks for the reminder. Of all the *vicani*, our potter Matugenus had most cause to resent Secundinius. Firmus, go fetch him."

Brocco slapped his palm on the table. "No need. I was with Matugenus. And we *were* plotting against Secundinius—plotting to smash his pots to bits." He pointed at Papias. "He had the real reason for wanting Secundinius dead. The Gaul knew something bad about him."

Papias looked indignant. "I've no idea what you mean."

"You stay out of this," Corvus told Brocco. "Was Secundinius interested in your 'family treasure,' Papias? Where *did* you get that ring?"

"I keep all contracts and receipts. I can prove it is mine. Son, get my case."

Calpurnius Firmus trailed after the boy, making certain he didn't run away.

Corvus turned to Tertullus. "You went out last night, too. I never dreamed our *vicus* had such a riotous nightlife."

"I visited the whorehouse," the African said. "Been there every night."

Corvus scratched his black, curly beard. "What of your threat to make Secundinius sorry for what he did to you?"

"Mere words, decurion. I wanted to do something childish, like piss in his *muria*, but I'm a mild man. I leave tantrums to Brocco here."

The Briton rose. Corvus snapped at him to get back in his seat. Firmus charged through the doorway, his big hand clamped securely on Papias' son's shoulder. The boy's face was ashen.

"Here's the case," Firmus said. "But *this* was also in their wagon, under the canvas cover." He held up a bloodstained knife.

The boy's discovery made Corvus realize it was time to talk to Flavius Antigonus Papias in private. He dismissed the other two merchants, sending them to the market under the watchful eyes of several cavalrymen. Then he and Firmus took Papias up to the sleeping quarters he shared with the others. The old Greek sighed. "At least you will not beat me in front of my son."

"Who said anything about beating you?" Corvus asked. "You're a citizen, not a slave. Just answer my questions. Is this knife from your stock?"

"No. I don't recognize it."

"Tell me about this ring. Why so secretive? Some of your brooches match it in value."

"This one isn't for sale. I am delivering it to a friend in Londinium."

Corvus paced the room, examining the ring. "An intriguing inscription: *vivas*. 'May you live.' And a CHI-RHO monogram, flanked by two fine pearls. Gift for a fellow Hellene?"

"Er, no."

Corvus rounded on him. "Gift for a fellow Christian?"

Papias blinked. "You knew. You knew from the moment you saw it! Yet you did nothing?"

Calpurnius Firmus looked from one to the other, his blue eyes puzzled. "I'm missing something. What's a Christian?"

"They're a *factio*," Corvus said. "Sort of like a burial club, except they keep themselves secret because they won't join in public religious rites. Their founder was one

Christus, who was crucified, so crosses are sacred to them, representing the tree of everlasting life. I suppose if he had been strangled, they would venerate the rope of immortality instead."

"They follow a criminal?" Firmus asked. "How bizarre."

"It's weirder than that," Corvus said. "He was a Jewish criminal."

"Oh, the Jews." Firmus brightened. "The ones who worship nothing but clouds and mutilate themselves."

The two soldiers turned at the sound of their prisoner laughing. "Gentlemen, your facts are muddled. But no matter. Yes, I follow Christus. For that reason alone, I could not have killed Secundinius. We are bound by oath to abstain from theft, adultery, and murder. When we meet in our assemblies, we Christians are united by our common hope of life after death. We pray, read our sacred writings, chant holy words. No harm comes to anyone from what we do."

Corvus and Firmus glanced at each other. Admittedly, Papias had given only a sketchy outline of whatever it was Christians did when together, but it sounded similar to what they and a select group of the men of Brocolitia did when gathered in the temple to Mithras near the fort.

"I doubt you murdered Secundinius," Corvus said. "You're intelligent. You wouldn't have left the knife where your son could find it. That strikes me as the act of someone who wanted to frame you, either Brocco or Tertullus. But the knife is the only evidence I have. Until something else turns up, I must hold you for the crime. Come to the fort with me."

Vestinus Corvus made his report about the murder to Claudius Appelinus. The prefect, as usual, left everything in Corvus's hands. The decurion went to the hospital next.

Archagathus greeted him. "Got a trinket from your dead man. Found this in his hand." The Greek physician gave Corvus a small piece of curved, flattened metal with a bit of writing scratched on it: the letters IVS.

"Broken off from something bigger, obviously," said Archagathus.

"I'm going back to Belatucadrus's shrine," Corvus said, fingering the fragment. "Perhaps we missed something in the darkness."

Corvus checked the ground where Secundinius's body had lain, but found nothing. He stepped back, trying to see if there were anything unusual about the surroundings as a whole. The outer wall of the shrine was studded with small rolled sheets of flattened lead, each carefully nailed in the center. One caught his eye: unlike the others, the nail was shiny and new, not rusty.

The sheets were curse tablets. If one hated an enemy enough, one could curse him in writing and nail the sheet to a temple wall or, even better, to a tomb, where the gods of the underworld would tie themselves to the victim. He hesitated before examining the new tablet. He did not know if Belatucadrus would take offense, or if the action might involve him in the curse. But Corvus, who'd once been falsely accused himself, loathed the idea of a man charged with a crime he did not commit.

He removed the sheet and unrolled it carefully. The nail obliterated several letters, but it was legible: *Belatucadrus, I conjure you, fix Secundinius of Trevera. His life and liver and lungs are fixed. His mind and memory are pinned down. That he may not be able again to cheat honest men. Secundin . . . is fixed.*

The fragment found in the Gaul's hand was the missing corner.

"How very interesting," Corvus murmured.

The decurion spent the rest of the day in the *vicus*. He spoke to Matugenus, Decuminus, Lemnus of the whorehouse and his girls, and he searched through Brocco and Tertullus's personal belongings while they were at the market.

When both merchants returned, he was waiting for them.

"How is Papias?" Tertullus asked.

"He's upstairs," Corvus said.

Brocco spluttered in surprise. "You've let him go?"

"A less curious decurion might have taken the knife as enough to prove Papias guilty. I, however, am relentlessly nosy. I wondered why Secundinius was killed at the shrine of one of our local gods. Why was there a fresh curse tablet on the wall of that shrine? Why was Secundinius clutching a piece of that tablet?" He walked across the room and stood in front of the Caesarean. "Why did a man buy lead to repair pots, though his pots show no sign of damage or recent repair? Where is the lead you bought from Cistomucus?"

"In my wagon," Tertullus said.

"Calpurnius Firmus just searched your wagon. It's not there, because you flattened it, scratched a curse on it, and nailed it to the shrine. But Secundinius must have tried to stop you—and you killed him."

"A bit of missing lead can't connect me to that," Tertullus said. "Brocco has often cursed Secundinius in public. He could have done it, or that *vicanus*."

"No. They can't write. But you have your letters. And Pluma, the whore you've visited, said you were asking about our local gods—their names, where their shrines were. Why? Because curse tablets are more effective if you invoke an unusual deity, like Belatucadrus."

"This is nonsense," Tertullus said, but some of the confidence had left his voice.

"You've a new cloak, too. Pluma said you forgot your old one, and she kept it, as she does with anything a customer might leave. But did you *really* forget it, or did you leave it on purpose, because of the bloodstains?"

"You dog!" Brocco said to Tertullus. "How could you make Papias take the blame? Coward!"

Tertullus hunched in on himself. "I didn't mean to kill him, but he followed me and overheard me recite the curse to the god. He knocked me down and yanked at the tablet. I hardly remember what happened next: only my knife plunging into his side. I dropped the knife in Papias' wagon, but I thought he'd get rid of it. I left the cloak with Pluma. Never imagined you'd bother talking to her. Who talks to whores?" He laid his hands flat on the table to keep them from trembling. "What happens now?"

"You face the courts at Eboracum," said Corvus. "Settle your debts with Decuminus; we'll hold you at Brocolitia until we can take you there."

As Tertullus gathered his belongings, Papias came downstairs. Tertullus stammered, "I beg your pardon for what happened, though I know it was an unforgivable act. I leave you my wagon and wares."

Papias bowed slightly. "Among my brethren, forgiveness is in limitless supply. Go, and may you find peace."

Corvus doubted the courts would be as accommodating as the Greek. He and Firmus escorted their prisoner out the door.

$\mathcal{H}$arry Turtledove first started publishing under the name "Eric Iverson" because his editor thought no one would believe his real name was Turtledove. In 1985, he decided to risk disbelief and began using Turtledove. Since then he has produced numerous books and short stories, many in the realm of alternate history or science fiction. In 1999 alone he published two books, Into the Darkness and The Great War: Walk in Hell, *plus* short stories. In 2000, there are three more—Colonization, Darkness Descending, *and* The Great War: Breakthroughs.

Harry got his doctorate at UCLA in Byzantine history, and many of his early science-fiction books reveal his interest in Roman and Byzantine society. Recently he has been writing a brilliant alternate-history series, starting with the premise in Guns of the South *that the South won the Civil War.* He has won both the Hugo and Nebula awards for science fiction. This is his first mystery story.

FARMERS' LAW

Harry Turtledove

Abrostola suited Father George well. The village lay only five or six miles north of Amorion, the capital of the Anatolic theme. That was close enough for George and his little flock to take refuge behind Amorion's stout walls when the Arabs raided Roman territory—and far enough away for them to go unnoticed most of the time.

Going unnoticed also suited Father George well. What with Constantine V following in the footsteps of his father, Leo III, and condemning the veneration of icons, a priest wanted to draw as little notice from Constantinople as he could. That was all the more true if he found the Emperor's theology unfortunate, as Father George did.

Every so often, officials would ride through Abrostola on their way from Amorion up to Ankyra, or from Ankyra coming down to Amorion. They never bothered to stop at the little church beside which George and his wife, Irene, lived. Because they never stopped, they never saw that the images remained in their places there. George never brought it to their attention, nor did any of the other villagers. They had trouble enough scratching a living from the thin, rocky soil of Asia Minor and worrying about the Arabs. They didn't care to risk Constantine's displeasure along with everything else.

George was eating barley bread and olive oil and drinking a cup of wine for breakfast when someone pounded on the door.

"Who's that?" Irene asked indignantly from across the table.

"Who's that?" their daughter, Maria, echoed. Rather than indignant, the three-year-old sounded blurry—she was trying to talk around a big mouthful of bread.

"I'd better find out." George rose from his stool with grace surprising in so big a man: he was almost six feet tall and broad as a bull through the shoulders. The pounding came again, louder and more insistently.

"Oh, dear God," Irene said. "I hope that doesn't mean Zoe's finally decided to run off with somebody."

"Alexander the potter should have got her married off years ago," George said, reaching for the latch. Zoe was the prettiest maiden in the village, and knew it too well.

But when George opened the door, it wasn't Alexander standing there, but a weedy little farmer named Basil. "He's dead, Father!" Basil cried. "He's dead!"

Automatically, the priest made the sign of the cross. Then he asked, "Who's dead?" Nobody in the village, so far as he knew, was even particularly sick. Rumor said plague was loose in Constantinople again, but—God be praised, George thought—it hadn't come to Abrostola.

"Who's dead?" Basil repeated, as if he couldn't believe his ears. "Who's dead?" He'd always had a habit of saying things twice. "Why, Theodore, of course." He stared at Father George as if the priest should have already known that.

"Theodore?" George crossed himself again. Theodore couldn't have been more than thirty-five—not far from his own age—and was one of the two or three most prosperous farmers in the village. If any man seemed a good bet to live out his full threescore and ten, he was the one. But, sure enough, the sound of women wailing came from the direction of his house. George shook his head in slow wonder. "God does as He would, not as we would have Him do."

But Basil said, "Not this time." He went on, "God didn't have anything to do with it. Nothing. I'd borrowed an ax from him, to chop some firewood with, and I brought it back to him at sunup, just a little while ago. You know how Theodore is—was. He lets you borrow things, sure enough, but he never lets you forget you did it, either."

"That's so," George admitted. Theodore hadn't overflowed with the milk of human kindness. The priest tried to make the peasant come to the point: "You went to give the ax back to Theodore. And . . . ?"

"And I found him lying there by his house with his head smashed in," Basil said. "Didn't I tell you that?"

"As a matter of fact, no," Father George said. Though he was wearing only the light knee-length tunic in which he'd slept, he hurried out the door and toward Theodore's house. Dust scuffed up under his bare feet. Basil had to go into a skipping half trot to keep up with him.

A crowd was already gathering. Theodore's wife, Anna, and his two daughters, Margarita and Martina, stood over the body, shrieking and tearing at their tunics, which reached down to the ground. Some of Theodore's neighbors stood there, too: Demetrios the smith and a couple of other farmers, John and Kostas. Demetrios' wife, Sophia, came out and began to wail, too; her brother was married to Theodore's sister.

George shouldered his way through them. He looked down at Theodore and crossed himself once more. The prosperous peasant stared up at the sky, but he wasn't seeing anything, and wouldn't ever again. Blood soaked into the ground from the blow that had smashed in the right front of his skull from the eye socket all the way back to above the ear. Flies were already buzzing around the body.

John grabbed Theodore's arm. "Murder!" he said hoarsely, which set everyone exclaiming and wailing anew. What had happened was obvious enough, but naming it somehow made it worse.

"What are we going to do?" Basil asked. "Send down to Amorion, so the *strategos* commanding the theme can order a man up here to find out who did it?"

That was what they should have done. They all knew it. But Lankinos, the governor of the Anatolic theme, was as much an iconoclast as the Emperor Constantine himself. Any man he sent to Abrostola would likely be an iconoclast, too. If he stepped into the church and saw the holy images of Christ and the saints still on the iconostasis . . .

"We can't do that to Father George!" Demetrios the blacksmith exclaimed. "We can't put our own souls in danger doing that, either."

Theodore's wife—no, his widow now—spoke for the first time: "We can't let a murderer walk free." She drew herself straight and wiped her tear-stained face on a tunic sleeve. "I will have vengeance on the man who killed my husband. I *will*, by the Mother of God."

Father George wouldn't have sworn an oath of vengeance in the Virgin's name, but he knew Anna wasn't thinking so clearly as she might have. Her older daughter, Margarita, said, "Why would anyone want to hurt Father? Why?" She sounded bewildered.

The question made people stir awkwardly. "Why?" Basil echoed. "Well, on account of he was rich, for starters, and—*ow!*" Father George didn't see what had happened, but guessed somebody'd stepped on Basil's foot.

"If we don't send down to Amorion, how will we find out who killed Theodore?" the farmer named Kostas asked.

No one answered, not in words. No one said anything at all, in fact, though Margarita and Martina kept weeping quietly. But everyone, including Theodore's daughters, looked straight at Father George.

"Kyrie, eleison!" the priest said, making the sign of the cross yet again. *"Christe, eleison!"*

"No one had mercy on my husband," Anna said bitterly. "Not the Lord, not Christ, not whoever killed him. No one."

She stood with George beside Theodore's corpse in the parlor of the house that had been the farmer's. She and her daughters had washed the body and wrapped it in white linen and bent Theodore's arms into a cross on his chest. He held a small, rather crudely painted icon showing Christ and Peter. He lay facing east on a couch by the bricks of the north wall, so the caved-in ruin that was the right side of his head showed as little as possible. Candles and incense burned by him.

"You heard nothing when he went out yesterday morning?" Father George asked.

"Nothing," Theodore's widow replied. "I don't know whether he went outside to ease himself or to see what he needed to do first in the morning, the way he sometimes did. Whatever the reason was, he hadn't been gone long enough for me or the girls even to think about it. Then Basil pounded on the door, shouting that he was dead."

"He must have come to me right afterward," the priest said. Anna nodded. Father George plucked at his thick black beard. "He didn't tell you he saw anyone running away?"

"No." Anna looked down at her husband's body. "What will become of us? We were doing so well, but now, without a man in the house . . . Hard times."

"I'll pray for you." Father George grimaced as soon as the words were out of his mouth. They were kindly meant, but felt flat and inadequate.

"Catch the man who did this to him—did it to all of us," Anna said. "He must have thought he would profit by it. Don't let him. Don't let Theodore go unavenged." Tears started streaming down her face again.

Gently, Father George quoted Romans: "Vengeance is mine; I will repay, saith the Lord."

But Anna quoted Scripture, too, the older, harder law of Exodus: "Eye for eye, tooth for tooth, hand for hand, foot for foot."

And George found himself nodding. He said, "No one heard anything. Basil didn't see anyone running off. No one else did, either, or no one's come forward. Whoever slew your husband got out of sight in a hurry."

"May he never show himself again, not till Judgment Day," Anna said.

"Here is a question I know you will not want to answer, but I hope you will think on it," Father George said. "Who might have wanted Theodore dead?"

"Half the village," the dead man's widow said at once, "and you know it as well as I do. When Theodore and I married, he was working a miserable little plot, and we almost starved a couple of times. But he worked hard— nobody ever worked harder—and he always had a good eye for land that would yield increase, so he made himself a man to be reckoned with in Abrostola—even a man people had heard of in Amorion. That was plenty to make lazy people jealous of him."

The priest nodded again. Theodore had been a great ox in harness. But not everyone said such gracious things about the land deals he'd made, though Father George didn't tax Anna with that now. He already knew some of those tales; he could learn more later. In the smithy close by, Demetrios' hammer clanged on iron. George said, "I'll leave you to your mourning."

"Find the man who killed my husband," Anna said. "If you don't . . . if you don't, I'll have to go down to Amorion to see if the *strategos* and his henchmen can help me."

"I understand." Father George bit the inside of his lower lip. With any luck, his luxuriant beard kept Theodore's widow from noticing. He couldn't blame her. Of course she wanted the murderer caught and punished. But if men from the capital of the Anatolic theme, men loyal to Constantine the iconoclast, started poking through Abrostola, George would have a thin time of it. The whole village would have a thin time of it, for supporting an iconophile priest. "I'll do everything I can."

Anna just waved him to the door, imperious as if she were an empress, not a peasant's widow. And George's retreat, to his own embarrassment, was something close to a rout. After the gloom of candlelight inside Theodore's house, he blinked in the strong sunshine outside.

He almost ran into Kostas, who was coming toward the

house. "Excuse me," he said, and got out of the farmer's way.

Kostas dipped his head. He was a lean gray wolf of a man, with hard, dark eyes and with scars on his cheeks and forearms that showed he'd done plenty of fighting against Arab raiders. "You're the man I came to see, Father George," he said. "Your wife told me you were here."

"Walk with me, then," the priest said, and Kostas did. They went past Demetrios' blacksmithery. The smith stopped hammering at whatever he was making. He raised his right hand from the tongs with which he held hot metal to the anvil to wave to the two men. Kostas nodded again. Father George waved back. As soon as Demetrios started clanking away with the hammer again, the priest gestured to Kostas. "Please, my friend—go on."

"Thanks." But Kostas didn't say anything right away. He stared at the brickwork houses of the village, some white-washed, some plain; at their red tile roofs; at the flocks and vineyards and pasturage that lay beyond, as if he'd never seen any of them before. At last, when George was wondering if he'd have to prompt the farmer again, Kostas said, "That business between Theodore and me last year, that wasn't so much of a much, not really."

"Has anyone said it was?" Father George asked.

Kostas ignored that. "I still don't think the plot I got from Theodore was as good as the one I gave him in exchange for it, but I never even reckoned it was worth going to law about, you know. Farmers' Law says I could have, and I think I would've won, too. But nobody wants those nosy buggers from Amorion mucking about here, and that's the Lord's truth."

"Seeing how things are these days, I'm glad you feel that way," George said.

Again, Kostas talked right through him: "If I wouldn't go to law over it, I wouldn't smash in Theodore's head over it, either, now would I?"

"I hope not," Father George answered. "But someone did."

"Not me," Kostas repeated, and walked, or rather loped,

away. A lone wolf, sure enough, the priest thought. He let out a long sigh. How many more denials would he hear over the next few days? And which villager would be lying like Ananias?

Like anyone else in the village, Father George kept a couple of pigs and some chickens. He was scattering barley for the chickens when Basil sidled up to him. Not even the chickens gave the scrawny little peasant much respect; he had to step smartly to keep them from pecking at his toes, which stuck out between the straps of his sandals.

"Good day, Basil." Father George tossed out another handful of grain.

"Same to you." Basil seemed to like the sound of the words. "Yes, same to you." He stood there watching the chickens for a minute or two, and kicked dirt at a bird that was eyeing his feet again. The hen squawked and fluttered back.

"You wanted something?" George asked.

Basil coughed and, to the priest's surprise, blushed red as a pomegranate. "You recall that business year before last, don't you? You know the business I mean."

"When you were tending Theodore's sheep?"

"That's right." Basil's head bobbed up and down. "People said I milked 'em without telling Theodore, and sold the milk and even sold off a couple of the sheep."

People said that because it was true. He'd got caught selling the milk and the sheep in the market square at Orkistos, more than ten miles northwest of Abrostola. Father George didn't bother mentioning that. With a grave nod, he said, "I remember."

"All right. All right, then," Basil said. "And after that, they gave me a good thumping, and Theodore took away my wages. That's what the Farmers' Law says to do, and that's what they did. I got what they said was coming to me, and that's the end. Fair enough, right?"

"So far as I know, no one has troubled you about it since," the priest replied. No one had hired Basil as a shepherd since, either, one more thing George didn't say.

"That's true enough—so it is," the skinny peasant agreed. "But do you know what's going round the village now? Do you know?" He hopped in the air, not because a chicken was after his toes but from outrage. "They're saying I smashed in Theodore's head on account of that business, is what they're saying."

"You found him dead," Father George observed. Did you find him dead because you killed him? he wondered. But he kept that to himself, too.

Basil dropped to his knees and clasped the priest's hand. "Not you, too!" he cried. "I couldn't've killed Theodore, not even with a club in my hand! He'd've grabbed it and thrashed me all over again. You know it, too."

"Not if you struck from behind." But George hesitated and shook his head. "No. The blow he got surely came from the front. I saw as much. I daresay he would have cried out against you, at any rate, if he saw you coming with a club in your hand."

"That's right! That's just right!" Basil said fervently. He kissed George's hand in an ecstasy of relief.

Is it? George wasn't so sure. Maybe Theodore wouldn't have taken scrawny Basil seriously till too late. But he lifted the peasant from the dirt and dusted him off. "Go your way. And stay away from sheep."

"Oh, I do," Basil said. And the priest believed him. Nobody in Abrostola let Basil near his sheep. Had Father George had sheep, he wouldn't have let Basil near them, either.

Theodore's funeral felt strange, unnatural. The procession to the burial ground outside the village seemed normal enough at first. Father George and the dead man's relatives led the way, all of them but the priest wailing and keening and beating their breasts. More villagers followed.

Some of them lamented, too. But others kept looking at one another. George knew what lay in their minds. It lay in his mind, too. They were wondering which of their number was a murderer. Was it someone they despised? Or was it a friend, a loved one, a brother? Only one man knew, and they were burying him.

No. Father George grimaced. Someone else knew, too: the killer himself. And he hoped to walk free, to escape human judgment. God would surely send him to hell for eternal torment, but he must have despised that, too.

George chanted psalms over Theodore's body as it lay in the grave, to protect his soul from demons. "Let us pray that he goes from here to a better place, to paradise, to the marriage chamber of the spirit," he said, and he and the mourners and the whole crowd of villagers made the sign of the cross together.

As the funeral ended, they straggled back toward Abrostola. Behind Father George, the grave diggers shoveled the earth down onto Theodore's shrouded body. The priest sighed and shook his head. That was always such a final sound, and worse here today because some wicked man had cut short Theodore's proper span of years.

Later that day Father George went to the dead man's house to console his widow and daughters. Anna met him at the door and gave him an earthenware cup of wine. She was dry-eyed now, dry-eyed and grim. "We are as well as we can be," she said when he asked. "I'll give you another few days to catch the killer. If you don't, I'm going down to Amorion." She sounded unbendably determined. In that, she'd been a good match for Theodore.

"I'm doing all I can, all I know how to do." George knew he sounded harried. His training was to fight sin, not crime. "If you go to Amorion . . ."

"The holy images are dear to me, too," Anna said. "But justice and vengeance are dearer still."

Father George bowed his head. He had no good answer for that, and no way to stop her if she chose to go. "I'll do all I can," he repeated. He finished the wine, gave her the cup, and turned to go.

Demetrios was already hammering away again. When George walked past his house and the smithy beside it, Sophia came out and stopped him. "Have you heard?" the smith's wife asked.

"I don't know," Father George said. "But I expect you'll tell me."

Sophia put her hands on her hips and cocked her head to one side as she studied George. Her dark eyes flashed. She remained one of the prettier, and one of the livelier, women in Abrostola. Fifteen years before, she'd been the prize catch in the village, as Zoe was now. George had eyed her back before she married Demetrios. So had a lot of the young men in Abrostola. She knew it, too, and used it now, making him pay more attention to her than he would have were she plainer. "Why, the lies John's spreading, of course." Her tone was intimate, too, as if she were the priest's wife, not the smith's.

"You'd better tell me more," Father George said. "John hasn't said anything to me." That was true. It didn't mean George hadn't heard anything, though he hoped Sophia would think it did.

She tossed her head. "Oh, no. He wouldn't tell you. That's not his way. He'll put poison in other people's ears, and let them put it in yours."

"I haven't heard any poison I know of," George said.

Sophia went on as if he hadn't spoken. "The mill Demetrios built last year has been sitting idle ever since, because the water it took out of the Lalandos kept Theodore's wheat fields from getting enough."

The priest nodded. "That's what the Farmers' Law says you do if a mill takes too much water out of a river—not that the Lalandos is much of a river, especially in summertime. It's a fair law, I think."

"So do I." Sophia reached out and set a hand on his arm, a startling intimacy. "And so does Demetrios. He never said a word when he had to let it rest idle. And why should he have? We make a good living from the smithy as is." Pride rang in her voice, as Demetrios' hammer rang off hot metal.

"I'm sure you do," George said, truthfully enough: Sophia's earrings were gold, not brass, and her tunic of fine, soft wool from the sheep near Ankyra.

"Well, then—Demetrios wouldn't have any reason to

hurt Theodore, and so he couldn't have." Sophia made it sound simple.

Father George wished it were. "By all the signs, nobody had any reason to hurt Theodore. But someone did."

"Someone certainly did," Sophia said sharply. "You might ask John about *his* dealings with Theodore. Yes, you might indeed."

"I intend to," George said. Sophia nodded. For a heart-beat, he thought she would kiss him. For half a heartbeat, he hoped she would. She didn't. She just turned and walked away. Shame filled him. *Whosoever looketh on a woman to lust after her hath committed adultery already with her in his heart.* He repented of his sin, but he would have to do penance for it, too.

As soon as the sun rose the next day, Father George went looking for John. He wasn't astonished to discover John walking toward his house. The farmer nodded to him. Like Kostas, John was a scarred veteran. Unlike Kostas, he was actively bad-tempered. "All right," he said now, by way of greeting. "I know that miserable bitch Sophia's been spreading lies about me, but I don't know what kind yet. I suppose you'll tell me, though."

"You didn't think she was a miserable bitch before she married Demetrios," Father George said. "None of the young men did." *I certainly didn't.* He remembered, and grimaced at, his own desirous thoughts the day before.

John dismissed that with a snort and a wave. "Just tell me what she said."

"That you were going on about Demetrios' mill, and why it's idle," the priest answered.

"By the Virgin, that's the truth," John said. "It's not like what *she's* been doing—talking about that ox of mine Theodore killed three years ago. He said it was in his field, and so he had the right, but the carcass was on *my* land. Farmers' Law says he should have paid me, but he's a big sneeze here. Did I ever see a copper follis? Not me."

"Why tell me this?" George asked. "Do you *want* me to think you bore a grudge?"

"Of course I bore a grudge." John tossed his head in scorn. "Like I'm the only one in Abrostola who did." George had to nod; he'd already seen as much there. John went on. "I've had it for years. Why should I all of a sudden decide to smash in his stinking, lying head? One of these days, I'd've found a revenge to make his heart burn for years. I want to kill whoever did him in, is what I want to do, on account of now I won't get the chance." He spat in the dirt. "What do you think of that?"

"I believe you." It wasn't what Father George had intended to say, but it was true.

"All right, then. Don't waste your time coming after me. Don't waste your time at all." John stalked off, leaving the priest staring after him.

"He could have done it," Irene said that night, over a supper of hot cheese pie with leeks and mushrooms. "He could be covering his tracks."

"John? I know he could." Father George nodded to his wife. He wasn't so sure about John as he had been that morning. "But so could plenty of other people. The longer Theodore's dead, the more it seems everyone hated him."

"Who hated him enough to kill him?" Irene said. "That's the question."

"I don't know," George said unhappily. "And if I don't find out soon, Anna will go down to Amorion, and the *strategos* or his people will come back up here, and . . ." He sighed. "And Abrostola won't be the same." He didn't dwell on what would happen to him.

"It's not fair. It's not right," Irene said. Then she gave a small gasp and grabbed for their daughter, who was helping herself to cheese pie with both hands. "Wash yourself off!" she exclaimed. "You're a horrible mess."

"Mess." Maria sounded cheerful, no matter how glum her parents were. She grabbed a rag and did a three-year-old's halfhearted job of wiping herself off. "There!"

Irene shook her head. "Not good enough. See that big glob of cheese on your left hand?"

Maria looked confused. "My best hand, Mama?"

"No, your *left* hand," Irene said, and cleaned it herself. The two words were close in Greek—*aristos* and *aristeros*. *Aristeros*, the word for left, was a euphemism, Father George knew: in pagan days, the left side had been reckoned unlucky. He looked down at his own left hand, on which he wore a wedding ring—to him, a sign of good luck, not bad.

He stared at the ring in dawning astonishment. Then he crossed himself. And then, solemnly, he kissed his wife and daughter. Maria giggled. Irene looked as confused as Maria had a moment before, till George began to explain.

Abrostola hadn't seen such a procession since Theodore's funeral, and not since Easter before that. Father George led this one, too. Kostas and John followed him like a couple of martial saints: they both carried shields and bore swords in their right hands. Basil capered along behind them. He had a light spear, the sort a shepherd might use against wolves—not that he got much chance to herd sheep these days. Several other villagers, all armed as best they might be, also followed the priest.

They stopped not at the church, but at Demetrios'. As usual, the blacksmith was pounding away at something—a plowshare, by the shape of it. He looked up in surprise, sweat streaming down his face, when Father George and Kostas and John strode into the smith. "What's this?" he demanded.

Sadly, George answered, "We've come to take you to Amorion for trial and punishment for the murder of Theodore."

"Me?" Demetrios scowled. "You've got the wrong man, priest. I figure it's likely John here, if you want to know the truth."

But Father George shook his head. "I'm sorry—I'm very sorry—but I'm afraid not, Demetrios. Theodore wouldn't think anything of seeing you with a hammer or an iron bar in your hand, because you carry one so often. And it would have been in your left hand, too, for the blow that killed him was surely struck by a left-handed man."

Demetrios stood over the anvil, breathing hard. As always, the tongs were in his right hand, the hammer in his left. With a sudden shouted curse, he flung that hammer at Father George. Quick as a cat, Kostas leaped sideways to ward the priest with his oval shield. As the hammer thudded off it, Demetrios ran past Kostas and John and out of the smithy.

John swung his sword, but missed. "Catch him!" he shouted. He and Kostas and Father George all rushed after Demetrios.

The smith hadn't gotten far. He'd knocked one man aside with the tongs, but the rest of the villagers swarmed over him and bore him to the ground. "Get some rope!" somebody shouted. "We'll tie him up, throw him over a mule's back, and take him to Amorion for what he deserves."

"They'll put him to the sword, sure enough." That was Basil, brandishing his spear so fiercely, he almost stabbed a couple of the men close by him. "Sure enough."

From under the pile of men holding him down, Demetrios shouted, "I gave Theodore what he deserved, the son of a pimp. Thought his turds didn't stink, screwed me out of the profit I deserved for the mill. His soul's burning in hell right now."

"And yours will keep it company." Three or four men said the same thing at the same time.

Kostas patted Father George on the back. "You did well here."

"Did I?" the priest asked. He wondered. Murder didn't come under the Farmers' Law, but this one had sprung from its provisions.

Just then, Sophia came out and started to shriek and wail and try to drag the villagers off her husband. A couple of them pulled her away from the pile, but not till after she'd raked them with her nails.

"What else could you have done?" Kostas asked.

Father George sighed. "That's a different question," he said, and started back toward his house.

Andrew Greeley is a priest, sociologist, author, and student of Irish history and culture. He writes the popular Bishop Blackie Ryan mysteries and a series featuring Nuala Anne McGrail, a Galway woman with more than a bit of the Sight, and her Irish-American suitor, Dermot Coyne, who spends most of his time trying to keep up with her. The first of these books, Irish Gold, *is a seamless joining of present-day Ireland and the troubled last days of Michael Collins. The most recent is* Irish Eyes.*

In "The Case of the Murdered Pope," Father Greeley introduces a new Irish detective, one Finbarr Mor O'Neill, a monk of the tenth century who, like many Irish scholars before and after, has left his homeland in search of knowledge. He discovers that the popes who rule Rome in his day are a far cry from Peter and Gregory the Great. This is the first Finbarr story, but I hope to read more about him and his travails in Rome. One Irish monk is more than a match for a papacy controlled by "killers of popes, bribers of popes, sons of popes, mistresses of popes, and mothers of popes."*

THE CASE OF THE MURDERED POPE:
A FINBARR MOR O'NEILL MYSTERY

Andrew Greeley

"Father Abbot wants to see you, Brother Scribe," the prior said, his aristocratic nose pointing at the Roman January sun, now lurking tentatively in the southern sky. "It is about the death of the pope."

Finbarr put aside his pen with a loud sigh. "Pope Benedict, poor dear man."

Finbarr knew very well that Benedict IV had been dead for several months, doubtless strangled by the usurpur Emperor Berengar, now himself dead of the fever. However, he liked to keep his Roman colleagues with their empty pretensions of virtue on the defensive.

"Oh, no, Brother. Pope Christopher. Pope Benedict was succeeded by Pope Leo in August."

Finbarr carefully covered his inks and eased away Pangur Ban, his pet cat who liked to sniff at the inks, often with disastrous results to his feline snoot.

"And Pope Leo . . . Let me see, he would be Leo V, would he not? When did he die?"

Pangur arched his back in anger.

"In September, Brother."

"Tragic," Finbarr muttered, wiping ink off his fingers.

Finbarr Mor O'Neill had come to the Abbey of St. Gregory on the Aventine Hill to copy manuscripts in 896. In the eight years since then, there had been eight popes. Three last year. Some of them, like both Leo and Benedict, had been good and holy men, which did not guarantee them long lives. On the other hand, the late Pope Christopher was a thug, and he had lasted only four months. Neither virtue nor vice made for longevity on the throne of the fisherman in the tenth century.

"For which death does Father Abbot hold me responsible?" Finbarr asked the prior.

He glanced out the window of the scriptorium through which flowed the warm Roman light. Excellent light for copying. No better than that in Ireland, only more of it. In the distance, across the thin silver line of the Tiber, the low and ugly Basilica of St. Peter glowed in the sun. It was a dangerous place and not just for popes.

The prior, good and pious man that he was, shook his head in dismay.

"I'm sure he does not suspect you at all, Brother. You spend all your time working on your manuscripts."

"Never trust an artist, Brother Prior," Finbarr warned. "Especially an artist from Ireland with red hair."

Finbarr had found it useful during his interlude in Rome to play the role of a crazy Celt. It made him a man of mystery to his Italian confreres who were inclined to leave him alone to do his own work. Moreover, it was an easy enough role for him to play.

"You put our holy abbey at great risk, Brother Finbarr," the short, round abbot informed him when he entered the abbot's presence.

"I'm sure St. Gregory will protect us."

The abbot was a nervous, fussy man who loved to play with his abbatial ring as though he were afraid that someone might snatch it off his finger. He meant no harm by his remark to Finbarr. In the abbot's haunted world, there was a risk to the abbey in the rising of the sun every morning.

."The senator himself wants to see you," the abbot whispered solemnly.

"I didn't know there were any senators still alive in Rome."

The great senatorial families had long since extinguished one another, only to be replaced by more recently arrived thugs. The current senator was a certain Theophylact, a man little better than a bandit, who had swooped down from his hill town outside of Rome and proclaimed himself protector of the city and the papacy. His name was Greek, and he was said to be the illegitimate son of a Greek bandit and a Saracen woman.

"Shh . . ." The abbot raised a trembling finger his lips. "The senator has brought peace to Rome."

"And the death of several popes."

"Do not say those things," the abbot begged. "You know how dangerous the lanes were before his police restored order."

Theophylact's men had driven the other Roman gangs into hiding and now monopolized terror.

"And he wants to see me? What use does he have for an Irish monk who copies manuscripts?"

Finbarr knew what Theophylact wanted. However, he wanted the abbot to tell him so that he could not later claim that he did not know.

"It is the matter of the death of Pope Christopher. You have gained some reputation in this city for solving mysteries . . ."

"Ah, the senator wants evidence that someone else killed that crooked priest so that he can bring his good friend Pope Sergius back to Rome?"

The abbot turned white. "Please, please, Brother Finbarr. Don't say that. Don't even think that. You know how dangerous this city is. You know what might happen to us . . . Please visit with the senator and hear him out. The poor Church needs a strong man to protect it. The senator and Pope Sergius will protect us all."

"As long as the senatrix tells them to . . ."

The abbot collapsed into his throne. "Theodora is a virtuous and holy woman," he sputtered.

"And I'm Queen Maeve!"

Having made his point, Finbarr collected a stout staff, a small loaf of bread, a jug of the abbey's Frascati, a pound of cheese, a sheaf of paper, and a piece of charcoal and, after a brief but fervent prayer for guidance in the monastery chapel, set out for the Theophylact house in the Lateran neighborhood. He was not afraid of the Theophylact clan or anyone else. Superstitious in the very marrow of their bones, the Romans feared the Irishman's green eyes even more than they feared the evil eye of those who lived across the Tiber. Moreover, he had learned from his Irish relatives, at least as dangerous as the Roman nobles, that an apparently fearless man could face down almost anyone and win.

Usually.

The difference between Italian thugs and Irish thugs seemed to be limited to the greater wit and style of the latter.

While he doubted very much that the senator and his family wanted him to solve a mystery, he was curious to see what they were like. In Rome, a thousand years after the coming of the savior, the question wasn't whether force would rule. Rather, it was whether force might perhaps be combined with intelligence. The city through which he was carefully picking his way was hardly a city at all. It was a wilderness of ruins, twisted lanes, ramshackle houses, decaying, fortresslike castles, collapsing churches, patches of farm- and pasture-land, pestilential swamps, and ancient city walls with so many breaches in them that the Saracen raiders could enter almost at will—though they were normally content with sacking only St. Peter's, which was outside the city walls.

It was now a hundred years since the pope had crowned the Emperor Charles the Great. Everyone, Finbarr had been told, thought that the greatness of Rome would be restored. When Charles died, however, the Frankish princelings who claimed him as an ancestor had fallen to killing one another. Chaos had returned to Europe as Frankish armies fought endless battles, and the Saracens and the Vikings roamed at will, even on occasion warring against each other. Rome was Europe in miniature, the final wreckage of itself and all it stood for.

Three unsavory-looking men in tattered livery and dirty armor trailed after Finbarr as he threaded his way down a narrow lane toward the Lateran. The black Benedictine robes were no protection. He turned, flipped aside his cowl, and stared at them. They stumbled away and then began to run.

Perhaps ten thousand humans lived in the rubble of Rome itself, most of them criminals of one sort or another. Yet there were monks and nuns and priests and anchorites, many holy men and women, and doubtless even a few saints. Presumably God knew what He was doing.

The principal income of Rome came from the pilgrims who flocked to the city at great peril, from warring armies, from Saracen and Viking invaders, from wandering bandits, and from the clergy of St. Peter's itself, including an occasional rogue pope. Yet they came anyway, eager to visit the place where the Fisherman had died and was buried.

To Finbarr Mor O'Neill it made little sense. Yet he admired faith that could persist in the face of such lawlessness and corruption. The Holy Spirit, he mused as he entered the scruffy piazza in front of the Theophylact castle, had His own ways. Certainly He did not deign to seek the opinion of a wandering Irish monk and artist. The winter sun was retreating quickly from the Roman sky, as if fearful of what it might see if it lingered too long. The tower of the castle cast a long accusing finger of a shadow at Finbarr, as if asking why he was not in Ireland where he belonged. Behind the castle the ancient Basilica of St. John Lateran, the cathedral of Rome, was already shrouded in darkness. Its new roof, which replaced the one that had been destroyed by the earthquake during the "Cadaver Synod," seemed ready to collapse at the first hint of trembling rocks. Nothing was permanent anymore in the eternal city.

Though he was capable of astonishing and mostly sincere meekness at the abbey, Finbarr saw no reason to adopt such a strategy as he approached the house of Theophylact. He strode up to the four tough-looking guards in black-and-gold armor and livery who stood guard at the low door of the old building, and announced, "Finbarr Mor O'Neill, monk, artist, and prince of Ireland!"

It was fair to claim that he was the son of a king and hence a prince, though in Ireland anyone with a hill fort and twenty head of cattle could claim to be a king. Actually, his father owned several hundred head of cattle.

The guards, if anything even more vicious seeming than the typical Roman men-at-arms, prepared to sneer, noted Finbarr's cat-green eyes glowing in the dusk, and hesitated.

"Do you carry a sword, Brother Monk?" the ugliest one of them asked.

"Only a staff, Brother Captain," Finbarr replied, gesturing with open arms to indicate that he was defenseless. The guard seemed skeptical, perhaps because the Roman had never met a man as tall as Finbarr was.

"I believe that the senator is expecting me," he said mildly. "A matter of a dead pope, though that seems to be almost a daily problem."

The guard grunted, "Follow me, Brother Monk!"

With considerable clanking of the guard's armor, they strode down a dark corridor and into a vaulted chamber brilliantly illuminated by flaming wall torches.

"Finbarr Mor O'Neill." The monk gestured with his staff. Then after the briefest of hesitations, he continued, "Monk, artist, and prince of Ireland!"

The striking triptych of the Theophylact family had caused his hesitation. The senator was at least as tall as Finbarr himself and much broader. Finbarr had once fled a band of Saracen raiders at dusk outside of St. Peter's. He knew a Saracen when he saw one. Senator Theophylact—massive, swarthy, bearded, with long black hair and blacker eyes—was undoubtedly a Saracen, despite the massive gold cross that hung around the neck of his crimson gown. He had the same crafty eyes and the same cruel smile of the Saracen leader who, having outrun his band, had finally caught up with Finbarr at the Tiber bank.

Finbarr was always ready for martyrdom. However, he did not think it appropriate that he die at the hands of a thief for whom religion was irrelevant. He had thrown the pagan into the river and then, taking pity on the man's inability to swim, fished him out and sent him running back to the sea coast.

"The Prince of Rome welcomes the prince of Ireland," Theophylact said, having taken the measure of the monk, in a rich voice that seemed to make the timbers of the room quiver with respect. He extended his vast hand and offered it to Finbarr. The two men shook hands vigorously, as if they were acknowledging each other's proper value.

"My wife, the virtuous Theodora, my maiden daughter of scarce fifteen summers, Mazoria, and, oh, yes, His Holiness Pope Sergius."

Finbarr nodded respectfully to the women and murmured "Holiness" with a modest show of respect. He doubted that any of the appellations were correct. Sergius had been elected pope and then chased out of Rome. Theodora's virtue was suspect. While Mazoria was surely only fifteen, Finbarr would not have wanted to wager on her maidenhood.

The so-called pope was a stout man with a low forehead, no more than thirty-five, and with thick arms and an expression of dangerous befuddlement on his face. He was not very intelligent and all the more a menace precisely because of his stupidity. He was dressed as a soldier with armor and sword, not as a cleric. Unlike the others in the room, he smelled of the latrine.

The two women were extraordinary, the main reason for Finbarr's slight hesitation when he had encountered the Theophylact family. They were both tall, full-bodied, and sensuous, the mother in a dark blue gown with gold trim and the daughter in white with her presumed virginal blond hair worn loosely. Theodora's fingers were decked with rings. Her dark eyes darted back and forth as she carefully pondered this new apparition who had swept into their room. Beautiful, intelligent, and deadly, thought Finbarr, a she-wolf who would snap through a neck without thinking twice about it.

Mazoria was the most beautiful woman Finbarr had ever seen, though her beauty was that of sculpted ice. She wore no rings. Her eyes were cold and lifeless, her hands folded in repose, a Viking goddess, perhaps, or an ancient Celtic warrior goddess. She seemed indifferent to everyone else in the room. She would kill with the silent bite of a snake instead of the howl of a she-wolf. Finbarr felt his palms sweat. So much disturbing beauty and so much evil. He restrained an impulse to make the sign of the cross in self-defense.

"Sit down, O Monk and Prince of Ireland. We were about to sup. You will join us, of course."

They sat on benches around a vast oak table. Servants brought in trays heaped with food, enough to feed all the men-at-arms in the city. The Theophylacts and their papal guest continued to stare at Finbarr's green eyes.

"I am under a vow," he pleaded, "and must eat only food from my abbey."

Mazoria giggled ominously. "The one with the green eyes fears we will poison him, Papa!"

"Only, my lady, if I should become a threat to your family. I'm sure you and your mother poison only when necessary."

The senator threw back his head and laughed. "Right you are, Sir Prince. They much prefer to amuse themselves with men who are alive. The dead are not interesting."

"Save if they are popes who will not stay dead," Theodora snapped.

"Your vow limits you to your own wine, too?" the senator asked, lifting a jug. "This is the best red wine in all of Latium."

"It would be wasted on me, Excellency."

"So much more for us." The senator shrugged and then drained the jug with a single swallow. The pope did the same and belched loudly. Neither woman did more than sip from her goblet. A lute player appeared at the door of the room and began to sing. Sad, sensual, romantic songs.

Love—of a certain sort—hung heavily in the room.

Savages, Finbarr told himself, different only from my wilder Irish relatives in the beauty of these women. He tried to concentrate on the self-anointed Prince of Rome. The women were distracting and noted every glance of his at them. Far from being frightened by his green eyes, they seemed to find them amusing in a sexual way. Finbarr muttered a quick prayer against the temptations of the demons.

"You have been in Rome long enough, O Prince and Monk, to understand our problems?"

"I have been here eight years, Excellency. Long enough to know that I do not understand them. Why do you not instruct me?"

"Rome must protect itself," the senator said with a sigh as he picked up a large dagger. "The Saracens and the Vikings attack us, the Franks like that accursed usurper Lothair of Spoleto treat us like playthings, my fellow nobles lack both principles and sense, the clergy—with the exception of the monks like yourself, of course—are corrupt. The mobs want only to pillage and loot. If someone like me does not see to the defense of the city and the church, we will soon cease to exist."

Finbarr put aside his crust of bread and his jug of wine, opened his parchment, and began rapidly to sketch the Prince of Rome as they talked.

"Surely the city needs order," he agreed, wondering why the Theophylacts needed a monk's verdict about the death of the last several popes.

"Only my husband has the wisdom to protect the people and the pope!" Theodora interjected.

"Without his power, the chaos will never end," Pope Sergius agreed.

With his army poised at the fringe of the city, Sergius was a major cause of the most current chaos. Apparently he and Theophylact were proposing an alliance, in the absence of any Frankish prince at the moment, to restore order to the city—or something that passed for order and provided them with steady revenue at the same time.

Finbarr noted that Sergius was too preoccupied with

lewd admiration of Mazoria to pay much attention to the conversation. The young woman ignored his leers, but was certainly well aware of them.

"It began with Pope Formosus," Theophylact began tentatively, waiting to see if the Irish monk would rise to the defense of that good and perhaps great man. Finbarr kept his thoughts on that subject to himself.

"He made an alliance with the Franks against the people of Rome," Theodora continued. "He imposed rules on the priests and the lay people. He took away our freedom. Soon everyone—nobles, clergy, people—regretted that they had elected him."

When a pope died, the leading clergy of the city met in St. John Lateran, consulted with the nobles, and nominated a new bishop for the city. The man was presented to the crowd, which was in fact little more than a mob. If they cheered loudly enough, the man would be crowned pope. There was nothing, except armed force, to prevent another group of priests, another band of nobles, and another mob from staging their own election. The Frankish emperors, loyal and devout Catholics whatever else they might be, often imposed order and supported an election which was more or less valid.

"Then Pope Formosus died, and Pope Stephen was elected," Theophylact went on sonorously. "Formosus had created so much disorder that it was necessary to summon a synod of bishops and priests to restore order to the city. That synod had no choice but to declare all the acts of Pope Formosus invalid."

"Including his appointments and ordinations."

"Of course . . ."

Theophylact had left out some of the details of the infamous synod. The dead pope had been dug up from his grave and put on public trial, dressed in full vestments and propped up on a throne. After he was convicted, his body was dismembered and thrown into the Tiber. During the deliberations, Rome had been shaken by a serious earthquake which had caused the roof of St. John Lateran to collapse. The Romans, not unreasonably, thought this was a sign of God's anger at the city. The clergy were now split into pro-Formosus and pro-Stephen factions, each denying the validity of the other's ordinations—and right to collect fees and stipends from tourists. Sergius, who had been made a bishop by Formosus, was delighted when Stephen came to power to seek ordination as a lowly deacon.

"For a time we had peace," Theophylact continued. "Then Stephen died . . . or was murdered by one of Formosus's accursed toadies . . . and we had confusion again. The good people of Rome elected Sergius here as pope because he had always been an ally of Stephen."

"But Lambert of Spoleto came to Rome," Theodora snapped, "and forced the poor pope to go into exile."

Now Lambert had been banished from Italy, and Theophylact, doubtless for reasons of his own, thought it wise to invite Sergius and his men-at-arms back to Rome as allies. The five men who had served briefly as pope after Stephen himself had been strangled could be conveniently dismissed as antipopes. Why would anyone want to be pope when it was a rare pope these days who served for as much as a year?

"It is time, I am convinced," the senator went on smoothly, "for the unfortunate matter of Formosus and Stephen to be forgotten. Even now, in Rome, the followers of both men are split into many factions. Both Pope Leo and Pope Christopher, so recently dead, are followers of Formosus, but they were bitter rivals. Sergius here, who in fact worked with both Formosus and Stephen, is the man to heal all wounds and restore unity to the clergy of Rome. Isn't that true, Sergius?"

"Uh, yes, of course," said the pope, taking his eyes momentarily away from the nubile body of the senator's daughter.

The senator apparently had no hesitation about turning his daughter over to the pope to seal their alliance. Her eyes were, however, consuming Finbarr, who avoided her gaze lest his powers of thought, already dulled by the sensuality of the hall of the Theophylacts, be snuffed out.

"What do you think of this plan, Finbarr Mor O'Neill?"

Theophylact asked expansively. "Does it not make excellent sense?"

"Any plan that would bring peace to this holy city and safety to the devout pilgrims would make excellent sense . . . Who would oppose it?"

"Those foolish priests," Theodora snarled, "who supported Pope Christopher and who believe he was poisoned in this house!"

Ah.

"Although he threw Pope Leo into a cistern and proclaimed himself pope without so much as a false conclave, he, ah, had a certain rough integrity about him which appealed to some of the priests and even some of the bishops. I invited him and Sergius here to supper two nights ago to see if some arrangement might be made. I guaranteed him and his supporters that nothing would befall him. Alas, my promise was frustrated!"

He slammed the table in fury, knocking several large chunks of meat to the floor. Several well-fed hunting dogs dashed off with them.

"I keep my word!" the senator insisted, his faced twisted in fury. "I will personally strangle the killer, whoever it may be."

"Pope Christopher," Mazoria giggled, "was not as cautious as you, O green-eyed monk. He did not bring his own food."

"Quiet, wench!" The senator struck his daughter with his massive hand, sending her sprawling to the floor. No one else in the room moved or spoke. Finbarr clenched his fist. In Ireland, a man who did that to a noblewoman would have put his life at risk. Rome, he reminded himself, was not Ireland.

"We all ate here at this very table last night!" Theophylact thundered on. "My wife, my daughter, the two popes, and myself. We ate the same beef, drank the same wine, nibbled at the same fruit, retired at the same time. Yet somehow Pope Christopher died of the almond poison, and no one else did."

"Ah," said Finbarr gently, not liking the situation at all.

He helped Mazoria back to her chair. The young woman's eyes were as icy as ever.

"We fed all the food that remained to the dogs. They are alive, as you can see. I must persuade Pope Christopher's followers that I did not kill their pope so that they will accept Pope Sergius's peace. Even now they await your verdict."

"Ah."

"I want you to tell me the name of the killer, O Prince of Ireland."

"Either your wife or your daughter or His Holiness here or yourself?"

"I assure you that I did not poison Pope Christopher!" he thundered.

"So there are only three suspects?"

"You must tell me which one is guilty."

The lutenist continued to sing soft songs of unrequited love. One of the hunting dogs curled up at Finbarr's feet. Mazoria stared at him hungrily. The situation made no sense. None of the three suspects seemed anxious. Theophylact was unlikely to strangle his wife or daughter or his chosen pope. Something sinister was happening. Theophylact wanted a suspect who would please the supporters of Pope Christopher and presumably the lay mobs who would shortly rally to them. It was up to Finbarr to find such a suspect, or *he* might be fed to the mobs.

"Where is the body of Christopher?" he asked, turning again to his drawing of the senator.

"We buried him already, behind my *casa*. We will transfer him to St. Peter's tomorrow."

"So soon?"

"He had begun to smell when we discovered him in his room here early this morning."

"He remained here last night?" Finbarr asked with a shiver.

"Yes, we negotiated most of the night. We were going to finish the final details of our peace treaty this morning and then sing a Te Deum in John Lateran. When Pope Christopher did not appear to break his fast, we sent servants to his room." The senator shrugged. "He smelled of almonds, and already his body had begun to bloat."

Finbarr's charcoal rapidly created a sketch of Theodora. He quickly erased it. His fingers were convinced that the senatrix was a slut.

"Then he could not have been poisoned here at dinner," Finbarr insisted. "That poison takes effect quickly. Someone must have brought him a drink of wine during the night. Or perhaps there was a jug left in his room."

"We always leave wine for our guests," Theodora said primly.

And only a fool would drink it, Finbarr thought to himself.

"You are telling me," said the senator, frowning, a serious man about to make a serious decision, "that no one who shared the table last night with Pope Christopher could have poisoned him?"

So that was the game, was it? The monk had cleared everyone. Perhaps a servant had slipped the deadly acid into Christopher's drink while he was preparing for bed. Who would believe that argument?

Those who wanted to believe it.

"I am saying that he was not poisoned here at table."

"Then anyone could have killed the pope—a servant perhaps, or someone who slipped into the *casa*?"

"Yes."

"You will tell the people that tomorrow?"

"After I have made other investigations."

Theophylact drew in his breath. Then he slowly exhaled. "Of course, we must be thorough."

"He was a worthless man," Sergius said with a grunt, his lips now only a few inches from Mazoria's breast. "He knew I was the true pope. He wanted a bigger bribe."

Despite the wishes of his mind, Finbarr's fingers sketched Mazoria. If her mother appeared as a tart, the young woman emerged as a goddess. *"Libera nos a mala,"* he whispered to himself.

"We were very close to a final agreement," Theophylact

insisted. "We parted last night as good friends. There was no need to kill him."

Someone thought there was a need.

The conversation turned to Ireland. They talked many long hours. Finbarr told stories about Ireland and its kings and its saints, including his favorite story of how Brendan, the Holy Navigator, had sailed to the Land of Promise in the west. Finally, Theophylact insisted that it was time to sleep. Tomorrow, when the cock crowed, the Irish monk would finish his investigation. A servant led him to a small room in the cellar, good enough for a monk. It was unlikely that the late pope had been sent to the same room the night before.

Finbarr did not lie on his pallet. Rather he sat in the corner of the tiny room and recited the psalms of the day from memory. There were two great joys in the monk's life—copying manuscripts and praising God. He needed to praise God to banish the emotions of corruption from that horrible dinner table.

Who had killed Pope Christopher? Finbarr thought he knew, though the thought brought him no consolation.

The door to the room opened softly. A woman's garment rustled softly as she sat on the pallet next to where she thought Finbarr was sleeping. Just one garment and that, he suspected, quite thin.

"I am honored, Lady Theodora," he hissed at her, "that you deign to visit me. You have perhaps brought me some wine, just as you brought the pope."

The woman gasped. "Those green eyes see in the dark!"

"What other purpose would there be in green eyes? Please lace up your gown. It is cold here in the cellar."

"Sergius did it. That should be obvious! Who else stands to gain from the death of that foolish priest? If my husband were not a fool, he would dispose of Sergius, too, and select a pope who is free from these insane Roman parties!"

"You have a candidate?"

"Of course I do. I will not tell you his name."

"I think you'd better leave, my lady."

"You spurn me?"

"No, I ask you very politely to leave so I can finish my prayers."

The senatrix snorted derisively and slipped away. Not many men had turned her away, especially not with the excuse that they had to say their prayers. Finbarr conceded himself some slight reason for pride. He had resisted the woman's charms. Pride, he warned himself, precedes the fall.

The next visitor was Pope Sergius. He promised Finbarr the city of Ostia and a cardinal's hat if he found Theodora guilty. She had her own candidate for pope, a priest named John who was her lover. Would the senator strangle his own wife? Cheerfully. He knew she was a slut. He had other women.

Finbarr made no promises. The pope slunk away with a curse. The monk still believed that Theophylact was looking to find someone to blame for an unsolved mystery in order to placate the fickle Roman mobs.

Suddenly he was aware that someone else was in the room with him, someone who had entered noiselessly and sat next to him, someone with a stunning womanly scent.

"I will make you pope, O green-eyed monk," Mazoria murmured. "Protect me from that monster and you will be pope and you and I will rule together—Rome, Italy, perhaps the world!"

She leaned against him, her hair soft against his face, her nipples hard against his chest.

Finbarr bounded away from her.

"Cover yourself," he ordered her, grabbing his staff.

"You cannot see me in the dark!"

He could not, thank God!

"Get out of here!"

"The man will beat me!"

"Only if you let him!"

"Please!"

Her plea seemed honest enough. She was but a child. She needed protection.

"Out!"

She left quietly.

Exhausted and trembling, Finbarr leaned against the wall. It was as he thought. The daughter had dreams far greater than the mother or the father could imagine.

Later the senator came to escort him to interviews with terrified servants. Theophylact concluded after these interviews that the killer was one of Christopher's servants who had been in the service of Pope Leo. The man had disappeared. Theophylact promised that he would be found and punished. Finbarr doubted that the search would be serious.

"I will tell the people that the Irish monk said that Pope Christopher did not die at table. None of us who broke bread with him killed him."

"Not while they were breaking bread with him," Finbarr reminded the senator.

"Of course," the senator said smoothly.

Back in his scriptorium on the Aventine Hill, Finbarr made peace with Pangur Ban by offering that offended worthy a saucer of milk. Did Theophylact know that his daughter had poisoned Pope Christopher so that her lover Sergius would not have to depend on her father? Did he realize that she was the only one who could gain from the complete elimination of the unfortunate Christopher? Possibly. Possibly not. Perhaps he suspected and did not want his suspicions confirmed. If he had asked Finbarr for the truth, the scribe would have told it to him. Could a father believe that his daughter was more vicious and more dangerous than he and his wife put together?

In a few years the young woman with the cold, empty eyes would dominate Rome.

Unless, as seemed likely to Finbarr, someone poisoned her first.

He looked at his charcoal sketch of her. She seemed so vulnerable, so innocent. Rome would see more of her. So far the gates of hell had been kept at bay. Rarely had hell appeared in such attractive form.

He sighed, as only an Irishman can sigh. He would pray for the woman. God was good and loved everyone. Surely he must love Mazoria, too.

He tore the sketch into tiny pieces and threw it out the

window of the scriptorium, where it joined the unexpected snow that was falling on Rome, on both the living and the dead of the eternal city.

Note

From 904 to 1048, Rome and the papacy were dominated by five generations of the Theophylact family. The gates of hell did not quite prevail against the Church. But it was, as Wellington remarked of Waterloo, a "damn near thing." One cannot reflect theologically on the papacy and not face this century and a half of history. It presents acute problems for those who argue that the Holy Spirit chooses each pope deliberately and that the pope is immediately and intimately connected to Jesus, for whom he speaks.

The Theophylacts were killers of popes, bribers of popes, sons of popes, mistresses of popes, mothers of popes. Five of them actually were popes, none of them prizes, and three of them, John XI, John XII, and Benedict IX, made Alexander VI, Rodrigo Borgia, look like a saint. Installed in their teens or early twenties, they were given to gambling, drinking, adultery, rape, and murder. They plundered the papal treasury and pilgrims who came to Rome. The Lateran Palace where they lived was reported to have become a brothel. They were alleged to have raped women pilgrims in St. Peter's. John XI is supposed to have died while committing an act of adultery. John XII was murdered, it is said, by an angry husband who caught him in adultery. Benedict IX sold the papacy to a man who wanted to succeed him.

The most deadly members of the family were the matriarch Theodora and her daughter Mazoria, who ran both civil and ecclesiastical Rome for the first third of the tenth century. The former was the mistress of John X, whom she installed as pope, only later to decree his death. The latter was the mistress (at the age of fifteen) of Pope Sergius III and the mother of John XI (Pope Sergius was his father). In tandem, these two women dominated papal appointments for thirty years, naming popes, deposing them, and ordering their deaths. Mazoria was called the senatrix of Rome from 1026 to 1032 while her son reigned as pope. Then another son, Alberic, overthrew and imprisoned her and treated his brother the pope like a slave. Nonetheless, Alberic and his sons (one of whom became John XII, a man as bad as his uncle John XI) and grandsons ran Rome for another hundred years with the same iron hands as their maternal ancestors, until the Emperor Conrad deposed Benedict IX, the great-great-grandson of Theodora and the great-grandson of Mazoria, and reform finally came to Rome. The power to name the Bishop of Rome was taken away from the priests, nobles, and people of Rome and given to the cardinals, a reform that was unquestionably necessary at the time.

These were dark times in Europe. The Danes were raiding northern Europe; the Saracens had invaded southern Italy and sacked Rome. Rome was a lawless jungle. The German emperors tried repeatedly to impose reform on the city, but the Roman populace, mostly an unruly mob, just as repeatedly revolted. The streets of Rome were dangerous both by day and night. Power came from the tips of swords and spears. Anyone of prominence used private armies to rise to power and the strength of the same armies to stay in power. The Theophylacts were no more murderous or corrupt or vicious or rapacious than any of the other nobles who lived in this jungle. They were only more successful. Given the times, the remarkable fact is that the papacy survived and that such visitors as Otto I and England's King Canute had enormous reverence for the office of the pope.

One can certainly argue with some justification that it was the Holy Spirit that preserved the papacy through these terrible times, no small achievement. But to see God doing much else during the reign of the Theophylacts is an insult to the deity.

The promise of Jesus is not that there will be great popes all the time, not that popes will necessarily be good men, not that they will be the best available choice for the office, not that they will speak for the Holy Spirit every time they say something, not that they will always reflect the wishes of God, but only that they will not destroy the Church. That promise has been kept, if only just barely on occasion. The Theophylacts did not destroy the papacy or the Church, but they sure gave it a try.

Sharyn McCrumb is a New York Times *best-selling author whose award-winning novels celebrating the history and folklore of Appalachia have received both academic and popular acclaim. She is the author of, among others, "The Ballad Books," consisting of* If Ever I Return, Pretty Peggy-O, The Hangman's Beautiful Daughter, She Walks These Hills, *and* The Rosewood Casket, *all of which were named* New York *or* Los Angeles Times *notable books. The most recent in this series is* The Ballad of Frankie Silver.

For this collection, Sharyn has reached further back into her ancestral heritage and created a tale of a woman who wished to leave the world but found that it, and the voice of an old friend, would not let her go. The story is based on another ballad, which may itself be the remnant of a true story, lost to history.

LARK IN THE MORNING

Sharyn McCrumb

It was a fine spring day, what I could see of it through the bars of my window. The grass had the feathery look of earliest spring, and the buds upon the oak bid fair to opening before the week was out. The light is different every morning. As the year passes, the shadows move upon the gravestones and the cloud patterns change like an ever-weaving tapestry of wool upon water. Mine is a world of simple pleasures.

I am within the village, but not of it. I watch it as I watch the mice in the churchyard grasses—and, like them, the village forgets that I am watching, and goes on about its business, absorbed in its daily cares. It has been five years since I walked out upon the grass or felt the sun on my face. Five years since I came into my little stone room beneath the church, from which only death can take me. To the village folk I must seem as eternal as the church tower: yet another stone thing looming on the periphery of their lives.

The men of the village speak to me in the low voices of

reverence, or else, according to their nature, with the bluff heartiness of unspoken pity as if I had reached a great age. 'Tis a great sacrifice she's made for Jesu our Lord, they're thinking as they stop by my little window, cap in hand, to ask for a prayer or a kind word of counsel. They hint sometimes at the angel who bade me leave the world so long ago, or at the memory of some long dead suitor, a fair young swain for whom I still must mourn. They do not ask me about any of it, for that would not be seemly, but I am the stuff of legends among the lads.

The womenfolk are different. They will take my prayers and my counsel readily enough, but they measure me with their eyes. They see little enough of a tragedy in being shut away in a simple room for all of your life, with nothing to do but pray and think about the hereafter. They kneel down to my barred window, some oftener than others, to pass the time of day with me, and they bring me a bit of cheese or a new-laid egg when they can spare it, but there isn't a one of them that hasn't said at least once: "It must be a fine thing to be shut away here, and not having to wear yourself out with weaving, and cooking, and birthing. To be freed from a woman's lot, and be thought holy for it in the bargain! A fine thing for some." They said it when they came to tell me that young Mary, the fletcher's wife, had died in childbed. *All right for you,* their eyes told me. *You are safe enough.*

When I was first called to live the life of a recluse, the bishop himself came and questioned me, to make sure that I had a good character and that I would be pious and disciplined, for there is no abbess to guide one's soul in a solitary life. I told the bishop of my visions and the voice that bade me do this, but he was more concerned with whether I could pay for my keep and retain a serving woman to see to my simple needs. He settled on the site of my hermitage—a little stone room attached to the foundation of the parish church, with one small window just at eye level with the gravestones, for I was as buried as they, folk said. There was a great ceremony initiating me into the life of an anchorite, and then it was done, and the tale of my existence had come to the last line: *and there she lived forever after.*

The men of the village think that *anchorite* is a pious word for madwoman, but their wives and daughters know better. I am saner than Eve, the mother of us all, and no one will drive me from my paradise. My prayers are words of thanksgiving—for my great deliverance, but I take care not to be overheard, for it does the village no harm to think I have made a great sacrifice in renouncing the world.

It is only very early in the morning that I have the peace and solitude to think of such philosophy, for the rest of my day is cluttered enough. At first light will come Eleanor, bringing bread and onions to break my fast. She will complain of the dampness in her bones, and the chill of the dawn air through which she must walk to bring me my meal, and I will smile and tell her what a treasure she is, which is no more than the truth, though I sometimes wish I could tell her so less often.

When the morning mist begins to clear, a shepherd or a plowman will stop by on his way to the fields to say a word or two. My fingers are busy with my handiwork as we speak. Four of the village children come to my window for a reading lesson at midmorning, and later on the women-folk come, with a bit of wool to card, like as not, and they sit upon the grass outside my window when the day is fine, carding their thoughts as well, so that one way and another, the life of the parish flows past me as if I were a rock in the river. I may have renounced the world—but indeed it has not returned the favor!

I am patient, though, with my trickle of visitors, for patience is a species of charity, and what else have I to give but time?

Through the grayness I saw Eleanor approaching, hunched in her cape against the chill of dawn and, as usual, giving no thought to the beauty of the world through which she passed. I, who ached for the sight of forest from the hilltop and for the chill of the stony brook on my bare feet, stayed pressed against my window, watching the light thicken.

"A lovely dawn," I told her as she passed the bundle of bread and cheese through my little window. "It will be a fine day,"

"Fine enough for some," she grumbled. "It will see Maud Longdon married—which is more than I ever thought *I* would."

"I did," I said. "Haven't I been making her a wedding gift for all of this past year?" I held up the little harp that I had carved so slowly and deliberately lo these many months. The body of the harp was hewn from oak, and I had worn away at it with my little knife until swirls of leaves and faces of angels adorned one side. At the top the winged lion of St. Mark curled its paw around an open book. The harp pegs were carved of bone, and they shone white in the dimness. The instrument lacked only the strings now to see it done. I had sent for strings, for I could not fashion them myself. It would sound its first notes at the wedding celebration.

"Of course Maud Longdon would marry, Eleanor. Her father is rich enough. She would have had suitors willing for that alone. And she is not ill-favored."

"No—but she isn't a patch on her younger sister. God rest poor Rosamund's soul." Eleanor crossed herself, and her eyes sparkled with a tear of remembrance. "I'm sure I hope she is in paradise, for she was a blithe and bonny girl."

"She was buried in consecrated ground." My eyes strayed to the wall that joined my cell to the parish church. Beyond those stones lay the crypt, and within it lay many folk of the village, but none so sorely missed by me as Rosamund. I fancied sometimes at night that I could hear her whispering to me from behind the wall, and I would rise and say the rosary and wish her peace until sleep overtook me or until the dawn light streamed into my cell, banishing the fancies of the night.

It had been a year already, since the body of poor Rosamund Longdon had been found in a stream in the forest. My faithful Eleanor had been the bearer of those tidings, too.

A year to the day, almost. Eleanor had come bustling through the mist with such a brisk and purposeful step that I knew she had some burden this morning besides her own ailments. She was big with news. I watched her from the shadows of my window, hoping that the bad tidings—*for what other kind were there?*—would not strike too close to heart.

"Well, now, here's a thing," she had said to me, handing me a wooden plate of apples and bread. "You'll never imagine what William Bewly has pulled from the river."

"Who was it?" I murmured, making a mental tally of the village. "Not a child, I hope."

Eleanor frowned, and I could see that I had not played my part to her liking. "I never said it was a body, did I? It could have been a stray lamb, or a great golden fish with a ring in its belly, or—or—"

"Or the feather of an angel's wing." I gave her a sad smile. "I wish it had been, Eleanor, but I fear that my first guess was right. Now tell me who of our flock has been lost."

"I'll never understand how you know these things. Nobody can ever steal a march on you, my lady. Anyone would think you went out creeping around the village of a night, instead of sitting there alone every hour that God sends in that coffin of a room. But you are right enough. A body it was. Poor William Bewly was whiter than a fish's belly from the shock of it. He's trembling still, I'll warrant. He had to carry her, you see. All the way back to the village. And her cold and lifeless in his arms."

I nodded. "Was it Maud Longdon, then? I have feared for her. I thought that either her pride or her passion would lead to her destruction."

"Ha!" said Eleanor. "Not she!"

"Who, then?"

"Her sister. Rosamund."

My hand tightened on the bar of the window, but I did not shed tears. I watched the morning light play upon the stones in the churchyard, and listened to the soft thudding of horses' hooves on the road beyond. A bright beautiful day, unheeded by those who toiled in it, as if existence were an endless gift to be taken for granted. How little may we take for granted in this world, but how seldom we remember that. Pretty, laughing Rosamund was dead. I had not known her before I began my vocation as an anchorite, but afterward she came often to visit at my window, and her gentle kindness was a welcome respite from my prayers and duties. To others in the parish I listened with all the patience I could muster for their troubles, and to the parish priest I made my confessions before God, but to Rosamund and Rosamund alone, I spoke as a friend. I would miss her greatly.

I had not expected this sorrowful news, though I did suspect that trouble was brewing at Longdon Grove. Of all the children sired on three wives by Sir Gervase Longdon, only two daughters had lived past infancy. There were no sons to carry on the family name, and no wife alive to offer hope for one. Maud, the eldest daughter, stood to inherit her father's lands, but Rosamund, the younger, had already inherited their mother's beauty. The village murmured at the pride of the one and the grace of the other, for we knew that there was strife between them, for all that Sir Gervase would overlook it. Proud Maud, chagrined by her plainness, was too fond of reminding Rosamund that one day she would be dependent upon Maud's charity. For her part, Rosamund replied that she would take care to marry well so as to escape her sister's grudging beneficence.

So matters stood when Alan Dacre came to Longdon. They say he had been at court, and knew all the fashions and could play upon a harp like the angel he well resembled. He was a tall young man with clear blue eyes and a ready smile for even the humblest of mortals, for all that he was a Norman born and bred. He had come on business to see the old squire, some business about horses, one of the stockmen told me, but as the days passed and the visit showed no signs of coming to an end, the village came to understand that other matters were delaying Alan Dacre's departure. Which of the sisters, we wondered, made him tarry?

The servants at the hall carried tales of his riding out with one of the Longdon sisters, and then of playing on his harp while the other one sang. He taught them both in turn the fashionable dances of the court, and if he had a favorite, he had been careful to give no evidence of the fact to the talebearers. For a young man of gentle birth but few prospects, the visit must have been an idyll of present beauty and future promise, but at last, of course, he must make his choice between two willing brides. Which prize would Alan Dacre choose: the proud landed lady who would one day command great wealth, or her fair and gentle sister?

I had thought I knew the answer to that, for Rosamund had whispered as much to me, the last time I saw her—the last I ever would. But perhaps she herself had been deceived by the ambiguous words of a cruel lover. Why else would her body be found in the forest stream?

I had made up my mind that Rosamund Longdon would lie in consecrated ground, for I would not give the Church any cause to suspect that she had taken her own life. I resolved to say nothing of our last talk together, except what I could say with perfect truth: that Rosamund when I saw her then was the flower of happiness, and that no hint of self-destruction lay in her eyes or in her voice. That much was true. If, after she left me, she learned that her lover proved false, I could not swear to it, and so I would say nothing of it.

"How did it happen, then?" I asked Eleanor.

"That's more than anyone knows," sighed Eleanor. "Miss Rosamund was missed this morning, when they found her bed not slept in, but there was not a trace of her until William came back from the wildwood with the body, lifeless as a lump of clay."

"Had there been a search for her?"

"Upon the grounds of Longdon Grove, I think. There's acres enough there to comb."

"And had Alan Dacre gone out to search for her?"

Eleanor gave me a puzzled look. "They do say that he had been taken ill the night before—and that he was taken worse when the sad news was brought to him. He is down with fever, and Miss Maud has put aside her grief to tend to him herself, so fearful are they for his life."

"I must pray for her soul and for his recovery, then," I said. "And you must bring me any news of Longdon."

There was little news thereafter, though. The churchmen met to talk about the fate of Rosamund. I was not present, of course, but her father spoke for her, insisting that the girl had met with an accident on a morning walk. He did not explain how a young gentlewoman might find herself in the swollen stream of a spring river, but the women who laid out the body swore that Rosamund had died a maiden, and as there was no proof otherwise on the manner of her death, her father's pronouncement of misadventure was accepted. No one spoke of suicide, for even the sternest of those present forbore to think of gentle Rosamund banished in death from the sight of God.

And so, three days after the news of her death had grieved the village, the sad procession of her funeral passed by my little window. She was laid to rest in the crypt with only the thickness of a wall between us.

And in my dreams she wept.

After seven nights of dreaming, I knew what I must do. I began to tell my visitors the materials that I required, and in due time, when they brought them, I began to fashion a beautiful harp in memory of my friend. In the beginning I sent for Tom the joiner, and told him that God had sent me a vision, instructing me to build a small harp, just the size to fit under one's arm, I said. It must be heavily carved, I told him, not a mere sounding board of strings, but a thing of beauty in itself.

I must make a harp. This pronouncement frightened poor Tom a bit, for he is a plain man, who thinks that angels should know their place as do the rest of us, but at last he drew out a pattern for me, telling me what I must do to turn wood into music. I listened, and at his direction I practiced a bit on scraps of soft pine wood that he brought. After a fortnight of daily visits to see my progress, Tom said I was fit enough for the task, though why the Almighty should wish such a chore on a woman was more than he could fathom.

I worked on the harp each day, between my prayers and my devotions, between my meals and my visitors, between waking and sleeping. I cut and carved and polished and fashioned the harp of oak and bone. I made swirls of wood in the likeness of leaves and flowers to adorn the sides of the instrument. Into the post where the stringing pegs go, I carved the winged lion of St. Mark, as I had seen it drawn once upon a manuscript. My fingers blistered from the rough work, and my knives went back and forth to the blacksmith to be resharpened as I wore them down upon the unyielding oak wood, but still I worked, and gradually, as the months passed, the instrument took shape beneath my hands.

It was nearly finished now. I knew it would be, for I knew nearly to the day how long I would have to see to its construction. I would like to have carved a face into the post of the harp, but that feat was beyond my skill. Still, it was a fair enough bit of craftsmanship, for I had labored long over it.

The death of gentle Rosamund was a nine days' wonder in the parish, and presently her name began to be mentioned less often. Other matters drifted into the conversation of my visitors, and presently a day or two went by altogether without my hearing her name upon the lips of anyone, save in my prayers.

But still in my dreams she wept.

After a time, Alan Dacre went away from Longdon, as if he could no longer think of reasons to delay his departure. Or perhaps the air of mourning in the house made his visit unseemly. He returned to London, folk told me, and although Miss Maud spent her time writing letters instead of dancing, it was thought in the village that we had seen the last of Alan Dacre. Those who blamed him for the death of Rosamund thought the parish well rid of him, but I said nothing to encourage such talk, for I thought we might not have seen the end of the matter yet.

I was right. Presently he came back. The current of village news ebbed and flowed past my window, and so, with all the other news of newborn children, strayed lambs, and parish ailments, I came to hear tales of happier times at Longdon Hall. The music had begun again. Alan the courtier had brought back new songs from afar, and he was teaching the lady Maud to play them on the lute. Together the pair of them took long rides across the fields, as spring struggled back from the little death of winter. It seemed to be spring in their hearts already, but they were watched by others who were slower to let go of the cold.

"Never a word about her that's gone, m'lady," an old servant from the hall whispered to me one morning as she handed me a bit of newly made sausage. "And for all that there's mourning worn by the family, there's no lack of laughter from some I could name, carrying on with that courtly gentleman as if she'd never had a Sister. And he all smiles to her. But I'll take my oath upon it, 'twas the other one he cared for. There! I've said it, and I hope it won't be held against me, for it's only the truth, and anyhow, telling you is like whispering to the grave, for you won't give away secrets, will you, m'lady?"

I promised that I would not, and the serving woman promised me a plump dove from the Longdon dovecote and went on her way.

The time of mourning was over, and the wedding would go on.

Over the years I have seen many a wedding procession through my little portal on the churchyard: happy people, who were God's gift to one another; trembling, tearful girl brides, marched to the altar by a stern father; implacable peasant girls, big with child, joyless in the coming marriage but full of dark satisfaction that the perpetrator should be brought to justice. Today I thought I knew what I would see: the triumphant face of one who has won the race and claimed the prize, not a lover but a possessor. I wondered if she knew that she had bought him with the promise of her inheritance, and would it matter to her if she did know?

There would be music at the revels after the ceremony itself had ended, and I knew that Jamie Ramsgate, the miller's son, would be first among the musicians summoned to play for the happy couple, for he could make the strings of an instrument speak with the tongues of angels. They said that he could hear a song once and could play it ever after.

The morning of the wedding I asked Eleanor to bid Jamie Ramsgate make haste to visit me at my window, and I took it as a sign of God's love of justice that he came straightaway.

"It should be a fair celebration, Sister," he said to me, cap in hand, for he was a respectful lad. "They have been roasting an ox since daybreak. Shall I bring you a bit of food by and by?"

"You can do more for me than that, Jamie," I said, pressing my face close against the window and speaking with soft urgency. "You can take my gift to the revels. Indeed, you must be part of the gift, if you are willing?"

The harp would just fit through the bars of my window. I had taken care that it should. With a sigh of admiration, Jamie ran his hands over the newly gilded wood. "It's a wonder," he whispered. "This is a gift to the wedding party? And have you done it yourself?"

I nodded.

"Do another like it and I'll find someone to wed myself," he said, smiling.

"There is more to the gift, though," I reminded him. "And you must deliver that as well."

I repeated my instructions three times, to make sure that he understood and that he was word-perfect in his mission, for there would be only the one chance to administer the justice of heaven. Jamie Ramsgate was an imperfect instrument to do the work of our Lord, but there was no help for it. I could not go with him. I could not even know if he had succeeded until someone in their charity remembered to come and tell me.

At last I thought him as ready as he was going to be, and I sent him off with a blessing—and a silent prayer for heaven's help when the moment came.

It seemed a long time to wait. Never had time hung so heavy on my hands as on that bright afternoon, as the shadows seemed not at all to lengthen within the churchyard as the day stretched on in eerie silence. All the village had gone to the wedding feast. I tidied my cell, and said my prayers three times, and I tried to get on with my needlework, but I pricked my fingers till they bled, for my hands were shaking so. At length I simply sat there staring out into the square of daylight and gave myself up to waiting— for patience is a virtue, and like many virtues it was difficult and unpleasant to attain.

It was Eleanor who broke my vigil. The sun lay well behind the oak branches when she marched up to my window, her eyes glinting like the sun on silver. "Well, my lady, you have done it now!" she cried. "There's talk of sending for the bishop, for 'tis a sin and a sacrilege you've done, for all the good that's come of it!"

"Tell me the good first," I said.

She made as if to dispute me, but after a moment she pursed her lips and said, "Very well. You shall hear of your miracle first. Much good may it do you, I'm sure. Young Jamie came to the wedding feast, carrying that great beast of a harp you've been slaving over. And the lady Maud, flushed with victory now she's a wife, says to him, 'Oh, have you come to play for the revels?' And Jamie says to her, 'I will, madam, but the harp is a gift from the anchoress herself. She made it. See. It is a fine bit of work, all carved wood, and bones to peg the strings. She says you'll know those bones when the harp plays. They come from Longdon.'"

I nodded. He had followed his instructions well.

"Jamie commences to play upon that harp then, and folk are gathered around him listening to a sad song, and suddenly Miss Maud tries to dash the harp from his hands. 'Stop that playing!' she cries. 'How have you made that harp say my sister's name? Stop!' Well, folk began staring at her, for her face is red, and the young gentleman, Dacre, tries to pull her away, but she shakes free, and begins to curse—well, she curses *you*, m'lady. In front of the priest and everybody."

"What did she say of me? You may tell me."

" 'The anchoress is a witch!' she screamed. 'She has robbed the grave of my sister Rosamund, and used her bones to make this devil's harp! Hear how it calls out, accusing me of drowning my sister. I did but push her into the water when she confessed her betrothal to my true love. It was God's will that she should drown, for He did not get her out. God's will!' "

"I am glad that she confessed." I said. "She may save her soul by it."

"But not her life. They have taken her away, right enough, for to be sure she murdered her sister for jealousy. But for all the good you did in avenging poor Rosamund, there's the charge of blasphemy to answer. Grave robbing. The bishop himself is sent for."

I smiled. "Let him come," I said. "For I have yet a bit of the evidence to show him. Jamie said that the harp's bones were from Longdon, and so they were. They came from a dove the serving woman brought me to eat a few weeks back."

Eleanor blinked. "Dove's bones? But—the miracle? How did they say the name of Rosamund?"

"A guilty mind hears more than the rest of us, perhaps. Or else it was a miracle wrought by God through the instrument of my harp."

Eleanor's scowl did not lessen. "A miracle, perhaps! But don't go counting on your sainthood yet, my lady. When Maud was taken away, the squire of Longdon and Dacre ended the feast then and there, and sent the village away hungry. Not many will bless you for that!"

No. But perhaps the weeping beyond the wall will cease. I will settle for that.

Maureen Jennings is a Canadian author whose first mystery, Except the Dying, *was nominated for both an Anthony Award in the United States and the prestigious Arthur Ellis Award in Canada.* Except the Dying *and a second book,* Under the Dragon's Tail, *are both set in Toronto at the end of the nineteenth century. Jennings's detective is an Irish-Catholic cop at a time in Canada when neither the Irish nor Catholics were popular.*

Maureen was sparked to write "The Weeping Time" when she read a brief biography of Margaret Roper, the scholarly daughter of Thomas More. "I was totally captivated by this story and its implications," she writes. "I have, of course, made up Ned Tingle and what he did, but the rest is true."

THE WEEPING TIME

Maureen Jennings

M aster James Kennett had hardly reached the door-step of the farmhouse when the door opened. Sarah, the old man's granddaughter, greeted him with a smile, but her voice was anxious.

"Come in. He hath been asking for you."

"Beg pardon, mistress, the path was icy, and we had to go with care."

He followed her gratefully into the kitchen, which was hot and so redolent with the smell of roasting mutton that the grease settled in a film on his lips. A small girl was turning a spit on the wide hearth, watched by two scrawny hounds.

"Warm yourself first," said Sarah. "And if it please you, sup with us afterward."

James went to the fire. The dogs slunk away, so he could hold out his hands to the flames. He would like to have turned and warmed his arse, but he had no wish to offend Sarah.

"He is up here," she said, and opened the stair door to lead him upstairs.

Unlike the kitchen, Tingle's chamber was chill, and the smell was rank and sour with his sickness. There was one small brazier for heat and one candle standing in the windowsill for light. Neither made a dint on the gloom of the winter afternoon. Sarah ushered James in and crossed to the bed where the man was lying.

"The scribe is here, Grandfather," she murmured.

Tingle opened his eyes. "It took him long enough. A man could have shuffled off in half the time."

James went to apologize again, but with a wave of his hand Tingle stopped him. His voice was hoarse but still full of authority. "We will waste time. You can leave us."

This last remark was addressed to the woman who was seated beside the bed. James recognized her as Tingle's daughter-in-law. She made no protest but took up the stitching she was doing and left the room. Sarah took a cloth from a bowl beside the bed and went to wipe her grandfather's forehead. He stopped her.

"No. Later. I hath a task to do. Leave us."

She, too, obeyed without demur.

"Bring the candle closer to the bed," he said to James.

He did so and was shocked to see how the disease had wasted Master Tingle's flesh. When he saw him last, he was big and broad-shouldered. Now he was shrunken to half his former size; his head was skull-like and his hands skeletal. From beneath his sleeping hood, his white hair straggled lank about his face.

A pain gripped him, and he groaned. "Give me the opiate." He motioned to the vial that was on a table next to the bed. James handed it to him and helped him sit up so he could swallow. His mouth was thick with cancres and stank abominably.

"Enough. I have need of my wit." His eyes were yellowish and sunken, but the look he fixed on the scribe was fierce. "No doubt you are full of wonderment as to the reason for this summons."

"Whatever is your wish, sire," said James, but his reply seemed to irritate the old man.

"Not too politic, Master Kennett. Too much politic rots

the soul." He sank back, gasping. "How long has our sovereign lady, the queen, reigned?" he asked suddenly.

"Almost seventeen years, Master Tingle," replied James, puzzled at the question.

"The holy maid of Kent prophesied the king would die within a month of his marriage to Mistress Boleyn, but he didn't. He lived on another twelve years."

He coughed violently and spat into a bowl lying next to him. There was bright red blood in the sputum. James waited until he was calm again.

"I beg pardon, sire, is it another testament you wish me to write?"

"Nay. That is settled."

James was relieved. Tingle had made his will when he first acknowledged the wasting sickness had afflicted him. He had only one son, and all his goods and chattel were left to him. There seemed no reason to think a dispute would arise.

"I heard him say it was the weeping time of the wretched world, but I do not believe it was so very different. Men die at this queen's whim with as much pain. And some with as much courage."

James could see that Master Tingle, although clear in his wits, was burdened with too many thoughts for them to come out clearly. To his surprise the old man smiled, the cadaverous face grimacing in a parody of a skull.

"You want your story seamless and orderly I can see, not tumbling out like pebbles in the spring thaw." He coughed again so harshly that James wondered if he was going to bring up his own bowels. "Very well. We can begin. But I have breath for only one telling of my tale. You must write it down as I say it and not question me at every stop."

James placed his scribe's box on his knees and took out a sheaf of paper and some quills. He dipped one into the inkwell.

"This document is as told by Mr. Ned Tingle who himself being unable to read or write has engaged the scribe Master James Kennett, who is recording only what is said and is not in any way complicitous with what is recounted."

The young scribe felt a twinge of fear. A disclaimer was all very well, but he had no fancy to be party to some traitorous secret.

Tingle continued. "I thought myself well favoured to be the king's servant. Steady wages, lodgings. I was married, two growing bairns, one suckling and another under the apron. I had found a position for my younger brother, Daniel, and he was taken on as a bridgekeeper."

He moaned quietly, reached for the opiate, changed his mind, and waited for the wave of pain to subside. Then he turned so he could see the scribe better. "Master Kennett, I put you this case. If the Antichrist himself appeared before you in this very room and said, 'Unless you swear to renounce all the teachings of God himself as we have received them, you will suffer a death so horrible it can hardly bear witness,' would you swear such an oath?"

The smoky candlelight was making pools of shadow on Tingle's face. Praying this was not a trap set by the devil, who was now inhabiting the old man's body, James considered the question. "If I knew for certain it was the Antichrist, I would not swear."

Tingle managed a smile. "Well said, my sprig. But what if I said that you would be hanged by the neck until you were between two worlds, the quick and the dead. And that then you would be pulled back to life but only sufficient to know that your pizzle was cut off and stuffed in your mouth. And that if you were not yet dead, your innards would be cut out and cast into a vat of boiling water. The stench from which is so vile, many who are witness vomit. And finally, if you are still alive, your very heart would be cut out and held before your eyes so it is the last thing you see on this earth."

He caught James by the sleeve of his doublet. "I put to you again, knowing full well this is the fate that will befall you, would you quail and swear the oath even to the devil himself? And, yeah, only for conscience' sake."

Mindful of Tingle's previous reprimand and also because he was an honest soul, James replied.

"Methinks I would so swear, sire. What are words but constructs of air here given out for another's connivance? My heart would know otherwise, and I trust my Saviour would know the true thoughts of my heart and grant me forgiveness."

Ned let go of James's arm. "A goodly answer. There were some few who did as you have so shrewdly posited. Then there were the hundreds of poor mortals such as myself, who did not give a jot what they would swear as long as they were not subject to these torments. The argument you have presented, however, was used by his daughter, whom he dearly loved, and his good wife. 'Take the oath in word only. Live for our sake.' But he refused their pleas and remained steadfast. Oh, this defiance was not because he was without imagination. Far from it. I had the night watch, and when he was first imprisoned, I oft heard him cry out in his sleep. When I was able, I would take him some small sustenance, bread sops or wine, for which he was most grateful. And he would hold discourse with me as if I were the keenest lawyer in the land."

He lay back on his pillow, and James could see his chest heaving, his breath raspy. He was keeping himself alive by sheer effort of will.

"Once I asked him why he, who had rejoiced at the burning of heretics, should see himself as so very different. Mr. Tyndale and Mr. Tunstall, after all, believed themselves to be right according to their conscience. He did not take offence but regarded me studiously. 'Tyndale was a heretic and an Antichrist, of that I am sure. But your point is well taken.' And methinks it was, because in the last months he concerned himself much less with such things as had before inflamed him."

Tingle sighed and waved his hand. "I have got away from my tale. Pray you write this down.

"I was one of the guards who helped him walk the way to his trial. I could see he thought even then he might be freed, as on a point of law he had committed no malice. And he was a lawyer first and foremost. A monkish lawyer for sure, but he was as adept as a dancing master at shifting and weaving. But we knew he would be found guilty. Even without Mr. Rich's lies. The jury were too afraid for their own lives to acquit him and displease the king.

"He was frail by now, his beard grown long and unkempt. He wore a coarse woolen gown, and foolish wights, who think noblemen must perforce wear only velvet and ermine, did not know him. The whispers went through the crowd. 'Who is it?' 'Who is it?' I answered one fellow. 'It is Sir Thomas More, the one who was the king's chancellor.' "

He paused. "I assume you know of him, Master Kennett?"

James shook his head. "I regret I do not, sir."

Tingle grimaced. "Methinks he would have been pleased with such an answer. He was never desirous of martyrdom. He wore a hair shirt all of his life, but secretly, so that no one would consider him like the Pharisee who wanted all the world to know of his righteousness."

"I see you much admired this Sir Thomas."

"I admired others equally as much. The priest John Fisher was nowhere near as comfortably off or as canny. He was a good old man and he should have died in his warm bed, surrounded by honor and love, not as he did, stripped naked before strangers and so thin that his neck could have been severed with a kitchen knife. And the five monks of the Charterhouse, who died in the manner I have described. These I sore pitied and loved for their courage. They each could see what was happening to the one before and they did not renounce their belief."

He stopped, and James could see he was remembering and wished he could give him comfort. Then the withered hand was raised again, the signal to continue.

"On the return journey the procession was led by the executioner, his great axe with the blade pointed toward the prisoner so the crowd would know the verdict . . ."

Tingle smiled slightly. "I am aware it has been whispered in the village that I wore the red horns, but there is no truth in it. I was never the king's executioner, merely one of the guards at the Tower . . . As we approached the prison gates, his son and his beloved daughter pushed through the throng of guards and halberders to say their final farewells. John More knelt for his father's blessing, but Margaret clung to his neck, kissing him and weeping sorely." Another pause and a wag of the finger. Kennett stopped writing.

"I understand," said Tingle, "that his son-in-law, Roper, in relating these events, wrote that for many of those present, this sight was so lamentable that it made them also mourn and shed tears. It was true that Margaret's love and her sorrow filled the very air we were breathing, and many did cry with her. But not all. Perhaps not near as many as Master Roper would have hoped for. What was it to them, who labored daily only to cover their own wretched bodies, to see such a one? The king and his court were the players, not they. And many more had long ago hardened their hearts to the suffering of other men. Various stories grew up after his death, as they always do. One was put out that on this day More smelled as sweetly odoriferous as one of the saints. But I can tell you, there was nothing supernatural about it. I was present when the lieutenant of the Tower, Mr. Kingston, gave him some rosewater and musk to perfume his clothes. Better than the stink of the Tower. The final story that has gone into the world concerns his head, but I will tell the truth of that in a moment. First give me some opiate. This biting in my stomach is like to distract me completely."

James brought the vial to the old man's mouth.

"They had no such ointments or salves when the rack had finished with them. I count myself fortunate. But quickly, I am not done. Six days later Thomas More went to the scaffold. The king in his clemency declared he would die by the axe and not the true death of a traitor, as Mr. Reynolds and the monks of the Charterhouse had so recently suffered. The time of the execution was nine of the clock in the morning. At mine own request, I was one of the guards attending him. Secretly, I offered to bring him wine or mandragora, but he refused. He was composed, walking to Tower Hill with his red cross in front of him. A wind coming up from the river ruffled his long beard. He was weak and needed to be helped to climb the scaffold, making a joke about it which pleased those around. The king had requested that he not speak long, so he did not. Why he obeyed I know not. Perhaps he was in a hurry now to go to the lap of God, where he would be merry for eternity. Perhaps even then he feared his innards could be ripped from him if he gave offence. The executioner received his piece of gold and his blessing. He was, after all, merely the king's servant and not to be blamed. He did his task well, and More's head fell into the basket on one fell stroke."

He ceased to talk, and James saw that once again he was remembering. His eyes glistened with tears he refused to shed. Outside, the wind soughed through the black-barked trees, and the snow pattered against the windowpane. The brazier needed more wood, but the scribe was afraid to interrupt the narrative that was now flowing so freely. He shifted his buttocks a little on the hard stool. Tingle raised his hand, and James picked out a fresh quill.

"As was done with all traitors, More's head was parboiled then stuck on a pike on top of London Bridge for all to see and take heed. It had been there more than a se'ennight when the events I am about to relate took place.

"I had finished my watch for the night and returned to my lodgings at seven of the clock. The summer sun had not shown its face for many days, and the morning proved drear, threatening rain. When I entered my chambers, I found my wife, Susanna, my two bairns, and my brother Daniel, who lodged with us, all seated at the table. When she saw me, my wife flew into my arms.

" 'Daniel will have us all burnt as traitors and our children orphaned or burnt with us!'

"I calmed her until she could speak sensibly. Daniel

meanwhile stared into the floor as if he could read his fate in the pattern of the rushes.

" 'He has agreed that More's daughter can have the head from off the bridge. She has offered him four angels of gold if he will throw it to her. I beseech you, Ned, forbid him. 'Tis not only him will be blamed. We all will die or be racked to tell.'

"I had seen Margaret Roper and her father together when she visited him in his cell. He lay with his head in her lap while she soothed and stroked his brow as she was wont to do when they were at home. Now her father was named a traitor, which he was not, and that same beloved face was soiled by birds and flies on top of London Bridge. Eventually, all of the heads were tossed into the river, but only at His Majesty's command, never before or at anyone else's say-so.

" 'Is this true, brother?' " I asked, although 'twas clear from Daniel's frightened face that it was.

" 'Tis a little thing, Ned. I shall say the wind blew it off.'

"I rushed at him and fetched him such a cuff across his head, he almost fell down.

" 'Has this same wind ever blown off a head that is so rammed on a pike, it cannot be turned? Answer me! So long as you have been walking the bridge length, have you known the wind to lift off one of these heads? Answer!' " Another hard slap that caused some flow of blood from his nose.

" 'Brother, please, this is of concern to me alone. She will pay well.'

"I shoved him to the floor in disgust. 'You are worse than a fool. Will gold stop the rack from ripping your limbs from their sockets and shredding your flesh like cloth? It will not!'

"I caught him by the hair, jerking back his head. 'Will gold put out the flames when *your* hair catches fire as they burn you for a traitor? It will not!'

"He tried to roll away, crying. ' 'Tis not just the gold, Ned. She is a good woman.'

"I banged his head to the floor. 'Was not the maid of

Kent a good woman? It did not save her. Nor Mr. Reynolds and the other monks. And were not they good men? And their death was horrible beyond imaging. You saw it.'

"My blood was running so hot I know not when I would have left off hurting him, but my wife caught me by the sleeve.

" 'Enough Ned.'

"My own bairns were wailing at her knees, and seeing them, I was sick in my heart. I stepped back and let Daniel get to his feet.

" 'Susanna is right. When the constable comes looking, he will blame all of us. And don't think it would be treated frivolously. The king will burn or hang anyone who sides against him. Especially with one such as Thomas More, who defied him to the end. And this was a man he had loved and favored. Do you think he gives a rush about a bridgekeeper or his family? I will answer for you, Master Daniel. He does not! We are as but the parings of his toe-nails.' " He wiped at his mouth.

" 'What shall I do? I have agreed. Mistress Roper will pass beneath the bridge at five of the clock today. I am to throw the head into the boat.'

"I turned away so as not to hit him again. Even in his whining, I did not trust him to be resolute.

" 'I will take your watch. You must feign sickness. Nay, more, you must be made ill. Susanna, go at once and make up a purge.' " Daniel protested no more. Susanna hurried to do what I said, and I went straightaway to the bridge. On some few prior occasions, I had taken his place when he was not able, and it mattered not to the other guard. I took up the halberd and walked to the centre of the bridge. Crows flapped away at my approach. A welcome wind blew away the stench of the rotting heads. More's head, distinguished by the long beard, was to the centre. He was flanked by the heads of the five monks of the Charterhouse. I looked up at them all, still recognizable for the men they had been in spite of the birds, and I hoped it was true what More had believed. That they were now together in heaven and making merry there.

"The hours crawled as I walked the watch. The air grew chiller, and the river was flowing fast and dark. Even by four of the clock, there was need for lights indoors. Finally, by the call of the watch, it was a quarter to the hour. Then the hour was sounded as I walked back to the gate. Heavy drops of rain began to fall, pocking the river. I wondered if she would come. As slowly as I dared, I once again marched to the centre of the bridge. And then I saw the boat coming fast down the river and I leaned over the wall. She saw me and stood up, keeping her balance in the bobbing boat by sheer wanting. They were within several yards of the bridge now, and pulling hard, the oarsman turned so that the bow was against the tide. They were strong men both, but even so they could not hold much longer, and the boat began to slip.

"She called something to me, but the wind seized her words, and I could not hear. It was apparent what she had said, however, and I shook my head, making it plain that I would not fulfill her request. Frantically, she reached down into the boat and lifted up a pouch, holding it up to me pleadingly. One of the boatsmen shouted. They could not hold much longer. The boat was being turned around. I waved my arms, indicating she must move away. In a moment she would have been gone, and I would have returned to the safety of my lodgings. But she dropped the pouch of money, and the hood of the dark monkish cloak she was wearing for secrecy fell back. The pelting rain was soaking her hair and streaking her face. She raised her hands, palms upward, beseechingly.

"Then, as if without my own will, my mouth opened, and a cry burst forth that I have never uttered before or since. I cannot say whence came such a sound, but it seized hold of my very flesh as if the wailing and my body were one and the same. I jumped up on the railing, seized the head from off the pike, and with yet another shout, 'Take it!' I tossed it from the bridge. There was a basket filled with straw in the bow, and the head landed there. The last sight I had was of Margaret Roper reaching forward to touch the beloved face she had caressed so often before. Then the boatsmen dipped their oars, and they shot away on the racing tide."

Tingle had been speaking so quickly, James had difficulty keeping up, and his fingers were cramping on the quill. But here the old man stopped.

"Were you punished, sire?" James asked.

"Verily. I was put in the pillory. Wishing to demonstrate their loyalty to the king, my fellow guards were strong in their revilement of me. I was pelted with their filth and the filth of the dogs of the street for three days. More's daughter, too, was imprisoned, but soon released. She said that her prayers had been answered, no doubt by an angel of God, and that is why the head had fallen into her boat. Later that is the story that some people believed. Others said it was indeed angels that caused the head to jump, but they were of solid gold. All were wrong."

"Did she not make good her promise?"

"Aye, she did. As soon as it was safe to do so, she sent money. Queen Anne's execution followed hard on More's, and soon after, I left the king's service and came here to this village. In the years that have followed, God has seen fit both to give and to take away. I have lost my wife and two bairns, but I have prospered."

He fought back another spate of coughing, which seemed to exhaust him more than ever. James waited patiently, sensing the story was not yet complete. Tingle raised his hand and pointed.

"See that cupboard by the window? Put down your box and go to it."

James obeyed.

"Open the drawer as far as it will go and feel with your hand behind it . . . Good. There is a strip of wood. Turn it widdershins and pull down gently."

James did so and felt the circlet of wood come loose in his hand.

"In that hole, you will find a pouch. Have you got it?"

"Yes, sire."

"Bring it here."

James took the pouch, which was of soft leather, all covered with dust. He placed it on the bed. With shaking hands, Tingle loosened the thong at the neck and upturned it on the coverlet. Out slipped four gold coins. James could see the stamp of His Majesty, King Henry.

"This was my payment. As you see, I have not touched it. There were many times when I was sorely tempted, when my own children were in want. But I did not do so."

Leaving the coins where they lay, he indicated to James to take up his quill.

"I leave this money herewith to one Master James Kennett, scribe, in payment for his services."

James gasped. "But, sire, that is one hundred times more than the fee."

"I am aware of that. And shortly I will call in witnesses to see that I am in sound mind and that you have not stolen the money. You are a goodly young fellow, Master Kennett. With this money you can go to London and study the law, as I have heard you have dreamed of doing."

His voice was now so low and hoarse he was almost inaudible.

"Fret not, master scribe. This is not a whim. It is my long-considered desire. Now I wish you to read through this account of mine as I have told it."

"Is there—is there any particular thing you would fain I do with the story, sire, after . . ."

"After I die? No. You can keep it or not as you wish, or as my son wishes, although he will not be happy for the giving of the money. A curate has shriven me, so I do not go to my death with my sins weighing on my soul as some men do. I could see by your look when you came that you expected I would have guilt to assuage. But my story is not of that."

He breathed as deeply as he could. "On the bridge that afternoon, I saw no winged angel . . . but I have held to my bosom a sliver of belief, fragile as icicles, that for one moment I was God's servant and I stayed the tears of the weeping world."

He tapped the coverlet. "Now, Mr. Kennett, please read back to me my tale. I would fain gaze into its glass and be merry therein."

Leonard Tourney has written eight novels featuring the Elizabethan constable Matthew Stock and his wife, Joan. Each one of them emphasizes an aspect of sixteenth-century society that is rarely covered in history texts or seminars on Shakespeare. Matthew and Joan are not nobility but solid English citizens who would prefer to get on with their clothier's business than solve murders. But Matthew's appointment as constable draws them into intrigue as well the machinations of the powerful. While all the books are splendid, the most recent, Frobisher's Savage, *is one of the most lyrical and touching that I've ever read.*

In his tradition of being true to the mentality of the times, Leonard has sent a very reluctant Joan and Matthew to Ireland for this story. What they find there is colored not only by the conditions of the society they live in, but also by a very English attitude toward the Irish and their stubborn refusal to realize that they have been made a part of Britain.

THE IRISH WIDOWER

Leonard Tourney

The Irish shipmaster had assured his two English passengers that according to all prognosticators of weather and wind, the crossing would be smooth as glass; no need to fret, he said, laughing. But the man and woman were sick through most of the voyage, undone by the churlish black swells, howling gales, and stench of the ship's innards, worse than a Smithfield muckhill. It was the year of grace, 1604. James I, the Scottish king, had sat on great Elizabeth's throne twelve months to the day.

Now, as the ship rounded a mist-shrouded promontory and the fullness of the land appeared, the wind whistled in the rigging, the ship leaned precariously in the turn, so that the salt spray dashed the Englishman's face, and from aloft a lookout pointed landward and sang out, "Ireland, Ireland"—more a lament than a cry of discovery.

The Englishman took in the graceful sweep of the bay fringed with black cliffs and green headlands, the whitewashed houses of the little town, the formidable castle guarding it, and he thanked God. The vessel could still be lost, he knew. Many a ship had foundered within hailing distance of port, drowning all aboard. Still, his spirits lifted. He had completed the first leg of his journey.

The Englishman was Sir Matthew Stock; the woman, his wife, Joan. He was stout and fortyish, with a pleasant, guileless expression and beardless in an age when beards were in fashion. She was of the same years, with a handsome oval face and dark eyes that always seemed to give full value to what they looked upon. The knighthood of her husband was newly minted, he being one of such a multitude of gentlemen raised to that distinction by the new king that they were disparagingly classed as "carpet knights" among those at court and city whose honors were had under the old queen of famous and revered memory. Sir Matthew had heard the derisive term, but had too little pride to bristle at the mockery. As for Joan, she was now a gentlewoman, more honor than this farmer's daughter and clothier's wife had ever looked to see.

Sir Matthew, was a clothier by trade, constable for many years by vote of his townsmen, and advanced by merit, of having saved in one swoop England's monarch and its most celebrated playwright from ignominious deaths. Those who were aware of the occasion of his knighthood readily allowed it was well deserved.

Now Sir Matthew, or plain Matthew as he still thought of himself, traveled in the king's service. His charge, to search out the Irishwoman who laid claim to healing the sick and being a queen of sorts. Her reputation had reached royal ears at Whitehall, royal ears always directed to Ireland and its persistent rebellious turmoil. Another king might have sent men to dispose of the troublemaker quickly enough, but Matthew had heard the double-mindedness in the king's scathing condemnation of the woman. Putrid Irish whore, the king called her, devilish fraud breeding an imp of treason in her womb. And yet, as Joan had said beyond the king's hearing, "He is afraid, husband. I warrant he thinks this Irish maid will slap him with a curse so his mind goes or body rots."

The king had some theory about women understanding

other women in ways no man could—a theory Joan endorsed and used as a lever to have her way about the voyage. Matthew had wanted her to stay at home in their pleasant new manor house in Essex and mind the servants didn't abscond with the silver. Joan had other plans, as wives so commonly do. She was not happy about Matthew's intended voyage, but she was determined that he would not voyage alone.

But now came a great pounding of feet on deck and raw cries from the men; the sails were quickly furled, ship heaved to and anchored, and within minutes knight and wife ushered into the longboat. The Irish shipmaster wished them well and promised to return within the week.

Matthew had the particulars of his mission from Sir Robert Cecil, the king's chief minister. Cecil, for whom Matthew had performed yeoman service more than once in the past dozen years, lectured him a good hour on Ireland. Cecil was full of facts and opinions about the weather, the Irish diet, and the peculiar nature of the Irish. He knew history, politics, topography. He said bluntly: "You won't like it, Matthew."

Matthew thought his not liking Ireland was beside the point. He told Cecil he would be taking Joan with him.

"Excellent! It will make your expedition seem more pilgrimage than a mission of espionage," Cecil said. "The king wishes to show a mild face—at least until such time as he can determine the fullness of this woman's intent, the true lineaments of treason's visage. He ever fears papist plots and homegrown conspiracies. Why shouldn't he? These honest fears run in his family."

"Is there no local magistrate or English lord to put these fears to rest?"

"There is, but there lies a mystery of its own."

"Mystery, Your Grace?"

"Thomas Manford, earl of Dunmaire and lord of the manor of Kilcuddy, wherein the girl dwells. An Irish earldom is a small pond for so ambitious a man to swim in. In youth he was a tolerable sailor, deflowering many a Spanish stronghold in the New World. Raleigh commanded him.

Now he takes this woman, once his servant, gives her the run of his house, and spreads word that she is queen of Ireland. God only knows what his wife thinks of it. She's his second or third, you know. A proficient widower, Manford is said to use wives up like a candle its tallow. As for the Irish wench, I hear she's a local beauty as well as a witch. Do not crowd the man, Matthew. Speak him softly. He could be dangerous, and he is certainly cunning."

Matthew was given a generous sum for expenses, the name of the Irish shipmaster, and a plausible cover for the tour: a gentleman of the court seeking to expand his mind with foreign travel.

More admonishment followed from the king's minister, which Matthew duly noted and thereafter, in the excitement of departure, forgot.

The Irish sky glowered and a light rain began to fall as the hirsute coxswain commanding the longboat delivered them to the pebbly shore along with their baggage and saluted them with a little bow. "This is Kilcuddy," he said, a broad derisive grin discernible through the thicket of monstrous whiskers.

Farther along, Matthew could see a road that climbed up rocks to what town there was and a dozen of the Irish, men shabbily dressed, observing their arrival. Fishing folk, Matthew surmised, wondering if any spoke the king's English.

"We'll be guests of the earl," Matthew reminded Joan, who looked worried.

"Indeed," Joan answered as she surveyed the welcoming committee. "If so, it shall be cold comfort if those yonder prophesy of what's to come."

Before they could reach the Irish, one decently dressed in leather jerkin and hose stepped out from among them and approached. He was a sturdy, thickset man, with red hair and pockmarked face, round like a great cheese. He walked with authority, like a mayor or magistrate. He said, "Welcome to Kilcuddy, Sir Matthew. I'm Daniel Tweed, the earl's bailiff."

Tweed gave a little bow, glanced at Joan, and then looked back at Matthew with a more solemn face. "The earl is expecting you these three days, ever since the king's letter arrived from England last month, saying you were to come."

Tweed motioned to two of the men behind him, and they came forward to carry the baggage to a rickety cart. The journey was a short one. They arrived at the castle within a quarter hour, which was just as well, given that the rain fell harder than before.

Castle Dunmaire was a marvel of masonry and military engineering. There was a bailey, a formidable keep, thick crenellated walls, and an iron portcullis, all perched above the bay on a sheer cliff of black rock, making the castle virtually impregnable. Matthew had seen many a castle in England, but never one so warlike in its uncompromising ferocity, and for the first time he thought of the wily Irishman who was presently to be his host, and was afraid.

The earl, however, did not condescend to greet them at their arrival; he was about some pressing business, Tweed explained apologetically. They were shown at once to their quarters, a cold, cheerless chamber with a narrow slit for a window, attained by climbing several flights of narrow stone stairs. Supper would be served in the great hall, said Tweed. They would be sent for, he said.

"Some warm welcome," Joan grumbled when they were alone at last.

"A welcome nonetheless," Matthew said. "Better here than with those somber townfolk. They did not look friendly."

"Not strange that this woman has bewitched them," Joan said, looking from the window out on the bay, half-dissolved in rainy mist. "I do not like great heights, the tumultuous sea, or the Irish."

"Nor do they like us," he said.

"It's not our country."

Her comment surprised him. He wasn't aware that his wife held such a view of Ireland—much less so unconventional a one. To his way of thinking, Ireland was England's by right of conquest, if not moral superiority. Was therefore

Ireland not as much their country as were the pleasant fields and copses of Essex?

They removed their great cloaks, found dry garments in their baggage, and changed. Then Matthew lay upon the bed and closed his eyes. He fell asleep.

Supper took place in the castle's great hall at a table beside a black, gaping hearth large enough to roast an ox. The hall was high-ceilinged, with smoky rafters, and had the dank, musty smell of ancient mold and violence. Massive wall hangings of richly embroidered but faded cloth tempered the severity of stone floor and walls. Outside the rain had become a monotonous drizzle, blurring the distinction between land and sea. Matthew was glad to be warm. Cecil had warned him that Ireland would be wet and the castle cold.

Thomas Manford, earl of Dunmaire, was a man of fifty or so, with hard resolute features, small, furtive gray eyes, and a square-cut beard that surely he must have trimmed each day, so neatly did the hairs match in length. He was a hale, energetic man who even in Irish weather managed to retain the tanned complexion of the seaman, and he spoke rapidly, as though in a constant state of excitement. Margaret Manford, his lady wife, was sick abed, according to the earl, and sent her regrets at not being able to take her place at table or greet the distinguished English knight and lady. In her place was the earl's daughter, Deirdre, a pale, sullen woman in her twenties, with as doleful a countenance as Matthew had ever looked upon. Deirdre said little through the meal, either to them or to her father, who, having introduced her to the English guests, acted as though she were as insensible as the stones about them.

Matthew noticed an empty place setting at table. The identity of this absent guest was not commented upon by the earl, and Matthew thought it impolitic to inquire. About a quarter hour into the chief of the courses—a suckling pig garnished with a variety of greens served before a strange, earthy-tasting soup—Matthew remembered Cecil's advice about the food. Beware of the unfamiliar. An English belly was a sensitive thing, Cecil had observed, having, he confessed, suffered much indigestion in his life. But the sea voyage with its Lenten fare and persistent seasickness had left Matthew ravenous. He threw caution to the wind and ate.

Later Matthew was aware of a stirring at the other end of the hall. He looked up and somehow knew that it was she, although no one had described her to him, a common serving wench and Ireland's queen.

His first impression was that Kathleen O'Rourke—yes, even the English king knew her name—was a child, perhaps of eleven or twelve, she was so small and thin. But as she approached he could see that she was older than that. She was strikingly beautiful, after the Irish fashion, with white skin and light eyes. Her mouth was small, her lips full and sensuous. Her chin was pointed; her arms were long and slender, as though her whole body was the barest covering of a luminescent soul. She wore a simple gown, of finer quality than a peasant might own, but it was clear that while the earl might have raised this former servant to a greater position in his household, he had yet to clothe her in the garments of gentility.

The earl explained that Kathleen O'Rourke spoke no English, a fact that was presently confirmed when she approached Matthew and began uttering a melodious stream of what he took to be Irish. She extended a small white hand, as though he was supposed to kiss it, or kneel, or fall upon his face in awe of her. He did none of these, but held the hand, feeling the delicate bones of her fingers and the soft, slightly moist palm and mumbled awkwardly, uncertain how to deal with the ambiguity of one who was both quondam servant and queen apparent. Her eyes fixed him with a bold, almost insolent regard, conveying no respect for his superior station, and he felt suddenly in her touch something threatening that caused him to pull away. He glanced sideways at Joan, who was studying Kathleen O'Rourke with a quiet intensity and had not bowed or curtsied to this strange young woman.

The earl came 'round the table and helped Kathleen to a

chair. A waiter scurried to remove the plates and bring in more food, as though more were needed—a course of fowl, something round and plump, awash in a savory sauce. Matthew thought partridges, or some Irish bird unknown to him. Unfamiliar foods Cecil had warned of.

After that there was little conversation at table. In the castle, talk was apparently not the custom at mealtimes.

Later still, the men took their leave of the women and retired to a small chamber adjoining the great hall. It was a kind of study, its walls adorned with swords, halberds, lances, pistols, and other firearms. Matthew noticed weapons of a kind he had never seen, but of which he had heard and read. Spears, not after the English or European fashion, but slender wooden shafts adorned with feathers and with points like needles, the kind used by the savages of America. Matthew asked about the collection, and the earl told him it was his father's doing, not his. He had little interest in such relics, he said, waving at the exhibit as though to dismiss it from his mind.

While Matthew still fixed his attention on the display of weapons, the earl explained that his wife had been ailing for several weeks, and that finally she had consented to be ministered to by the maid of Kilcuddy.

"In the beginning," said the earl, "my wife would have naught to do with Kathleen, scorning her as a mere servant. Then, when my daughter fell sick like the others, I brought Kathleen to the castle. It was only a fortnight before her condition improved. Now my wife believes."

In the light of several torches, the earl's hard features softened to give an impression of personal triumph. "Oh, she is a great wonder. No more than a scullery maid when the plague came. A strange, wasting disease, striking adult and child."

The earl described the symptoms, which are appalling. Cramps in the gut, boils and pustules on the flesh, racking pain in the extremities. Matthew was glad the earl saved this gruesome inventory for after supper. "Kathleen O'Rourke ministered unto each," the earl continued. "The evil passed. I saw it with my own eyes. Otherwise I would not have believed it."

"Not witchcraft, you think?" said Matthew.

The earl related the local legend, how a queen would someday come forth from among the common folk of Ireland, be recognized by her powers to heal, and unite the contentious tribes under a single banner.

And rid the country of the English?

The earl stopped short of saying so much, but to Matthew, the whiff of rebellion filled the room with its intimidating hints of savage cruelty and hostile territory.

The piercing shriek woke him sometime before dawn. Joan had heard it, too, sitting up in the bed and breathing heavily, clutching at her chest to still her racing heart, wanting to know of her husband what it was, the unearthly howl, as though he could tell.

In the passage, they encountered the earl, who was still dressed, and walked unsteadily, as though he were quite drunk. The source of the alarm was the daughter. She shuddered as the earl comforted her. "She's dead. She's dead," the young woman declared, not loudly now, but in a child's miserable whimper.

Matthew and Joan followed them to another chamber, larger and well furnished, where a handful of servants gathered 'round a bed, making a shrill keening. A very pale woman of about thirty lay there, her coverlets all askew, as though she had been fighting with them. Her stark open eyes examined the ceiling; her mouth gaped as though the shrieks had come from her. But it was her lips and what was on them that everyone noticed.

Matthew went forward to examine the woman and then drew back. "Joan, look."

Joan bent over the dead woman, hesitated, and then leaned even farther toward the cold vacant eyes. She turned to Matthew. "This poor lady has been poisoned," she said.

The earl groaned, then commanded the servants to stop their wailing and peered at his dead wife's face. He turned to look at Joan questioningly.

"Hellebore, I judge. Or something like unto it," Joan said. "Look at the chalky rime about the lady's lips. That's nothing natural, but a foreign substance, coated and deadly and noxious if inhaled, the worse if consumed."

Matthew commended his wife's knowledge of herbs and physic, but the earl's mind was in another place now. He stared about the chamber wildly, looking first at this servant and then at another, as if someone might tell him why his wife was dead. Finally, his eyes fixed upon Kathleen O'Rourke, who had come into the room quietly, in a long white nightgown and bare white feet.

"You have killed my wife," he said in a voice charged with righteous indignation, pointing his finger accusingly at the healer of Kilcuddy.

Deirdre Manford joined her father in the accusation while the other household servants stood astonished and mute. Then one of them declared that she had witnessed Kathleen in the very act that night, giving her mistress a vial of some substance the odor of which was identical to that which reeked from the dead woman's breathless mouth. This servant's charge opened the door for others. Everyone began to berate Kathleen O'Rourke as a murderess and a deceiver, as though all former adulation was finally revealed to have been gross misunderstanding.

In the bedlam of accusations and denunciations, Kathleen O'Rourke started to defend herself, but before she was able, the earl ordered two of the menservants to silence her and remove her to another part of the castle.

When the alleged malefactor was gone, the earl dismissed the servants and then said to his English guests: "Oh, this is plain murder. You are witnesses to this wickedness. Note she did not deny the accusations."

Joan was tempted to observe that the girl hardly had the chance, but decided to agree with the earl's reasoning. With the man's wife so newly dead, it was hardly the time for a debate upon the evidence.

"Hellebore, you say," repeated the earl in a dry whisper, as if saying the word could reverse what the poison had wrought.

"Or something like," said Joan. "I have used it myself in small amounts as a cure for dropsy and melancholy. In smaller doses it sickens, in larger it kills."

"And how obtained?"

"Any herbalist or apothecary," said Joan.

The earl sat down on the edge of the dead woman's bed, buried his face in his hands, and began to sob as though his grief were more than he could bear. Joan remembered that the dead woman was the earl's third wife. The earl had gone through this before—the grief, the wrenching anguish, the drama. A proficient widower, Cecil had called the man.

"Kathleen O'Rourke must have her own story," Joan reasoned, when she and Matthew had returned to their chamber. "We must hear it."

"Easier said than done," Matthew said. "The earl said she spoke no English. You'd need a translator, and who could tell if the translator rendered her words faithfully, or if she'd tell the truth? A prisoner in her position—there's a powerful motivation to lie."

"Press him, Matthew. You have the king's warrant. Besides, did you not hear the earl? The earl accused her of being guilty because she would not deny the charge, yet I heard only English spoken. How then could Kathleen O'Rourke deny what she had no understanding of?"

"Maybe she guessed," Matthew ventured.

Joan scoffed. "And maybe she speaks English as well as you or I."

"I'll speak to the earl. In the morning. I promise."

During the night the storm spent itself. The new day was cold but awash in a stark, uncompromising light that seemed to leave little room for confusion or treachery. When the Stocks descended to breakfast, they heard from their escort that Kathleen O'Rourke was to be tried straightaway. The whole castle was buzzing with the news, although out of the earl's hearing. If English justice was swift, Irish justice was swifter. The funeral for Margaret, countess of Dunmaire, was to be held the day after. Margaret's murderer would lie in her grave before her victim.

The earl wore mourning garments. A chain of office rounded his neck, yet he showed little sign of melancholy, for one bereaved. Matthew thought perhaps the anticipation of exercising his judicial function had stirred him. He had known men who rose to such occasions, shedding melancholy for the warmth of public attention as a man sheds a cloak in summer weather.

He asked the earl if he and Joan could speak to the accused woman, just as he had promised.

"But why, sir?" replied the earl sharply. "What can she say for herself who is so clearly fraud and traitor?"

"Traitor?" inquired Joan, amazed at this sudden shift.

"Traitor without a doubt," said the earl, as though it were his position from the beginning. "She presented herself as a healer and had commenced to represent herself as a queen. It is certain some in Kilcuddy so regarded her. I trust you will convey to His Majesty my own loyalty."

"Your loyalty, sir?"

"Well, she's to hang."

Matthew heard the urgency in the earl's voice, as though he were fishing for some kind of reassurance, the understanding between gentlemen of the terms of survival. Silence might imply consent, but it did not demonstrate loyalty. Ireland was far removed from the English court, but the king of England had a long arm. Matthew realized suddenly he might be of great use to this Irish earl.

"But may I speak to Kathleen O'Rourke?" Matthew asked.

"Regrettably, she speaks no English."

"Perhaps a translator could be provided," Joan ventured.

The earl scowled and looked doubtful.

"The king would wish it," Matthew said. "He would be interested in the girl's confession—whether she was laid on to this, whether there be some larger plot against him. Surely I will be asked to report when I return to England. Any help you might render would not go unrecognized or unappreciated by His Majesty."

Further discussion of this point was now halted with the

entrance of Deirdre Manford. She was dressed in black, and the melancholy expression she had worn the first time Matthew had seen her had now become even more a picture of devastation. She said nothing in response to her father's greetings. She did not partake of the food, speak, or look up to meet her father's gaze. Her manner had become a statement, a rebuke, its meaning more impenetrable than Kathleen O'Rourke's Irish.

The bailiff Tweed entered and exchanged whispers with his master. The earl announced that the trial of Kathleen O'Rourke would commence within the hour—in the great hall of the castle, outside the public eye. Sir Matthew and his lady might find attendance instructive, entertaining. In the meantime, he said, his English visitor could question the accused. Tweed would translate, showing the way to the hall since it was so easy to become lost in the castle's labyrinthine interior.

While Matthew followed Tweed to where Kathleen O'Rourke languished, Joan climbed to her and her husband's chamber, out of sorts because she had not been invited to interview the prisoner. Within, a new servant busily made up the bed. This girl was about the age of Kathleen O'Rourke, but plump and rosy of face where Kathleen was pale and thin. Kilcuddy was a small town; Joan thought that the two girls probably knew each other. She said something about the bedding and was pleased to see the girl understood.

"You speak English well," Joan said.

The girl curtsied and said that her mother and father also spoke English. They had been servants at the castle and were much devoted to the earl's lady.

The girl crossed herself, and Joan thought this simple soul was more grieved by her mistress's death than was the unfortunate woman's husband, who now seemed so caught up in his administrative duties and courtly ambitions.

"What think you of Kathleen O'Rourke?"

The girl started at the question, perhaps because she was accustomed merely to receiving orders to and not engaging in conversation. Joan was also aware that an English lady might appear quite intimidating to an Irish peasant. After all, this simple girl could not know—nor perhaps even imagine—how Joan began life as a farmer's daughter, milking cows, slopping pigs, baking bread, her elbows deep in dough.

"What's your name, child?"

"Mary Tone, if it please you, m'lady."

"Mary, you must know Kathleen O'Rourke. You are of about the same years, and the town is no more than a village of how many souls—say two hundred?"

Mary Tone did not know how many souls inhabited Kilcuddy, but she did know Kathleen. Who in Kilcuddy did not? Kathleen's father was once the earl's bailiff, Mary Tone said, her mother a maid to the earl's second wife, she who came before the lady who had just died and whose body remained to be buried. Kathleen's own mother died shortly after Kathleen was born. "She took her own life, she did," whispered Mary Tone, as though this information were a dark secret of the castle.

Joan murmured sympathetically and considered this new information. Mary Tone had learned English from her parents—who knew it because of their employment with an Irish earl who well understood the value of knowing English and using it well. Why would a bailiff's daughter not learn it?

"Did you and Kathleen often speak?"

"Oh, not much, m'lady. Not much at all."

"You spoke Irish?"

"Yes, m'lady,"

"English, too?"

"Sometimes," she admitted, as though the practice were a vulgar habit. "But mostly in Irish we spoke, since Ireland this is."

"You said Kathleen's mother died—what of her father? Does the earl still employ him?"

"No, he's old. He was so when he married Kathleen's mother, for so my own parents have said."

"He lives in Kilcuddy?"

"He does. Everybody knows him, but he's not liked at all."

"And why not?" asked Joan.

"Because when he was bailiff he was mighty and proud, but now in his dotage he's a bitter tongue lashing out at one and all."

"Can you tell me where he lives?"

"Anyone can, m'lady. Everyone knows where to find Sean O'Rourke."

Matthew returned with the news. There would be no trial in the great hall, no public execution of the healer of Kilcuddy. When Tweed had led him to the place where she was being confined, they found her slender body dangling, her feet a span from the floor. Her prison had been a small, dank room in the lower regions of the castle, without window or furnishings. Tweed had been unable to account for the rope that was the instrument of her death or explain how she was able to lift herself toward the wooden beam 'round which the rope was tied. The rope was new, had mysteriously appeared in her cell, and the hangman's knot was wrought with a sailor's deftness.

The earl, upon hearing the news, had seemed disappointed that there would be no trial or public execution, but said the girl's death by her own hand further confirmed her guilt, should there have been any doubt before. He had urged Matthew to convey to the king that he had done all that he could to bring the malefactor to justice, since he had been a principal victim of her treason in the loss of a wife. The earl had wanted Matthew to know that. He said he planned to erect a monument to his beloved countess, perhaps more than one.

"We'll sail for England the day after tomorrow," Matthew told Joan later. "We wait now only for the funeral of the earl's lady."

"Did you say anything to the earl about the curious circumstances, the new rope, or how the wretched girl was able to get up to hang herself?"

Matthew said he hadn't. Tweed had said nothing to his

master about the curious circumstances of the hanging, nor
had the earl asked, after learning that the prisoner was dead.
It was clear enough to Matthew what had really happened
in Kathleen O'Rourke's cell, but he thought it wise not to
trouble the waters. Joan agreed.

Joan told Matthew all she had learned from Mary Tone
about Sean O'Rourke.

"Let's find the man," Matthew said.

Sean O'Rourke lived at the poor end of Kilcuddy, where
the low whitewashed houses became huts and finally mere
hovels, barely rising above the earth like little rocky
mounds in the furze. He was an old man with a dirty beard
and dirty hands, and his miserable abode was dirty, too,
dark and rank with his own smells and that of the two
scrawny goats he kept. He had not heard the news of his
daughter's murderous act and suicide, but responded to
both without apparent emotion, as though it were a stranger
the English couple had brought him word of and not his
own flesh and blood.

Despite his decrepitude, the former bailiff was not un-
willing to talk, and seemed to welcome the attention and
company as a refreshing change from the ordinary. He had
obviously lived alone for a long time as an outcast. Bitterness had etched deep lines in his face. All three of them
stood outside in the warm morning sun. He had not invited
them to come in, nor would Joan have accepted the invitation, nor would the three of them been able to fit where
Sean O'Rourke lived in his bitter old age.

The old man didn't deny his daughter was a poisoner,
but he did say she wasn't a suicide. "She would have never
done as much as that," he said. "She would not have used
a rope, but leaped into the sea or swallowed poison first.
No, hanging herself was not what she would do. It was the
way her mother died, and she would not have done it. She
even said as much. 'I'll not hang, Father,' she said, 'no
matter how black the night or deep the grief.' "

"Why did her mother take her own life?" Joan said.

The old man shook his head and scratched his dirty beard. "She had her sorrows."

Matthew asked for an explanation.

"For the child. *Her* child."

"You mean Kathleen?" Joan said.

"Kathleen was hers, not mine. She was with child when I married her, but I didn't know it. She played me for a fool."

"Did you complain to your master, the earl? Surely he would care that his bailiff was tricked."

"Hah." O'Rourke laughed in a dry, raspy voice. " 'Twas the earl who urged me on. 'She needs a husband,' said he, and I was it. But when the child came, I knew it was none of mine. I was old then, too old for a young wife, too old to beget a child, but not too old to count the months of our marriage and find them wanting. Besides, the child looked nothing like me, never did."

Matthew asked outright who O'Rourke thought the father was.

The old bailiff looked at his English visitors as though they had just asked a question any simpleton should be able to answer. "A lord must have his way with the virgins of his house. Is it not the same in England? And must not dogs lap up the crumbs from the rich man's table, as it says in holy writ? A bailiff, though he's high and mighty on his lord's estate, he's but a dog at last. To be thrown his master's leftovers, and then be cast out into the cold when age comes upon him."

There was a silence then. The old bailiff stared toward the castle, as though remembering other slights and outrages of his service to the earls of Dunmaire. Joan reflected gloomily on the miseries of old age, then shifted subjects. "How did Kathleen come by her knowledge of cures?" she asked.

"She had none," O'Rourke said. "Her mother was dead. I knew naught of such things."

"But the cures she supplied to the townspeople?" Joan protested.

O'Rourke shrugged. "Oh, I never believed that nonsense

about her being queen of Ireland. Few in the town did. Sure they were agog over her cures and such, but a queen is another matter. Besides which, whoever heard such a legend until the earl told it, and I've lived in Kilcuddy for seventy years or more? As for Kathleen, though she were fair as her mother, yet she was an idle girl with a cold heart. She never spoke of herbs or cures or any such matter before she went up to the castle."

"That's strange," Joan said.

"She changed when she went up to the castle," O'Rourke said.

"In what way?" Matthew asked.

"She changed," O'Rourke repeated. "The new earl brought new ways into the house. He would tell her of his adventures. He had sailed, you see, with the great captains and brought back strange things."

"What strange things?"

"The devil's things, things used by the savages of the western Indies and of Peru, in the dark forests. He called them souvenirs, but name them what he would, I knew whence they came. I was gone from the castle then, cast out like an old dog, replaced by Daniel Tweed, but I heard the stories."

The old bailiff settled into a stony meditation. Joan thought he was probably thinking about Tweed, his successor. He sat in the sun outside his hovel with his dirty hands on his bony knees. Then, suddenly, he looked up and asked Matthew if he had money to give him, for he badly needed a drink, now that his daughter was disgraced and dead, and he thought he deserved it. He had talked a long time to the English knight and his lady and his mouth was as dry as bone.

"Will ya not give an old dog a drink, sir?" he said bitterly.

The funeral of Margaret Manford, third countess of Dunmaire, wanted the pomp and circumstance Joan had expected from the burial rite of a woman of her station. The castle's builders had been too bloody-minded to provide it with a chapel, and the disrepair of the local church, half-crumbled and with the rain leaking through the roof in the chantry, hardly lent itself to anything decorous, much less grand. The service was said by an aging, mumbling cleric whose name, as Joan remembered it, was Hall or Hull. Interment would be within the castle grounds, where, Joan had noticed earlier, there was an orchard of lichen-covered stones and mossy mounds, the markers of which had long ago dissolved into the earth like half-remembered dreams. It was as depressing a funeral as she had attended, and when it was done, the drizzling rain was replaced by a steady downpour so violent that the aged building seemed to shake to its foundations.

Returned to the castle and soaked to the bone, Joan stood a long time before the fire in their chamber, thinking doleful thoughts about Ireland, the bitter old bailiff, and the murders of Margaret Manford and, almost certainly, Kathleen O'Rourke. Matthew was in the great hall at the request of the earl. When Joan's husband appeared again, he carried with him an object clothed in a finely woven scarlet cloth.

"How does the widowed earl?" she asked as her husband entered.

"Well enough. He's quite philosophical about his wife's death, and plans to remarry. Already he talks about it, as though it were the next order of business."

"A proficient widower, Lord Cecil called him. What's beneath that cloth, pray tell?" Joan asked.

Matthew lifted the covering to reveal a round silver goblet, very ornately worked.

"That's a fine piece," she said. "It must be worth a great sum. A present for the king?"

"It's mine."

"Yours!"

"A token of the earl's appreciation. It's booty. Taken from a Spanish treasure ship. See, there's an inscription 'round the lip. In Spanish, I think."

"A token of appreciation! For what? What good have we done him that his generosity should overflow in silver goblets?"

"Not what we've done, but what we may yet do."

"Say on."

"The earl urges me to convey to the king his absolute loyalty, the evidence of which is his suppression of the dangerous rebellion Kathleen O'Rourke might have led had she lived."

"And that the earl would doubtless have joined," Joan said.

"He claims he was working to expose her all the while. Kathleen learned of his true intent, and murdered his wife to avenge herself on him."

"Oh, that's a fine notion from one who, from Sean O'Rourke's account, invented the legend to begin with," Joan said scornfully. "Will you convey the earl's earnest assurances to His Majesty?"

"The truth, not his assurances."

"I think we're of the same mind, husband."

"I think we are," Matthew said. "Have you had enough of Castle Dunmaire?"

"More than enough."

"Then we're best gone before the earl sees us as more danger to his reputation than agent for his advancement."

"He will be occupied planning his next nuptials, the jolly thriving bridegroom," Joan said.

But then Tweed came with another manservant to take their baggage below to where the cart waited. The ship Cecil had promised had just anchored in the bay. Tweed had arranged for them to board by noon. He said the earl was eager for Sir Matthew to put in a good word for him with the king.

"Speaking to the king about your master the earl will be my first order of business," Matthew said to the bailiff, who looked very pleased at the English visitor's answer.

A month later London bloomed in April light. The king hunted somewhere in Kent, and Matthew and Joan told their story to Lord Cecil, who said he would convey Matthew's report—and an excellent goblet of fine workmanship—to His Majesty when he should choose to return.

They were seated in Cecil's study in his stately house on the Strand, and Cecil's normally tired, brooding face was alight with satisfaction. He was obviously pleased with the results of their expedition, confident that the truth was now known and treason and murder on the verge of getting their just deserts.

Joan wanted to know whether she and Matthew would be again sent to Ireland, given all that had happened.

"I have another in mind for the next envoy to the earl of Dunmaire," Cecil said. "He will bear no gifts but His Majesty's warrant for high treason and murder against this most treacherous earl."

"It was Kathleen O'Rourke who poisoned the earl's wife," Matthew said.

"It was the same wife's husband who put Kathleen onto it," Cecil responded, acknowledging Joan's part in shaping the story. "The instigator is as guilty as the actor. That's good English law. And Irish."

For an hour or more Matthew and Joan had taken turns giving Cecil the evidence. Joan had said with a good measure of disgust, "The earl bedded his wife's maid, then foisted the maid and her child off on the old bailiff, who by his own confession could not have fathered a grave thought, much less a lively daughter. In time, the earl brought her up to the castle, taught her what he knew of poisons strange and subtle, for there was none else to teach her, and probably exercised his lordly rights upon her body, caring little that she was his own true daughter, if only to confirm the bargain."

Matthew told Cecil about the earl's collection of weapons, especially the savage-looking spears. Cecil, too, had heard that such weapons were tipped with poison, that the fabrication of poisons were an art among the savages. Cecil said that Raleigh and his lieutenants had taken a great deal of interest in such arcane knowledge and often boasted of it. Cecil agreed it was likely the earl of Dunmaire had acquired such knowledge on his voyages, for certainly no one else in Kilcuddy had it.

"Kathleen O'Rourke administered her medicinals 'round the village, people sickened, then she seemed to cure them, although she did no more than stop the noxious contagion she herself began. And all this to manufacture a false legend that finally even the ignorant Irish were loath to swallow," Matthew said.

"A plot beyond a simple serving girl's conception, I warrant," Joan said disdainfully, "but not beyond that of an ambitious earl. Doubtless the man planned to make a great thing of Kathleen's queenship, but when it was not fully credited even by the people of Kilcuddy, he despaired of convincing other of his countrymen. He had to resort to a second plan—murder his wife and make the best of his failed attempt at rebellion by representing himself as its suppressor."

"With his wife dead," Matthew continued, "at least he could replenish his finances with a fourth wife's dowry and let the prosecution of his third wife's murder testify to his loyalty to the king."

Cecil could not help laughing at this. A shrewd and sober counselor, he was not above enjoying the wit—and sometimes witlessness—of the criminal mind. "Thus the poisoner becomes the savior," he said, "the rebel the loyal subject. *O tempora, O mores!* Were one to see this in the theater, it would not be believed possible save the best actor in England played the earl. Not since Iago have I seen such calculated villainy."

Cecil explained that Iago was a character in Mr. Shakespeare's new play, a devious lieutenant to a general undone by jealousy. Theater had not been on the Stocks' agenda during the past months.

Cecil asked what first put the Stocks onto the earl's design.

"Small things, a tissue of lies, mostly about language," Joan said. "Lies about Kathleen O'Rourke, about his own father and his own knowledge. The earl said Kathleen could speak no English, nor understand it, but we learned from her father that she spoke it well enough, and another servant who had come to replace her let the truth out, too. Besides, the earl had accused Kathleen of failing to deny a charge she could only have understood had she understood English. It was a foolish slip of the tongue on the earl's part, but telling enough. My thinking was this: Why should the earl lie about such a matter, save he wanted to keep her silent? And why care unless they were in it together and he feared she'd betray him?"

Matthew joined in. "The earl hesitated even to supply a translator, and when finally he agreed, already he was taking steps to send Kathleen to hell before she could betray him. Her suicide was bold murder, plain and simple to anyone with eyes."

"Tweed's work, doubtless," Cecil said. "Again the earl prefers to have others do his dirty work. It makes you wonder about the deaths of his earlier wives, doesn't it? Yet since the earl can hang but once, we'll be satisfied with a sole count to his indictment. The earl may choose between being hanged for murder—or for treason."

"Hobson's choice," Matthew said.

"Sin narrows a man's options," Cecil said. "He hardly deserves our sympathy. Here, Matthew, the goblet's yours. Look upon me as the king's purse. There's enough silver there to compensate you for your time in Ireland."

Joan thought of the damp and dark of that country and said she wasn't sure there was enough silver in the goblet to compensate her. The voyage home had been as rough as the voyage out, and she still dreamed of the stark white face of the queen of Ireland, the poisoned countess of Dunmaire, and poor Deirdre Manford, the earl's sullen daughter, who might have known more truth about her wicked father's proficient widowerhood than she let on.

William Sanders has ridden various literary horses during the quarter century that he has been writing professionally. A successful sports and outdoor writer for many years, he turned to fiction in 1988 with the alternate-history farce Journey to Fusang, *for which he was nominated for the John W. Campbell Award. After several more SF titles, he turned to adventure and suspense novels, then to mysteries, winning wide critical acclaim with his short-lived and much-mourned Taggart Roper series, the first two of which (*The Next Victim *and* A Death on 66*) were finalists for the Oklahoma Book Award.*

In the mid-nineties he returned to science fiction and fantasy, publishing short stories—mostly on traditional Cherokee themes—in various magazines and anthologies. His story "The Undiscovered" won the Sidewise Award for Alternate History in 1998 and was nominated for the Nebula, Hugo, and Sturgeon awards as well. His sixteenth book, The Ballad of Billy Badass and the Rose of Turkestan, *was published in January 1999 by Yandro House.*

In the story that follows, he takes us to a Cherokee village of the 1790s, where an old shaman must solve a mystery that threatens to tear his world apart.

SMOKE

William Sanders

Standing on the bank of the little stream, facing the sun that was just beginning to rise over the nearest ridge, the old man named Smoke poured tobacco into his palm, cautiously shaking the little buckskin bag until it was empty and tucking it into a fold of his fringed hunting coat. He raised both hands to face level, so that the rays of the rising sun shone full on the small mound of dark Cherokee leaf.

Now he stuck the forefinger of his free hand into the little pile of tobacco and began stirring gently. As he stirred, he raised his dry old voice in an *igawesdi* medicine song, chanting the secret words that were not Cherokee but a much older language.

At the end of the song he paused and blew very lightly on the tobacco; then he raised it to the sun again and began the *igawesdi* once more. Four times in all he sang the song, always stirring, always keeping the tobacco in the sunlight; four times he blew on the acrid-smelling crumbled leaves.

Done, he got out the little bag and carefully refilled it,

making sure not to spill so much as a flake of the tobacco. It was good strong tobacco; he had grown it himself, in a secret mountainside clearing, protected by a charm to keep hunters and others away, since of course serious tobacco had to be grown absolutely unseen by anyone but the one who would be using it.

Now, however, it was "doctored" tobacco, "remade" for a particular purpose, and needing only to be smoked in order to release its power. And so it was to be treated with respect; it would have been very bad to drop any.

Stowing the buckskin pouch in the bigger medicine bag that hung at his hip, he turned and started down the narrow trail that ran alongside the fast-running little creek. But he had taken only a few steps when he heard the high young voice from somewhere downstream: *"Ni, edutsi!"*

He stopped, his dark, lined face registering anger. Then his expression cleared and he smiled very slightly. *"Ni,"* he called back.

A moment later the spring-green bushes parted and a half-grown boy appeared. *"Osiyo, Inoli,"* Smoke said. "What do you mean, coming up here and hollering when I'm making medicine? You know better than that."

The boy called Badger said, "I heard you singing, Uncle. I waited till you were through."

"How did you know I was done?" Smoke asked, trying to sound angry but not doing it very well. Badger was his only sister's daughter's boy and his favorite of all his younger relations.

"You taught me that *igawesdi*," Badger said. "For finding lost things, right? Did you lose something?"

"Never mind that." In fact, Smoke had lost a treasured ear ornament the other night at a stomp dance and was hoping to use the tobacco to help him find it, but he wasn't going to admit that to the boy. "Anyway," he added, "you shouldn't trail your elders and sneak up on them like that."

Badger tossed his shaggy black hair back. It was a warm day, and he wore only a buckskin breechclout and moccasins. He said, "Nine Killer wants you. Something bad has happened."

"*Doyu?* Then let's go." Nine Killer was the town headman. Not that that gave him any right to issue orders to Smoke or anyone else: A Cherokee headman's power was very limited, a matter of personal prestige rather than any vested authority. But Nine Killer was a good, smart headman, and respectful of custom; he wouldn't have sent for the town's senior medicine man without good reason. "What's the matter?" Smoke asked as Badger led the way back down the trail.

"Otter's dead," the boy said over his shoulder. "Somebody killed him."

"*Eee,*" Smoke said, surprised. "Who did it?"

Badger stepped over a fallen log and looked back. "Nobody knows," he said. "That's why Nine Killer wants you."

"Big Head found him," Badger told Smoke. "He was going fishing this morning, and when he went down to the river, there was Otter, lying on that sandbar below the bluff, with a knife stuck in him."

By now they were passing through the town, which had come unusually alive this morning, though nobody seemed to be doing any useful work; people talked excitedly in little groups while others were walking in the direction of the river. News of Otter's death must have spread like a brushfire in a dry summer.

The town was a fairly typical Overhill Cherokee community of the time: a loose collection of houses strung out along the river, between the high-water mark and the cultivated fields beyond. Most of the houses were solid log cabins, chinked with mud and roofed with pine bark, though a few families still lived in the old-style wattle-walled homes.

In Smoke's youth the town had been a closer place, the houses clustered tightly together around the big central council house, and surrounded by a high palisade for protection against attack. But the raiding days were all but over now; most of the traditional enemy tribes—such as the distant but dreaded Iroquois nations to the north—were paying a brutal price for having helped the English king in his recently ended war with the white colonists, and were having all they could do just to survive, never mind bothering anybody else.

As was true for the Cherokees as well, of course; the final peace with the Americans had cost the Principal People much of their best lands, and yet still the pressure continued from the insatiable white settlers . . . but at least the days of blood were more or less at an end. Now the People could live in peace while they tried to adjust to the enormous changes in their world.

Only now something had happened that might destroy that peace. Smoke pulled his hunting coat closer about him; warm as the day was, he suddenly felt a little cold.

There was a considerable crowd down by the riverbank when Smoke and Badger arrived. They all stood well back, though, up in the shadow of the trees, above the still-fresh marks of the last spring flood.

The little sandbar lay white and clean in the sunlight, sloping gently down to the water's edge. It would have been quite a pretty little scene if it hadn't been for the dead man lying on his back on the sand, a few bowstrings' length back from the water's edge. Even from the high-water line, Smoke could see the knife handle protruding from the body.

Nine Killer stood beside the corpse, along with the man named Big Head. Both of them were looking very serious. So was everybody in sight, come to that. Except for the dead man, who didn't look any particular way but dead.

"Stay back there," Nine Killer called as Badger pushed through the crowd. Then he recognized Smoke. *"Osiyo, Gog'sgi,"* he said, relief in his voice. "Come see."

Smoke walked slowly down the bar, watching the ground, keeping well clear of the lines of tracks that already marked the sand. *"Osiyo,"* he greeted Nine Killer and Big Head, and looked down at the body. *"Osiyo,* Otter, you drunken fool," he muttered. "What did you get yourself into this time?"

"I found him," Big Head said. His voice was a little unsteady. "He was just lying here like this."

"Anybody else around?" Smoke asked.

"No," Big Head said. His head wasn't particularly big; the name came from a dream he had had. "Didn't see anybody at all, all the way to the river."

"I made everybody stay clear," Nine Killer said to Smoke, "until you could get here. Figured we didn't need a lot of people tracking around, messing up the sign."

Smoke gave a quick nod of approval, without looking at Nine Killer. He was studying the body at his feet. Otter lay with his arms flung out to either side, his eyes open, staring blankly at the sky; a thin, long-limbed young man dressed in badly fitting trousers of dark blue broadcloth, such as the traders sold, but no shirt. His hair was chopped off at neck length, in the style some of the young men now favored.

The knife had gone in just below his breastbone; the angle of the handle showed that the killer had given an upward thrust, to be sure of striking the heart. The sand beneath and around the body was soaked with blood; the flies were already swarming, paying little attention to Big Head's attempts to shoo them away.

"This is bad," Nine Killer said in a low voice.

Smoke looked up sharply, switching his attention momentarily from Otter to the headman. Nine Killer was an imposing figure, tall and powerfully built; although no longer the young warrior who had killed nine Catawbas in a single battle, he was still a man in the prime of life, and age had only added dignity to his bearing. Standing there now, wearing only a breechclout and a blanket thrown over his shoulders—Smoke guessed he had come quickly when he heard about Otter, not waiting to dress properly—he could not have been mistaken for anything but an important man.

But just now he looked worried; there were lines about his eyes besides the ones the years had put there.

"A very bad thing," he said, and shook his head. "There could be big trouble."

Smoke knew exactly what Nine Killer meant; he had been thinking along the same lines, all the way down the hill with Badger. The situation had all sorts of ugly possibilities.

Murder was not unknown among the Cherokees, but it was far from common. Killing an enemy was an honored act—probably half the men in the town had names incorporating the verb "to kill"—but among themselves the Principal People were expected to keep their violent impulses firmly in check.

The penalty for transgression was simple and, except in very unusual cases, without appeal: the victim's clan kin would take blood vengeance, a life for a life. It was not merely their right but their absolute duty.

If possible, the avenging clan would kill the slayer; but if this proved impracticable, any member of the killer's clan could be taken instead. Either way, the execution would be a privileged act; no counterretaliation would take place. There would be no long-running blood feud.

Still, as Nine Killer said, there could be much trouble before this affair was settled. Tensions always ran high in the wake of a killing, and the sacred harmony of the community would be endangered. Nine Killer was right to be worried.

"Otter was Wolf Clan," he said to Smoke. "They'll be demanding blood. And right now we don't even know who did it. Is there any way you can tell?"

Smoke looked at the headman for a moment. "A finding medicine for the truth?"

"Something like that."

"Huh. Maybe." Smoke kept his face straight. "Maybe we won't need it. Let's try using our own eyes first, and our good sense. Sometimes that's all the medicine you need."

He studied the ground for a moment. "Look at the tracks," he said. "What do they tell you?"

The other two men glanced briefly at the lines of footprints in the crumbling sand. That was all it took; they were, after all, Cherokees.

"One set of tracks," Big Head said. "Came out here, walked back."

"A lot deeper coming out than going back," Nine Killer added. His forehead wrinkled itself up like a folded blanket. "Somebody killed Otter and then carried him out here? That's crazy."

"Crazier than that. Look at all the blood," Smoke said. "All of it right here, not a drop anywhere else. Otter was carried here while he was still alive. Then the other man stabbed him."

Big Head and Nine Killer stared at him. "*Eee*," Big Head said finally. "Why would anybody do that?"

"And *how*?" Nine Killer asked. "Otter wouldn't just let himself be carried around, like a baby, and then lie there and let somebody stick a knife in him." He looked down at the body again. "Maybe he was tied?" he said doubtfully.

"*Unh-tla,*" Smoke said, and pointed. "No marks on his arms or legs. Besides, tied or not, he'd have struggled. And the sand under him isn't disturbed at all."

A voice said, "I can tell you that part."

All three men turned as a short, stocky young man came through the crowd and stepped out onto the sand. He was dressed in ragged, rather dirty white-style shirt and trousers. His face was a bad color and he moved slowly, as if in pain.

"Yellow Bird," Nine Killer said. "What can you tell us?"

Yellow Bird started toward them, stumbling a little, walking right across the line of footprints. Nine Killer started to speak, but Smoke said quietly, "It's all right. The tracks have told us all they're going to."

"Otter was drunk," Yellow Bird said as he came near. His voice was thick and dry. "We got drunk last night, Otter and me, out at Fenn's place."

The three older men looked at one another. Jack Fenn was a half-breed, the son of a white trader—killed, some years ago, by a Creek raiding party—and a Deer Clan woman. He lived just outside of town in a big house his father had built, like a white man's home; there he sold the usual trade goods—powder, beads, cloth, metal pots, knives, whatever the People wanted—in exchange for furs and deerskins.

All of which was fine, but he also sold whiskey and rum; he even kept a room where people could buy the stuff by the drink. Fenn's place had been the scene of many fights and other troubles, and the liquor he sold had caused endless problems among the people of the town. There had been talk of running him off; but he was still one of the People—even if he didn't act like it—and under the protection of the powerful Deer Clan.

"We got drunk," Yellow Bird repeated. His eyes were red, and his face looked swollen. "We got a jug and we came back this way and we sat down under a tree, up by the river trail, and drank some more, and finally we went to sleep on the ground. Anybody could have picked Otter up and carried him off," Yellow Bird said. "The shape he was in, he wouldn't have known it."

Nine Killer was looking disgusted. "And you didn't see or hear anything?"

"I was as drunk as he was," Yellow Bird confessed. "Whoever did it could have done the same to me if he wanted."

He looked down at the body. "Can I see that knife?"

Smoke said, "Sure," and bent down and pulled the knife from Otter's body, feeling the back edge of the blade grate slightly on bone. The handle was covered with sticky drying blood, and he didn't like the thought that he was getting it on his hand, but he'd have to smoke himself clean after this anyway.

The knife was an ordinary butcher knife, of the kind sold by traders throughout the First Nations, with a wide curving blade and a plain wooden handle. The edge had been resharpened in the usual way, so that the bevel was all on one side, for skinning—or for scalping, which after all was basically a skinning job.

There was nothing unusual about it except the rawhide wrapping around the handle. But Yellow Bird said, "That's Otter's own knife. I remember when he put that rawhide on, after he dropped it on some rocks and broke a piece off the handle."

"Huh." Smoke looked at the knife a moment longer and then turned and spun the bloody weapon out across the river, where it skipped a couple of times before disappearing beneath the cool green water. Nobody objected.

"Could it have been an enemy raid?" Big Head mused. "No, they'd have scalped him. White men, maybe?"

"No white men could have come through here without our knowing it," Smoke told him. "Anyway, those tracks were made by moccasins. No, it wasn't an outsider. Whoever did it is right here in this town."

Turning back to Yellow Bird, he said, "Did anything happen out at Fenn's place? A fight, maybe?"

Yellow Bird rubbed his eyes with both hands, like a sleepy child. "There was something," he mumbled. "Some trouble between Otter and Fenn. I don't remember much, though. It's all like a fog inside my head."

"What's inside your head," Nine Killer said angrily, "is that buzzard piss you got from Jack Fenn. If you—"

He stopped suddenly, looking back up the sandbar. "Panther Shooter," he said in a different voice. "I was wondering when he would show up."

A big, heavyset man was walking down the bar toward them with slow, deliberate steps. His upper body was wrapped in a red trade blanket, though his muscular legs were bare. His head was down as he studied the footprints in the sand. There would be no need to explain their meaning to him; as the town's most successful hunter, Panther Shooter could read sign as well as any man alive.

He was also Otter's mother's eldest brother, and the leading warrior of the Wolf Clan. Now, Smoke thought, the trouble begins.

Sure enough, Panther Shooter's first words to Nine Killer were, "Who did this?"

"We don't know yet," the headman said.

"He was drunk," Yellow Bird put in stupidly.

Panther Shooter gave the younger man a look that would have withered a whole cornfield. "With you, I guess?

Drinking Fenn's whiskey again?" He spat on the sand. "No matter," he said, speaking to Nine Killer again. "He was a worthless fool but he was the Wolf Clan's worthless fool. We will do the right thing. We will cover Otter's bones with blood."

"Yes," Smoke told him, "but whose blood? That's what we're trying to find out."

Nine Killer began walking back up the sandbar, toward the still-growing crowd of onlookers. The other men followed close behind.

"Listen," he cried, "we want to know what happened here! Does anybody know anything about it?"

From the back of the crowd a strong, deep voice said, "I can tell you a little."

The crowd parted, with a certain amount of jostling, and a lean, handsome-faced young man came striding through. He wore the old-fashioned buckskin breechclout and leggings. That was no surprise; Little Dog was one of the conservative faction among the People, opposed to the growing tendency to adopt white ways, and he made a point of dressing in traditional style.

"I was at Fenn's place last night," he said. "I saw what happened there."

"You?" Nine Killer said. "At Fenn's? Why?"

Little Dog looked away. "My sister," he said, and everyone sighed in understanding. Little Dog's sister Walela had been Otter's wife; still was, strictly speaking, but just barely, because a couple of moons ago she had taken up with Jack Fenn.

Cherokee marriages tended to be pretty loose and short-lived; there was no penalty for adultery, and either spouse could call it quits at any time, for any reason or none. Walela, however, had been particularly shameless, ever since she first tasted whiskey, first lying with any man who would get her a drink, then going right to the source. Nowadays it was common knowledge that she spent more nights at Fenn's than at home.

"I went to Fenn's to see if she was all right," Little Dog said, "and to try to get her to stop shaming the family. She wouldn't listen. She was already pretty drunk herself."

"And Otter was there?" Smoke asked.

"No. He came in just as I was about to leave. Yellow Bird was with him," Little Dog said. "They were drunk, too. Otter wanted Walela to come home with him. She said no, and he grabbed her arm and started to pull her toward the door. Fenn told him to stop it, and he let go Walela's arm and pulled out his knife."

Several people sucked in their breath and exchanged looks. Nine Killer said, "He went after Fenn with a knife?"

"Not really. He just waved it around, made a lot of talk, said he was going to kill Fenn. You know how he was when he was drinking." Little Dog's voice was level and without expression, but his face showed profound contempt. "Then he picked up a jug of whiskey and said he was taking that in payment for Walela lying with Fenn." His voice did waver a little now. "He said," Little Dog added with obvious difficulty, "that Fenn had to pay for riding his mare."

Little Dog paused; you could see him pulling himself together. "And then," he went on, "when Otter and Yellow Bird were going out the door, Fenn said, 'Someday somebody's going to take that knife away from you and kill you with it.'"

He looked past Nine Killer and Smoke, at the body lying on the sandbar. "And it looks like somebody did."

"Fenn." Panther Shooter's voice was low and harsh, like the growl of an angry bear. "That's who did it. Good. I was afraid it would be somebody I wouldn't enjoy killing."

"Wait, wait," Smoke protested. "We don't know that yet."

"Good enough for me," Panther Shooter said impatiently. "Otter threatened Fenn. Fenn followed him and killed him when he was too drunk to fight back. Everybody knows what a coward Fenn is."

A murmur ran through the crowd, getting louder. But Smoke said again, "Wait," and held up both hands. "This is wrong. It's not fitting to be arguing like this in the presence of the dead."

"Smoke is right," Nine Killer said decisively. "We'll talk this out in the proper way, tonight in the council house."

He looked at Panther Shooter. "You will wait until then before you do anything?"

Panther Shooter didn't look happy about it, but after a moment he took a deep breath and let it out. "All right. Tonight."

"I didn't do it," Jack Fenn insisted. "I didn't kill him."

Evening now, and everybody was gathered in the council house, each clan sitting together in its section around the big seven-sided building: elders in front, everyone else to the rear. Nine Killer sat on his bench in the center, and for this occasion, Smoke sat to his right.

Jack Fenn stood in front of the Deer Clan's section, facing Nine Killer and Smoke. "Why would I kill him?" he asked. "To get his wife? I already had her. Because he insulted me? I pay no attention to the barking of a scabby dog."

He was a short, wiry man, about thirty summers of age, dressed in white-style clothing—ruffled white shirt and dark trousers—though his feet were shod in center-seam Cherokee moccasins and copper ornaments dangled from his earlobes. His hair was a dark reddish brown rather than the glossy black of a full-blood; his skin was on the light side, too, and his features were small like those of a white man. But his eyes were the dark brown eyes of the People, and just now they showed desperation and fear. As well they might; here and now he was safe—it was absolutely forbidden to bring weapons into the council house, or to commit any sort of violence in its sacred space—but if the decision went against him, he was a dead man as soon as he walked out the door.

Panther Shooter said, "Otter told you he was going to kill you. You saw a chance and killed him first."

Sitting to the rear, among the women of the Paint Clan, Otter's wife, Walela, spoke up. "He didn't do it," she said. She had once been a pretty woman, but drink had aged her badly. "He was with me all night."

Panther Shooter snorted loudly. "You would say black was white for this half-*yoneg*," he said scornfully. "Besides, you were probably too drunk yourself to know anything."

Nine Killer said sharply, "None of that kind of talk inside the council house. Panther Shooter, you know better than that."

He looked at Jack Fenn. "Little Dog says you talked about killing Otter with his own knife."

"That's right," Yellow Bird put in. He looked a little better than he had that morning but not much. "I remember now," he said.

Fenn swung around to face Yellow Bird. "And how do we know *you* didn't kill him?"

"Me?" Yellow Bird looked shocked. "He was my friend."

Smoke cleared his throat. "Whiskey has led more than one man to kill a friend," he said pointedly. "But Yellow Bird was very drunk. And those footprints were not made by a staggering man."

"Locust, then," Fenn said, and gestured toward a broad-shouldered young man who sat in the middle of the Blue Clan's section. "He could have done it. He and Otter were enemies, ever since that business with the horse."

Everyone fell silent for a moment, considering this. It was true that there was bad blood between Otter and the man named Locust. A favorite horse of Locust's had disappeared one night and had later turned up in the possession of a white settler, who refused to give it up. The white man hadn't known the name of the Cherokee who had sold the horse to him, but his description had sounded a lot like Otter; and Otter had vanished the same night as the horse, and had returned to town many days later, dressed in fancy new clothes—somewhat the worse for wear—and showing signs of having been on a long drunk.

Locust had accused Otter to his face of stealing the horse and selling it to the white man; Otter had laughed and told Locust a man shouldn't have a horse if he couldn't hold on to it. Locust had said that the same thing ought to apply to wives, and the two men had scuffled in the town street before being separated by Nine Killer and others.

Locust rose to his feet in the middle of the Blue Clan's section. "It's true I hated Otter," he said calmly. "And I say right now that his death is no loss. But"—he raised his voice over the general muttering—"I didn't kill him last night. If I had wanted to kill him, I would have done it in the open, for everybody to see, and then admitted it like a man."

He sat back down. There was an uncertain pause. Fenn's eyes were those of a trapped animal, flickering now here, now there. He seemed about to speak.

But then Black Fox stood up beside Jack Fenn. A husky, middle-aged full-blood, he was the brother of Fenn's dead mother and therefore Fenn's closest clan kin.

"I speak for the Deer Clan," he said. "We are not satisfied that our brother here is guilty of killing Otter. We have heard no one say they saw him do it. We have heard only a lot of guessing, like the gossip of old women."

He looked straight at Panther Shooter. "We do not accept our brother's guilt. If his life is taken, or that of any other of the *Ani-awi,* we will take a life in turn."

Before Panther Shooter could reply, old Drowning Bear of the Blue Clan said, "We say the same, with regard to our brother Locust."

It was a bad moment. All about the big council house people were looking this way and that, and their faces, in the flickering light of the torches and the central fire, were not good to see. Violence and blood were in the air, held in check only by the sanctity of the council house.

But Nine Killer had risen from his split-log seat. *"Gusdi idadaduhni!"* he shouted. "Stop this!"

When quiet had been more or less restored, he added, "People, this will not do. This is not right."

He turned slowly, looking at all of them in turn. "In all my life," he said, "I have never heard of such a thing, that one of the Principal People should kill another in secret. Or that any man should fail to step forward and accept the consequences of his acts. I think it must always have been unknown among us, because there is no tradition to guide us in this matter."

He reached out a hand and touched Smoke on the shoulder. "And so I am asking my old friend Smoke to help us. Perhaps his medicine can reveal the truth."

Smoke remained seated—enough people, he thought irritably, were popping up and down tonight, like so many ground squirrels—but he inclined his head. "I will try," he said.

Panther Shooter was talking in low tones with some of the other Wolf Clan men. After a moment he turned back to face Nine Killer. "All right," he said. "We can't do anything for the next three days and nights anyway. We have to bury our brother."

He folded his arms and looked at Smoke. "You have that long, then. In three days, if you can tell us the name of the killer, we will be in your debt. If not—" He glanced at Jack Fenn, then at Locust. "Then we will do as we see fit. *Nasgi nusdi*," he finished. "That's how it is."

Walking away from the council house, Nine Killer said, "Can you do it?"

"I'll try," Smoke said again.

"Good. I hope you succeed." Nine Killer's voice was heavy with worry. "Otherwise something very bad is going to happen . . . Fenn!" He fairly spat the name. "I could kill him myself."

"You think he did it?" Smoke asked mildly.

"Probably. I don't care," Nine Killer admitted. "Whoever actually did it, it was caused by that evil stuff he sells. I'd be glad to see the Wolf Clan rid us of Fenn," he added. "But then the Deer Clan will take a life in return, and then we'll have a blood feud that will destroy this town. Unless Black Fox and his brothers can be convinced that Fenn is really blood-guilty."

He gave Smoke a sidelong look. "So if you should find some way . . . you know what I'm saying."

"You want me to make false medicine?"

"Did I say that?"

The two men grinned at each other in the darkness.

Smoke laid a hand on Nine Killer's arm. "Don't worry," he said gently.

"Truth is a funny thing. It comes out in the strangest ways. I have some ideas."

Three nights later Smoke stood in the center of the council house and said, "I guess you're all wondering why I called you all together here."

There was a chorus of chuckles, especially from the older men. Everybody in the council house—it was packed tonight; people were standing up or sitting on the floor, and a few young boys even sat in the rafters overhead—knew exactly why they were there. The old medicine man's sarcasm was what was needed, though, to ease the tension in the air.

Everybody was dressed in their best tonight, as befitted such a serious occasion. Most of the elders wore trade-blanket robes and fancy turbans with egret or eagle feathers. Shiny silver gorgets swung at the men's throats, and elaborate ornaments dangled from their stretched earlobes. The women, too, were decked out in their best dresses, and even the children had been cleaned up a bit.

Smoke still wore his old fringed hunting coat, but he had put on his best turban and a couple of white egret feathers, and his good moccasins. He thought he looked pretty good.

He gestured to the boy named Badger, who stood behind him, next to a big honeysuckle-vine basket with a tight-fitting lid. Badger picked up the basket, looking a little nervous, and held it up at waist level.

Smoke said, "Jack Fenn, come here. Locust, too. *Ehena.*"

Jack Fenn rose from his seat and came forward. His face was almost green, but he held himself straight and he moved with a steady pace. Locust joined him with an air of almost bored calm; he might have been on a visit to an unusually dull bunch of relatives.

"Now," Smoke said, "we're going to settle this—"

With his left hand he removed the lid from the basket. Reaching inside with his right, moving very fast for an old man, he pulled out the biggest rattlesnake anyone there had ever seen.

"*Inada,* here," he said over the sudden chorus of gasps and exclamations and the buzz of the snake's rattles, "is going to help us. I doctored him with a special medicine I learned from my grandfather."

Nobody was listening all that closely; they were all looking at the snake. It lay lazily across Smoke's hands—which were not gripping it, only supporting it—its big flat head slightly raised, seeming to look this way and that. Its tongue flicked in and out, in and out, almost too fast to see. Its dangling tail vibrated gently, sending out a low-pitched whir. It didn't give the impression of being angry, but how could you tell with a snake?

"Locust," Snake said, "come lay your hand on this snake and tell us whether you are guilty of Otter's death. Tell the truth, and you have nothing to fear. But if you lie," he warned as Locust stepped forward, "he'll bite you. The medicine will tell him."

Locust shrugged. "And should I be afraid?" He reached out and laid a hand on the rattlesnake's body, midway between Smoke's hands. "I tell you, I did not kill Otter."

"Good," Smoke said approvingly. "Spoken like an honorable man. Go sit down."

He turned to Fenn. "And now—?"

Jack Fenn was staring at the snake. His face had gone whiter than ever, like the belly of a fish; his eyes were huge. "No," he said. "No." He said it first in English, then in Cherokee.

Behind Smoke, sitting on his bench, Nine Killer said, "You have to do it, Fenn. Or else we'll know why."

Fenn licked his lips with a long tongue. "No," he said once more, his voice gone hoarse.

His hand dived suddenly into the front of his broadcloth jacket and came out clutching a pistol. "Nobody touches me," he said, swinging the weapon from side to side, while everybody sat stunned by the incredible sacrilege. "Stay away."

He began backing toward the doorway. Behind him, a

couple of men got to their feet, ready to jump him, but Smoke waved to them to sit down. "Let him go," he commanded. "No violence in the council house."

At the door Fenn called, "Don't come after me. I'll kill anybody who gets on my trail."

A moment later he was gone. Immediately the Wolf Clan men began getting to their feet, their faces furious; but Smoke cried, *"Hesdi!"* and they all stopped moving.

"You can go after him later if you want," he told them. "Right now we are not finished with this medicine. Sit down."

As they reluctantly reseated themselves, he said, "Little Dog, come here."

"What?" Little Dog stood up, but he looked confused, and he made no move to come forward. "Why?"

"Yes," Panther Shooter said, "what does Little Dog have to do with this? We know now that Fenn killed Otter."

"Do we? Or do we only know," Smoke said, his voice rising, "what everyone here already knew—that Jack Fenn is afraid of snakes?"

That got a moment's quiet. "It's so," a man said, somewhere over among the Hair Clan. "When he was a boy, even the girls used to scare him with little green grass snakes."

"Little Dog," Smoke said, "you said something that morning when we were looking at Otter's body. You told us Fenn had said somebody was going to kill Otter with his own knife, and then you said somebody had done it."

"I said that," Little Dog assented. "What of it?"

"But," Smoke said, "the knife was already gone. I threw it in the river myself. *So how did you know it was Otter's knife?*"

Everybody was staring at Little Dog now. They had even forgotten the rattlesnake.

"I—" Little Dog said, and stopped. "I must have seen it—"

"You couldn't have seen it from where you were," Nine Killer spoke up. "Not well enough to recognize it. And you were too far away to hear Yellow Bird telling us whose knife it was. So how *did* you know?"

Little Dog's eyes were very strange. His mouth opened and then closed without any sound coming out.

"But you can settle these questions," Smoke said in a reassuring voice. "Just come up here and lay your hand on *inada,* same way Locust did. If you didn't do it . . ."

Little Dog looked at the snake, which looked back at him. He started to take a step forward. Then he stopped.

"No," he said. His voice was almost steady. "No, I'd rather have a clean death. Put the snake away, old man. It's true. I killed Otter."

He turned to face the Wolf Clan men. "I stayed at Fenn's place a little while, after Otter and Yellow Bird left, trying to talk Walela into coming with me. When I left, I took the trail by the river."

He glanced over at Yellow Bird. "I saw those two drunken fools lying asleep under a tree, and I thought of what Otter had done to my sister, how he had been the first one to give her the whiskey that ruined her. I picked him up and carried him down to the river and stabbed him with his own knife."

The council house was absolutely silent now. Even the rattlesnake had quit buzzing.

"I was going to throw him into the river," Little Dog added, "but then I remembered the fight, and I thought maybe Fenn would be blamed. Then he would be killed, too, and then maybe Walela would become an honorable woman again."

He came forward then, but not toward Smoke; he walked over and stood facing Panther Shooter. "I have some things I need to do," he said, "to make sure my family is all right. Will you give me until the next full moon?"

Panther Shooter didn't hesitate. "Yes."

"Then I'll be waiting for you. Down by the river, on the same sandbar, I think that's the best place, don't you?"

He turned and walked toward the door, not looking to either side. There was no need for further assurances. In all the long history of the Principal People, no man had ever failed to keep an appointment of that kind.

"Uncle," Badger said on the way home, "will you teach me that medicine sometime? What you did with the snake?"

Smoke laughed softly. "Oh, yes, the snake. Hold on."

He stopped, looked both ways up and down the trail, and took the basket from Badger's hands. He took off the lid and tipped the rattlesnake gently out onto the ground. It made no move to coil or strike; it only lay there a moment and then slithered off into the brush, without so much as a rattle.

"I can teach you," Smoke said, "how to make a snake stupid with tobacco and some other herbs, till you can handle him without getting bit. And I can teach you how to milk his poison, so even if he does bite you, it won't hurt. That's all the medicine I did tonight."

Badger said, "But you knew already that Little Dog was the one. Why did you go through all the rest of it?"

"It was a chance to get rid of Jack Fenn," Smoke said candidly. "A worthless fellow, and a danger to the People with that whiskey of his. I remembered he was afraid of snakes. I figured he'd run, and he did. He won't be back."

He sighed. "And as for Little Dog, I fear the snakes are in his own head." He reached out a hand and ruffled the boy's hair. "Come on. Let's see what your mama can give us to eat."

$\mathcal{B}$*ruce Alexander first introduced us to Sir John Fielding in* Blind Justice. *The title referred both to the literal blindness of Sir John and to his reputation as one of the finest magistrates in late-eighteenth-century London. While the cases are fictional, Sir John was a real person, the brother of the novelist Henry Fielding. Bruce has created an amanuensis for Fielding, one Jeremy Proctor, who is the narrator.*

The second in the series, Murder in Grub Street, *was a* New York Times *notable book, and all have garnered excellent reviews. There are now six books about Sir John and Jeremy Proctor, the most recent being* Death of a Colonial. *In the following story, we find Sir John in the ironic position of being a man who is truly blind to racial differences.*

THE EPISODE OF THE WATER CLOSET

Bruce Alexander

"It's simple enough, Lady Kilcoyne," said Sir John Fielding. "If a man lacks one of his senses, then he must compensate by strengthening the other four."

This was not the first time I had heard this, or something quite like it, from his lips during the few years I had been in his service. It was, however, the first time I had heard him make a remark of that sort in such august company. With Lady Fielding nearby, he sat at the table of Lord Kilcoyne, a Scottish earl. It was indeed a grand occasion, one of a number that had taken place in the grandest London residences during the month of September in the year of 1771, and all of them in honor of Prince Govinda, the Maharajah of Bangalore.

The prince, who was rumored to be one of the world's wealthiest men, had arrived from the continent without a great retinue of servants, yet in a manner that could hardly be called quiet or modest. A great caravan of wagons, heavily laden with bags, cases, and portmanteaus trailed a coach-and-four specially decorated with painted flowers

162

and a smiling sun; all wended their way from the docks, across London Bridge, then on to the Globe and Anchor, grandest hostelry on the Strand. Along the way, dray wagons halted in respect, and pedestrians gawked in awe. A colorfully dressed blackamoor oversaw the unloading of the wagons and assisted the prince from his coach and into the hostelry.

The prince let it be known that he had made this long journey that he might meet the King of England, and was sore disappointed to learn that His Royal Highness would be, until the end of the month, at the family seat in Hanover. In the meantime, what was the prince to do? How was he to spend his time?

This proved to be no problem, for Prince Govinda soon found himself quite inundated with invitations to London's finest houses. All the best people were eager to entertain him—and why not? A picturesque individual he was in his robes and glittering red stones (rubies, surely), velvet slippers, and brocaded waistcoat. He had a ready wit after his fashion, though it was somewhat disguised by the curious manner in which he expressed himself in English. One could hardly tell what word Prince Govinda might choose, or how he might pronounce it in his high, fluting voice. It was said he would blabber on to his host and to the table at large, keeping all quite amused, though somewhat confused as to the precise content of his anecdotes and comments. It was not what he said, but how he said it at which they laughed with such delight.

I had been no little surprised when Sir John received the invitation to Lord Kilcoyne's dinner. He, a mere magistrate, was seldom welcomed into the homes of the mighty. Yet, when I read to him the message, he seemed not in the least taken by the occasion. He had simply listened, nodded, and told me to pen an acceptance and he would sign it.

You may have guessed, reader, from the remark made by him at the beginning of this little narrative, that Sir John did indeed lack one of his senses. And further, from the fact that it fell to me to read him the invitation from Lord Kilcoyne and write Sir John's reply to it, that the missing faculty was the power of sight. Alas, so it was. He had been thus deprived since late adolescence. Nevertheless he had assembled and now directed a force of constables, known locally as the Bow Street Runners, that brought order to Westminster and the City of London, where the forces of lawlessness had previously prevailed. For this and in recognition of certain schemes put forward for the common weal, he had been knighted some years before.

As to who I might happen to be, my name is Jeremy Proctor. Orphaned at the age of thirteen, I first attached to Sir John as a ward of his court but soon won a place in his household as houseboy, amanuensis, runner of all possible errands, and general factotum, Best of all I liked the chances I was given to serve him in his investigations of criminal doings in and about London. Least of all did I like the sort of thing I was called upon to do that evening in question, and that was to play Sir John's personal manservant and stand in rigid attendance behind his chair at Lord Kilcoyne's table. From that vantage point I had naught to do but watch the rich and powerful eat, and listen to their chatter, which was not greatly edifying.

The guest of honor's table talk I have already described. It was only when, three courses into dinner, the maharajah excused himself abruptly and ran up to the water closet, of which Lady Kilcoyne had earlier boasted, that the others took the opportunity to prove themselves at the art of conversation.

"Well!" shouted Lord Kilcoyne as soon as the door closed behind the princeling. "Tell me all, what do you think of the little fellow?"

A great hubbub of comment exploded forth from the eleven seated round the table, all of it rather vehement in expression, yet none of it—even what was meant in approval—which could fairly be termed "polite."

"Why," said the Duke of Dingle, "I must say he's a cute little bugger. I'll give him that."

"Indeed," said the duchess, "did you see him jump up from the table and hop out of here? Quite like a little monkey, wasn't he?"

"Oh, wasn't he, though!" said Lady Lydingham, decorating her contribution with a proper little giggle.

"Altogether precious!"

"But for the most part he talked utter nonsense," complained a gentleman quite unknown to me, "Couldn't understand half what the fellow said."

"You, Sir John," said Lord Kilcoyne to the magistrate, "what thought you of him? I noted you laughed little, and now you keep silent. Did you not find him entertaining?"

The powdered and painted faces of guests of both sexes turned to Sir John as he gave thought and made ready to speak. "Indeed, Lord Kilcoyne," said he at last, "I was well entertained. Prince Govinda, if I have his name aright, gave quite a performance. That is what you sought from him, and that is what he provided—but it could not have been easy for him. I sensed the strain in our guest of honor as he sought to provide further non sequiturs and malapropos comments for your entertainment. You must all have seen it. He had it writ plain upon his face."

"How can you say that?" demanded Lady Kilcoyne. She seemed to smart at the criticism implicit in Sir John's remarks. "You, a blind man? How can you presume to tell us what was plain upon the maharajah's face when you could not see that face?"

And that, reader, is when he spoke the words quoted above: "It's simple enough, Lady Kilcoyne. If a man lacks one of his senses, then he must compensate by strengthening the other four."

"You claim, then, to see without the aid of your eyes? That, sir, sounds a bit farfetched to me."

"Perhaps I should demonstrate, using you as a subject," said he to her. He then turned to Lady Kilcoyne so that he appeared to be studying her. (Yet, could he have claimed the power of sight, the band of black silk over his eyes would have prevented him from seeing her face and form.) He remained in this posture for near a minute. There came a hush over the table.

Lady Kilcoyne smirked rather unpleasantly. "I am ready," she said. "Ready and waiting."

"You have hair of a reddish hue," began Sir John. "Your front teeth are prominent—they protrude. Your eyes, whose color are blue, I believe, or perhaps green, show a sharp expression. You lean forward in an aggressive attitude, and your face is twisted in a frown."

It was then as if all at the table had caught their breath in the same instant, for his description was quite accurate. All at the table, that is, except for her husband, Lord Kilcoyne, who at that moment quite roared with laughter. "Good God, Maggie," he shouted out the length of the table, "he has you down for fair!"

"How did you do that?" Lady Kilcoyne put the question rather coldly to Sir John.

"Quite simply," said he. "First of all, you are known in society for your red hair. Blue eyes or green usually accompany hair of that hue. My ears detected a certain minor speech impediment which could only be caused by protrusive teeth. And as for the rest—your sharp expression, your posture—they are as one in the hostile state you would indeed be in. I may say, by the by, that when I speak of strengthening the other senses, I mean also to include common sense."

So absorbed were they all in discussing this, each with his dinner partners, that the maharajah's return to the table was given little notice. I watched him, curious, as he padded silently across the floor; he seemed as interested in the animated behavior of those at the table as they were now uninterested in him. He had lost their attention, yet as he resumed his place at the table he made one last effort to retrieve it.

Speaking to Lord Kilcoyne, his high voice carried the length of the table: "Oh, yes, my good lord, Your Earlship, I must congratulate you on your new water closet, sir. Nowhere in India, I believe, do we have such devices. I should like to be the first, oh, yes, the professor of the principal water closet in all India. Then shall the other princes visit me in their gold coats with spots which should be rubies, but seeing me, then making use of my water closet, they shall come away amazed and envious. Up and down, I will lead them up and down, I will show them all."

This he said to his host, yet his host had little to say in reply. Lord Kilcoyne smiled indulgently and nodded at Prince Govinda as the latter began his paean to water closets, but he soon wearied, and finding his guest no longer amusing, turned his back on him and continued his conversation with Sir James Bigelow, a baronet, who had the stud services of a prize stallion to offer. This sort of thing interested Lord Kilcoyne far more.

The maharajah seemed not to be hurt by this. He continued until he had had his say, speaking out to whomever wished to listen; these seemed then to number only Sir John and myself. But, having done, he smiled and nodded at us both and fell to his neglected dinner.

It was a proper ten-course meal, and the diners took ample time to consume it. Freed now from any obligation to the guest of honor, the ladies gave their attention to gossip and the gentlemen to matters of the hunt, to shooting, and to horse raising. A dinner of such size and duration allows time for those around the table to ease themselves as they proceed. Thus Prince Govinda was simply the first of many to leave the table, climb the stairs, and visit Lord and Lady Kilcoyne's new water closet up at the top.

(Now, it should be explained that this small room, so much admired by the prince, had to it three doors: the first opening into the hall, the second into the lord's bedchamber, and the third into his lady's. In the hall, a manservant and a maidservant stood in attendance on either side of the door so that one or the other might provide assistance, should it be needed. Placed so, they also served as guardians of the two bedchambers.)

As the evening wore on, and the diners had only the dessert course to look forward to, Lady Kilcoyne happened to look up and became very cross when she saw her maid intrude into the dining room. From the foot of the table, her angry eyes followed the poor creature, who was near quaking in fright, as she made her way toward her. There must, I reflected, be some dire event to report. The servant bent to whisper into the ear of her mistress.

Having heard her out, Lady Kilcoyne went suddenly erect in her chair. A look of terrible consternation came upon her face. She stood and announced to the table: "My emerald pendant is gone from its place in my bedchamber. It must surely have been stolen!"

Before any other response could be made to the announcement, Sir John Fielding leaped up from his chair. "In my capacity as magistrate of the Bow Street Court," he bellowed forth, "I must insist upon talking to each and every one of you who has journeyed up the stairs to make use of the water closet. All are suspect."

Then did he call me to him and say to me in a much quieter voice, much less intimidating, "Jeremy, you I must ask to hasten off to Bow Street. Take Lady Fielding with you, and come back with a constable."

When I approached her and asked her to accompany me, Lady Kate objected strenuously.

"Why must I always leave just when things become most interesting?" she asked. "It's not fair!"

"P'rhaps not, mum, but it will soon be a good deal less than interesting hereabouts, for Sir John must talk to a great many, which will no doubt take half the night."

"I see your point," said she, conceding.

As we left I noted that six had grouped themselves about Sir John and were waiting to be interviewed. The maharajah, however, was not among them. I wondered where he might be.

Yet when I returned in less than a half of an hour with Mr. Benjamin Bailey, the captain of the Bow Street Runners, I found Prince Govinda quite prominently present. He had been discovered by the butler seeking to exit through a window; when returned to the dining room, he was found to have the emerald pendant in the pocket of his waistcoat. A small crowd of peers, patricians, and their ladies surrounded him. The Duke of Dingle held a huge old fowling piece—a proper blunderbuss it was—trained upon the Indian prince. Lord Kilcoyne had in his hand a sizable length of stout hemp rope which he shook most threateningly at him who only a short time before had sat at his right hand.

Sir John lectured them one and all on the need for due process, warning that if they were to execute Mr. Binney without benefit of trial, he would have no choice but to arrest all present on charges of homicide. Then did he add: "Mr. Bailey, did I hear you enter with Jeremy?"

"I am here, Sir John."

"Take charge of the prisoner, Charles Binney, and let us be on our way. If any of these distinguished gentlemen should attempt to impede you, you have my permission to use your club upon them."

At that, all fell back from the prince. (Could he be the Charles Binney named by Sir John?) The ladies let out little yelps of outrage. Their husbands grumbled. Lord Kilcoyne threatened to have Sir John removed from his position as magistrate and "disknighted"—if such a thing were possible.

"Why such a passion for punishment?" Sir John asked him. "You got back your emerald. Could it be the wound given your pride still bleeds? You were, after all, properly duped."

In response, the peer could do no more than glower. Sir John shrugged at his silence and charged Mr. Bailey to march the prisoner outside, and he summoned me to him, "Jeremy," said he, "let us follow close upon those two. This mob of nobles quite frightens me."

Once out of the mansion in Bloomsbury Square and into the warm night, the false prince became suddenly quite talkative. "Could it be as you told 'em, Sir John, sir?" he asked in a manner quite unlike I had heard earlier from him. "Did you truly find me out by the sound of my voice?"

"You made a big mistake in trying to scarper from the house, Charlie—but I had you before that. I said to myself, 'Now that voice is familiar. Who does it belong to?' Yet I was still wondering about that when you dropped a couple of lines of Shakespeare into your recital, and then I knew exactly who you were."

"From *Midsummer Night's Dream,* of course."

"Ah, yes, Robin Goodfellow—from Act Two, Scene One, and Act Three, Scene Two."

"It was my best role, no question of it. But I must say, sir, you do know your Shakespeare."

Sir John dismissed Mr. Binney's flattery with an easy wave of his hand. "I would go so far as to say you were a magnificent Puck," said he, "but also rather a good Ariel."

"That was *The Tempest* two seasons back, which was my last role at the Drury Lane. Mr. Garrick always said he was sorry he couldn't use me more, but a fellow of my size . . ."

"And you made a fine Indian prince—Govinda, was it?" said Sir John. "If you could only have left out the Shakespeare, perhaps you would have fooled me."

"But I'm an actor, and an actor needs a script. I'd run out of words of my own to say, and I always have the Bard in mind. I could always spout a bit of him at the wink of an eye."

"A pity," said the magistrate, referring, I assumed, to Mr. Binney's predicament. "But tell me, Charlie, who put you up to this?"

"I've nobody to blame but myself, sir. I got this idea at a place where I used to take my grub and bub, which was run by a pair of Lascars—right over from India, they were. I had a great old time listening to them and getting down the way they messed the King's English. Pretty soon I could talk it as bad as they could. And I got to thinking, what if I was to make one of those state visits with all sorts of folderol and fancy dinners and whatever betide? Now, wouldn't that be a lark? So one night I snuck into the costume room of the Drury Lane and found myself all the finery a fellow like me could need or want. I arranged a grand landing with some empty trunks and got the services of big black Samson for the show—and we put on a good one, we did."

"Ah, from all reports, indeed you did," said Sir John. "I hear the invitations fair poured in. Honestly, how many dinners were given in your honor? What more have you stolen?"

"Naught worth mentioning, Beak, upon my soul, sir,"

said the prisoner. "A gold chain here, a ring there, all of them from three of the grand houses. All that's under me mattress at the Crown and Anchor. I thought of them as keepsakes, I did, souvenirs of my adventures among the rich and powerful. I wanted to see them up close." At that he hesitated and then added: "I found I didn't like them much."

"Nor do I," said Sir John with a sigh.

"But I reckon it's the rope for me now, no matter what."

"Oh, perhaps not."

"Sir?" Mr. Binney perked up a bit at that, "Did I hear right?"

"Charlie, how quickly could you get out of London?"

"Quick as you could wink an eye." Then realizing that in effect Sir John had no eye to wink, he added quickly: "Sorry, sir, no offense meant."

"And none taken. If you can be out of the city by morning, then you have my permission to escape. My advice is that you try Dublin or New York in the colonies. Each has a thriving theater life, or so I'm told." He waited a moment, then: "What? Still here?" He clapped his hands thrice. "Away with you, man! Away!"

Mr. Bailey at last loosed his grip on the prisoner's shoulder, and swift as Robin Goodfellow did Prince Govinda disappear from sight.

*M*ichael Coney is best known as the author of more than sixty science-fiction novels and short stories. He has won the British Science Fiction Association Award for best novel and been a finalist for the American Nebula and the Canadian Aurora awards. Recently he has begun writing mystery stories, one of which was published in Crime Through Time II *and another in* Alfred Hitchcock's Mystery Magazine. *His style ranges from black humor to dark tragedy, sometimes in the same book.*

In "Suspicion," Michael writes about the time of the Clearances in Scotland, a place that fascinates him and that he has visited often.

SUSPICION

Michael Coney

When they dragged old Mattie out of her home screaming, I finally realized the Highlands would never be the same again.

The soldier threw a blazing torch onto the roof while other soldiers held her. She kicked and struggled and spat, and called upon the Lord to visit his wrath on her tormentors—and the torch guttered and went out. Mattie's tiny stone cottage had a sod roof.

The sergeant said, "Try lighting it from inside," and the soldier nodded. Soon smoke began to ooze through the sod and drift away in the damp October air. Mattie uttered a great yell of despair.

"My things!"

"Let her go," said the sergeant.

The soldiers released their grip. The old woman darted into the cottage and began to hurl her possessions outside. Moments passed. Smoke puffed through the ill-fitting shutters.

"Have your men help her, Sergeant," I said. "There's not much time."

He regarded me coldly. "You have no authority over me, man."

A rough chair skidded over the short grass. Mattie appeared, eyes streaming, flinging blackened pots. Smoke billowed around her. She disappeared inside again.

"For God's sake . . . !" I ran forward.

The roof collapsed with a roar.

A great gout of smoke and flame burst from the doorway, halting me in my tracks. I doubled up, coughing, eyes streaming, and ducked away, the heat searing my back. A strong hand seized my arm and dragged me away into cooler air.

When eventually I could speak, I said, "Mattie . . . ?"

"One less passenger for the boat," the sergeant said. "I doubt that she'd have survived the journey, anyway."

As I said, the Highlands would never be the same. We'd had our share of wars, but there had never been anything so heartless as this cold-blooded eviction of our people by their own landlords. People in the uncaring Lowland cities were already calling it the Clearances, as though the crofters were no better than scrub to be hacked and burned and tossed aside to make room for a more worthwhile crop.

And I, Hamish Morrison, factor to the McPhail, was a party to all this mischief.

In fairness to myself, I hadn't expected it to happen quite like this. Certainly there had been reports of terrible doings elsewhere in the Highlands, but this was Achnabrae, and Achnabrae folk were peaceable and respected their laird. The McPhail had assured me that suitable arrangements had been made for them in the New World, and in my turn I'd assured the clansfolk of Achnabrae.

But Achnabrae people, though peaceable, are stubborn. I hadn't realized how stubborn. As I stood sick with horror, watching old Mattie's cottage burn around her, I began to wonder about all the others. And particularly my friend Iain McBain, probably the most stubborn of the lot.

"Must you burn the cottages?" I asked.

"The laird's orders. It's the only way to get them out,"

replied the sergeant, "and to make sure they don't come back."

I rode away with a heavy heart.

My wife, Aileen, was already at the McBain house, having perhaps had the same thought as I. But there was no urgency in the scene that met my eyes. Morag was tossing sticks on the fire, Iain was sharpening his mattock with deft strokes of the stone. Aileen saw me, raised her eyebrows, and shrugged. Iain smiled.

"Welcome, Hamish! Morag has already put on the pot for your lady wife. You'll take a mug with us?"

The vision of Mattie's burning cottage rose before me, and I felt a slow, helpless anger. "You've not packed your belongings?"

"Why would we pack? We're not leaving. Today I'm breaking new ground for the spring planting." He bent over his mattock again, and the sparks showered in the darkness of the tiny room.

"Pack now, Iain," I said as steadily as I could. "The laird and his son arrived at my house at first light, and his soldiers have already burned old Mattie's cottage, and Mattie with it. There's devilry afoot in the glen."

They gazed at me, incredulous. "That's not a pretty jest, Hamish," said Iain.

"We all heard they put fire to the cottages in Inverloch with the people still inside. Now it's happened here. Believe me or not, they'll be here before midday. Pack for Morag and the baby's sake, if you don't care for yourself, Iain. Take your belongings down to the quay and get aboard the boat like everyone else." I appealed to his fresh-faced wife. "For God's sake, tell him, Morag!"

"You'll not blaspheme in this house, Hamish!" She advanced on me as if to throw me out physically.

Aileen said, God bless her, "That's not the point, Morag. The point is the laird and his soldiers."

"My man and I have no fear of the laird or his lapdogs."

"The laird owns the land! It's his right!" I realized I'd shouted, and said more quietly, "We've been friends a long time, Iain."

"You're the laird's factor," snapped Morag. "You speak the laird's words. You live in the big house on the hill. Where's the friendship there?"

"No, be fair, Hen," said Iain. "Hamish had no part of this. It's happening all over the Highlands, the greed. The landlords hatch out their plans in Edinburgh and London, and they say: the clansmen must make room for the sheep. But there's a thing they haven't bargained for—we two are staying. And whatever foulness the laird and his men might visit on me and Morag, I charge you with telling the world, Hamish. You are an educated man and you have the right ears in Edinburgh. They will listen, and the laird's name will be shame."

"That's an unfair thing to ask of Hamish," said Aileen.

"This is an unfair world, don't you think? What of it, Hamish? Will you do it?"

Aileen and I had a good life here in this remote glen rolling down to the sea. The laird lived far away in Edinburgh, and he'd been a fair enough master, leaving me to collect the rents and deal with the small problems of Achnabrae in my own way. I'd walked the fine line between loyalty to him and fair dealing with people scratching a living from the poor soil and the unforgiving sea. And now I was being asked to make a choice between this loyalty and the people who had become my friends.

Cravenly I thought the choice might not be necessary. The laird might see reason if I made a special plea on behalf of one good tenant who might equally well become a good shepherd in the changing times.

I heard myself say, "I will do it."

And I heard Aileen's angry cry, "You fool, Hamish!"

As if in apology, Iain said, "You must understand, we can't leave our croft. My kinfolk have lived here for more generations than I can count. We've tilled the land and we've fed it with the seaweed and manure and we've tended our crops and our animals and we've kept our cottage fresh and our roof sound and, Hamish, we love this place almost as much as we love each other. How can we leave?"

Morag went to his side and put her arm around his waist. She looked up at him, and the love in her eyes embarrassed me. She said quietly, "The Lord will not allow us to be thrown out of our home to make room for a rabble of bleating, pissing sheep, and that's an end to it."

I didn't think Morag made much sense, not being a religious man myself. But from that moment on, nothing made much sense anyway. Aileen and I went in opposite directions to visit the rest of the crofts and ensure there was no further stubbornness—and for this I was glad, because there had been a look in her eyes that boded me ill.

Most of the tenant crofters had accepted their lot. Near the end of a busy morning I was speeding the departure of the McLeods, away up the glen, when three soldiers came riding up on steaming horses.

"Mr. Morrison, you're to come to the McBain house now! There's been devilment done!"

"Devilment?"

"The laird's been done to death, Mr. Morrison!"

I felt a sick apprehension as I mounted my horse. "Who did this thing?"

"Why, the McBains, of course," the man jerked out as we galloped northward. "Who else?"

When I arrived at the cottage I found a host of soldiers gathered outside. The laird's tasselled stick leaned against the wall. As I pushed my way through the doorway, the first person I saw was Iain, held firmly by two soldiers. The laird's eldest son stood near the fireplace, head bowed, his face hidden.

On the floor, stretched out on his back as though sleeping, lay the laird, the McPhail of McPhail, a knife protruding from his chest and the blood still weeping slowly across his plaid.

Nobody spoke, so I asked Iain, "Who did it?" It could not have been Iain. I waited for him to tell me so.

"Does it matter, Hamish?" he said. "The bastard is dead, and the world is a better place for it."

The laird's son swung around to face us. He was a lad

of twenty, good-looking like his father, with a shock of red hair and a complexion to match. But now the face was twisted with grief, and tears forged trails down the freckled cheeks.

"Take soldiers and take McBain to your house, Factor," he said unsteadily. "Question him, find out what devil possessed him, then hang him."

I spoke first to the soldier who had found the body.

"The cottage was empty, so we thought," he said, "so the sergeant told me to put it to the torch. I went inside and held the torch to the roof timbers, and then I saw the McPhail lying there. Stabbed. I threw the torch outside and called the sergeant in. We sent runners for the"—he hesitated—"the young laird and yourself."

"What of Iain McBain?"

"We sent out a search party. We found him beyond the burn to the east, breaking new ground. As though the laird were of no account," said the man wonderingly.

"I doubt that he confessed," I said, skeptical.

The young laird broke in, "Did he have need? The laird lies dead in McBain's own house!"

I turned back to Iain, who had remained silent all the way here. "Did you murder the McPhail?"

"No doubt he did!" shouted the laird's son.

There was an interruption at that point. The door opened and the sergeant came in, followed by two soldiers keeping a firm grip on Morag McBain. I was relieved to see Aileen with them. The men would have shown some gentleness, with my wife as witness.

"We have the woman," said the sergeant unnecessarily. "We found her gathering firewood, bold as brass."

Before the young laird could speak, I said quickly, "Aileen, will you take Morag into the other room and find out what she knows about this, if anything?"

My wife led Morag away. I turned to the laird. "It will go better if I handle this matter, sir, with your permission," I said quietly. "If there's hanging to be done, it must be seen that judgment is independent. There has been too much killing in the Highlands recently. Too many summary executions. Edinburgh is beginning to talk; London, too. You take my meaning?"

He nodded.

I asked Iain again, "Did you murder the laird?"

He seemed to have composed himself. He'd relaxed slightly, and the soldiers, sensing this, released his arms. I waited for some word that might help me solve this problem, for I knew Iain could not have done this deed. It was not in him.

He faced me calmly. "For sure I killed him, Hamish. I tell you again, the bastard deserved to die."

"Take him, men!" the young laird burst out. "Hang him!"

"Not yet, sir," I said. There was something wrong here. "Iain," I said, "you will tell me exactly how this came about." The young laird made an explosive noise, compounded of exasperation, sorrow, and despair, and strode from the room.

Iain watched him go, then turned back to me. "I stuck him, Hamish," he said, "with the knife we use for butchering the game. It's simple enough. What more do you want to know?"

"Why did you do it?"

"You know why. He walked into our house as though he . . . Well, anyway, he walked in and told me to get out. Just like that."

"Was Morag there?"

"No!" It was a shout of denial. "She was after gathering the firewood, down in Blaney's wood. I was alone when the laird came in. He asked why we hadn't put our possessions outside for the cart to take down to the quay. I said we weren't going. We had words. Use your imagination, man! He swung his stick at me, and I ducked. The knife was on the table. I picked it up to hold him off. He was off balance and he fell toward me. I held my ground with the knife and he fell to the floor. And that's the truth of it."

"So he fell on the knife. It was an accident."

"Mebbe I could have turned the knife aside. I felt no sorrow."

Why was he so determined to hang himself? "There's no blood on you."

"Mebbe the laird's a little short of blood. Or mebbe I washed it off."

I sighed. "Have you no will to help yourself, Iain? Because that story will not convince the young laird, and there's not a thing I can do to help."

"And mebbe I don't want your help, Hamish Morrison," he said.

We found the young laird leaning against the doorpost, gazing down to the sea where the barque lay at anchor. A tender plied between the quay and the ship, ferrying people and their belongings.

"McBain has confessed," I told him heavily.

Without looking at us, he said, "And the woman?"

"She had nothing to do with it."

"Have the sergeant see to the hanging."

The men took Iain back indoors. I said tentatively, "McBain is a stubborn man, and there's no doubt he had no love for your father, but it seems it might well have been an accident. There is reason for doubt. And it was a wee bit foolhardy, your father going to the house of the McBains alone, knowing how the feelings ran."

His eyes blazed at me. "The McPhail was frightened of no man, and he knew the McBains for ringleaders. It would have been his way to deal with them in person!"

Yes, I could see that. And then the thought occurred to me that in the absence of suitable trees in this part of the world, the soldiers might think to hang Iain from a beam in my own house. I hurried to dissuade them, and found Aileen and Morag in the big room. There were tears in my wife's eyes.

"You can let Iain go, Hamish," she said. "Morag has confessed to the deed. She killed the McPhail. Iain was nowhere near. He was working beyond the burn at the time."

*   *   *

"Morag!" Iain roared his despair.

She wouldn't look at him. "We have no need to lie, Iain."

This was far beyond my ken. I asked Aileen, "How did it happen?"

"Morag returned from gathering wood. The laird arrived soon after, alone."

"Wait a moment, Aileen." I saw the young laird enter and stand against the wall, watching silently. "Perhaps we should hear this from Morag herself."

"Be quiet, Morag!" shouted Iain.

But his wife took up the story. "The laird became angry when he found we'd made no preparations. I told him not to fash himself, because we weren't leaving anyway. He said it was his land and his to say who left and when. He was very angry. He pushed me, and I fell to the floor. He said he would teach me a lesson I wouldn't forget. He took hold of my clothes as I lay there—" She hesitated.

"It seemed he intended to exercise his view of droit de seigneur," said my educated wife helpfully.

"Not my father!" the young laird burst out. "You're lying, woman!"

Morag continued, "He came down toward me. I cast around for something, anything to hold him off. I felt the knife we'd been using to skin a deer. It lay under my hand. I picked it up, and as the laird descended I . . . used it. He fell on me and I rolled him off with some difficulty. He was a heavy man."

I said quickly, "So it was self-defense."

The young laird said suddenly, "Out of here, all of you! Except my factor and his wife. You two I must speak with." His manner had changed. When the room was clear, he seated himself in my favourite chair and regarded us somberly. "Perhaps it would be best," he said quietly, "if you told me exactly what McBain told you, Factor."

I repeated Iain's story as best I could.

"So my father made to attack McBain, did he now? With his stick? And McBain stabbed him when he overbalanced?" There was no expression on his face. "Well, Factor, can you explain how my father's stick came to be outside the door of the McBain cottage when we arrived?"

I said nothing. I can see that stick to this day, tasselled and heavy, leaning against the gray stone wall.

"I'll tell you how," continued the young laird. "Because he placed it there before entering. He never made to attack McBain. There was no accident. McBain lied to cover up a cold-blooded murder!

"And as for the woman, Morag," he snapped, "I have no time for her or her story either. It was my father's misfortune to have been injured a certain way in battle some years ago. There is no longer any place for women in his life. She lied, and in lying attempted to soil my father's reputation. I cannot forgive that."

He sat there, that young man, and there was no triumph on his face; merely disgust. "They are a pair of rouges," he told us, "and they are in it together. I don't know which one struck the blow, and it is of no account. They are both guilty."

Aileen spoke hesitantly. "Excuse me, my lord. If they had both been present at the time of the killing, they would have told the same story. They are not fools. And they were both found some distance from the cottage, in opposite directions. So there is no question of them being interrupted before they had time to discuss their defence."

"What are you trying to say, woman?"

"That one of them is guilty, certainly. But which one?"

"The matter is simple. They will both hang."

Aileen's face went white. "But we know one of the McBains was far from the cottage when the deed was done! Hang them both and you'll hang the innocent with the guilty! There's been enough killing in the Highlands, my lord. Let the McBains go. Let them leave on the barque for the New World. You'll be well rid of them!"

"I will not let the murderer of my father go free. I cannot."

"Then," said Aileen tightly, moving toward him, "I will make sure that the whole of Scotland knows what you have done—and England, too. Iain and I have friends in Edinburgh, and believe me, if you do this thing, I will make sure your name will go down in history as a murderous rogue who hanged his tenants to make room for sheep. For all you know, you've killed the whole village already, sending them off in that cockleshell boat. There's enough disgust at people like you already, and when I've said my piece, you'll find there's no place in society for you anymore. I will make sure you can never hide from your deed so long as you live, McPhail, you bastard!"

Was this Aileen? Was this the same woman who had challenged a similar promise I'd made to Iain McBain, this very morning? I wondered what had come over her, and I feared for her.

Sure enough, the young laird said quite casually, "Mebbe it would solve that problem if I hanged you, too."

"And mebbe it would!" shouted Aileen. "But how much more blood can your conscience take, McPhail?"

All he did was to sigh, watching her thoughtfully.

In silence, the young McPhail and I stood on the rain-swept hillside, watching the people embarking. In happier days the ancient wharf had been used for landing fish, but these were not happy days. A dank gloaming glittered on the Hebridean sea; the moored barque appeared black, almost menacing, rocking sluggishly on the tide. I heard the sound of weeping borne on the onshore wind. A man shouted angrily down there. A host of dark figures clustered on deck; surely too many people for that small vessel? I felt a moment of uncertainty. The captain had assured me the boat was sound, the voyage to the New World a mere formality.

I could see Iain McBain tossing bundled possessions onto the barque's tender. Morag stood at the end of the quay, staring at the empty sea. They would be the last to leave.

The McBains, standing apart. The McBains who had each confessed to knifing the old laird. The McBains, once lovers, separated one from the other by a gulf of suspicion and horror.

"They killed my father," said the young laird somberly.

I said, "One of them killed your father."

"So you say, Morrison."

I glanced at my companion with a sympathy I would not have afforded his father. This was not a bad man, this fair-skinned lad with authority beyond his ability to exercise wisely, and sorrow beyond his ability to conceal well.

"Maybe they've found their own punishment," I said, wishing I would see the McBains touch hands, kiss, *anything,* before the people left their old home to the sheep. It was a strange victory for the brainless animals. As if emphasizing the permanence of this victory, smoke drifted from the smouldering shells of the cottages scattered over the bleak hillside.

On an impulse I said, "There's still time. Bring the people back to their land. Give them back their crofts."

Now he swung round to face me. "*My* land! *My* crofts!"

"*Your* people."

"The devil's murdering people, Morrison, and good riddance to them!"

I found myself plodding slowly down the hillside toward the quay, wet heather dragging at my breeks, leaving the McPhail alone with his anger and sorrow.

"Iain," I called. "Morag. We must talk."

They met me on the wet stones, not looking at each other. "Good-bye, Hamish," said Iain. "And I thank you and your wife for swaying the young laird."

Now the moment had come, I found I was trembling. I didn't know how to say what I had to say. But I could not let these two good people leave this place with their love soured by a suspicion that would remain all their lives.

In the end I said bluntly, "Iain, Morag, it is a terrible thing to think of a person, that they are capable of murder. It can ruin your lives together."

"The McPhail deserved what he got," muttered Iain.

"Mebbe. But he did not get it from you, Iain. Nor you, Morag."

There followed a long silence. Then: "Explain yourself," said Morag.

"I'm saying that neither of you killed the McPhail, but

each of you thinks the other is the murderer. Each of you believes the story the other told the young laird. But you, Iain, told your story to protect Morag, just as she told hers to protect you. You were both far from the cottage when the deed was done. You may be guilty of loving each other too much, but you are innocent of murder. Because I know who did the deed, and it was not you."

For a moment they stared at each other quite blankly. A gust of wind swept cold rain across the quay.

"Is this true, Iain?" asked Morag. "It was not you?"

"I think Hamish has a greater knowledge than us, my love."

"I have that," I said. "I have indeed."

And so—thank the Lord—I saw the suspicion melt away, and the love come back into their eyes. Their hands touched.

"Are you coming aboard or no?" called the boatman.

Morag scrambled into the rocking tender and seated herself. Looking up at me, she asked, "Then who did it, Hamish?"

"Get into the boat, Iain," I said. "The tide does not wait."

"Who did it, Hamish?" asked Morag again as the boat pulled away from the quay. Only when the oarsmen were well into their stroke did I call out quietly.

"It was I. I killed the McPhail."

They took those words with them to the New World, and the Old World never heard them, so I was never held to account for them. I saw Iain lean forward and kiss his wife on the lips, and for them the most important thing was their trust restored. Maybe later they would think to blame me for allowing them to come under suspicion for my own act . . .

Picture it: soldiers, the laird, his son, myself, my wife, the crofters, all scattered over the glens and hillsides; a time of turbulence and sorrow and confusion, and driving rain. People don't notice much in times like that. People are too busy with their own problems.

Picture me visiting the McBains' cottage and finding nobody there, nothing packed. Sitting down and waiting for them, practicing my reproving words. Hearing a step outside, seeing—of all people—the laird entering . . . Words rising to a quarrel, he and me standing face-to-face, then me taking up a knife and driving it into his chest . . .

Not very probable, is it?

No, because it didn't happen.

I know that, and what the McBains think they know doesn't matter, because they are gone.

I climbed back up the hillside, and the young laird and I watched the barque making sail. He said quietly, "Everybody's doing it, all the landowners. It's the way of the future, Morrison. The world is changing fast, and my clansfolk would be left behind if they'd stayed here. At least in the New World they'll have a chance to keep pace."

I said, "It could have been handled better."

"We can't always predict the consequences, man. It's cost me, too." He glanced at me. "Your wife is a good woman, Morrison."

"She is that." And the fear was with me now, gripping my stomach with hot fingers so that I almost groaned.

. . . *Aileen, beside herself with anger when I made my promise to Iain and Morag, seeing me throwing away our comfortable position for the sake of a friendship. Yet Aileen suddenly challenging the young laird and putting that same comfortable position in jeopardy when he spoke of hanging the McBains for the murder of his father.*

Why the transformation? Was it a strong sense of justice?

Or was it because she *knew* the McBains were innocent, and her conscience had got the better of her caution?

I pictured Aileen visiting the McBains' cottage and finding nobody there, nothing packed. Sitting down and waiting for them, practicing her reproving words. Hearing a step outside, seeing—of all people—the laird entering . . .

I had accepted the inevitability of the Clearances because I am that kind of man. Aileen had not. It was wrong, so she would fight it tooth and nail. She might think that with the laird dead, Achnabrae would return to normal. And there was my promise to the McBains, the loss of my job and our house. Did she feel the young laird might be a more compassionate man than the old? I could have told her: A laird is a laird.

Was there a quarrel? Was it self-defence? Was it simply an accident? I'll never know, because I can never talk to Aileen about it. It would be disloyal to let her know I even suspect her, just as it would have been disloyal to call her name out to Iain and Morag as their boat pulled away from the quay.

I was able to lift the cloud from the McBains' love, but I can never lift the cloud from my own. I tell myself I have no proof; only suspicion.

Suspicion is a slow killer of love, but a sure one.

As the barque's sails filled to the breeze, I found myself envying the McBains.

$\mathcal{P}$eter Robinson is best known for his books about Yorkshire detective Alan Banks. He received an Edgar nomination for Wednesday's Child *and* won the Arthur Ellis award for Past Reason Hated. *While he now lives in Canada, he grew up in York-shire and the books show his deep familiarity with the region.*

When I first asked Peter to do a story for Crime Through Time, I expected him to take it as a chance to go back to his academic roots as a scholar of Anglo-Saxon. However, he surprised me with a depiction of a more recent event in English history. "Murder in Utopia" is about a mid-nineteenth century attempt at creating a perfect society for workers. It is based on a number of well-meaning but doomed "model communities" that existed on both sides of the Atlantic during this period.

Peter Robinson's most recent Banks book is In a Dry Season. *He has also published a collection of short stories,* Not Safe After Dark.

MURDER IN UTOPIA

Peter Robinson

I had just finished cauterizing the stump of Ezekiel Metcalfe's left arm, which I had had to amputate after it was shredded in one of the combing machines, when young Billy Ratcliffe came running in to tell me that a man had fallen over the weir.

Believing my medical skills might be required, I left my assistant Benjamin to take care of Ezekiel and tried to keep up with young Billy as he led me down Victoria Road at a breakneck pace. I was not an old man at that time, but I fear I had led a rather sedentary life, and I was panting by the time we passed the allotment gardens in front of the mill. A little more slowly now, we crossed the railway lines and the canal before arriving at the cast-iron bridge that spanned the River Aire.

Several men had gathered on the bridge, and they were looking down into the water, some of them pointing at a dark shape that seemed to bob and twist in the current. As soon as I got my first look at the scene, I knew that none of my skills would be of any use to the poor soul whose coat had snagged on a tree root poking out from the riverbank.

"Did anyone see him fall?" I asked.

They all shook their heads. I picked a couple of stout lads and led them down through the bushes to the riverbank. With a little maneuvering, they were able to lie on their bellies and reach over the shallow edge to grab hold of an arm each. Slowly they raised the dripping body from the water.

When they had completed their task, a gasp arose from the crowd on the bridge. Though his white face was badly marked with cuts and bruises, there could be hardly a person present who didn't recognize Richard Ellerby, one of Sir Titus Salt's chief wool buyers.

Saltaire, where the events of which I am about to speak occurred in the spring of 1873, was then a "model" village, a millworkers' utopia of some four or five thousand souls, built by Sir Titus Salt in the valley of the River Aire between Leeds and Bradford. The village, laid out in a simple grid system, still stands, looking much the same as it did then, across the railway lines a little to the southwest of the colossal, six-storey woollen mill to which it owes its existence.

As there was no crime in Utopia, no police force was required, and we relied on constables from nearby townships in the unlikely event that any real unpleasantness or unrest should arise. There was certainly no reason to suspect foul play in Richard Ellerby's death, but legal procedures must be followed in all cases where the circumstances of death are not immediately apparent.

My name is Dr. William Oulton, and I was employed by the Saltaire Hospital both as a physician and as a scientist conducting research into the link between raw wool and the transmission of anthrax. I also acted as coroner; therefore, I took it as my responsibility to inquire into the facts of Richard Ellerby's death.

In this case, I also had a personal interest, as the deceased was a close acquaintance of mine and I had dined with him and his charming wife, Caroline, on a number of occasions. Richard and I both belonged to the Saltaire Institute—Sir Titus's enlightened alternative to the evils of public houses—and we often attended chamber-music concerts there together, played a game of billiards, or relaxed in the smoking room, where we had on occasion discussed the possible health problems associated with importing wool. I wouldn't say I knew Richard *well*—he was, in many ways, reserved and private in my company—but I knew him to be an honest and industrious man who believed whole-heartedly in Sir Titus's vision.

My postmortem examination the following day indicated only that Richard Ellerby had enough water in his lungs to support a verdict of death by drowning. Let me repeat: *There was no reason whatsoever to suspect foul play.* People had fallen over the weir and died in this way before. Assault and murder were crimes that rarely crossed the minds of the denizens of Utopia. That the back of Richard's skull was fractured, and that his face and body were covered with scratches and bruises, could easily be explained by the tumble he took over the weir. It was May, and the thaw had created a spate of meltwater, which thundered down from its sources high in the Pennines with such force as easily to cause those injuries I witnessed on the body.

Of course, there *could* be another explanation, and that, perhaps, was why I was loath to let matters stand.

If you have imagined from my tone that I was less fully convinced of Saltaire's standing as a latter-day utopia than some of my contemporaries, then you may compliment yourself on your sensitivity to the nuances of the English language. As I look back on those days, though, I wonder if I am not allowing my present opinions to cloud the glass through which I peer at the past. Perhaps a little. I do know that I certainly believed in Sir Titus's absolute commitment to the idea, but I also think that even back then, even after only thirty years on this earth, I had seen far too much of human nature to believe in utopias like Saltaire.

Besides, I had another quality that would not permit me

to let things rest: If I were a cat, believe me, I would be dead by now, nine lives notwithstanding.

It was another fine morning when I left Benjamin in charge of the ward rounds and stepped out of the hospital on a matter that had been occupying my mind for the past two days. The almshouses over the road made a pretty sight, set back behind their broad swath of grass. A few pensioners sat on the benches smoking their pipes under trees bearing pink-and-white blossoms. Men of "good moral character," they benefitted from Sir Titus's largess to the extent of free accommodation and a pension of 7/6 per week, but only as long as they continued to show their "good moral character." Charity, after all, is not for everyone, but only for those who merit it.

Lest you think I was a complete cynic at such an early age, I must admit that I found much to admire about Saltaire. Unlike the cramped, airless, and filthy back-to-back slums of Bradford, where I myself had seen ten or more people sharing a dark, dank cellar that flooded every time it rained, Saltaire was designed as an open and airy environment. The streets were all paved and well drained, avoiding the filthy conditions that breed disease. Each house had its own outdoor lavatory, which was cleared regularly, again averting the possibility of sickness caused by the sharing of such facilities. Sir Titus also insisted on special measures to reduce the output of smoke from the mill so that we didn't live under a pall of suffocating fumes and our pretty sandstone houses were not crusted over with a layer of grime. Still, there is a price to pay for everything, and in Saltaire it was the sense of constantly living out another man's moral vision.

I turned left on Titus Street, passing by the house with the "spy" tower on top. This extra room was almost all windows, like the top of a lighthouse, and I had often spotted a shadowy figure up there. Rumour has it that Sir Titus employed a man with a telescope to survey the village, to look for signs of trouble and report any infringements to him. I thought I saw someone up there as I passed, but it could have been a trick of sunlight on glass.

Several women had hung out their washing to dry across Ada Street, as usual. Though everyone knew that Sir Titus frowned on this practice—indeed, he had generously provided public washhouses in an attempt to discourage it—this was their little way of asserting their independence, of cocking a snook at authority.

As befitted a wool buyer, Richard Ellerby had lived with his wife and two children in one of the grander houses on Albert Road, facing westward, away from the mill toward the open country. According to local practice after bereavement, the upstairs curtains were drawn.

I knocked on the door and waited. Caroline Ellerby opened it herself, wearing her widow's black, and bade me enter. She was a handsome woman, but today her skin was pale and her eyes red-rimmed from weeping. When I was seated in her spacious living room, she asked me if I would care for a small sherry. While Sir Titus would allow no public houses in Saltaire, convinced that they encouraged vice, idleness, and profligacy, he held no objection to people serving alcohol in their own homes. Indeed, he was known to keep a well-stocked wine cellar himself. On this occasion, I declined, citing the earliness of the hour and the volume of work awaiting me back at the hospital.

Caroline Ellerby smoothed her voluminous black skirts and sat on the chesterfield. After I had expressed my sorrow over her loss and she had inclined her head in acceptance, I moved on to the business that had been occupying my thoughts.

"I need to ask you a few questions about Richard's accident," I explained to her. "Only if, that is, you feel up to answering them?"

"Of course," she said, folding her hands on her lap. "Please, go ahead."

"When did you last see your husband?"

"The evening before . . . before he was discovered."

"He was away from the house all night?"

She nodded.

"But surely you must have noticed he was missing?" I

realized I was perhaps on the verge of being offensive, or even well beyond the verge, but the matter puzzled me, and when things puzzle me I worry away at them until they yield a solution. I could no more help myself than a tiger can change its stripes.

"I took a sleeping draught," she said. "I'm afraid I wouldn't have woken up if you'd set me down in the weaving shed."

Given that the weaving shed contained twelve hundred power looms, all thrumming and clattering at once, I rather suspected Caroline of hyperbole, but she got her point across.

"Believe me," she went on, "I have been tormenting myself ever since . . . *If* I hadn't taken the sleeping draught. *If* I had noticed he hadn't come home. *If* I had tried to find him . . ."

"It wouldn't have helped, Caroline," I said. "His death must have been very swift. There was nothing you could have done. There's no use torturing yourself."

"You're very kind, but even so . . ."

"When *did* you notice that Richard hadn't come home?"

"Not until George Walker from the office came to tell me."

I paused before going on, uncertain how to soften my line of inquiry. "Caroline, believe me, I don't mean to pry unnecessarily, or to cause you any distress, but do you have any idea where Richard went that night?"

She seemed puzzled at my question. "Went? Why, he went to the Travellers' Rest, of course, out on the Otley Road."

It was my turn to be surprised. I thought I had known Richard Ellerby, but I didn't know he was a frequenter of public houses; the subject had simply never come up between us. "The Travellers' Rest? Did he go there often?"

"Not *often*, no, but he enjoyed the atmosphere of a good tavern on occasion. According to Richard, the Travellers' Rest was a respectable establishment. I had no reason not to believe him."

"Of course not." I knew of the place, and had certainly heard nothing to blacken its character.

"You seem puzzled, Dr. Oulton."

"Only because your husband never mentioned it to me."

Caroline summoned up a brief smile. "Richard comes from humble origins, as I'm sure you know. He has worked very hard, both in Bradford and here at Saltaire, to achieve the elevated position he has attained. He is a great believer in Mr. Samuel Smiles and his doctrine of self-help. Despite his personal success and advancement, though, he is not a snob. He has never lost touch with his origins. Richard enjoys the company of his fellow workingmen in the cheery atmosphere of a good tavern. That is all."

I nodded. There was nothing unusual in that. I myself ventured to the Shoulder of Mutton, up on the Bingley Road, on occasion. After all, the village was not intended as a prison. It was beginning to dawn on me, though, that Richard probably assumed I was above such things as public houses because I was a member of the professional classes, or that I disapproved of them on health grounds because I was a doctor. I felt a pang of regret that we had never been able to get together over a pipe and a pint of ale. Now that he was dead, we never would.

"Did he ever overindulge?" I went on. "I ask only because I'm searching for a reason for what happened. If Richard had, perhaps, had too much to drink that night and missed his footing . . . ?"

Caroline pursed her lips and frowned, deep in thought for a moment. "I'll not say he's *never* had a few too many," she admitted, "but I *can* say that he was not in the habit of overindulging."

"And there was nothing on his mind, nothing that might tempt him to have more than his share that night?"

"There were many things on Richard's mind, especially as regarded his work, but nothing unusual, nothing that would drive him to drink, of that I can assure you." She paused. "Dr. Oulton, is there anything else? I'm afraid I'm very tired. Even with the sleeping draught . . . the past couple of nights . . . I'm sure you can understand. I've had to send the children to Mother's. I just can't handle them at the moment."

I got to my feet. "Of course. You've been a great help already. Just one small thing?"

She tilted her head. "Yes?"

"Did Richard have any enemies?"

"Enemies? No. Not that I know of. Surely you can't be suggesting someone did this to him?"

"I don't know, Caroline. I just don't know. That's the problem. Please, stay where you are. I'll see myself out."

As I walked back to the hospital, I realized that *was* the problem: I *didn't know*. I also found myself wondering what on earth Richard was doing by the weir if he was coming home from the Travellers' Rest. The canal towpath would certainly be an ideal route to the tavern and back, but the river was north of the canal, and Richard Ellerby's house was south of it.

On my way to the Travellers' Rest that evening, I considered the theory that Richard may have attracted the attention of a villain, or a group of villains, who had subsequently followed him, robbed him, and tossed his body over the weir. The only problem with my theory, as far as I could see, was that he still had several gold sovereigns in his pocket, and no self-respecting thieves would have overlooked a haul that big.

As it turned out, the Travellers' Rest was as respectable a tavern as Richard had told his wife, and as cheery a one as I could have hoped for after my gloomy thoughts. It certainly didn't seem to be a haunt of cutpurses and ruffians. On the contrary, the gaslit public bar was full of warm laughter and conversation, and I recognized several groups of millworkers, many of whom I had treated for one minor ailment or another. Some of them looked up, surprised to see me there, and muttered sheepish hellos. Others were brash and greeted me more loudly, taking my presence as an endorsement of their own indulgence. Jack Liversedge was there, sitting alone in a corner nursing his drink. My heart went out to him; poor Jack had been severely depressed ever since he lost his wife to anthrax two months ago, and there seemed nothing anyone could do to console him. He didn't even look up when I entered.

I made my way to the bar and engaged the landlord's attention. He was a plump man with a veined red nose, rather like a radish, which seemed to me to indicate that he was perhaps a whit too fond of his own product. He nodded a crisp greeting, and I asked for a pint of ale. When I had been served, noticing a slight lull in business, I introduced myself and asked him if he remembered Richard Ellerby's last visit. Once I had described my late colleague, he said that he did.

"Proper gentleman, Mr. Ellerby was, sir. I were right sorry to hear about what happened."

"I was wondering if anything unusual happened that evening."

"Unusual?"

"Did he drink too much?"

"No, sir. Two or three ales. That's his limit."

"So he wasn't drunk when he left here, unsteady in his gait?"

"No, sir. Excuse me a moment." He went to serve another customer, then came back. "No, sir, I can't say as I've ever seen Mr. Ellerby inebriated."

"Were there any rough elements in here that night?"

He shook his head. "Any rough elements I send packing, up to The Feathers on the Leeds Road. That's a proper rough sort of place, that is. But this is a respectable establishment." He leaned forward across the bar. "I'll tell thee summat for nowt: If Mr. Salt won't have public houses in his village, there's no better place for his workers to pass an hour or two than the Travellers' Rest, and that's God's honest truth."

"I'm sure you're right," I said, "but surely things must get a little out of hand on occasion?"

He laughed. "Nothing I can't handle."

"And you're sure nothing strange happened the last night Mr. Ellerby was here?"

"You'd be better off asking him over there about that."

He nodded toward Jack Liversedge, who seemed engaged in a muttered dispute with himself. "I've as much pity as the next man for a fellow who's lost his wife, poor beggar, but the way he's carrying on . . ." He shook his head.

"What happened?"

"They got into a bit of a barney."

"What about?"

He shrugged. "I heard Mr. Liversedge call Mr. Ellerby no better than a murderer, then he finished his drink and walked out."

"How much longer before Mr. Ellerby left?"

"Five minutes, mebbe. Not long."

I mulled this over as he excused himself to serve more customers. Jack Liversedge's wife, Florence, a wool sorter, had died of anthrax two months ago. It is a terrible disease, and one we were only slowly coming to understand. Through my own research, I had been in correspondence with two important scientists working in the field: Monsieur Casimir-Joseph Davaine, in France, and Herr Robert Koch, in Germany. Thus far we had been able to determine that the disease is caused by living microorganisms, most likely hiding in the alpaca wool of the South American llamas and the mohair of the Angora goats, both of which Sir Titus imported to make his fine cloths, but we were a long way from finding a prevention or a cure.

As I sipped my ale and looked at Jack Liversedge, I began to wonder. Richard Ellerby was a wool buyer. Had Jack, in his distraught and confused state, considered him culpable for Florence's death? Certainly, from what I had seen and heard of Jack's erratic behaviour since her death, it was possible, and he was a big, strong fellow.

I was just about to go over to him, without having any clear plan in mind of what to say, when he seemed to come to a pause in his argument with himself, slammed his tankard down, and left, bumping into several people on his way out. I decided to go after him.

I followed Jack down the stone steps to the towpath and called out his name, at which he turned and asked who I was. I introduced myself.

"Ah," he said, " 'Tis thee, Doctor."

The towpath was unlit, but the canal was straight, and the light of a three-quarter moon lay on the still water like a shroud. It was enough to enable us to see our way.

"I saw you in the Travellers' Rest," I said. "You seemed upset. I thought we might share the walk home, if that's all right?"

"As you will."

We walked in silence, all the while growing closer to the mill, which rose ahead in the silvery light, a ghostly block of sandstone against the black, starlit sky. I didn't know how to broach the subject that was on my mind, fearing that if I were right, Jack would put up a fight, and if I were wrong, he would be justly offended. Finally, I decided to muddle along as best I could.

"I hear Richard Ellerby was in the Travellers' the other night, Jack."

"Is that so?"

"Yes. I hear you argued with him."

"Mebbe I did."

"What was it about, Jack? Did you get into a fight with him?"

Jack paused on the path to face me, and for a moment I thought he was going to come at me. I braced myself, but nothing happened. The mill loomed over his shoulder. I could see a number of emotions cross his features in the moonlight, from fear and sorrow to resignation. He seemed somehow *relieved* that I had asked him about Richard.

"He were the wool buyer, weren't he?" he said, with gritted anger in his voice. "He should've known."

I sighed. "Oh, Jack. Nobody could have known. He just buys the wool. There are no tests. There's no way of *knowing*."

"It's not right. He bought the wool that killed her. Someone had to pay."

He turned his back to me and walked on. I followed. We got to the bottom of Victoria Road, and I could hear the weir roaring to our right. Jack walked to the cast-iron bridge, where he stood gazing into the rushing water. I went and stood beside him. "And whose place is it to decide who pays, Jack?" I asked, raising my voice over the water's roar. "Whose job do you think it is to play God? Yours?"

He looked at me with pity and contempt, then shook his head and said, "You don't understand."

I looked down into water, its foam tipped with moonlight. "Did you kill him?" I asked. "Did you kill Richard Ellerby because you blamed him for Florence's death?"

He said nothing for a moment, then gave a brief, jerky nod. "There he were," he said, "standing there in his finest coat, drinking and laughing, while my Florence were rotting in her grave."

"How did it happen?"

"I told him he were no better than a murderer, buying up wool that kills people. I mean, it weren't the first time, were it? He said it weren't his fault, that nobody could've known. Then, when I told him he should take more care, he said I didn't understand, that it were just a hazard of the job, like, and that she should've known she were taking a risk before she took it on."

If Richard really *had* spoken that way to Jack, then he had certainly been guilty of exhibiting a gross insensitivity I had not suspected to be part of his character. Even if that were the case, we are all capable of saying the wrong thing at the wrong time, especially if we are pushed as far as Jack probably pushed Richard. What he had done had certainly not justified his murder.

"*How* did it happen, Jack?" I asked him.

After a short pause he said, "I waited for him on the towpath. All the way home we argued, and in the end I lost my temper. There were a long bit of wood from a packing crate or summat by the bushes. He turned his back on me and started walking away. I picked it up and clouted him and down he went."

"But why the weir?"

"I realized what I'd done." He gave a harsh laugh. "It's funny, you know, especially now it doesn't matter. But back then, when I'd just done it, when I knew I'd *killed* a man, I panicked. I thought if I threw his body over the weir, then people would think he'd fallen. It weren't far, and he weren't a heavy man."

"He wasn't dead, Jack," I said. "He had water in his lungs. That meant he was alive when he went into the water."

"It's no matter," said Jack. "One way or another, it was me who killed him."

The water roared in my ears. Jack turned toward me. I flinched and stepped back again, thrusting my arm out to keep him at a distance.

He shook his head slowly, tears in his eyes, and spoke so softly I had to strain to hear him. "Nay, Doctor, you've nowt to fear from me. It's me who's got summat to fear from you."

I shook my head. I really didn't know what to do, and my heart was still beating fast from the fear he had been going to tip me over the railing.

"Well," he said, "all I ask is that you leave it till morning. One more night in the house me an' Florence shared. Will you do that for me, at least, Doctor?"

As I nodded numbly, he turned and began to walk away.

Early the following morning, after a miserable night spent tossing and turning, grappling with my conscience, I was summoned from the hospital to the works office building, attached to the west side of the mill. I hurried down Victoria Road, wondering what on earth it could be about, and soon found myself ushered into a large, well-appointed office with a thick Turkish carpet, dark wainscoting, and a number of local landscapes hanging on the walls. Sitting behind the huge teak desk was Sir Titus himself, still a grand, imposing figure despite his years and his declining health.

"Dr. Oulton," he said, without looking up from his papers, "please sit down."

I wondered what had brought him the twelve miles or so from Crows Nest, where he lived. He rarely appeared at the mill in those days.

"I understand," he said in his deep, commanding voice,

still not looking at me, "that you have been inquiring into the circumstances surrounding Richard Ellerby's death."

I nodded. "Yes, Sir Titus."

"And what, pray, have you discovered?"

I took a deep breath, then told him everything. As I spoke he got up, clasped his hands behind his back, and paced the room, head hanging so that his grey beard almost reached his waist. Though his cheeks and eyes looked sunken, as if he were ill, his presence dominated the room. When I had finished, he sat down again and treated me to a long silence before he said, "And what are we going to do about it?"

"The police will have to be notified."

"As yet, then, you and I are the only ones who know the full truth?"

"And Jack himself."

"Yes, of course." Sir Titus stroked his beard. I could heard the muffled noise of the mill and feel the vibrations of the power looms shaking the office. It was a warm day, and despite the open window, the room was stuffy. I felt the sweat gather on my brow and upper lip. I gazed out of the window and saw the weir where Richard Ellerby had met his death. "This is not good," Sir Titus said finally. "Not good at all."

"Sir?"

He gestured with his arm to take in the whole of Saltaire. "What I mean, Dr. Oulton, is that this could be very bad for the village. Very bad. Do you have faith in the experiment?"

"The experiment, sir?"

"The moral experiment that is Saltaire."

"I have never doubted your motive in wanting to do good, sir."

Sir Titus managed a thin smile. "A very revealing answer." Another long silence followed. He got up and started pacing again. "If a man visits a public house and becomes so intoxicated that he falls in a river and drowns, then that is an exemplary tale for all of us, wouldn't you say?"

"I would, sir."

"And if a man, after visiting a public house, is followed by a group of ruffians who attack him, rob him, and throw him in a river to drown, then again we have an exemplary—nay, a *cautionary*—tale, do we not?"

"We do, sir. But Richard Ellerby wasn't robbed."

He waved his hand impatiently. "Yes, yes, of course. I know that. I'm merely thinking out loud. Please forgive an old man his indulgence. This place—Saltaire—means the world to me, Dr. Oulton. Can you understand that? The *world*."

"I think I can, sir."

"It's not just a matter of profits, though I'll not deny it's profitable enough. But I think I have created something unique. I call it my 'experiment,' of course, yet for others it is a home, a way of life. At least I hope it is. It was my aim to make Saltaire everything Bradford was not. It was designed to nurture self-improvement, decency, orderly behaviour, and good health among my workers. I wanted to prove that making my own fortune was not incompatible with the material and spiritual well-being of the working classes. I saw it as my duty, my God-given duty. If the Lord looks so favourably upon me, then I take that as an obligation to look favourably upon my workers. Do you follow me?"

"Yes, sir."

"And now this. Murder. Manslaughter. Call it what you will. It disrupts the fabric of things. It could destroy any trust that might have built up in the community. No doubt you remember the troubles we had over anthrax some years ago?"

"I do, sir." In 1868, a man called Sutcliffe Rhodes had garnered much support from the village in his campaign against anthrax, and Sir Titus had been seriously embarrassed by the whole matter. "But surely you can't expect me to ignore what I know, sir?" I said. "To lie."

Sir Titus smiled grimly. "I could never ask a man to go against his beliefs, Doctor. All I ask is that you follow the dictates of your own conscience, but that you please bear in mind the consequences. If this issue surfaces again, especially in this way, then we're done for. Nobody will *believe* in the goodness of Saltaire anymore, and I meant it to be a *good* place, a place where there would never be any reason for murder to occur."

He shook his head in sadness and let the silence stretch again. Above the noise of the mill I suddenly heard men shouting. Someone hammered on the door and dashed into the office without ceremony. I couldn't be certain, but my first impression was that it was the same shadowy figure I had seen in the "spy" tower.

"Sir Titus," the interloper said, after a quick bow, "my apologies for barging in like this, but you must come. There's a man on the mill roof."

Sir Titus and I frowned at one another, then we followed him outside. I walked slowly, in deference to Sir Titus's age, and it took us several minutes to get around to the allotment gardens, from where we had a clear view.

The man stood atop the mill roof, full six storeys up between the two decorative lanterns. I could also make out another figure inside one of the lanterns, perhaps talking to him. But the man on the roof didn't appear to be listening. He stood right at the edge, and even as we watched, he spread out his arms as if to attempt to fly, or dive into a swimming pool, then he sprang off the roof and seemed to hover in the air for a moment before falling with a thud in the forecourt.

It was a curious sensation. Though I knew in my heart and mind that I was witnessing the death of a fellow human being, there was a distant quality about the whole event. The figure was dwarfed by the mill, for a start, and just in front of us, a dog scratched at the dirt, as if digging for its bone, and it didn't cease during the man's entire fall to earth.

A mill hand came running up and told us that the man who had jumped was Jack Liversedge. Again, it was an eerie feeling, but I suppose, in a way, I already knew that.

"An accident and a suicide," muttered Sir Titus, fixing me with his deep-set eyes. "It's bad enough, but we can weather it, wouldn't you say, Doctor?" There was hope in his voice.

My jaw tensed. I was tempted to tell him to go to hell, that his vision, his *experiment,* wasn't worth lying for. But I saw in front of me a sick old man who had at least tried to do *something* for the people who made him rich. Whether it was enough or not was not for me to say. Saltaire wasn't perfect—perfection is a state we will never find on this earth—but it was better than most mill towns.

Swallowing my bile, I gave Sir Titus a curt nod and set off back up Victoria Road to the hospital.

In the days and weeks that followed, I tried to continue with my work—after all, the people of Saltaire still needed a hospital and a doctor—but after Jack Liversedge's pointless death, my heart just didn't seem to be in it anymore. Jack's dramatic suicide lowered the morale of the town for a short while—there were long faces everywhere and some mutterings of dissent—but eventually it was forgotten, and the townspeople threw themselves back into their work: weaving fine cloths of alpaca and mohair for those well-off enough to be able to afford them.

Still, no matter how much I tried to convince myself to put the matter behind me and carry on, I felt there was something missing from the community; something more than a mere man had died the day Jack killed himself.

One day, after I had spent a wearying few hours tending to one of the wool sorters dying of anthrax, I made my decision to leave. A month later, after sorting out my affairs and helping my replacement settle in, I left Saltaire for South Africa, where I eventually met the woman who was to become my wife. We raised our three children, and I practised my profession in Capetown for thirty years. After my retirement, we decided to move back to England, where we settled comfortably in a small Cornish fishing village. Now my children are grown up, married and gone away, my wife is dead, and I am an old man who spends his days wandering the cliffs above the sea, watching the birds soar and dip.

And sometimes the sound of the waves reminds me of the roar of the Saltaire weir.

More than forty years have now passed since that night by the weir, when Jack Liversedge told me he had killed Richard Ellerby; more than forty years have passed since Sir Titus and I stood by the allotments and saw Jack's body fall and break on the forecourt of the mill.

Forty years. Long enough to keep a secret.

Besides, the world has changed so much since then that what happened that day long ago in Saltaire seems of little consequence now. Sir Titus died three years after Jack's fall, and his dream died with him. Fashions changed, and the ladies no longer wanted the bright, radiant fabrics that Sir Titus had produced. His son, Titus Junior, struggled with the business until he, too, died in 1887, and the mill was taken over by a consortium of Bradford businessmen. Today Saltaire is no longer a moral experiment or a mill-workers' Utopia; it is merely another business.

And today, in July 1916, nobody believes in utopias anymore.

*P*eter Lovesey has won or been nominated for almost every award in mystery writing. He has won the Golden Dagger in England and the Macavity in the United States. And he has done so for both novels and stories, modern and Victorian. On top of that, he can juggle—truly a man of many talents.

Peter's Victorian mystery detectives range from the dour compassion of Inspector Cribb to the totally oblivious complacence of Bertie, Prince of Wales. If Bertie is the essence of insulated wealth, the modern policeman, Peter Diamond, is all too aware of the realities of life and death. It seems impossible that both these marvelous characters were created by the same man.

For this collection, Peter has written a tale that he describes as "Grand Guignol." I call it mesmerizing.

DR. DEATH

Peter Lovesey

I am alone in the house with a madman, and I don't know
what to do. My poor husband, Charles, has been murdered, his throat cut after he went to open the door. Please
God, may I be spared!

I am at the mercy of the monster who has butchered no
fewer than twelve people in their own homes since March
of 1873. The newspapers call him Dr. Death. Of course, he
cannot be a doctor. That is a wicked slur against the medical profession. He is a murderer who knocks on doors and
kills at random with a cutthroat razor, attacking whoever
comes to the door. In the streets the children chant a horrid
rhyme:

> *Dr. Death will cure your ills.*
> *He's very quick.*
> *He calls, he kills.*
> *He never gives you stomach pills.*
> *He just turns up*
> *And calls, and kills.*

• • •

Our night of terror began at twenty-five past nine, less than half an hour ago. Charles and I were in the drawing room playing cribbage, as we do most Sunday evenings. Some will disapprove of cards on the Sabbath; I can only say in mitigation that this is the only evening we have together. From Monday to Saturday, Charlie supplements our meagre income by working long hours as a billiard marker at the mateur Athletic Club premises at Lillie Bridge. It is a humble occupation, keeping the score for gentlemen of leisure in the hope that they will be generous with gratuities, but in these difficult times a man is glad of anything that keeps him from the workhouse. We live—thank God—in a nice detached house on Putney Hill. Charles's family has owned the house for generations. We were playing cribbage, then, and eating some nuts I had kept from Christmas, enjoying the modest comfort of a wood fire and a chance to be alone, with just our little Shetland terrier, Snowy, for company. We have no servants.

There was a knock on the door, an urgent *rat-a-tat* that startled us both and caused Snowy to bark. I was in no state to receive a visitor. I had taken a bath earlier in the evening and had not gone to the bother of dressing again. In my nightdress and dressing gown I was relaxing with my dear husband. One feels so secure, so content in one's privacy, at home behind locked doors and thick curtains.

"Who can that be?" Charles said.

I shook my head and spread my hands. It did not cross my mind that Dr. Death was on our doorstep.

One Sunday evening a few weeks ago we talked about him. I asked Charles what he would do if the madman called at our house, and Charles said, "I would protect you, of course."

"But what if I were alone, as I am most evenings?"

"Don't answer the door. It's bolted, and the windows are shuttered. You're safe here."

I believed him.

Tonight we were proved wrong.

He got up and reached for his jacket. "I expect it's William."

His brother William is our mainstay, our Good Samaritan. He gives us money, pays our doctor's bills, and even hands on his old suits to Charlie. He found Charlie the job at Lillie Bridge. Without his help, we would have been on the streets years ago. I call him Sweet William.

Charles said, "You'd better leave the room, just in case it's someone else."

I obeyed willingly. It was possible Charles would feel obliged to admit the caller, and dressed as I was I had no wish to receive anyone. I withdrew at once to the dining room. In there, without a fire, it was chilly, but I could remain out of sight until Charles had dealt with the visitor. I hoped it was just some hawker who could be sent on his way at once. People come quite late hoping to interest us in anything from bootlaces to kittens, or even expecting us to pay them something to remove their caterwauling hurdy-gurdy to another street. I suppose they think we must be comfortably placed, living in a house with a gravel drive. Little do they know the long hours Charles has to work to keep us from penury. He walks two miles to work every day, to save the fares.

Charles withdrew the bolt on the front door and opened it. From the dining room I strained to hear who the caller was. The words were modulated at first, and then they increased in volume; although I could not hear them distinctly, I was sure they were not friendly in tone. In vain my poor husband, who is not the most patient of souls, tried to get rid of the visitor. The exchange of opinions turned to ranting. Still I had no suspicion as to who the caller might be. Then, to my horror, the argument was joined by sounds of a physical struggle. Some piece of furniture in the hall—probably the umbrella stand—was toppled over. Then a picture or a mirror fell and shattered. I cowered in a corner, shaking uncontrollably. How I wish now that I had gone to Charles's assistance; feeble as I am, I might have created some distraction, enabling him to gather his resources. You see, horrible as it was to hear sounds of violence, I had no conception that anything so dreadful as murder was being done.

Neither did it cross my mind that we were being invaded by Dr. Death. Why should he choose our house, of all the homes in London? I know the answer now, of course. He didn't choose it at all. He calls and kills indiscriminately, men and women, taking perverted pleasure in the power he feels when he produces his razor and sees the uncomprehending terror in their eyes. He'll knock at anyone's door. It must give him a sense of power, not knowing who will be next to feel the blade across their throats. That is why the police are having such difficulty catching him. He is unpredictable.

I *should* have been alert to the danger. Like everyone else, I have read about the killings in the newspaper and tut-tutted and shaken my head, but I never seriously thought we would be his next victims.

There was a bloodcurdling scream that stopped abruptly, followed by silence. I shall hear it forever if I live through this experience, the scream and the silence. It must have been the moment my beloved Charlie's throat was cut. Then the thump of his body hitting the floor, followed by the beastlike panting of his killer.

Petrified, I pressed my fists against my teeth, trying to understand what had just happened. There could be no doubt that terrible violence had been done. I wanted to shriek in terror, but the slightest sound would have revealed me as a witness, and put me in danger.

I waited, trying desperately not to swoon and praying that this evil presence would leave the house. Presently I heard a door being opened. Then, faintly, the sound of running water. He had gone to the kitchen to wash away the worst of the blood, as I now realise.

It was my opportunity. Without regard to the risk, I left the dining room and went to assist my poor husband. Broken glass crunched under my carpet slippers. My heart sank fathoms when I saw the scene, the lifeless form lying across the hall with a dark pool spreading beneath his head, and blood all over the wall, running down in streaks. The smell of it was sickening. It must have gushed from an artery. No one could survive such a massive loss.

Now I knew for certain that Dr. Death had called, and killed. Numb, petrified, ready to faint, I could not bring myself to touch my poor husband. I just stood staring at the back of his head.

Then I heard the tap turned off in the kitchen and steps across the tiled floor. What was I to do? Charlie was beyond help. The madman would kill me next. I had seen in the papers that he has twice before slit the throats of a man and his wife together.

I ran up the stairs. It was a stupid action, I admit, for where could I go if he pursued me? I went to our bedroom and looked for a place to hide, and in my distracted state I could think of nothing more original than the wardrobe, a huge mahogany thing we inherited with the house. Charlie's late father was quite well-to-do; he was deeply disappointed when Charlie failed his exam for the Civil Service and had to seek unsalaried work. We are not all good at passing exams. I was so grateful that he left us the house in his will. It is the one secure thing in our existence. The family money, the stocks and shares and so on, were left to William, who is a chartered accountant and understands the world of finance, and helps us to survive. We have practically no money, but we have a roof over our heads. It was a wise decision.

Here I squat, at the bottom of the wardrobe, trying to hide under the spare blanket. I have been here ten minutes at least, weeping silently, trying to tell myself not to give way to my troubled thoughts. I must stay in control.

If Dr. Death comes looking for me, I am going to die. I pray that he will leave the house. Surely his desire for blood is sated. Yet I know he is still here. Occasional sounds come from downstairs. I suppose he is looking for money or valuables. He won't find any.

Suddenly there is a sound nearby, here, in the bedroom. My flesh prickles. I want to scream.

It is not a heavy sound, but it is close, extremely close. The wardrobe door rattles. There is a scratching sound outside, followed by whimpering.

Snowy.

My little dog has found me. If I don't do something about him, he'll give me away, for sure. He will start barking any second.

I open the wardrobe door and get a terrible shock. Snowy has a gash across his middle, from the top of his back to right under his stomach. It seems unspeakably cruel. Then I look closer and see that what I am looking at is not a wound, but a streak of my poor husband's blood. Snowy climbs up and nudges against me, seeking comfort, and some of it marks my nightdress. He continues to whimper. The sound will surely bring the killer upstairs.

I must think of something. I can't stay here, now that Snowy has found me, and I can't silence him. If the madman comes anywhere near, Snowy will bark. He barks at the slightest thing. Oh, God, am I starting to panic?

I dare not go downstairs again.

Above me, there is the attic, but I can't get up there without the stepladder, and that is kept in the cupboard under the stairs. If there was a balcony to this bedroom, I would step outside, but there is not.

I have just remembered the fire escape. It is at the back of the house. You get to it from the little bedroom, the one we use as a box room. If I can open the window, I can climb down the ladder to the ground and run for help. That is what I must do.

With as much stealth as I am capable of, I emerge from my hiding place and cross the bedroom to the landing. Snowy follows me. Mercifully he is silent.

Then—oh, God!—I hear footsteps on the stairs. Dr. Death has heard me and is coming.

Abandoning caution, I rush across the landing to the box room and fling open the door. Our box room is, of course, crammed with portmanteaux and trunks filled with bric-a-brac, summer curtains, old clothing, rolls of carpet, discarded ornaments, cracked mirrors, a dressmaker's dummy. There is scarcely room for a person to move in there, and I must get to the window.

I slam the door after me, hoping to hamper my pursuer. Finding strength I did not know I possessed, I slide an enormous cabin trunk across the doorway and heap things on it, at the same time clearing a route to the window. Snowy is beside me, barking furiously now. I don't know what I shall do with him. He will have to be left here and take his chances. In my frenzy I knock over a tower of hatboxes, and they crash against some brass stair rods with a clatter that sounds all over the house. I *must* get to the window.

I have to climb over an old armchair heaped with magazines to reach it. My foot slides on the paper, and I fall against an iron bedstead. Pain shoots through my arm and shoulder. I try again.

Now Dr. Death is at the door, rattling it. Brave little Snowy barks and growls. I don't look 'round. I am at the window trying to get my fingers under the brass handles. The sash cord is broken, I think. I have to force it upward by brute strength, if I have any left. It is very stiff, but it moves a few inches, and I wedge a book into the gap and try again.

I can hear the madman straining outside the door. He has it open a fraction and is crashing his shoulder against it.

I succeed in heaving the window upward and putting my leg over the sill. It is pitch-black out there. I tug my nightdress to the top of my legs, all decorum abandoned, and get a foot onto one of the top rungs of the fire-escape ladder. Squeezing myself under the window, I climb fully out. The window slams down, just missing my hand. The last thing I hear is my little dog still inside the room. He has stopped barking and is whimpering.

On the ladder I feel the chill of the night air. I am so hot from my exertions that I welcome it. Down the iron rungs I hurry, feeling chips of rust flaking off under my already sore hands. My feet hurt terribly. Slippers were never meant for this sort of activity. I don't know how far down I am when the window above me is thrust open. I suppose he is looking down, deciding whether to come after me. All I can do is keep descending until I feel the ground under my feet.

At last I am down and running around the side of the

house to the front, where it is better lit. I shall stop the first person I see. I run across the drive, sobbing now. I can't stop myself from crying.

On Putney Hill the gas lamps show me an empty street. Nobody is about. What can I do except run to my neighbours? I cross the road to the Tylers' house. We don't know them well, but they have two grown-up sons. Surely one can be sent to summon the police.

Their manservant opens the door.

"Help me!" I say. "My husband is murdered, and the man is still inside the house." I point toward where we live.

He asks me to wait, but I follow him inside.

Mr. and Mrs. Tyler are magnificent. They grasp the urgency of the matter at once, and the men go out to deal with the emergency. One son will go for the police, just a short way down Putney Hill. The others will keep watch. Mrs. Tyler wraps me in a blanket and brings me brandy. I have given way to weeping hysteria again, but by degrees I lapse into a shocked silence.

I can't say how much time passes before the front door opens. I jump at the sound, but it is only Mr. Tyler, with a policeman. Mr. Tyler has Snowy tucked under his arm.

"It's all over, my dear," he says, releasing my little dog, who runs to me and licks my ankle. "This is Inspector Reed."

"You caught the man?"

"Yes," says the policeman. "He's in custody now. We forced an entry into the house and took him. You must be in a state of shock, ma'am, but I need to speak to you."

I take Snowy into my arms. "It's all right. I feel much better."

"Did you see the man who came to the house?"

"See him? No. Charles, my husband, went to the door. It was savage, what happened. He was murdered almost at once."

"We saw for ourselves, ma'am."

"I heard everything. I was in the next room."

"Heard what was said?"

"No, that was indistinct. Raised voices, and the sound of violence."

There is a pause, as if they hesitate to tell me some new horror.

"Your husband had a brother William. Is that correct?"

I frown and hug Snowy to my chest. "What does William have to do with it?"

"He's older than your husband?"

"Yes. He's twenty-eight, I think."

"Comes to visit you, does he?"

"Yes, he takes a brotherly interest in our lives. He's a lovely man, generous and caring." I don't mention that William sometimes helps us with money. That's private, and the Tylers don't have to hear of it.

"It was William who came to your house this evening."

I am astounded. "What? William? I don't understand."

"He came out of a sense of responsibility, ma'am. We've spoken to his wife, and she told us they were deeply troubled by your husband's conduct."

"This can't be true!" I say.

"Will you hear me out, ma'am? People at Lillie Bridge, where your husband is known—he works there sometimes, I believe—saw him last week using the bathing facilities, washing blood from his hands and arms on the day the man was murdered in Chelsea."

"No!"

"They reasoned that a billiard marker doesn't get bloody hands. They suspected him of the crimes we've heard so much about. It was only suspicion, so they didn't come to us as they should have done. They went to your brother-in-law."

"To William?"

"William came to your house tonight to seek an explanation and was savagely attacked. Your husband must have had his cutthroat razor at the ready, in his jacket pocket. He murdered William."

"No!" I cry out. "You're mistaken. It's Charlie who is dead."

"Did you look at the face of the dead man?"

I am speechless. I *didn't* look at his face. I couldn't bear to see the cruel gash across his throat. How could I mistake my own husband for his brother? My brain is racing now. They have similar-coloured hair. William is slightly taller, but their physiques are similar. And Charlie wears William's handed-down suits. Black pinstripes always, as you would expect a professional man to wear.

The policeman says, "Your husband is alive. He's the man we have in custody, ma'am."

Mr. Tyler says, "It's true."

I scream, a long, piercing scream, a scream of horror, and despair, and mental agony.

Mrs. Tyler tries to comfort me. I push her away. I stare at them all, shaking my head, sobbing convulsively.

Over my sounds of grief, the policeman adds. "We believe him to be responsible for the deaths of thirteen people. You're going to ask me why he did it, and I can only say that he's obviously insane."

"He's not," I plead. "He's a perfect husband to me."

"He has a double life, then," the policeman insists.

Now Mr. Tyler tries to make me understand. "My dear, such cases are not unknown to those who study the criminal mind. They are perfectly reasonable ninety-nine percent of the time. Then something happens in the brain. An uncontrollable anger makes them attack innocent people for quite trivial reasons. It seems that tonight your husband's brother came to face him with the truth, a brave but misguided action. There was a struggle, and William was killed with a vicious slash across the throat, just like the other victims."

The policeman says, "He would have killed you, too."

"Never. Not Charlie."

Will I ever believe it? I stare at the policeman, hating him for what he is saying, and knowing, deep inside, that he is right.

Mr. Tyler says, "It's going to be hard for you to accept. However intimate we are with another human being, we never know them fully."

Wise, intolerable words. I have the rest of my devastated life to reflect on them.

Canadian writer Eileen Kernaghan has lived for most of her life on the West Coast. Though she's a devoted reader of mystery novels, most of her work has been in the field of historical fantasy. Her novels Songs from the Drowned Lands, the second of a trilogy set in prehistoric England, won the Canadian Science Fiction and Fantasy Award. From time to time she also writes horror Fiction— hence her curiosity about the occult.

Victorian traveler and author Alexandra David-Neel's real-life adventures provided source material for Eileen's young-adult fantasy, Dance of the Snow Dragon, based on Tibetan Buddhist myth. The young Alexandra was a student in London during the final flowering of Madame Blavatsky's Lansdowne Road salon. Though no record exists of this particular encounter, the two almost certainly met.

DINNER WITH
H. P. B.

Eileen Kernaghan

Madame Helena Blavatsky's London establishment at
17 Landsdowne Road in Notting Hill proved to be
a pleasant villa overlooking Holland Park, with private gardens behind.

Alexandra took her printed invitation out of her skirt
pocket and glanced nervously at the inscription.

*Madame Blavatsky: At Home, Saturday 4:00 to 10:00
o'clock.*

"This Madame Blavatsky," said Alexandra, lingering on
the bottom step, "they say she is *très formidable.*"

"Indeed she is," said Elisabeth Morgan, "but, my dear,
you must not let her intimidate you. You, too, can be *très
formidable.*" So saying, she lifted the knocker.

The door was opened by a slim, attractive woman in her
fifties. Her dinner gown of lace and moiré silk was lavishly
beaded and flounced, her ash-blond hair modishly coiffed.

"Mrs. Morgan, do come in. How pleasant to see you
again!"

"My dear countess," said Elisabeth Morgan as they

stepped into the entrance hall. "May I present my young friend and protégé, Mademoiselle Alexandra David. Alexandra, this is the Countess Constance Wachmeister, who looks after this household, and Madame Blavatsky, with quite miraculous efficiency."

"H. P. B. is in her office," said the countess in a charmingly accented voice. Her elaborate, beruffled gown seemed a little at odds with her capable, take-charge manner. "Come, I will take you downstairs. She has especially asked to meet you, mademoiselle."

"Courage, my dear," said Mrs. Morgan *sotto voce* as the countess led Alexandra away.

This evening the doyenne of the London Theosophical Society had chosen to hold court in her private ground-floor rooms. Alexandra, approaching tentatively, found her seated at a large and extraordinarily cluttered desk. Behind her, a bay window with half-drawn curtains looked out into the shadowy park. Every shelf and table in this inner sanctum was heaped with reference books, and more volumes were stacked haphazardly on the floor. As well, Madame Blavatsky had surrounded herself with souvenirs of the years she had spent in the East: a golden Buddha, Benares bronzes, Palghat mats, wall plaques from Kashmir. The close air of the room held a lingering odour of hashish—a scent that Alexandra had lately learned to recognize. On one wall, looking curiously out of place, was a Swiss cuckoo clock.

Still more out of place in that fashionably exotic room was Madame Blavatsky herself: a huge, shapeless bulk draped in a baggy black gown girdled with black rope, the hem riding up to reveal grotesquely swollen ankles and feet. Her bush of crinkly grey hair was pulled back into an untidy knot; her massive double-chinned face was deeply pitted and yellow-tinged. Yet what caught and held Alexandra's gaze were the luminous azure eyes that looked out of that ruined face with a shrewd intelligence and an almost hypnotic force of personality.

"Here is the young lady from Belgium," said the countess, and abandoning Alexandra to Madame Blavatsky's mercies, she flounced briskly up the stairs.

"Where exactly in Belgium?" Nicotine-stained fingers tapped a cigarette into an overflowing ashtray. Clearly the redoubtable H. P. B. had no time for social niceties.

"From Brussels, madame." Alexandra loathed Brussels. How depressing, she thought, to be introduced as a resident of that grey bourgeois city. She added, "But I was born in Paris, and lived there until I was five."

"Paris," said Madame Blavatsky, with faint distaste. "I understand they are ruining the view with some sort of enormous metal excrescence."

"Monsieur Eiffel's tower," said Alexandra, smiling. "Indeed," she added, in her correct but hesitant English, "it is the centre of much controversy. There are those who call it the 'junkman's Notre Dame.'"

"Exactly so," said Madame Blavatsky. "And you, Mademoiselle David. Mrs. Morgan tells me you are a student of the occult."

Alexandra recoiled a little under the intensity of that bright blue gaze, but Madame Blavatsky's expression was unexpectedly benign.

"It interests me a great deal, that is true."

"And you plan to make it your career?"

"Au contraire," said Alexandra. "I have trained for a career in music—but now I believe I would like to study medicine, perhaps to become a medical missionary."

She thought it best not to mention a more immediate aim: to escape from her parents' cold and stultifying Brussels home.

"A doctor—now there is a worthy undertaking!"

"It's difficult, of course, for a woman . . ."

"Flapdoodle!" said H. P. B. fiercely. "These days a woman can do anything she wishes. I myself am a living example of that. Did you know that I fought with Garibaldi's army at the Battle of Mentana, was wounded five times, and was left for dead in a ditch?"

"I am amazed," murmured Alexandra, who had heard this improbable tale from Elisabeth Morgan.

"Furthermore, I have a dear friend, Anna Kingsford, who is an eminent doctor. You may meet her tonight."

Alexandra felt herself warming to this immense, untidy, blunt-spoken woman. How different was Madame Blavatsky's reaction from that of Alexandra's mother, who had said discouragingly, "You want to be a doctor? But men themselves don't know anything. Just think . . . a woman!"

"When you have finished your medical studies," said H. P. B., "you must come and see me again. By then my good Dr. Mennell will have retired, and perhaps I will take you on as my personal physician. That is, if these rotting kidneys have not already finished me off."

"I had thought," said Alexandra politely, "that I might use my skills in the Orient. Even perhaps Tibet."

"Ah, yes, Tibet," said Madame Blavatsky, with sudden animation. "I myself have travelled extensively in the Forbidden Kingdom."

Alexandra said nothing. She was trying to imagine those elephantine lower limbs transporting their owner over the Himalayas.

"But there is the dinner bell," said H. P. B. "We must see what guests have come to amuse us tonight. Let me have your arm. These stairs are an abomination." Leaning heavily on Alexandra's shoulder, she began her laborious ascent.

Folding doors opened from the airy drawing room into the dining room, where gas chandeliers cast a warm glow over a table set for twenty. A dozen or so guests in evening dress were just preparing to sit down.

Alexandra observed among the female guests a certain individualism of style that verged on the eccentric: stayless, high-waisted Directoire gowns à la Sarah Bernhardt; loose, diaphanous tea gowns; and draped Grecian costumes lavishly embroidered with gold thread. As befitted a young woman of intellectual aspirations and anarchist leanings, Alexandra had dressed in a plain serge skirt, high-collared white blouse, and sensible boots. Now she felt like a pigeon who had strayed into a flock of macaws.

How many unexpected paths had opened up to her since

she had stumbled, at fifteen, across the journal of the Society of the Supreme Gnosis. At first, as she worked her way in English through the twists and tangles of occult theory—made still more confusing by random bits of Sanskrit—she had thought, These people are crazy! But when Elisabeth Morgan wrote and offered her cheap accommodations at the home of the Supreme Gnosis while she studied in London, Alexandra seized the opportunity. After all, Alexandra herself had a reputation as an eccentric—an odd bookish child who at twelve read St. Augustine and Proudhon, a reluctant debutante who at seventeen, to the despair of her parents, hiked alone across the Alps to Italy, carrying an umbrella and the *Maxims* of Epictetus.

The Gnostics had a large library, fragrant and dim from incense smoke and Turkish cigarettes, and stocked with books on alchemy, metaphysics, and astrology. Her lodgings there were cheap, safe, and convenient to the British Museum. They suited Alexandra very well. And when Mrs. Morgan brought her an invitation to dine at 17 Lansdowne Road, the very epicentre of London occultism, Alexandra was quick to accept.

Madame Blavatsky settled herself at the head of the table, ashtray at hand, and immediately launched into a spirited lecture. "The whole universe is filled with spirits," she declaimed loudly. "It is nonsense to suppose that we are the only intelligent beings in the world. I believe there is latent spirit in all matter."

Mrs. Morgan, who was listening intently, turned to Alexandra with an encouraging smile. Alexandra found an empty place and sat down. A moment later she heard the silvery chime of an invisible bell, and a long-stemmed red rose plummeted onto the table next to her wineglass. Startled, she stared up at the ceiling.

"Aha," said the lean, bespectacled gentleman on Alexandra's left hand. He sounded amused. "H. P. B. is up to her parlour tricks again. Doesn't she know we're all thoroughly bored by them?"

Alexandra pushed the rose nervously to one side, just in time to see a plain white envelope fall with a small thud onto her plate. She thrust her chair back from the table in alarm. Madame Blavatsky, who had ignored the mysterious chimes and the apparently heaven-sent rose, looked straight down the table at Alexandra and smiled expansively.

"Look," she said, in her hoarse smoker's voice. "The Mahatma has sent our young guest a letter. You must open it and read it to us, mademoiselle."

Inside the envelope was a sheet of a shell-pink writing paper with a message in heavy black script: *To Mlle. David. Master Koot Hoomi Singh sends a warm welcome to the young visitor from abroad.* Where the signature should have been were some rather badly formed Tibetan symbols.

"What," said Alexandra to her neighbour, "in the name of heaven is going on?"

"You should feel honoured, mademoiselle. You hold in your hand one of the famous—or should I say infamous?— Mahatma letters. According to H. P. B., they are written somewhere in the Himalayas by a mysterious holy man, an initiate of the Brotherhood of the Snowy Range. And delivered, as you observe, by means of the astral post office."

"What utter nonsense," Alexandra burst out.

"Quite so," said her neighbour. "But you would be astounded, mademoiselle, at how many otherwise sensible people have been duped into believing this Mahatma is real."

Alexandra looked more closely at the writing. The black letters were hastily scrawled, and there was a large inkblot in one corner.

"But how is the trick done? Do you suppose this could be an instance of telekinesis?"

"Ah, I see you are familiar with the term."

"Indeed, we are not entirely cut off from such research on the continent. I have read with great interest the works of Dr. Charles Richet on metapsychics. He cites some fascinating instances of table-tilting, levitation of furniture, music from invisible instruments . . . If tables and chairs can drift in midair or walk about the room, is a floating letter so astonishing?"

Her neighbour smiled uncertainly. Clearly, he was struggling to decide whether or not Alexandra spoke in jest.

"I am a man of science, mademoiselle. If I am to accept these 'miracles' that Madame Blavatsky is thought to perform, they must be subject to scientific proof. I have seen no such evidence."

"And what branch of science do you study, monsieur?"

"I am a zoologist—forgive me, mademoiselle, I have not introduced myself, my name is Charles Barker. I lecture in zoology at Cambridge."

"Then, Dr. Barker," said Alexandra, "you will be familiar with the other works of Dr. Charles Richet."

"I have read his monographs."

"I, too," said Alexandra, "and attended his lectures. In fact," she said, "it was through reading his papers on experimental pathology and serotherapeutic injections that I first stumbled upon his spiritualist writings."

"Heavy reading indeed," remarked Barker, "for one so young."

Alexandra's smile was distant. How she hated being patronized! She remembered that her father had once said, when her mother was wringing her hands over Alexandra's eccentricities, "Alexandra has never been young."

A heavyset, rubicund man across the table from Barker set down his glass. "I also have read the work of Dr. Richet. The controlled psychical experiments of a respected physiologist, the editor of the *Revue Scientifique,* are naturally of the greatest interest."

"So you will concede," said Alexandra, "that science and spiritualism are not necessarily in conflict, if a scientist of Dr. Richet's stature can believe in both."

"My mind is entirely open on the subject," said the florid gentleman. "Like Dr. Barker, all I ask is evidence that will stand up to scientific examination."

"Allow me to introduce Dr. Wilfred Forbes-Grant," said Barker. "He is a colleague of mine at Cambridge."

"And are you a member of the Theosophical Society, Dr. Forbes-Grant?"

"Most definitely not," said Forbes-Grant, ladling out a generous serving of mulligatawny soup. "Dr. Barker and I are members of the Society for Psychical Research."

"Or the Spookical Research Society, as H. P. B. would have it," said Barker with a smile.

"And what is this society?" Alexandra sipped her soup. It was excellent.

"We are a group of like-minded scientists and scholars, dedicated to investigating paranormal phenomena."

"Par exemple . . . ?"

"In the main, four areas: astral appearances, transportation of physical substances by occult means, precipitation of letters, and occult sounds and voices. All of which," he added, "Madame Blavatsky lays claim to. And so we are part of a committee formed to look specifically into Madame Blavatsky's psychic abilities."

"And what has your research shown?"

"So far, we have reached no firm conclusions. However"—he dropped his voice and leaned in confidentially—"we are very much inclined to think she is a fraud."

"On what grounds?"

"My dear young lady, one scarcely knows where to begin. Her entire history is a series of exaggerations and falsehoods and outrageous behaviour. Take, for example, these letters she insists are written by her 'Tibetan Masters'— blatant forgeries, according to the report prepared for our society by Mr. Richard Hodgson, who travelled to India to interview Madame Blavatsky and investigate her claims. In fact, he suspects she may be a Russian spy. Certainly she has been shown to be a plagiarist. It seems that in this much-touted book of hers, *Isis Unveiled,* there are some two thousand passages copied verbatim from other people's books without credit. In his conclusion, he describes her as one of the most accomplished, ingenious, and interesting impostors in history."

People continued to arrive without ceremony in the middle of the soup course. They would find an empty chair, chat for a while, and then leave without waiting for the pudding. There was, as well, a good deal of changing places around the table. Alexandra, who at one moment was deep in conversation with a pale, intense young poet called Willie Yeats, at the next moment found herself talking to Lady Wilde, the mother of Oscar, who seemed convinced she was at a séance. It was all, she thought, very much like Mr. Dodgson's Mad Hatter's tea party.

Nonetheless, she was encouraged by the lavish display of enticing dishes. The Gnostics set a sparse table and had a gaunt, attenuated look about them. Their president, someone had told Alexandra, lived on a handful of almonds a day, and an occasional orange.

"Do try this lentil stew," said Dr. Forbes-Grant, helping himself from the tureen. "And these, I believe, are H. P. B.'s famous curried mussels." He took a modest portion, hesitated, then added another spoonful. "Though, of course, this vegetarianism is simply another fraud. The woman was raised on sausage and smoked goose, and until recently insisted that large amounts of meat were essential to her health."

"Are you fond of shellfish?" asked Alexandra. Madame Blavatsky's misdemeanours had made Dr. Forbes-Grant quite agitated and red in the face. Fearing apoplexy in a gentleman of his age and girth, she thought it wise to change the subject.

"As a matter of fact, I've always avoided it, on my physician's advice, as I've inherited an unfortunate tendency to gout. But I sampled this special Indian recipe of Madame Blavatsky's a few Saturdays ago, and I declare, it was well worth the risk."

Alexandra, who had a delicate stomach, tried a cautious forkful of the mussels, and declared them delicious.

She sat contentedly sipping her wine, and chatting with a bearded student of Oriental languages. Meanwhile, at the far end of the table, H. P. B.'s voice gained steadily in volume as she warmed to her subject. "It is recorded of some patients suffering from nervous diseases that they have been raised from their beds by some undiscoverable power, and it has been impossible to force them down. Thus we see that there is no such thing as the law of gravitation, as it is generally understood . . ."

Suddenly, from across the table, came painful sounds of

wheezing. Alexandra turned, alarmed, to Dr. Forbes-Grant. He was deeply flushed and seemed to be having trouble getting his breath.

"Oh, monsieur," she cried out, "shall I thump you on the back? Have you a bone stuck in your throat?"

Dr. Forbes-Grant shook his head in silent anguish. His eyes bulged. "Something . . . disagreed . . ." he managed to gasp out. Clutching his throat with both hands, he fought desperately for air.

"Give him room," said Countess Wachmeister, motioning back the other diners, who had half risen from their seats.

"Loosen his collar," she told Alexandra, who hastened to obey.

Forbes-Grant drew an agonized, rattling breath and slipped sideways in his chair. As he fell, one hand struck his empty wineglass and knocked it into Alexandra's lap.

"Help me," said the countess. "We must get him to a sofa. And send for Dr. Mennell."

Charles Barker and the young poet Willie Yeats sprang to her assistance. Between them they carried Forbes-Grant to a chaise-longue. Suddenly he went into convulsions, his whole body jerking and writhing, limbs flailing. White froth speckled his lips.

Charles Barker looked up in horror from his colleague's body. "Too late for the doctor," he said in a hushed, shocked voice. "You must send for the police."

"A murderer has just passed below our windows," remarked Madame Blavatsky obscurely. They all stared at her.

"An inspector from Scotland Yard?" Alexandra turned in surprise to the poet George Russell, with whom she was sharing a sofa. "Is this usual in such cases?"

"I confess I am scarcely familiar with what is usual in such cases," said Russell, with a trace of irony. "It is not as though they are an everyday occurrence in Dublin literary circles. But I believe discretion is the watchword here. Madame Blavatsky is very much a public figure—moreover the focus of a great deal of scandal. And some of her guests, as you can see, are influential." As he said this he nodded in Lady Margot Asquith's direction. She was sitting by the window, elegant in crepe de chine and velvet, looking as though she very much wished to be somewhere else. "If the newspapers get so much as a whiff of this, our little dinner party will push the Whitechapel affair onto the second page."

"All except for the *Telegraph*," said Willie Yeats's dinner partner, a Valkyrian beauty called Maude Gonne. There was amusement in her rich Irish tones. "We can depend on Oscar's brother Willie to see that the *Telegraph* is discreet."

Inspector Murdoch was a slim, softspoken man of middle years. His accent was educated, his manners unobtrusive. A good choice, decided Alexandra. He looked to be the very soul of discretion.

He addressed his first question to Alexandra: "You were seated across the table from him, mademoiselle?"

Alexandra nodded.

"Can you tell me what you observed just before he collapsed—what his symptoms appeared to be?"

"At first I thought he had choked on his food or was having an asthma attack. But I believe he was also trying to complain of nausea. His face was flushed and somewhat mottled, as though he were running a fever. Almost at once he began to have extreme difficulty in breathing. This was followed by convulsions and collapse."

"Indeed, mademoiselle," said the inspector. "You are to be commended on your powers of observation."

Madame Blavatsky, an impassive presence at the head of the table, spoke for the first time. "More flapdoodle," she said emphatically. "It's perfectly clear what happened. A man of his age and girth—obviously his heart gave out."

"I'm sorry to contradict you, madame," said Murdoch, "but the symptoms this young lady has described do not sound like heart failure or apoplexy. We shall know more when we have the medical examiner's report. In the meantime, we cannot rule out the possibility of foul play."

"Are you saying there will be a police investigation? An

inquest?" The speaker was a sharp-faced man of soldierly bearing, with a clipped beard and long, curving moustache. At dinner he had been sitting at H. P. B.'s left hand.

"It's possible. It will depend on the medical report."

"I must protest," said the man with the moustache, "in the strongest possible terms. As Madame Blavatsky has just told you, Dr. Forbes-Grant, while apparently vigorous, was by no means a young man; his death, while unfortunate, is quite obviously the result of natural causes. To suggest otherwise, at a public inquiry, would cause irreparable damage to Madame Blavatsky's reputation, and the reputation of the Theosophical Society."

"Who is that?" whispered Alexandra to her seat mate.

"That is H. P. B.'s private secretary, George Mead," replied Russell. "A classics scholar who has taken up Hindu philosophy—and a bit of a poseur, I gather. Willie Yeats can't abide him—says he has the intellect of a good-size whelk."

Charles Barker had risen from his chair. With barely repressed fury, he said, "Certainly there will have to be an inquest. There is every possible reason to suspect foul play."

Inspector Murdoch turned to him with an expression of polite interest. "Indeed, sir? How can you be so sure?"

"How can there be any doubt? Madame Blavatsky has the motive—who had better reason to revenge herself against the researchers who have revealed her as a charlatan? Who even now are collecting evidence of still worse misdeeds? She has the capability—a woman of dubious morals and outrageous reputation, who smokes and uses foul language, who has lied about every aspect of her history, who even in her own country was the subject of police investigations . . . And most importantly"—here he paused for dramatic effect, and pointed to the door of Madame B's bedroom—"she has the means. On her bedside table is an empty bottle that contained strychnia."

"The man is a complete idiot," said H. P. B. "He's talking about my kidney medicine. You can ask Dr. Mennell, who prescribed it. Constance, fetch this fellow my prescription."

With a look of sad perplexity, the countess rose to obey.

"Nonetheless," persisted Barker, "it is clearly labelled strychnine, and the bottle is empty."

"But," Alexandra pointed out, "we all served ourselves from the same dishes. Dr. Forbes-Grant ate nothing that I did not eat myself."

"It would be a simple matter," said Barker, "for her to slip the strychnine into Dr. Forbes-Grant's wineglass. She is, after all, a mistress of legerdemain. That is how Mr. Hodgson accounts for the occult phenomena—the mysterious letters, the objects appearing out of nowhere."

"But surely you are overlooking the bitterness of strychnine," said one of the poets. "He would immediately have noticed the taste." How was it, Alexandra wondered briefly, that he was able to speak with such authority?

"Not if he drank it straight down," drawled Margot Asquith unexpectedly from her window seat. "It was, after all, cheap wine, not the kind one is tempted to sip."

Barker gave her a look of gratitude. "And remember Madame Blavatsky's words, just as Dr. Forbes-Grant was breathing his last? As I recall, she said, 'A murderer has passed below our windows.' Obviously a tactic to divert suspicion from herself."

George Mead drew himself up to his full height. His moustache bristled. "Sir, you have gone too far. Am I to understand you are actually accusing Madame Blavatsky of murder?"

"I am not the first to do so."

Murdoch's eyes narrowed. "Indeed? Perhaps you would care to elaborate?"

"Anyone who has followed Madame Blavatsky's history is familiar with the case. It happened at her sister's country house near St. Petersburg, about thirty years ago. A man had been murdered in a local gin shop, and Madame Blavatsky's father suggested to the police that, using her occult powers, his daughter might help locate the murderer. Curiously enough, she not only named the murderer, but was able to reveal his hiding place. Naturally the St. Petersburg police were anxious to question Madame Blavatsky about her sources; it took some effort on the part of her father to convince them of her purported innocence."

"What do you mean, 'purported innocence'?" Madame Blavatsky ground her cigarette furiously into a saucer. "If you had followed the case as closely as you say, you would know that his name and his hiding place were revealed through my Ouija board. The spirits themselves provided the answer to the mystery."

The friction match shook in her hand as she lit a fresh cigarette. Her heavy face had gone a sickly shade of yellow grey. "But why do I bother to defend myself?" she said plaintively. "So much mud has already rained down upon me that I no longer bother to open an umbrella."

What Alexandra saw before her was not the blustering, arrogant, outrageous figure of the popular press, but a tired, sick old woman, fearfully awaiting the approach of death. She is not a murderer, Alexandra thought with sudden conviction. She is capable of almost anything else, but not of murder.

"Perhaps," H. P. B. was saying with desperate bravado, "if the spirits can find one murderer, they can find another. Constance, fetch the Ouija board."

"No need, madame," said Inspector Murdoch hastily. He motioned to the countess to sit down. "This is a matter for the civil authorities, I think—not the astral ones."

"Then let me consult the Mahatmas," said H. P. B, gazing up at the ceiling with a remote and contemplative expression.

"This is outrageous," said Charles Barker. "Ouija boards, Mahatmas . . ." Just then the countess ushered in the medical examiner. "At last," said Barker. "Now we will arrive at the truth of the matter."

"And what that might be?" The medical examiner, Dr. Graves, wore well-cut evening clothes that smelled faintly of cigar smoke. He looked ill-pleased at being called away from what Alexandra surmised had been an excellent dinner.

"My colleague," said Barker, "has been poisoned. In the bedroom you will find an empty strychnine bottle."

Dr. Graves raised an ironic eyebrow. "And are you in the habit, sir, of wandering uninvited into your hostess's bedroom?"

Barker flushed. "The door was ajar. As I passed by I saw the bottle sitting on the bureau, in full view. Under the circumstances, I thought it wise to check the label, before anyone saw fit to remove it. As we all observed, Dr. Forbes-Grant was seized with violent convulsions, his lips and face turned blue, he frothed at the mouth, and he apparently died of asphyxiation. I need not remind you, those are precisely the effects of strychnine poisoning."

"But," said Alexandra, "I believe that dying of a strychnine overdose takes at least an hour. Dr. Forbes-Grant succumbed in a matter of mere minutes."

The medical examiner held up an impatient hand. "With so much medical expertise at hand," he remarked, "I wonder at the need to call me in at all."

"Miss . . ."

"David," supplied Alexandra, rising from the sofa.

"Miss David, since I'm told you observed Dr. Forbes-Grant's difficulties from the outset—and you seem familiar with toxology—"

"I have made a study of it, but only as an amateur," said Alexandra modestly.

"Did you observe, in Dr. Forbes-Grant's final moments, the characteristic *risus sardonicus* of strychnine poisoning?"

Alexandra shook her head. "And I fear that as to the cause of death, Dr. Barker and I are in serious disagreement. I would like to suggest another less sinister, though equally tragic, explanation."

At that moment Madame Blavatsky, who had been half sitting, half reclining on a chaise longue, gave a kind of strangled groan and toppled sideways. The countess and George Mead rushed to her assistance. Inspector Murdoch pocketed his notebook and moved quickly to join them.

"There's no cause for alarm," said the countess, waving everyone back. Alexandra saw that in spite of her calm demeanour all the colour had drained from her face. "A touch of indigestion, nothing more. Mr. Mead, will you fetch me the smelling salts? And then we must put her to bed."

After a moment H. P. B. rallied. "What a lot of flapdoodle," she muttered as she tottered out on George Mead's arm, with the countess following anxiously behind.

Alexandra drew Dr. Graves aside. "As you see, Madame Blavatsky is not a young woman, and her health is precarious. She has endured a great deal of late—there have been slanderous press articles, threatened lawsuits . . . Mrs. Morgan tells me that on more than one occasion these cruel attacks on her reputation have endangered her life. I fear she may not survive the physical stress, and the humiliation, of an inquest."

"But, mademoiselle, if there is any indication of unnatural causes . . ."

"Hear me out, *M'sieur le docteur*," said Alexandra. "I am convinced that Dr. Forbes-Grant's death was not unnatural, and that there is no need for a police inquiry."

"You seem very confident of that, Mademoiselle David."

"But what evidence is there of foul play?"

"And your theory, mademoiselle?"

"I believe it was the mussels."

"Are you saying that the mussels were poisoned, or tainted in some way? But surely others at the table must have eaten them."

"Indeed, almost everyone, myself included. But when Dr. Forbes-Grant tried to tell me that something had disagreed with him, that is precisely what he meant. He had just eaten a large portion of curried mussels. It's common knowledge that some people react violently, even fatally, to shellfish. I read of a man who almost died from eating a single fresh prawn."

"But that is nonsense," Charles Barker suddenly burst out. Alexandra realized, too late, that he had been listening intently to their conversation. "Dr. Forbes-Grant and I ate curried mussels in this very house not three weeks ago, and he suffered no ill effects whatever."

"I fear, mademoiselle, that would seem to undermine your theory," said Dr. Graves.

Alexandra bridled—suspecting, as she so often did, that she was being patronized. But Dr. Graves was listening attentively, and his expression was serious. Pointedly ignoring Charles Barker, she addressed her remarks to the medical examiner. "Dr. Graves, are you by any chance familiar with the work of Dr. Charles Richet?"

"No, really, I must protest," said Barker. "A man has been murdered. If we are to waste time listening to more of this spiritualist claptrap . . ."

Alexandra gave him a scathing look. "I refer, Dr. Barker, to Dr. Richet's medical research, not to his interest in metempsychosis. In particular, I am thinking of his experiments with sero-therapeutic injections, in which he successfully immunized laboratory animals against infectious disease."

Dr. Graves nodded. "I understand Dr. Richet is about to publish a paper on his research. I hope to obtain a copy—his work on immunology has caused quite a stir in the medical community. But what does this have to do with the matter at hand?"

"Hear me out," said Alexandra. "When you read Dr. Richet's paper, you may well find references to earlier work, by a Dr. Majendie. He, too, experimented with injecting foreign substances into animals. And he found, curiously enough, that while rabbits suffered no ill effects from a first injection, a second smaller dose, a few days later, often proved fatal."

"In other words," said Graves, "they had become sensitized?"

"*Précisément!*" cried Alexandra, forgetting her English in her determination to drive home her point. "Is it not possible, then, that the same might apply to human beings? That a food that was harmless enough when first eaten might prove deadly when ingested for a second time?"

The room had fallen silent. Alexandra saw that every eye was riveted upon her. It was a not entirely unpleasant realization.

"You see," she said, looking squarely at Charles Barker, "the essential point is not that Dr. Forbes-Grant ate mussels tonight, *but that he had eaten them before*."

It was long past midnight, the hour at which Madame Blavatsky had decreed that everyone in her otherwise eccentric household should be in bed. Dr. Forbes-Grant's body had been removed to the morgue, the dinner guests had at last been excused, and Alexandra stood in the quiet dining room with Inspector Murdoch and the medical examiner.

"You realize, of course, that I can't promise anything until I have completed my medical report. However—based on what you've told me—I shall be very surprised to find anything suspicious, and therefore it seems unlikely that Madame Blavatsky will have to endure an inquest. Would you agree, Inspector Murdoch?"

"You'll get no argument from me," Murdoch said. "With this Whitechapel business, we have enough on our plates."

"I know she will be immensely grateful for that assurance," Alexandra told them.

The medical examiner looked down at her with a faintly sardonic smile. "From what I've heard of Madame H. P. B., I doubt I will receive any letters of thanks. And in any case, mademoiselle, it is you who deserve her gratitude."

At that moment a faint papery rustling, a movement of air like a cool draft in the close, hot room, caused them both to glance up.

"What on earth . . . ?" Alexandra followed the direction of the medical examiner's startled gaze.

From somewhere in the shadowy heights above the gaslight, an envelope was spinning slowly downward. Alexandra reached out and caught it as it drifted into reach.

It smelled of incense—sandalwood, perhaps, or myrrh. She opened it carefully, drew out a folded sheet of rose-pink paper, and glanced down at the heavily inked salutation: *Sister Neophyte, we greet thee*. She scanned the hastily scrawled message and the blotted signature: *Master Koot Hoomi Singh, for the Brotherhood of the Snowy Range*.

Graves looked inquiringly at Alexandra.

"A personal greeting," she said. "From the Tibetan Masters, I believe. They convey their gratitude, in most gracious terms. And it seems I am invited to another dinner party."

"In London, mademoiselle?"

Alexandra looked up at him, smiling. "*Mais non.* In the Himalayas, somewhere south of Lhasa." She folded the letter, returned it to its envelope, and tucked it into her pocket. "If I am able to find my own way there."

"I have no doubt you will, mademoiselle," said Graves as he accepted his hat and gloves from the hovering countess and turned to go. "I have no doubt at all."

Jan Burke is the author of popular contemporary mysteries featuring reporter Irene Kelly. Goodnight, Irene, *the first in the series,* Hocus, *and* Liar *have all been nominated for awards. Her short stories have won the Macavity and Ellery Queen Mystery Magazine Readers awards. She is also a closet historian who enjoys the chance to use her training in her fiction. The most recent in the Irene series is* Bones.

Paul Sledzik is the curator of the anatomical collection at the National Museum of Health and Medicine as well as being a consultant in forensic anthropology. One of his research topics is the physical evidence of the New England vampire folklore that forms the basis for this eerie story.

The authors state that "while Carrick Hollow and its inhabitants are entirely fictional, some New Englanders were ascribing the cause of consumption (tuberculosis) to vampires late into the nineteenth century; newspaper accounts and other evidence indicate rituals such as the one described here occurred at least as late as the 1890s in rural Rhode Island."

THE HAUNTING OF CARRICK HOLLOW

Jan Burke and Paul Sledzik

❦

I reached the end of the drive and pulled the buggy to a halt, looking back at the old house, the modest structure where I had been born. At another time I might have spent these moments at the end of the drive in fond remembrance of my childhood on Arden Farm, recalling the games and mischief I entered into with my brothers and sisters, and the wise and gentle care of my loving parents. But other, less pleasant memories had been forged since those happier days, and now my concerns for the welfare of my one surviving brother kept all other thoughts from me.

Noah stood on the porch, solemn-faced, looking forlorn as he watched me go. It troubled me to see him there; Noah had never concerned himself overmuch with formal leave-takings—only a year ago he would have all but pushed me out the door, anxious to return to his work in the apple orchards.

Upon our father's death six months ago, Noah had inherited Arden Farm. From childhood, we had all of us known that Noah would one day own this land, and the house upon it. The eldest sons of generation upon generation of Ardens before him had worked in these same orchards. In our childhood, I had been the one whose future seemed uncertain: no one was sure what useful purpose such a bookish boy could serve. Now Noah spoke of leaving Arden Farm, of moving far away from the village of Carrick Hollow.

At one time this notion would have been nearly unthinkable. Noah had always seemed to me a steadfast man who did not waver under any burden, as sturdy as the apple trees he tended. But then, as children we never could have imagined the weight that would come to rest on him—indeed, on everyone who lived in our simple New England village.

I pulled my cloak closer about me, and told myself I should not dwell on such matters. I turned my thoughts to my work. When I first returned to Carrick Hollow after medical school, I wondered if my neighbors would be inclined to think of me as little Johnny Arden, Amos Arden's studious fourth son, rather than Dr. John Arden, their new physician—but my fears of being treated as a schoolboy were soon allayed. I attributed their readiness to seek my care to the fact that the nearest alternative, Dr. Ashford, an elderly doctor who lived some thirty miles away, was less and less inclined to make the journey to Carrick Hollow since I had set up my practice there.

Now, driving down the lane, I considered the patients I would visit tomorrow morning. Horace Smith, who had injured his hand while mending a wagon wheel, would be the first. Next I'd call on old Mrs. Compstead, to see if the medicine I had given her for her palsy had been effective.

A distant clanging and clattering interrupted these reveries. The sounds steadily grew louder as we neared a bend in the road, until my gentle and usually well-mannered horse decided he would take exception to this rumbling hubbub. He shied just as the source of this commotion came trundling into view—an unwieldy peddler's wagon, swaying down the rough lane, pulled by a lanky, weary mule.

My horse seemed to take even greater exception to this plodding, ill-favored cousin in harness. The peddler swore and pulled up sharply. I have never claimed to be a masterful handler of the reins, and it took all my limited skill to maneuver my small rig to the side of the narrow lane, which I managed to do just in time to avoid a collision. The mule halted and heaved a sigh. And there, once my horse had regained his dignity, we found ourselves at an impasse.

This was obviously not, by the peddler's reckoning, any sort of calamity. After profuse apologies, but making no effort to budge his wagon—which now blocked my progress completely—he chatted amiably for some minutes on matters of little consequence. He then ventured to offer to me—a gentleman he was so sorry to have inconvenienced—several of his wares at especially reduced prices. "Far lower," he assured me, "than any you could find by mail-order catalogue. If you will only consider the additional savings in shipping costs, and how readily you might obtain the goods you need! Consider, too—you may inspect any item before purchase! You will find only the finest-quality workmanship in the items I offer, sir! And you must own that buying from one with whom you are acquainted must be seen to be superior to purchasing by catalogue!"

"Pardon me," I said, a little loftily, hoping to stem any further flow of conversation, "but we are not at all acquainted. Now, if you would be so good as to—"

"But we *are* acquainted!" he said, with a clever look in his eye. "You are Dr. John Arden."

I was only momentarily at a loss. Sitting at my side, in plain view, was my medical bag. Any local he had visited might have told him that the village physician, Dr. John Arden, had urged them not to buy patent medicines or to be taken in by the claims of those who peddled tonics.

"Forgive me, Mr."—I squinted to read the fading paint on the side of his wagon—"Mr. Otis Merriweather, but I cannot agree that knowing one another's name truly acquaints us."

He grinned and shook his head. "As near as, sir, as near as! You've been away to study, and were not here on the occasion of my last visit to Carrick Hollow. You are young

Johnny Arden, son of Mr. Amos Arden, an apple farmer whom I am on my way to see."

"Perhaps I can spare you some trouble, then," I said coolly. "My father has been dead some months now."

He was immediately crestfallen. "I'm sorry to hear it, sir. Very sorry to hear it indeed." I was ready to believe that his remorse was over the loss of further business, but then he added, "Mr. Arden was a quiet man, never said much, and little though I knew him, he struck me as a sorrowing one. But he was proud of you, boy—and I regret to hear of your loss."

I murmured a polite reply, but lowered my eyes in shame over my uncharitable thoughts of Mr. Merriweather.

"And Mr. Winston gone now, too," he said.

My head came up sharply, but the peddler was thoughtfully gazing off in the direction of the Winston farm and did not see the effect this short speech had on me.

"Do you know what has become of him?" Mr. Merriweather asked. "I'll own I was not fond of him, but he gave me a good deal of custom. It seems so strange—"

"Not at all strange," I said firmly. "These are difficult times for apple growers—for farmers of any kind. Have you not seen many abandoned orchards in Carrick Hollow? Indeed, we aren't the only district to suffer—you travel throughout the countryside in Rhode Island, and you must see empty farms everywhere. Scores of men have left their family lands and moved to cities, to try their luck there."

"Aye, I've seen them," he said, "but—but upon my oath, something's different here in Carrick Hollow! The people here are skittish—jumping at shadows!" He laughed a little nervously, and shook his head. "Old Winston often told me that this place was haunted by . . . well, he called them *vampires*."

"Winston spoke to you of vampires?" I asked, raising my chin a little.

He shifted a bit on the wagon seat. "I wouldn't expect a man of science to believe in such superstitious nonsense, of course! But old Winston used to prose on about it, you see, until my hair fairly stood up on end!"

"Mr. Winston was always a convincing storyteller."

"Yes—but nonsense, pure nonsense!" He paused and added, "Isn't it?"

"I never used to believe in such things," I said.

"And now?"

"And now perhaps I do."

Merriweather's eyes widened. He laughed again, and said, "Oh, I see! You pay me back for guessing your name!"

I smiled.

"Here now," he said, "I've left you standing here in the lane, taking up your time with this idle talk. Otis Merriweather's all balderdash, you'll be thinking." He cast a quick, uneasy look at the sky. "Growing dark, too. Hadn't realized it had grown so late. I hoped to be in the next town by now, and I'm sure you've patients to attend to. Good day, to you, Doctor!"

With a snap of his reins, he set the mule into motion. Soon the clattering, jangling wagon was traveling down the lane at a pace that made me realize I had underestimated the homely mule.

My own vehicle's pace was much more sedate. I wondered how much faster the peddler would have driven if he had known how much I knew of vampires. I had long made it my business to make a study of the subject. I knew that tales of vampires had been whispered here and there in New England for more than a hundred years, just as they had been told in Egypt, Greece, Polynesia, and a dozen other places. The New England vampire has little in common with those that caused such panic in Turkish Serbia and Hungary in the last century—no fanged or winged creature bites the necks of unwitting strangers here. No, our Rhode Island vampires have always more closely resembled ghosts—spirits of the dead who leave their tombs in the night, to visit their nearest and dearest as they dream. Our vampires are believed by some to cause the disease of consumption; it is they, we are told, who drain the blood of living victims into their own hearts, and who thereby cause their victims' rapid decline. The Ardens were never among the believers of such superstitions, never held with any talk of vampires. Indeed, how clearly I remembered a winter's night five years ago, when I assured my youngest brother there wasn't any such thing.

"Mr. Winston said that Mother will come for me," Nathan said. "Will she, Johnny?"

"Pay no attention to him," I said, smoothing his fair hair from his damp forehead. His eyes were bright, and his cheeks ruddy, but he was far too frail for a six-year-old boy. His cough was growing worse. He needed his sleep, but Winston's talk of vampires had frightened him. I tried to keep my anger at our neighbor's thoughtlessness from my voice. "Mother loved you, and would never harm you, you know that, Nate. And she's up in heaven, with all the angels. You must not worry so. Just try to get well."

"But Mr. Winston said—"

"Mr. Winston is a mean-spirited old busybody," I said with some exasperation. "He only means to frighten you, Nate."

Nathan said nothing, but frowned, as if making a decision. After a while he took hold of my hand. "I'm glad you've come home, Johnny," he whispered. "I know you wish you were away at school—"

"No, Sprout, I could not wish to be anywhere else if you need me."

He smiled at the nickname. "You'll stay with me tonight, won't you?"

"Of course I'll stay with you," I said, and reached into one of my pockets. "And see here—I'm armed—look what I've brought with me!"

"The slingshot I made for you!"

"Yes, and I've gathered a few stones for ammunition," I said, winking at him. "So you're safe now. Only get some sleep, Sprout. I'll stay right here."

He slept soundly. Noah came in to spell me, even though I protested I would be fine. "I know, but please go downstairs to see to Father, Johnny," he whispered. "Try to talk him into getting some sleep."

Downstairs, my father stood near the window, staring out into the moonlit night. I thought he looked more haggard than I had ever seen him. The previous year had taken a great toll on him, and when Nathan fell ill early in 1892, Father could barely take care of himself, let alone a small boy with consumption. So I came home from the private school for which my godfather had so generously paid my tuition; my instructors had been understanding—my family, they knew, had suffered greatly of late. Even though this was not the first occasion upon which I had been called home, my marks were high, and I was well ahead of most of my classmates in my studies; the dean assured me that I would be allowed to return.

I found my father greatly changed—indeed, Arden Farm itself seemed changed. Winter was the time he usually pruned the trees, but now as I stood next to him at the window, I saw the sucker branches reaching sharply into the winter sky, casting strange shadows everywhere.

"Half my orchard has been felled," he remarked, and I knew he was not talking of the trees, but of the toll consumption had taken on his family. "First Rebecca, then Robert and Daniel. Last month, your mother—dearest Sarah! I've said prayers and made my peace with the Lord. And still he wants more. Is this my God?"

"Noah and I are healthy," I replied, trying to keep his spirits up. "And Julia is with her husband in Peacedale. She's well."

From the other room, we heard the sound of Nathan's cough. "Now my youngest!" my father said.

"Noah and I will care for Nathan. He'll get better."

But neither of us could easily hope that Nathan would recover. Too many times in the past year, consumption had robbed us of those we loved. Ten-year-old Rebecca's cough started early in 1891, and her illness progressed slowly at first. She rallied in the spring, and we thought all would be well. But in August, the cough came back. She was soon coughing up blood—we knew she would not live long after the blood started. By the end of the month, she was dead.

Robert and Daniel, my older brothers, took ill the week

before Rebecca's funeral. Mother wrote to me less often, her time taken up with care of them. When she did write, her letters were filled with news of neighbors who had also taken ill, or of the advice given to her by Dr. Ashford. *He tells me to give to them fresh air, to keep them clean, to change their clothes often,* she wrote. *I confess to you, dear John, that I am quite worn down—each day, I take them outdoors, read to them, and try to keep their spirits up. This is the most difficult of all my duties. They miss Rebecca, and they know their own symptoms are identical to hers. Still, I will do all I can to keep my boys alive. God keep you safe, John!*

But despite all her efforts, by October I came home again—for Robert's funeral. And thus I was there, three days later, when Daniel told us he had dreamed of Rebecca and Robert.

"They were here, sitting on my bed. They weren't sick. They said I had helped them to get better." Two days later he passed away during the night.

I returned to school, but Mother's letters grew fewer still. I thought it was grief that kept her from writing, but when I came home for the Christmas holidays, I immediately realized that the cause was otherwise: the racking cough of consumption was no longer an unfamiliar sound to any of us.

"Why did you not tell me?" I asked my father.

"She did not want us to take you from your school," he said. "She has come to believe you will be safer there than here."

I hurried to her bedside. She looked so thin and weak.

"John, you are home!" she whispered to me as I sat beside her. "Rebecca, Daniel, and Robert are with the Lord. I'll be with them soon. They are good children. They'll not bother me. I have not dreamt of them. They won't come and take me."

"What does she mean?" I asked my father when she fell asleep again.

"Winston!" he said angrily. "He's all about the village,

telling everyone that the consumption is caused by vampires."

"Vampires!"

"Yes. He tells his tales to any who will hear him. Gets the most ignorant of them to believe that the spirits of the dead consume the living, and thus the living are weakened!"

"But surely no one believes such things!"

"In the absence of any cure, do you blame them for grasping at any explanation offered to them? Grief and fear will lead men to strange ways, Johnny, and Winston can persuade like the devil himself!"

"Yes, he was ever one to seek attention," I agreed.

"He has gained a great deal of it during this crisis," my father said. "And the rituals he has driven some of the more superstitious ones to perform! It sickens me!" He shivered in disgust.

Mother died two nights after Christmas, as Father held her, singing hymns to her. The next day, he dressed her in her favorite dress and sent word to the undertaker. The stone carver had already completed her headstone, and her burial place had long been chosen.

Noah wrote to me of Nathan's illness in late January of 1892, and I hurried home again. That first night back home, as I studied my father's face, etched in grief, I saw that my mother's death had wounded him even more deeply than I had imagined. I had never doubted their love or devotion to one another, but I had not before realized how much of his strength must have come from her. If this great man could be made so weak, what would become of us? I suddenly felt as small and frightened as a boy of Nathan's age.

"Papa!" I said, placing a hand on his shoulder.

He looked at me and smiled a little. "It is some time since you called me 'Papa.'"

"You—you need your sleep," I said. "Won't you go up to bed?"

The smile faded. "So empty, that room . . ." he murmured.

"Please, it's so late, and you seem so tired—"

"I cannot—I will not be able to sleep there."

Understanding dawned. "Then I'll make a place up for you here, near the fire. But you must sleep. Please. Nathan and Noah need you. I need you."

And so he consented, but when I left him to go back to Nathan, he was staring into the fire.

The next morning, my father gently shook me awake. I sat up stiffly in the chair next to the bed where Nathan still slept. I could hear our dogs barking. Father gestured for me to step into the hallway.

"Winston is on his way up the drive! I've asked Noah to delay him all he can. But I must tell you this—make sure Nathan hears nothing of his foolish talk."

I started to tell him that Nathan's head was already full of Winston's foolish talk, but he had hurried off.

I stood near the window of Nathan's room, straining to hear the conversation that was taking place below. Winston was a large man, whose new derby, well-made coat, and fine boots signaled his prosperity, but could not improve his rough features. As my father approached, Winston's pockmarked cheeks were flushed. He eyed the dogs warily, until Noah called them to heel.

"Will you not ask me in, neighbor?" Winston asked, fingering his heavy gold watch chain.

"My youngest is ill," my father said firmly. "I would not have you disturb him."

My father's lack of hospitality did not delay Winston from his mission. He took a deep breath and said in a loud voice, "I fear for my community, for my neighbors and their families! I know you're scared for what remains of yours, too. I can see it in your eyes, Arden. Rebecca took the boys, then they took Sarah. Now Sarah's taking Nathan. John and Noah will follow, and you'll be last. Julia may be far away enough to be safe, but there is no certainty of that."

"My family's safety is my own concern, Winston."

"Your obligation is greater than you perceive, Arden!"

Winston shot back. "The vampires look beyond your family! Lavinia Gardner has the consumption."

"Isaac's wife is ill?" my father asked, dismayed.

"Yes. And she's dreamt of your wife! There's only one way to stop this: the ritual must be performed! It has worked for Robinson, and others as well. This is a warning, Arden! If you're afraid to do what is necessary, I'll do it myself!"

"You'll go nowhere near the graves of my beloved!" Father shouted. "I know of your ritual, Winston. I've spoken with Robinson. He's not the same man; he's alive, but he looks for all the world as if he believes himself damned."

"Nonsense!" Winston blustered. "What's more important, Arden? Maintaining your own selfish prejudices, or the survival of Carrick Hollow? Our eldest sons and daughters are fleeing; they've taken factory jobs in Providence and Fall River."

"There are many reasons they leave. You have no wife or children, Winston. Allow me to take care of my own."

"A fine job you're doing of it! Half of them dead!"

Noah stepped forward, his fists clenched. I could not make out what he said to Winston.

"Noah," my father said, "it's all right. Try though he may, Mr. Winston cannot harm me with his words."

"Think of your neighbors, Arden!" Winston said. "Think of Isaac if you won't think of your own sons!" He turned on his heel and strode quickly down the lane, dried leaves swirling in his wake.

"Johnny?" I heard a small voice say.

I turned from the window to see Nathan watching me. "So you're awake, Mr. Sleepyhead!"

"I heard Mr. Winston yelling at Papa."

"Yes, and had I known you were awake, I would have opened the window and used this fine slingshot to knock old Thunderpuss's fancy derby right off his silly head."

Nathan smiled. "I should have liked to have seen you do it," he said, and went back to sleep.

The thaw broke the day Lavinia Gardner died. Isaac Gardner came to visit us two weeks later. Noah stayed with

Nathan as I sat with Father, watching Isaac wring his hands.

"You know what I think of Winston," he began. "And I would not come to trouble you, Amos, except—except that, before she died, Lavinia called Sarah's name several times."

"Our wives were good friends," my father said.

Isaac shook his head. "That's not what I mean, Amos. I mean, called her name as if she were within speaking distance. I'd tell her, 'Sarah's dead,' and she'd say, 'No, Sarah Arden is rattling me again. She comes at night and shakes me, and the cough starts up.' "

My father sat in stunned silence.

"Your wife was very ill—" I began gently.

"Yes, John," Isaac said, "and I told myself that she was right out of her head, although of course Neighbor Winston had a good deal to say otherwise, and he's caught my daughter's ear. Even before Jane was took ill, she was asking me if perhaps we should pay attention to what Winston had to say."

"The news of Jane's illness only reached us yesterday," my father said. "I was sorry to hear of it, Isaac," my father said. "I had always hoped that she and Noah—well, I can only offer my prayers for her recovery."

"She's all I have left in the world, Amos," Isaac said. "As hard on you as it has been, losing so many—well, I don't know what I'll do if Jane suffers like her mother did." He paused, then said, "But I'm here, Amos, because I want you to know what things have come to—and God forgive me, but I need your help. Jane no longer doubts that Winston's right."

"What?"

"Yes. Just last night, she told me, 'Mother will take me just like Sarah Arden took her.' And she pleaded with me, Amos: 'Mr. Winston knows the way to stop this. You can't let me die!' "

My father was silent.

"I told her," Isaac said, his voice breaking, "I told her, 'Jane, think of it! Think what you ask me to do! Your mother—let her rest in peace!' And she said, 'But, Father, she's not resting in peace now. She can only rest forever with your help.' "

"Good God, Isaac!"

"I don't believe in it, not for a minute, Amos. But *she* does. And what's worse, now more than half the village does, too! Winston's got them all stirred up. What they say of you, I'll not repeat."

"I'd as soon you didn't!" Father said, casting a glance at me.

"I've gone to Pastor Williams. He doesn't promote the ritual, but he doesn't oppose it, either. He's only human, and Winston holds some sway with him, too."

"With his coffers, you mean. I hear Winston's most recent donation makes up what is needed for the new roof on the church."

"Amos!"

"Yes, yes, I'm ashamed of making such a remark. Forgive me, Isaac." He sighed. "What do you need from me?"

"Help me to do it."

"The ritual?" my father asked, horrified.

"Amos, you're my best friend in all the world, else I wouldn't ask it. But I need someone there—someone who hasn't lost his mind in all this vampire madness. Otherwise, God knows what is to become of me! I need your strength!"

His strength is failing! I wanted to protest, but my father was already agreeing to help his old friend.

Father would not let us go with him on the day the ritual was performed. When he came home, his pallor frightened me. I gave him soup and warm bread, but he did not eat. He would not speak of what happened, but late that night, I heard him weeping.

Jane Gardner died two days later.

If we had thought this would put an end to Winston's cause, we were mistaken. A town meeting was held the next week. I sat next to Father, near the front of the room, when Winston presented his case. Father had told Noah that Winston could not hurt him with his words, but how wrong he had been!

"The future of our community is at risk!" Winston declared, fingering his gold watch chain. "Many of our dearest friends and family members have died from consumption. We've taken action against the vampires, with one notable exception." He stared hard at my father. "Those in the Arden family!"

There was a low murmur, a mixture of protest and agreement.

Winston held his hands out flat, making a calming motion. "Now," he said silkily, "I have great sympathy for my neighbor Amos Arden. The death of his wife and three children is a terrible loss for him. But in consumption, the living are food for the dead, and we must think of the living! The graves must be opened, and the bodies examined! If none of their hearts is found to hold blood, we may all be at peace, knowing that none are vampires. But if there is a vampire coming to us from the Arden graves, the ritual must be performed! This is our only recourse." The room fell silent. No one rose to speak, but many heads nodded in agreement.

Father stood slowly, grasping the chair beside me. "The thought of disturbing the peace of my wife and children sickens me. I do not believe in this superstition, but I see no other way." He glanced toward Winston, then said, "If I refuse, I have no doubt that some other will take the task upon himself. He takes a great deal upon himself, but the thought of his hands on my wife's remains—" He broke off, and I saw that he was trembling, not in fear, but in anger. He looked around the room, but many of our neighbors would not meet his gaze. "I will agree to the ritual," he said at last, "but no one else will touch my wife."

The exhumation was set for two days hence and, under other circumstances, would have occupied all my thoughts. Instead, all my energies were taken up with the care of Nathan, whose condition suddenly worsened. He bore it bravely, worrying more about his father than himself.

"Papa is troubled," he said, and pleaded again and again with me to tell him what had so disturbed our parent.

On the night before the exhumation, I told my father that

Nathan's condition terrified me. "He needs a doctor! He has night sweats now, and the coughing is ceaseless. He has so little strength and—"

"I know, John. I know."

I was silent.

"With all that has befallen us," my father said, "I'm sorry, John, I cannot afford to bring Ashford here again, even if he would come."

"What do you mean, 'if he would come'? Of course he would!"

My father shook his head. "I have not wanted to tell you this, son, but—the last time Dr. Ashford saw him, three weeks ago, he told me Nathan's case is hopeless. Your brother is dying."

I had known it, of course, without being told, but still it was a blow. Childishly, I struck back. "So you resort to Winston's witchcraft!"

He looked into my eyes. "Do you think I would hesitate for a moment to save any of your lives by any means I could? By God, I'd offer my own life if it would save his!"

"Papa—I'm sorry! I just can't understand why you've agreed to this ritual. It did not work for Jane Gardner. I've heard of other unsuccessful cases—"

"I don't do this because I believe it will cure consumption. But it is a cure for mistrust. A bitter remedy, but a necessary one."

"I don't understand."

"You will go back to school soon, and perhaps you will never return to Carrick Hollow. No, don't protest—whether you do or not, Noah and I will continue to live here. We who live in the countryside depend upon our friends and neighbors. My neighbors are depending on me now, to do something which they have come to believe will keep them safe and well. No matter how repulsive I find it, John, I must do this to keep their trust."

That night, my sleep was fitful. Nathan's cough was horrible, and nothing I did could bring him any relief. My brief dreams were filled with images of decaying flesh and bones, of coffins unearthed, of Winston's thick hands reaching into my mother's grave.

The morning broke bright and warm, unusual for an early-spring day in New England. We had agreed that Noah would stay with Nathan; a suggestion that he met with both relief and some guilt. But my father knew that Noah's anger toward Winston had already nearly led to blows, and asked him to stay home.

A group of ten men, including poor Isaac Gardner, gathered in the village. Winston tried to lead the way to the cemetery, but Isaac shouldered him aside and let my father go ahead of them. I saw my father hesitate. I took his hand, and together we walked to the familiar section of the churchyard, the one I knew so well from the winter's toll. As we stood at the foot of the four newest Arden graves, Winston's voice interrupted my silent prayers.

"Dig up all four coffins," he directed.

"All four!" my father protested.

"We must be certain!" Winston said. "We'll place them under that tree. Once they are all exhumed, we'll open them one at a time. Start with the children."

Father, Isaac, and I stood away from the group. At a nod from Winston, their picks and shovels struck the earth. They began to dig, never looking up at us. My father swayed a little on his feet, and Isaac moved nearer, placing a firm hand on his shoulder. Together we stood listening to the rhythm of the digging, the downward scrape and lift, the thudding fall of the soil as they attacked my sister's grave.

Soon the top of Rebecca's coffin was struck. How small that coffin looked! The earth was moved from around its sides, and ropes were placed under the ends. The coffin was lifted from the grave and placed under a nearby tree. In two more hours two other coffins were taken from the earth—the larger coffins of my brothers, Robert, who had been but eighteen, and Daniel, a year younger; the age I was now. As each coffin was brought up, my prayers became more urgent and the fact of the exhumations more real.

The group moved to Mother's grave. Again shovels broke into the soil. The digging slowed now—the first frenzy long past, the men grew tired. At last they pulled her coffin from the earth and set it with the others, beneath the tree. I moved toward it, and placed my hand on the lid of her box. I felt the cool, damp wood and the small indentations made by each nail. I broke out in a cold sweat, and my hand shook. I turned when I heard the creak of the nails being pried from the other coffins.

Father's hand gently touched my shoulder. I moved away.

When they had finished loosening all the nails on the top of each of the coffins, Winston directed the men to remove the lid of Rebecca's. With horror, I gazed at the unrecognizable form that—had it not been for her dress and the color of her hair—I would not have known as my sister. All that remained was a skull and dried sinew. My throat constricted—I could not swallow, could not breathe. Rebecca! Little Rebecca! My memories of her could not be reconciled with what I saw. I had taught her to write her name, I thought wildly—I had heard her laughter. This could not be my sister . . .

Winston was studying her. I wanted to claw his filthy eyes out.

"No," he said, and the lid was quickly replaced.

He said the same thing when he gazed upon the remains of my brothers, who appeared mummified, their dry skin stretched tight over their bony frames.

I tried hard to control my emotions, but this was increasingly difficult. By the time we reached my mother's coffin, only my desire to deny Winston any glimpse of weakness kept me on my feet.

They slid the coffin lid off the edge of the box. Father and I looked down at Mother's face. She looked peaceful, remarkably like the day we buried her, despite the three cold months that had passed. Her nails and hair appeared longer, and in places her skin had turned reddish.

"Ahh," Winston said, moving closer. "As I suspected. But we must examine the heart to be certain."

"You'll not touch her!" my father cried.

Winston smiled, and turned to the others. "Light the fire."

"By God, Winston—"

"Oh, indeed, I'll not touch your vampire wife. You must be the one." He handed my father a long knife.

My father stared at it.

"Get on with it, man!" Winston ordered.

"John," my father said, anguished, "leave us. Go home. It was wrong of me to bring you here—"

"I'll not leave you, Father."

He shook his head, but turned back to the open coffin. He set the knife aside and, with trembling fingers, gently moved her burial gown down from her neck. I heard him sob, then lift the knife. He cut a gash in her chest.

"The heart, the heart!" Winston said eagerly.

Father's face seemed to turn to stone—cold and gray. He pried the wound open, then took the knife and cut away her heart. Bloody fluid ran from the wound onto her dress.

"You see! She's the one, she's a vampire!"

As from a distance, I heard the other men gasp, and saw their quick gestures—signs against evil.

"Put it in the fire, Arden!" Winston directed.

"No!" I said weakly, but Father carried her heart to the fire. He let it drop from his fingers; the fire hissed and sparked as the heart fell into the center of the flames.

Father walked back to Mother's coffin, placed the lid on it, and began to hammer it shut. I picked up one of the other hammers, and did the same, tears blinding me as I worked at his side. Without speaking, several men did the same for the other coffins. Each coffin was slowly lowered back into its grave, and in silence we began to cover them again—but Father buried Mother's coffin alone, refusing the others' help with a steely look in his eyes.

I saw Winston warming his hands over the fire. He caught me looking at him and smiled. "You should thank me. I've saved your life this day, John."

Before the others could stop me, I slammed my fist into his jaw.

My father led me away from them, and with Isaac we made our way back home. All the way down the lane, I could not help but be troubled over what I had seen, and wondered at it. That my mother could be a vampire, I did not for a moment believe. I knew there must be a rational, scientific explanation for the blood that had been in my mother's heart. I swore to myself that I would study anatomy and medicine—yes, and vampires, too—and learn all I could about consumption and its causes.

When we returned to the house, Noah held Nathan's body in his arms.

My medical schooling was the best in New England. The Boston area had many fine schools, and Springhaven University was among them. Springhaven was the choice of my godfather, as it was his alma mater, and he was a respected alumnus and benefactor.

Medical school was not easy for me. The work itself was not difficult, though much harder than my earlier schooling, to be sure. I took to the reading, lectures, and discussions with great interest, but it was the hustle and bustle of Boston that caused me discomfort. The size of the city, its noises and smells, always left me ill at ease. Although I loved the work, I was homesick.

Early on, I learned that there had been nothing unusual about the appearance of my mother's body, given the conditions of her burial—the coldness of the ground, the brief length of time she had been buried. The heart is a pump, my anatomy instructor said, and at death, blood and other fluids often settle there as the heart ceases beating.

My professors called consumption by another name—tuberculosis, or TB. Tuberculosis was not an enigma to these men of science. Over forty years before my brother's death, sanitariums were being established in Europe, and TB patients were living longer lives. But of all the discoveries that had been made about the disease, perhaps the most exciting had come in 1882, when Robert Koch identified its true cause—*Mycobacterium tuberculosis*. Koch's discovery proved that TB was transmitted from a consumptive to a healthy person through germs contained in the consumptive's cough—not by vampires.

Although saddened that my knowledge had come too late to save my family, I had no difficulty accepting these new discoveries. But educating the public, whether the poor of Boston or the farmers of Carrick Hollow, was the bigger challenge. I determined to practice medicine in Carrick Hollow upon graduation, to do my best to counter the superstitious remedies that offered no real hope to its inhabitants.

I stopped to visit with one of my chief correspondents and supporters soon after my return; old Dr. Ashford received me gladly, and we talked at length about the medical histories of families in the area and exchanged information on the latest medical supplies and pharmaceuticals. We also discussed my schooling and how much medical education had changed since he had taken the title "doctor."

"The War of the Rebellion was where I learned medicine," he said. "We learned on our feet, not from the books. I haven't been much for the science of it, but I know that folks here are quite independent, even when it comes to medicine. They take care of their own problems, using the same remedies their grandparents used. It's hard to fight their traditions, John."

"I suspect that will be the hardest part of my job," I replied. "I have confidence that I can do some good here, if my neighbors will only accept me."

"You've always had both the mind and the countenance for medicine," he said proudly. "You'll do well in Carrick Hollow. It's time they had a doctor as fine as yourself."

As it happened, the residents of the village took me in with open arms, proud of my accomplishments and glad to have a physician so nearby. Several of them helped me to convert a building formerly used by a lawyer into a small clinic, which had the advantage of living quarters on the upper story.

I had the good fortune to be of some help to my first patients, and soon others were ready to follow my medical advice and help me to establish my practice. I fell easily into life in Carrick Hollow, surrounded by the sense of community I so missed in Boston.

Only one problem continued to trouble me—my father's state of mind.

Father had never fully recovered from the deaths in our family, especially not from the loss of my mother. Noah had been greatly relieved when I told him that I meant to set up my practice in the village. "Perhaps you will be able to cheer him," he said. "He has not been the same since—since the day Nathan died."

But although he was always kind to me in those months, my father never smiled, and seldom spoke. His sleep was often disturbed by nightmares, and if not for our constant coaxing, I do not know that he would have eaten enough food to sustain himself. He worked hard, but the joy he had once taken in his labors was gone. There was a lost look in his eyes, and the smallest happiness seemed beyond his reach. It was as if, on that long-ago day at the cemetery, his own heart had fallen on those flames, and turned to ashes with my mother's.

His lifelessness was a condition that was mimicked in others in Carrick Hollow as well—Isaac Gardner, Robinson, and those who had performed Winston's brutal ritual. Bitterly I reflected that nothing in my medical training would cure these men. I vowed that no one in Carrick Hollow would ever be forced to endure that ritual again.

Soon after I had opened my office, I was given an opportunity to make good on that vow. I was visited by Jacob Wilcox, a middle-aged man just returned to Carrick Hollow from factory work in Fall River. His rumbling cough spoke the telltale sign of tuberculosis, but my examination revealed that the disease was in its early stages.

I recommended the best hope for his recovery—the strict regimen of a sanitarium. I suggested one in the Adirondack Mountains, which had the advantages of being close to Rhode Island and less costly than those in the western United States. He thanked me, took the information, and went on his way.

A few days later, at my father's request, I visited the

farm. Coming down the drive, hearing the welcoming bark of our old dogs, I felt what had become a customary mixture of sadness and deep comfort in returning to my childhood home. Noah and my father came out to help me stable the horse, and my brother and I spoke of inconsequential things. I could not help but notice that Father seemed agitated, and Noah wary.

My father did not broach the subject that concerned him until we had finished eating our simple meal—a meal he had barely touched. He put a log on the fire, then turned to me and said, "I'm told that you saw a patient with consumption today."

"Yes," I answered hesitantly. I had not previously told him of my devotion to the study of consumption, and I was concerned that he would be touched on the raw by any mention of it.

He frowned. "I talked to young Wilcox after you saw him. What is this treatment you prescribed? Why do you send him to the mountains?"

"In hope of curing his consumption," I said.

"Curing! Is it possible?"

"Sometimes, yes." I began to tell him of the benefits the TB patient might find in life in a sanitarium—exposure to a healthful climate, enforced rest, fresh air, proper care, and good nutrition. "And of course the sanitarium separates those who have this contagion from any who might be vulnerable to it, so the disease is less likely to be spread to others."

"You have especially concerned yourself with the study of—you call it 'TB'?"

"Yes."

His questions became more persistent, and soon I was talking to him of Brehmer, Villemin, Koch, and all the others whose discoveries had brought us to our present understanding of the disease. My father listened with rapt attention, but I saw that he became more and more agitated as I spoke. Soon, however, I recognized that he was dismayed not by what I had learned about TB, but by his own previous ignorance.

"Dr. Ashford did not know of this!" he said bitterly. "Your mother, the children—their consumption was a death sentence! I should have sought another physician, a younger man such as yourself. If we had known of these sanitariums—"

"It still might not have helped; sanitariums only give consumptives a *chance* to recover. Some people survive, others arrive only to die a few weeks later."

"But Nathan—your mother, Robert, and Daniel; all of them, even Rebecca—they might have lived had we sent Rebecca away?"

"I don't know. There were so many others in Carrick Hollow who were ill that winter. Perhaps they would have caught TB from Mrs. Gardner, or Jane, or another. We cannot always cure this disease, Papa. I can't say for certain who would live and who would die. For all that men in my profession have learned, life and death are still in God's hands."

He was silent.

"We cannot change the past, Papa. I only hope to save others from the horror our family experienced. In truth, my most difficult battle is not against the disease, but rather the ignorance—the sort of ignorance which allows men like Winston to convince others that the afflicted are beset by vampires. As long as he spouts his nonsense, others will die, because he will have his neighbors believing that spiritual mumbo jumbo—and not infection—are at the root of the disease."

"You are too kind, John," he said slowly. "You fail to mention the truly damned. Men like your father, who will be persuaded that barbaric rituals must be performed on the bodies of their dead—"

"Papa, you never believed him. You had other reasons. Do not torture yourself so!"

"There is no escape from it."

"Then try to find some peace where I have—in helping the living. That is how my mother's memory is best served: the sooner we educate our neighbors in the truth of this matter, the less influence men of Winston's stripe will have over them."

I was gratified, the next day, to see that he seemed to have taken up this cause, and that he was to some degree transformed by his devotion to it. Whenever I happened to glance out my office window, I saw my father talking in an animated fashion to any who would hear him. He was a respected member of the community, and had no shortage of listeners. Isaac Gardner was with him, and he, too, seemed to have taken up the banner.

By the early afternoon, Mr. Robinson had stopped into my office, to ask if what my father said was true—that vampires had nothing to do with consumption, that some people were being cured of it in sanitariums. I verified that it was so, and watched his eyes cloud with tears. "Then what Winston told me to do to Louisa's body—the ritual—that was all for naught?"

"I'm afraid so," I said gently.

He swore rather violently regarding Mr. Winston, then begged my pardon and left. I watched him walk across the street to join the growing crowd that had gathered around my parent. I smiled. My father, Isaac Gardner, and Mr. Robinson would all do a better job of convincing the others than I ever could.

I was vaguely aware that the crowd was moving off down the street, but I was soon caught up in the care of a young patient who had fallen from a tree, and forgot all about vampires and consumption. I set his broken arm and sent him and his grateful mother on their way. I had just finished straightening my examination room when the door to my office burst open, and my father, Noah, Isaac Gardner, Robinson, and a great many others came crowding into the room. They carried between them a man whose face was so battered and clothing so bloodied that I would not have recognized him were it not for a memorable piece of ostentation he was never without—a heavy gold watch chain.

"Winston!"

The others looked at me, their eyes full of fear.

"Lay him on the table!" I ordered.

It took only the briefest examination to realize that he was beyond any help I could offer. He was already growing cold. "He's dead."

I thought I heard sighs of relief, and I turned to face them. They all stood silently, hats in hand.

"Who did this?" I asked.

No one answered, and all lowered their eyes.

"Who did this?" I asked again.

"Vampires," I heard someone whisper, but I was never to know who spoke the word. No matter what I asked, no matter how I pleaded to be told the truth, they remained resolutely silent. Winston's blood was on all of them; there was no way to distinguish a single killer from among the group. I went to my basin, to wash his blood from my own hands. The thought arrested me. These were neighbors, friends—my father, my brother. I knew what had driven them to this—I knew. Had I not lived in Carrick Hollow almost all my life?

"What shall we do with him?" one of them asked.

I dried my hands and said, in a voice of complete calm, "I believe it is said that for the good of the community, one who is made into a vampire must be cremated."

I could show you the place in the woods where it was done, where the earth has not yet healed over the burning. Nature works to reclaim it, though, as nature ever works to reclaim us all.

I would like to tell you that the last vampire of Carrick Hollow had been laid to rest there, and that we now live in peace. But it is not so.

Not long after Winston's death, people who had lived in our village all their lives began to leave it. Farms were abandoned. We would tell strangers that it was the economy—and in truth, some left because it was easier to make a living in the cities. But that would not explain the mistrust the inhabitants sometimes seem to feel toward one another, or the guilty look one might surprise in the eye of those who traveled past Winston's farm.

I thought the peddler was unlikely to return. He had seen something that frightened him, though he might not know enough to put a name to the emptiness in a young doctor's eyes. I knew it for what it was, for I had seen it in my father and Isaac and Mr. Robinson and so many others—for Carrick Hollow is a haunted place, haunted by the living as well as the dead.

Oh, yes, I believe in vampires—though not the sort of bogeyman imagined by fanatics like the late and unlamented Winston.

But if vampires are the animated dead, dead who walk upon the earth—restless, hungry, and longing to be alive again—then I could never deny their existence. You see, I know so very many of them.

Indeed, I am one.

H.R.F. Keating is the creator of Bombay's Inspector Ganesh Ghote, a policeman caught between two very different cultures. The first book in this series, **The Perfect Murder**, appeared in 1964 and is still going strong. Keating has won both the British Golden Dagger and the American Edgar awards and received the Diamond Dagger Lifetime Achievement Award. Recently he published a delightful compilation of stories set, not in India, but London's Kensington Gardens.

"Howard" is set in colonial India at the turn of the last century. Inspector Ghote is not there to solve the crime, but fortunately, Keating has found another clear-thinking detective, not bound by cultural bias, to investigate the crime.

HOWARD

H.R.F. Keating

Howard's first murder case came to him only because
it landed smack on his plate as if it had been a fat
helping of mutton curry dumped in front of him by a
clumsy bearer. It would have pretty certainly been his last
case, too, except that in the nick of time he saw the solution
to the mystery that was, as it were, under his nose all the
while. He would never in the ordinary way have been given
the investigation, a youngster only just a full member of
the Indian Police Service and, perhaps more damning than
that, "country-born." one who, however solidly of British
stock, had never been sent to school in cold, bracing Britain.

Yet District Superintendent of Police Mellish, brought to
India when it had been suggested to the viceroy that with
the new century—the twentieth century!—the Indian police
needed new thinking, had summoned him and put him in
charge. Not that he had done so without expressing his
doubts, partly of Howard's inexperience but much more
because of that stigma, "country-born." However, the fact

was that for the past six months Howard had actually been posted at the same small station from which, out riding at first light two days before, Mrs. Mabel Fellows had totally disappeared. As the sole other chess player in the station besides John Fellows—unless you counted little, impish Lucy, John's daughter by his first marriage—he had even been a frequent visitor to their bungalow.

"Now, Howard," D.S.P. Mellish barked, "you searched in person the whole length of Mrs. Fellows's morning ride when she was missed and found nothing, so there can be no doubt the poor lady must have been set upon by a gang of dacoits intent on robbing her of the few pieces of jewelry she may have been wearing. Very well, swine of that sort will be known in at least one of the villages in the area of your station. Bound to be. Quartered themselves there for the night no doubt, raped a few women, stole anything worth stealing and swore to silence every ryot in the place if they complained before going off and chancing to come upon Mrs. Fellows. So go out and ask questions. Get the truth out of whoever looks most likely. You've got a riding whip. If necessary, use it."

He may have seen on Howard's youthfully fresh face the tiny frown that had appeared, despite efforts made to suppress it, because he gave him a ferocious glare from his boiled blue eyes.

"Oh, yes, I daresay you think, because you were born and bred out here, you've some sort of special feeling for your so-called simple natives. Think we're too hard on 'em. That sort of rot. So, let me tell you: Disabuse yourself of all that right from the start. Every step you take, remember a police officer is first and foremost just that. If a police officer suspected his own mother of a crime, it'd be his duty to arrest her without turning so much as a hair."

"Yes, sir. Of course, sir."

The D.S.P. grunted, half-appeased.

"And remember this, too, young man. I'm not having a white woman murdered in my district and no one brought to justice."

"No, sir. I understand."

"Then off with you. Bring me the name of the leader of whichever pack of black swine did this, and you can count on me to hunt him down, and every last man jack of his gang."

Howard did not use the riding whip D.S.P. Mellish had recommended. But at the end of two days of going 'round to every village in the area—no need of a local constable to interpret—he felt altogether sure there had not been any marauding gang of dacoits anywhere on the morning Mabel Fellows had disappeared, leaving her pony to be found far away hours later. He knew the simple ryots he was seeing. If dacoits had come to their village, a glance aside from one among them at the wrong moment, or a child's words quickly muffled, any of a dozen such hints, would have betrayed the secret.

But who, in the long boredom of village life, does not like to talk over anything new? And Howard had things he wanted to know. So by the end of his two days of seemingly idle gossip, laced with an occasional deft question, he felt certain not only that Mrs. Fellows had not been killed by dacoits but that, hard-galloping rider though she was, she had not been the victim of an accident either. If two days ago she had fallen from her pony and broken her neck, her body would long before have been pinpointed by hovering vultures, hovering and then descending. And that descending, clumsy spiral of ungainly, long-necked birds would have been noted by every villager within sight. Fearing a lost buffalo or other disaster, they would have gone to find out what the birds' prey was. And they had seen nothing.

So, Howard thought with a sudden sinking feeling, the body of Mabel Fellows, former nurse at the district hospital, brusquely determined second wife of his chess mentor, dutiful second mother, too, to that ten-year-old imp of a girl, Lucy, had not been the victim of a dacoity, nor had her body been lying somewhere under the growing heat of the sun. No, riding out that fatal morning, she had—could it be?—met at some point someone from the station, most probably like herself out for early-morning exercise. And something then, surely, must have happened.

Yet on the day of Mrs. Fellows's disappearance, when his immediate search had failed to find any sign of her, bar her wandering pony, he had—this was beginning to seem more significant now—gone 'round asking every single rider in the small community of the station whether, out at exercise, they had happened to see her. No one said they had, and none of them, as he remembered, had been without some sort of an account of why they could not have met her.

All he had learnt was that Mabel Fellows never varied her ride. First, the sharp downward half mile to the river, then a mile-long canter beside its muddy bank. And next— what made it all worthwhile—the straight run, a delight to gallop, of two solid miles, rising gently to a knot of neem trees standing out against the skyline. Then at last coming back more slowly along the low ridge above the station, before dropping down to her bungalow, where she would tether the pony for the syce to see to, safe from snakes inside a garden where they were habitually caught and killed.

So what had happened? Had someone waited for her beside that clump of neem trees? There had been no dacoits in the area, that was certain. So can it have been—almost unthinkable—a sahib from the station who, for some unimaginable reason, had attacked her and later concocted some sort of account of his movements? Had he, after killing her, slung her body across his own horse and taken it to a place where it would not easily be discovered? But, no. Where was there in all the area 'round where a body could be left, however hidden, which jackals would not scent out? Scent out, drag to light, and gather to their feast, soon to be seen by the ever-vigilant circling vultures in the sky above? And no vultures had gone swooping down. That he knew.

And, besides, who among the men of the station and at the nearby district hospital—or, for that matter, the women in either place—had any sort of motive for wanting Mabel

Fellows dead? He could think of nothing, and he felt that living among them for six months or more, meeting most of them every day at the club, he had got to know who disliked and even hated whom, who had some sort of covert relationship with whom, who was a loner perhaps with a secret. There were not all that many people to have got to know about. And, more, Mabel Fellows played no great part in the station's life. She had her few friends among the nurses she had worked with at the hospital, and, more than this, burrowing into her recently acquired role as the memsahib at the Fellows' bungalow was still her almost total absorption.

Yet she had been murdered. There could be hardly any doubt about that. In the unlikely event that she had survived a fall from her pony and gone wandering off, she would have been found long before this. Of course, too, wives did desert their husbands, sometimes with little warning. Five years ago John Fellows's own first wife had, indeed, gone gallivanting off with one of the medicos at the hospital. But she had not left taking nothing at all with her.

Already Howard was beginning to fear this first murder case of his was either going to produce a solution which no one at all would like, or, perhaps more probable, produce no solution at all. Systematically, as he rode his own sturdy waler back to the station after yet another fruitless search for clues along the path of Mabel Fellows's ride, he went over in his mind all that he knew about her. Something in her life, however ordinary and everyday that had seemed to be, must have led to this vanishing. Yes, vanishing. It was the only word for it. Here was the distinguished archaeologist's respectable wife, who, as his own anxious inquiries had established even before he had been summoned to D.S.P. Mellish, had done nothing out of her ordinary routine. But she had just disappeared, as it were, into thin air.

Early each morning except Sunday, when with Lucy she attended matins at the church, Mabel Fellows had gone out on her pony. On her return, after taking a bath and changing, she had seen the khansamah and arranged with him the meals for the day. Next, still according to custom, she had made her inspection of the garden. Questioning the mali, an old, old man, thin, as they said, as a bamboo lathi, employed at the Fellows' bungalow for as long as anyone could remember. Fellows Memsahib, believing the pigeons sheltering in niches and projections inside the wide, ancient walls of the well in the garden were unhygienic, had become determined to condemn it. Mali, who needed a bulging goatskin for his watering each evening, had been desperately slow to find stones to fill the well in, much disliking the prospect of toiling up the long slope from the river. The tussle of wills had been going on for weeks, its outcome not certain to go to the seemingly more powerful.

After her garden inspection, Mabel used to take an hour's relaxation, reading or, in the absence of her husband who liked silence to work in, playing her piano—abominably thumpingly, Howard, who had sat through one or two evenings of music, guessed; tiffin came next. Then an afternoon rest under the flapping punkah in the bedroom, the punkahwallah rhythmically working as he squatted outside. As the day began to get cooler, lessons would follow for Lucy, sternly summoned from watching her friend Mali weeding away with his little axe-shaped kulhari, and then more reading or piano playing until it was time to snatch Lucy from a last hour spent crouching beside her crouching friend in the garden and send her off to bed. Finally it would be time to dress for dinner, unless there was bridge at the club with her friends among the hospital nurses.

An apparently unvarying routine. And nothing in it, if it was everything it seemed, to give the least clue to why Mabel Fellows had not returned from that morning ride.

Dismounting at the bungalow and giving his horse's reins to the hastily running-up syce, a terrible thought entered Howard's head. John Fellows was at this moment coming back to the family home, painfully slowly by train from one of the Indian Archaeological Institute meetings he attended in Calcutta. But what if on this occasion he had not gone to Calcutta? What if he had pretended he was going to a meeting, had departed, and then had left the train at the first convenient station and surreptitiously made his way back? No one would have thought to question an extra trip among the ones he took regularly. So could he . . . ? After all, though married for less than two years, he was not exactly a husband head over heels in love. No, when Susan had run off with her medico, he had, quite quickly, proposed marriage to the most suitable of the nurses from the hospital. He had needed someone to look after little Lucy, and himself. And in Mabel he had got just that, a formidably efficient housekeeper-cum-governess. It was not too cynical to say as much. Ask almost anyone at the club, and that would be their verdict. So what if she had ridden John on too tight a rein? Had pressed too often to have his much-cherished Lucy sent back home to school? Had at last aroused his slow resentment?

What was it Mr. Mellish said as he gave him his orders? *If a police officer suspected his own mother of a crime, it'd be his his duty to arrest her without turning so much as a hair.*

But, no. No, this was nonsense. He was never going to have to arrest John. John was not the sort of man to commit murder. Or was he? The chess player, with a chess player's cunning, farsightedness, and even perhaps ruthlessness. He certainly never gave as much as a pawn advantage to Howard, though he was scarcely better at the game than bright little Lucy. But before long the night train from Calcutta would arrive. Or . . . or did he board it in Calcutta? What if in truth he had never been there at all?

Well, it could easily be checked. One telegram to the right person in the Indian Archaeological Institute asking if John Fellows had received an earlier telegram telling him of his wife's disappearance, and at least this nightmare— who could have been more decent to him than John in the time he'd been there?—would be over. Even though the spectre of failure at his first big chance would still be there, hard to accept as ever.

And with that thought came another. No use him sending a telegram to Calcutta. To begin with, Howard had no idea who to send it to at the institute, and a discreet inquiry of this sort could hardly be sent to just anybody. It would have to go to a person of standing, and it would have to come from a person of standing, too. It would have to come, in fact, from D.S.P. Mellish, and no one else.

But asking Mr. Mellish to make the inquiry would be tantamount to telling him he was wrong about the death being a dacoity. Howard knew that he was wrong. But telling him so was quite another matter.

Yet the impossibly awkward task had to be done.

So he sent a message, strictly confidential, as fast as a constable could ride to district HQ. And in a very short time, just as he was leaving the Fellows bungalow after once more questioning all the servants, a reply came.

He tore the letter open.

Have you failed to wear your sola topee out in the sun? There can be no other explanation for your outrageous suggestion, which I have no intention of complying with whatsoever. Mrs. Fellows was the victim of an attack by dacoits. That is my instruction. Unless I hear within twenty-four hours that you have located the village where these men were harboured, I shall order you here to headquarters and take whatever disciplinary action I see fit.

J. R. Mellish, D.S.P.

He stood there in the heat of the sun. With, of course, his topee firmly on his head. And blank despair flooded through him. His career in the Indian police, like his father before him, was it to be ended before it had properly begun? What would his mother, back now at home, a widow with only her hopes for him to comfort her, say when she heard?

And what would Howard do? He was fit for nothing else but police work, police work here in India where he knew how life was led. Up among the sahibs. Down among the people. The humble ones like the old mali there. The Britons in their clubs.

He stood looking at the mali, emerging from the nasturtium bed where he had been grubbing away with his kulhari, a figure such as he had been aware of right from the days when he had just been able to toddle out into the garden of his own father's bungalow. A man so much of the parched Indian earth that he might have grown from out of it, or have been a spindly desiccated tree that had at last heaved its roots up from the harsh soil and begun slowly to move. A man who was in truth the soul of India, patient under all the burdens of the pitiless sun, the enraged monsoons, striving to keep alive, to go on from day to day snatching enough to eat, providing for wife and family and often enough seeing them die before him, taking a few hours of rest when and where he could, going on. Going on. Until the end came. Afterward to be born again to a new life and hopefully a better one, the reward of duty done.

Was he to lose all contact with such men? Would he, unemployable in India, have to make some wretched living in inhospitable England? A master at some second-rate prep school? Agent to some small-time landowner? Even a gentleman trooper in the British army?

And then he realised what the frail old man, unaccompanied for once by the warlike form of Lucy, was doing now. He was coming back into the garden, hefting a basket of large stones on his head, tramping with step-by-step slowness over toward the well.

He was taking another basket of stones—the implications of that burdened walk, slow as the progress of a lumbering, worn-out, half-starved bullock, bloomed in Howard's head—to add to those in the well which Mabel Fellows had ordered to be filled up for hygienic reasons. But Mabel Fellows was no longer there. The strict taskmistress, with whom long battle over weeks and weeks had been joined, was no longer there. She could not now order the well, with its easy supply of sweet water, to be closed. Knowing all he did of the wily, defensive evasiveness of the oppressed worker, it was clear that the old mali should have been hauling stones *out* of the well rather than adding to those already there.

So why was he not doing that?

Could the answer be that it was necessary to add a substantial layer of stones to those already at the bottom? Necessary in order to hide from wheeling vultures, snout-lifting jackals, that there was a body there? And—could it be?—that it was the old man who had put that body there? Or rather that Mabel Fellows had, after all, returned from her morning ride and, going past the well, had peered in to see what progress had been made in filling it? Could Mali have unthinkingly seized his opportunity to make sure Fellows Memsahib never won her battle with him? Only paradoxically to ensure, with her body lying there at the bottom, that the stone-filling had to go on?

Then, as there came a loud rattling as the old man tipped out the contents of his basket, Howard saw the snag.

Yes, Mali putting a body in the well could certainly account for his lugging that heavy basket of stones all the way there. And, all right, if this was what was happening for the reason he had guessed, the stones could be removed. Half a dozen constables would undo Mali's work in a quarter of an hour. But that did not account in any way for the fact that he himself had found Mabel Fellows's pony miles away from the Fellows bungalow, up near the cluster of neem trees on the ridge. So how could she have both abandoned the pony there, for whatever reason, and been simultaneously down in the bungalow garden, pony tethered, peering over the wall of the well?

What he needed now was a little time. Enough to try to work out if that snag could be got 'round or not. So, let the old man go slow step by slow step under the sun to fetch another basket load. And another, and another.

And, come to think, there might be a second snag, too. Little Lucy. Lucy at almost every hour of the day, unless she had been dragooned into her lessons or sent with her ayah off to bed, out in the garden crouching where Mali crouched, talking to him as easily as she talked English to her father over the chessboard. If Mali had indeed killed Mabel Fellows and tipped her body into the wide mouth of the well, then in all probability Lucy would have been there at the time. And that was simply an impossibility.

He stood wrestling with these likelinesses and unlikelinesses, watching old Mali come back from beyond the garden, another loaded basket dwarfing his thin, stooping body.

Yes, the old, old man—murderer or not—was making even slower progress with this load than with the last. In fact, he was at this moment standing stock-still, regaining his—

No. No, he was not. Quite suddenly the lathi-thin figure had toppled forward onto his face, sending the basket of stones rolling down the slight incline toward the well.

Howard set off at a run. And, half a minute later, kneeling beside the recumbent form he found, as he had known he would, a dead body. He paused a moment before summoning help, paying the old man who had laboured so long in this garden the tribute of . . . Of what? He hardly knew. A Christian prayer? A Hindu sloka of farewell. *Farewell, gardener. Farewell, murderer.*

And then, running toward the frail inert body, running like the will-of-the-wisp that she was, there was Lucy. There had been no possibility of stopping her. She must have been at one of the upstairs windows of the big bungalow, probably looking out for the tonga bringing her father from the train. And, like himself, she had seen that toppling collapse.

"Lucy," he said. "Yes, it is Mali. And I'm afraid he's dead. That last basket of stones was too much for him, poor fellow."

Then, with the words coming from he knew not where, he added something more. "You know, don't you, why he was going on filling in the well?"

"Yes," Lucy answered, with all the solemnity a child can sometimes muster. "Mali had to make sure the jackals didn't find her."

And, knowing now what he knew, he saw in that same instant the solution to the riddle he had, not five minutes earlier, found himself maddeningly puzzling at. Yes, of course Lucy had actually been there when Mali, her con-

stant companion, had ended the life of the intrusive new-
comer who had tormented both him and her. And, yes, she
had accepted that act, as she had accepted the facts when
her friend Mali killed a snake. So, at once the quick-
thinking, coolheaded little chess player had gone to Mabel's
pony, tethered where she had left it at the end of her ride,
had scrambled up onto its back, dug her naked heels into
its sides, and ridden hell-for-leather, unseen, up to the
clump of neem trees on the distant ridge. And then, sneak-
ing and sliding, she had made her way back the long two
miles and more, the now well-risen sun beating down on
her.

"Well, yes, Howard," D.S.P. Mellish said, "it was a good
thing I sat pretty firmly on that first notion of yours about
John Fellows not going to Calcutta. Damn lot of rot, of
course. But you seem to have made a decent fist of it all
in the end. Better than I expected. When those constables
taking the stones out of that well found the body with the
wound in the neck fitting that black devil's weeding tool,
there could be no question what had happened. And you
say you've got an explanation, too, for the pony being
found where it was? Not going to tell me it just wandered
away all that far, are you?"

"No, sir, no. No, I rather think this is what happened.
The little Fellows girl must have seen the pony tethered
where Mabel Fellows had left it, and—she's a bit of a monkey, you know—she must have simply gone for a ride on
her own. Something she's forbidden to do, of course. But
you know youngsters. And then, as was only to be expected, she evidently came a cropper somewhere up near
the ridge there, and, the little wretch, she just made her way
home on foot and said not a word about it. I hinted to her
that I'd guessed about that bit of naughtiness, and though
she didn't admit it, I saw the look in her eye. Little minx."

"Yes. Yes, no doubt that was it. So, well done, Howard.
You know, I see this as being the first in a string of suc-
cesses for you going on till you get to retirement. Yes, we'll
make something of you yet."

Elizabeth Foxwell's first short story, "Unsinkable," appeared in Crime Through Time. *Since then she has published stories elsewhere, along with several articles on mysteries and on independent women, such as her protagonist in the following story, Alice Roosevelt, about whom her father, Theodore, once said, "I can run the country or I can control Alice; I can't do both."*

Elizabeth has also edited magazines and edited or coedited several anthology series, including Malice Domestic 7 *and* Murder, They Wrote. *She is a serious student of the women's movement in the early 1900s, but that doesn't mean she can't have fun with the subject as well, as "Come Flit by Me" clearly proves.*

COME FLIT BY ME

Elizabeth Foxwell

I was smoking on the White House roof, contemplating the towering obelisk of the Washington Monument in the twilight and the eternal question of how to pay my overdue clothing account, when the summons came.

"Alice!"

I did not answer. My clothing allowance was a serious matter, worthy of deep and undisturbed concentration. As the president's eldest and much-photographed daughter, I had an obligation to look my best. Unfortunately my parents had a more limited view, simply not grasping that $50,000—Father's salary—was insufficient to meet my pressing needs, especially with my imminent debut. Like Father, I had a public to consider. Like Father, I was plain stubborn.

"Alice Lee Roosevelt!" Ethel's head poked out the window. "Are you smoking again?"

"Just keeping my word." I took another delicious drag. "I promised I would not smoke under Father's roof. *Voilà*— cigarette *al fresco*."

Her little forehead creased in consternation. Ethel was my opposite—the obedient, good-hearted daughter who, at ten years of age, mothered our tribe of eight and worried over any dissension in our close family ranks.

"Shouldn't you be in bed?" I asked.

"Archie and Quentin are. Kermit and Ted are waiting for the carriages—I think dropping water balloons on the coachmen is their plan, the naughty boys." Her tone was affectionate. "I offered to fetch you. They're waiting for you downstairs."

"Oh, bother." Although I was the first daughter of the president to have her debut in the White House, I was dreading it. Mother—my stepmother, actually, because my mother, Alice Lee, had died at my birth—had forbidden champagne and the *de rigueur* expensive party favors for the guests, and since there was no hardwood floor in that hideous mausoleum of an East Room, we would be dancing on a colorless, coarse fabric called crash. The term was appropriate—I would fall on my face in the scornful eyes of the Four Hundred with this fancy-dress wake. My sense of gloom deepened.

"ALICE!" A stentorian roar erupted from below, shaking the stately white columns—and I had no doubt who belonged to the Executive Bellow.

"Please tell them I'm dressing," I told Ethel, and she complied like the good little soul she was, ducking inside. Reluctantly, I stubbed out the cigarette, climbed over the windowsill, and eyed the white chiffon dress embroidered with rosebuds and beached on the bed like a dead whale. I had wanted black—a dramatic departure from the usual debutante insipidness—but Mother, who would rather be run through with a sword than accused of impropriety, had nearly swooned at the suggestion.

As my maid slithered the dress over my head, I considered whether to wheedle Grandpa Lee again for the dress money. He was a Cabot and usually indulgent, but the check would come with the inevitable lecture about extravagant companions, and I did not care for a repeat performance. I worried at the question as my blondish hair (the newspapers had not yet decided on the color) was drawn up into an elegant pompadour and the obligatory debutante pearls were placed around my neck. Tilting my chin to a defiant angle, I yanked on my gloves, then walked down the stairs to face The Ordeal.

Pink and white roses and narcissus frothed over the mantel of the East Room, and green garlands wound through the sparkling crystal chandeliers. The portrait of General Washington veiled in smilax seem to appeal for release. I knew how he felt. With a suppressed shudder, I avoided looking at the floor with its horrid shroud and hurried through to the Blue Room, which bore a more dainty and welcoming touch in its yards of asparagus-vine garlands and palms.

Mother, in white lace and purple orchids, and Father, bristling and barrel-chested in evening dress, stood among a gaggle of Roosevelt relatives. It was still quite early, well before the bewitching hour of ten o'clock when Mother and I would receive over three hundred guests. "Straighten up, dear—you look positively sulky," was Mother's hissed version of a welcome, fidgeting with her pendant with its three large diamonds.

I glanced in the glass, which revealed a figure all in frothy white with smoldering gray-blue eyes. Far from slouching, I always walked and stood very upright, a legacy from a childhood onslaught of heavy leg braces. Mother's nerves must be overwrought, I decided. I had a warmer reception from my female cousins and Aunt Bamie, Father's sister, her plain but charming features illuminated by white silk.

Hovering near Mother were Cousin Franklin and a knot of Harvard boys. He detached himself and walked about me as if appraising a fine piece of art. With his chiseled features and carefully brilliantined hair, Franklin reminded me of—and dressed like—Little Lord Fauntleroy, and he provoked me into being outrageous if only to keep him and his invincible ego off balance.

"Tally-ho, Alice. The bachelors are afoot."

"Franklin," I said *sotto voce*, with my sweetest smile.

"Go run for something. Preferably a brick wall."

"My, someone *is* in a disagreeable temper," he observed, unperturbed. "Did your snake forget to bite a Republican today?"

"A small problem with an overdue account—stand *still*, Franklin." I rapped him sharply on his flitting knuckles with my fan. "You will keep fluttering. It's no wonder we call you Feather Duster—you can't remain still for two minutes."

He displayed his unquenchable grin. "The better to appreciate your beauty, my dear Alice."

"Does Eleanor know you're flirting with her own cousin?" I asked, undiverted. "Pity she's at school and unable to oversee you personally."

"Ah, but she knows your dainty hand is firmly on the reins," said he with a soulful wink, and I pealed with laughter and gave him another rap across the knuckles for good measure. Both Mother and Father frowned, not pleased when I attracted attention to myself. But Franklin could be awfully fun, when he forgot about being a prig.

"Who has been torn away from the *Harvard Crimson* for this occasion?" I inquired, looking at the delegation from Boston. The knot had re-formed around Mother, and Franklin took my elbow and steered me over to them.

"I believe you know Jay . . ."

I smiled politely and Jay—DeLancey Jay, great-great-grandson of John Jay, first chief justice of the Supreme Court—returned it with a dazzled sheen to his eyes. Oh blast, I thought.

"Miss Alice, what a pleasure to see you again."

"And you, Mr. Jay."

He looked hurt, like a kicked puppy. "I thought you would call me by my first name."

Mentally I consigned Mr. Jay to his great-great-grandfather's mausoleum, and turned my head gratefully for Franklin's next introduction, praying for rescue.

"And Arthur Crowe. Arthur refused me the pearly gates of the Porcellian."

The Porcellian Club was the premiere club at Harvard—
Father's own, and Franklin's father's.

The rather porcine Arthur blinked out of piggy, good-
natured eyes. "Aw, Franklin, you said you'd forgotten all
about it, there's a good fellow."

"My dear Arthur." Franklin slung a comradely arm
around him. "Of course I have. Just my feeble attempt at
a joke. Arthur's family is in bacon," he explained to me.

"How appropriate," I commented. As Franklin's face
contorted and the porcine Arthur beamed beatifically at me,
I decided that Arthur did not specialize in deep cogitation.
He probably had been told by his club brethren to be a
good fellow and vote as they decreed. Well, a little rejection
would do the supremely confident Franklin no harm.

Alan Whitbourne and David Hayes Sutton both followed
Arthur, and Franklin retired to pay respectful attention to
Mother.

"Hello," said the very tall Whitbourne, fascinated by the
white rosebuds on my sleeve.

"Hello," said the very short Hayes Sutton, engrossed by
the hem of my skirt.

"Good-bye," I said, turning a limp shoulder as they
laughed nervously. Unprepossessing but rather callow
youths. I resigned myself to an unspectacular and dull evening of platitudes.

Suddenly one of my cousins swooned, neatly collapsing
in a crumple of pink satin, shifting the attention and a number of people to her side. Fool, I reflected crossly as Arthur
fanned an ineffectual handkerchief in her face and Aunt
Bamie waved smelling salts under her nose. She will keep
her stays too tight, I thought. Ridiculous things.

On the edge of the group I heard Mother give a little
gasp and I moved to her side. "What is it?"

"Oh, dear. I thought I had worn my diamond pendant . . ."

She had. I now looked at her throat, which bore the
obligatory pearls, but not the pendant. I looked at the floor.
No pendant.

"I'll find it."

"It's not important."

Yes, it was. Mother would worry and sigh about the missing jewelry all evening, and Father would turn up the crash *and* the muddy carpet underneath it, and overturn every basket of carnations, searching while the reporters' pencils raced across their pads, and Franklin's branch of the family would turn up their well-bred noses at "those Oyster Bay Roosevelts." The crash was bad enough; I could not allow my debut to become a complete disaster.

"I'll take care of it, Mother," I said firmly.

"Don't make a spectacle of yourself and *don't* accuse anyone of theft," she ordered.

"I shall be dainty and demure as the first breath of spring," I said, dropping a perfect if saucy curtsy, and moved away to consult with my aunts.

Yes, they had remembered the pendant but not it dropping from Mother's throat. I turned to Father—or rather tried to. He was declaiming about the Panama Canal, and I could not catch his eye without calling attention to Mother's predicament. I would be unable to for at least an hour, if Father had a typically full head of steam.

Turning on my heel, my eye fell on the adoring Mr. Jay. I smiled encouragingly, and he moved so quickly he nearly tripped over his own feet. "Mr. Jay," I murmured, trying to peer discreetly into his coat.

"DeLancey," he insisted.

"Of course," I said smoothly, brushing a finger lightly across his lapel. No. Nothing incriminating there. "I wonder if you would be so kind as to fetch me a cup of that delicious punch."

"My pleasure, Miss Alice." He hurried off.

"I never knew you for a fondness for punch," remarked Franklin in passing.

"Only if it has a healthy shot of whiskey in it." I drifted over to Mr. Hayes Sutton and Mr. Whitbourne, peppering them with a stream of bright questions about college life and examining their pockets at the same time. Then it was on to Mr. Crowe.

"Shocking," he mumbled, returning his handkerchief to

his breast pocket, and I realized he meant my cousin's swoon. His right pocket bulged, but whether it was due to jewelry or excess flesh I was not certain. I fluttered my fan in a weak fashion.

"Mr. Crowe, I fear I, too, may be a bit faint. Would you lend me your arm?"

The small eyes widened at the alarming prospect of further maidenly distress. "Oh! Certainly, Miss Roosevelt."

"Let's just step from the room for a breath of air," I suggested cozily, and he readily agreed.

Once we were in the hall, I leaned heavily on Crowe's arm. I am taller than most of my delicate contemporaries and a hearty eater. So when he staggered from the additional mass of weight and whalebone, I slipped my hand easily into his pocket. Mother's pendant appeared, glittering, between my fingers.

"Alice, are you unwell?" Franklin paused, looking from the pendant in my perfectly steady and unswooning hand to his sweating friend and back again.

"Thank you, Franklin. I am quite fit." I fixed my gaze on Crowe. "Mr. Crowe, may I ask what my mother's necklace is doing in your jacket?"

Rivulets of sweat ran down his porcine features.

"Dear me, Arthur." Franklin shook his head mournfully. "And I thought you had recovered from your 'little problem' of picking up what does not belong to you. How distressing."

"En . . . look here, Miss Roosevelt. I have this little . . . weakness. Don't even know I'm doing it. I honestly don't remember removing Mrs. Roosevelt's pendant. I'd count it a favor if you would—ahem—perhaps overlook this unfortunate occurrence?"

I remembered that Mr. Crowe's family was rolling in bacon, and a little pork might not be inappropriate applied to my own position. I fanned myself briskly. "With my overdue dress account weighing so *heavily* on my mind, it's a wonder I can remember anything."

Arthur's face went blank as his mind worked mightily to

absorb this intelligence, then the light gradually dawned and he reached for his checkbook.

I turned to Franklin. "For heaven's sake, hold your tongue or you'll have Father nosing into this matter personally. He still fancies himself the commissioner of police."

"Right," promised Franklin, and Arthur blanched at the thought of Father's formidable breath on his neck. He fanned the check to dry the ink, then handed it to me. "I trust this remedies any . . . misunderstanding? Perhaps we might have a dance later, Miss Roosevelt?"

I glimpsed the amount, folded the check, and tucked it neatly into my glove without any unseemly gloating, although I was sorely tested. "I shouldn't be at all surprised, Mr. Crowe."

He beamed with relief and waddled—er, walked—back to the Blue Room. Franklin made as if to follow him, but I grasped his arm. The firm reins.

"I want to know something."

"What is it?"

"How you removed Mother's necklace and slipped it into Arthur's pocket."

His eyes widened in elaborate innocent astonishment.

"Oh, spare me the theatrics, Franklin," I snapped. "I'm not feeble, unlike poor Arthur, who doesn't have the nerve or the brains to lift a valuable necklace from the first lady's throat in full view of a roomful of people. And our cousin's swoon was remarkably timely. Of course she insists on lacing herself into apoplexy, but she is very agreeable, is she not, for doing a turn for a favorite relative? That faint was remarkably artistic—as artistic as your removing Mother's necklace while she was distracted, and replanting it in Arthur's pocket."

I leveled my eyes at him—the straight, piercing gaze that Father always insisted on. "Arthur blackballed you from Porcellian. That must have smarted, with all the Roosevelt history in the club, and especially excruciating when facing Father, if you have any political ambitions at all, which I believe you do. Confounding Crowe before the president's daughter must have been too delicious an opportunity to miss."

"Guilty as charged." He bowed, hand over his heart. "Why didn't you give the game away?"

"I can hardly make a scene at my own debut. Mother was quite specific about that."

"Although it's quite all right to indulge in blackmail."

I opened up my eyes very wide, imitating his gesture. "My dear Franklin, what a vulgar word. I merely offered an opportunity to salve his guilty conscience." I adjusted my gloves serenely. "It just so happened to coincide with my own fish to fry. Designer fish."

He laughed. "You are incorrigible, Alice." He offered me his arm, and I accepted it graciously. En route to the Blue Room, he added, "Perhaps you should investigate as a rule. You have a gift for it."

I snorted. "Alice Lee Roosevelt, a Pinkerton? The idea." But the compliment held a certain appeal. Certainly tonight had been diverting. It would be a matter for further, smoky reflection on the White House roof.

Poor Mr. Jay waited patiently with the long-forgotten cup of punch. I managed a polite sip and handed it back to him with a dazzling smile that promised amends. Then I slipped behind Mother and refastened the necklace behind her neck. Arthur contrived to look elsewhere.

"Oh, you found it." She sighed, fingering it with relief. "Thank you, dear."

Touched by her gratitude, I kissed her cheek. "My pleasure, Mother."

"Did the catch loosen?"

Franklin winked and strolled off, whistling what the press considered my personal tune, the tiresome "Alice, Where Art Thou?"

"In a manner of speaking," I answered, frowning at Franklin's cheeky back, and smoothing into place a strand of hair loosened during the night's events.

"Oh, Alice," she said, closing her eyes in long-suffering patience. "You are a trial."

"I hope so, Mother. I certainly hope so." I craned my

head, very unladylike, scrutinizing the growing receiving line. "Good Lord, is that Daisy Leiter in red satin? She looks like a madam."

"ALICE!" bellowed the chief executive. And I smiled.

Before writing mystery novels, Margaret Coel published four nonfiction books on the history of Colorado and the American West. Her articles have appeared in such publications as The New York Times *and* American Heritage of Invention & Technology *and have been included in numerous anthologies.*

She is the author of the acclaimed Wind River mystery series set among the Arapaho on the Wind River Reservation in Wyoming. The novels feature Jesuit priest Father John O'Malley and Arapaho attorney Vicky Holden. The Dallas Morning News has called Coel "a vivid voice for the West, its struggles to retain its past and at the same time enjoy the fruits of the future."

For this story, Margaret goes back to one of her early nonfiction books on the early railroad in Colorado. As an extra bit of spice, she adds as her sleuth the unsinkable and unflappable Molly Brown.

MURDER ON THE DENVER EXPRESS

Margaret Coel

"Looks like you got yourself some toned traveling companions, Mol," Daniel said.

Molly Brown followed her brother's gaze across the platform of the Leadville depot. The Denver Express stood on the near track, steam belching along the coach and the first-class cars. A plume of gray smoke, dense and ash-scented, cut through the cold morning air. Passengers surged about the conductor at the foot of the steps.

Molly knew it wasn't the miners in bulky coats and slouch hats or the women struggling to hold on to squirming children that her brother was referring to. It was the pair of elderly women starting up the steps, heads aloft under wide-brimmed hats, gloved hands daintily lifting the skirts of their traveling coats, and the handsome middle-aged couple, both swathed in long gray coats, who followed the women into the first-class car.

"You're gonna have yourself a real boring trip," Daniel went on in that teasing voice that had made her pummel him with tiny fists when they were growing up. "If you wasn't so toned yourself, Mol, you'd be ridin' in the coach where you'd have a good visit with some real folks."

"The likes of yourself, I suppose." Molly laid a gloved hand on her favorite brother's arm and tried to ignore the cloud of gloom that always settled over her at the conclusion of each visit home. Leadville still felt like home. The narrow, sloped-roof houses, wagons rattling through the streets, whistles shrieking from mines carved into the mountains above town, miners bellowing outside the saloons day and night—all welcome and familiar, unlike the quiet around her new home on Denver's Pennsylvania Street.

She and her husband, J.J., had lived in Denver two years now, since 1894 when J.J. had struck gold in the Little Jonny Mine. The strike had surprised everyone, with the exception of J.J. Leadville was a silver town. Even after the silver market collapsed the year before—plunging Colorado's millionaires into bankruptcy—most mining engineers had clung to the belief that Leadville's mountains would disgorge only silver—not gold. But J.J. had believed otherwise, a happy circumstance that had made the Browns rich beyond imagining.

"Why, there's Charles Langford," Molly said, her attention diverted to the tall, light-haired gentleman in the chinchilla coat striding alongside the train. He held a small black case.

Daniel's expression took on that blank look that always appeared when she had leapt ahead. "President of the Denver Western Bank," she explained. "Must've come to Leadville on business. I saw him yesterday, too, outside the Vendome Hotel." She blinked back the image of Langford darting around the corner of Harrison Avenue. Most likely he hadn't seen her.

Daniel looked away, but not before she had caught the disappointment shadowing his eyes. "You and J.J. sure got a lot of fancy new friends now," her brother said.

"Oh, I'm sure the Langfords and the Browns will soon be friends." Molly tried for a cheerful tone. "The Langfords live only a block away—on Logan Street. Yes, we're certain to become friends, and you'll surely meet them one day, too." She let her gaze roam over the platform, hoping to see Clarissa Langford. What a stroke of luck it would be to travel with a prominent member of Denver's Sacred Thirty-six. Why, she could convince Clarissa that the Browns had more than a gold mine to recommend them to society. After all, J.J. was a brilliant mining engineer, and she had read dozens of books and was learning to speak French. Molly sighed. Clarissa Langford was nowhere in sight.

As the locomotive emitted a series of shrill whistles, the depot door flew open and two women hurried across the platform. They couldn't have been more than eighteen or nineteen, Molly realized, only a few years younger than herself. Obviously women with their own living to get: the black cloaks neatly brushed and patched, the worn, polished boots, the everyday struggle to appear respectable.

For the briefest moment Molly caught the eye of the smaller woman as she hurried by. She had a pale, delicately shaped face, almost like a child's, and long golden hair that fell around the folds of her hood. She carried a brown canvas grip, holding it ahead in both hands. The cloak swung open to reveal a dress as blue as the Leadville sky.

The taller girl had pulled her hood forward around a mass of dark hair. She allowed her companion to board while she stood at the foot of the steps, glancing up and down the platform, eyes wide in fright. Finally she followed the other girl into the coach car.

Molly noticed the round-shouldered man in the red plaid coat standing in the depot doorway, his gaze trailing the two young women. He was hatless, black hair slicked back from a fleshy, mottled face with the gray pallor of a man who has spent too many days underground. He flipped aside a cigarette and started for the train.

"All aboard!" the conductor shouted. Molly planted a kiss on Daniel's cheek. No doubt he was right, but she would take a vow of silence before she would give him the satisfaction of hearing her admit that she was in for a boring trip in the first-class car.

The conductor doffed his blue cap as she approached the train. "Welcome aboard, Mrs. Brown."

Molly tossed aside the small red-leather copy of *Easy Lessons in French Grammar*. She glanced at the silver watch pinned to the bodice of her black traveling dress. Four more hours to Denver. The oil lantern swayed overhead, and sounds of wheels on rails filled the private compartment— *clickety-clack, clickety-clack*. In the distance, brakes squealed and a whistle bleated. The little station at the top of Kenosha Pass slid by the window, and the train started on the downgrade, winding along a narrow ledge blasted out of the mountainside. Far below, a mosaic of sunlight and shadow lay over the South Park.

She had been cooped up in the small compartment now for almost six hours, except for the twenty-minute stopover in Como, where she had disembarked and gone to the Pacific Hotel dining room for a slice of apple pie and a cup of coffee. None of the other first-class passengers had left the train. Obviously they were content being cooped up in small compartments.

"What the hell," Molly said out loud, startled by the sound of her own voice. Perhaps there were rules for a lady traveling alone, but sometimes rules had to be broken. She decided to visit the coach car and find some real folks to talk to. She withdrew a silver compact from her pocketbook and dabbed at her cheeks with the powder puff. Tiny laugh lines fanned from the corners of her eyes, which were the blue of morning glories. She patted back the red curls that sprang around her face and fixed them into place with ivory combs. Then she slid the compact back into her pocketbook.

As she started to her feet, the train banked into a curve, swaying on the outside rail toward the mountain drop-off. The lantern swung wildly on its chain. Molly grasped the window bar to keep from being pitched to the floor. She froze, disbelieving her own eyes. Outside, a girl was soaring over the ledge, face turned heavenward, blue dress and long, golden hair flowing in space. In a half instant she was gone, a bird swooping into the shadows far below.

Molly pressed herself against the cold windowpane. She could hear her heart drumming. "Saints preserve us," she whispered. Either the girl had jumped from the train backward—a notion Molly dismissed as ridiculous—or someone had flung her from the train.

Molly crossed the compartment and threw open the door. "Conductor!" she shouted. From somewhere came the sharp, unmistakable snap of a door closing.

She hurried along the corridor, shouting again for the conductor. As she stepped into the gangway, the rush of cold air whipped at her skirt and plucked her hair loose from the ivory combs. The floor bucked beneath her feet. With a kind of horror, Molly realized she was leaning against the railing over which the poor girl must have been thrown.

"Conductor!" Molly shouted again as she plunged into the coach car. The odors of damp wool, cigar smoke, and sausage filled the air. Heads snapped around and eyes stared at her. The man in the red plaid coat leaned over his armrest and framed her in his gaze. " 'Spect you'll find the conductor back with the fine folks," he said.

She swung around and retraced her steps into the first-class car, shouting again and again for the conductor. The door at the far end creaked open, and the elderly women appeared around the frame and stared at her over tiny wire-rimmed glasses perched halfway down their noses. Another door opened. The man in the gray suit stepped out, blocking her way. "What's the meaning of this disturbance?" he demanded.

"A girl's been murdered," Molly said. Her frankness surprised her. She hadn't wanted to admit what she knew must be true: No one could survive being hurled from the train over the steep mountainside. The two elderly women darted back inside their compartment.

"Ridiculous," the man said. "This is a first-class car."

Molly felt the pressure of a hand on her arm. "Allow me to be of assistance, Mrs. Brown." It was a man's voice, low and close to her ear.

Molly pivoted about and stared up at Charles Langford, who lifted his chin, as if, with a snap of his fingers, he might banish the cause of her alarm. He was boyishly handsome, with a long, patrician nose, deeply set brown eyes, and sand-colored hair parted in the middle above a high forehead that gave him the look of intelligence. "Whatever is the matter?" he asked.

"A girl was thrown from the train." Molly heard her words tumbling together. Her breath came in quick, sharp jabs that pricked her chest like needles.

"You saw it?" Langford's forehead creased in thought.

"Yes," Molly said. "Well, not exactly. But I saw the girl flying over the ledge. We must stop the train."

"You mustn't concern yourself further, Mrs. Brown," Langford said in a low tone meant to soothe her. "I'll notify the conductor. You can return to your compartment now."

"Please do so," said the man in gray. "And allow us to complete our trip without further disturbance."

Molly felt a sting of anger and disappointment. "You don't understand." She kept her eyes on Langford. "The girl may still be alive." She doubted that was the case. "We have to go back."

"Now, now, Mrs. Brown." Langford took her arm again and began tugging her toward her own compartment. "The conductor will follow the proper procedures."

"The conductor! He's nowhere around. We have to stop now." Molly jerked herself free and started running along the corridor, eyes fastened on the small box tucked under the ceiling near the gangway door. A red handle protruded from the box, and underneath, black letters swayed with the train: EMERGENCY BRAKE.

"No!" Langford shouted as Molly reached up and pulled on the handle with all of her strength. The handle snapped downward.

A loud screech ripped through the sounds of the whistle and the blasts of steam coming from the locomotive. The train began to contract and reassemble, swaying sideways, jerking forward and back again. Metal squealed against metal; wood groaned and snapped. Molly huddled against the window as the two men stumbled against her, then righted themselves. Somewhere a woman was screaming. Gradually the train came to a stop, and the sounds gave way to the shrill blasts of the whistle.

The gangway door crashed open, sending a burst of cold air into the corridor. The conductor stood in the opening, his mouth forming words that appeared to be stuck in his throat. "What . . . what . . . what . . ." he stuttered. "What have you done?" He threw both hands into the air.

"This woman is mad." It was the voice of the man in the gray suit.

"I'm so sorry," Langford said. "I tried to prevent this."

Molly grabbed the lapels of the conductor's blue coat. "A girl was thrown off the train at the big curve. We must back up and find her."

"Back up?" The conductor stared at her in disbelief—she might have uttered an obscenity. His massive chest rose and fell as he took in great gulps of air. "That is impossible," he said, withdrawing a white handkerchief from inside his waistcoat and mopping at his face.

"Stout! Where are you?" The man's voice came from outside.

"My engineer," the conductor muttered. He stepped into the gangway, opened the gate, and started down, boots thumping on the steps. Molly followed. She hurried to keep up as they strode alongside the train. Tongues of steam flicked from the underside of the cars, but the wind stabbing at her face and hands was as cold as ice. A few feet away, the ledge dropped off into the chasm below.

The engineer came toward them, clapping mittened hands together against the cold. He wore a padded coat buttoned to the neck and a slouch hat pulled low over his ears. "What's the meaning of this?" he yelled. "There's an extra freight coming behind us. I whistled out the brakemen to set the warning flares, but if the engineer misses 'em, we're gonna be knocked off the mountain."

The conductor tilted his head back toward Molly. "This woman says she saw a girl thrown off the train at the big curve."

Molly stepped forward. "I am Mrs. J. J. Brown," she said, struggling to keep her voice steady in the cold. "I demand you back up and attend to the poor girl."

"J. J. Brown of Leadville?" A look of respect and admiration came into the engineer's eyes.

"Formerly of Leadville. We are wasting time, sir."

The engineer shook his head. "It is impossible to back up, Mrs. Brown. We'll telegraph the police from Pine Grove. Now we must proceed." He gave a little bow and started again for the locomotive.

"All aboard, all aboard," the conductor called as Molly followed him back through the knots of passengers who had also disembarked. Suddenly a chill unrelated to the cold ran down her spine. What had she done? Given the killer a chance to walk away? She stepped toward the ledge, eyes searching the track that stretched in both directions from the train. No sign of anyone walking away. But where could the killer walk to? They were on a narrow ledge, high on a mountainside, miles from the nearest town. The killer would wait until they pulled into Pine Grove.

Molly caught up with the conductor. "There's a murderer on board," she said. "You must not allow anyone to leave the train. You must telegraph the Denver police to meet us."

"Madam, you will allow me to do my job." The conductor took her arm and turned her toward the steps where Charles Langford was waiting.

"I'll see Mrs. Brown on board," Langford said, looking back at the conductor. Then he guided Molly up the steps and into the first-class corridor. They stopped at the first door. The sound of three long whistles filled the air as the train started to lurch forward.

Molly said, "I saw the girl boarding in Leadville. She was with a traveling companion, a tall, dark-haired girl."

"A traveling companion." Langford seemed to turn the idea over in his mind a moment. "My dear Mrs. Brown, the authorities will look into the details of this unfortunate incident."

Molly studied the relaxed, confident face—the face of a

man who understood the world into which she and J.J. had taken only the first tentative steps. There was so much to learn. Still . . . "It would seem a simple matter to find the companion and learn what she may know," she said.

A gentle smile spread across Langford's handsome face. "If, indeed, the girl was thrown from the train, as you insist, Mrs. Brown"—a slight hesitation—"she could hardly be one of our sort. I am certain Mr. Brown would not approve of your meddling in this matter. Unfortunately, you are bereft of his wise guidance at this moment. As a gentleman, I must stand in for your good husband and shield you from your womanly inclinations."

Langford opened the compartment door. "Allow me to fetch you a tonic for your nerves," he said, stepping past her. The compartment was almost a duplicate of hers: green plush seat, lantern swaying overhead as the train gathered speed. Stuffed in the overhead rack was the chinchilla coat.

"No need to put yourself to any further trouble." Molly had no intention of drinking something that might dull her senses. She wanted to make certain the conductor did not allow anyone to leave the train at Pine Grove.

"Nonsense. It's no trouble at all. You will find the tonic most soothing." The man had opened a black case on the seat and was pouring a ginger-colored liquid from a small crystal decanter into a glass. A pungent odor that Molly couldn't identify drifted across the compartment.

"Here you are," he said, holding out the glass. "This will help you recover from your shock. You have only to open your mouth."

"Undoubtedly some people on this train would prefer me with my mouth closed, Mr. Langford," Molly said, giving him a polite smile and starting toward her own compartment. Footsteps sounded behind her, and she realized he was following her.

Molly opened her door, then hesitated. A cold understanding flooded over her: The murdered girl's companion was also in danger. Molly had seen the anxious way the dark-haired girl had looked around the platform, as if she had wanted to make certain no one was following. Unfortunately, the girl hadn't seen the man in the plaid coat watching from the depot doorway.

Turning back to Langford, Molly said, "I'm sure some-one was after the murdered girl. He must've gotten her in the gangway, where he threw her overboard. He may try to kill her companion to keep her from telling what she knows."

"My dear Mrs. Brown," Langford began, a condescending note in his tone, "you have a most vivid imagination. If you choose to pursue this matter, I must warn you that it will harm your reputation. No one whose name appears in the newspaper in connection with a scandal could expect an invitation to the holiday dance at the Denver Country Club."

Molly backed into her compartment, closed the door, and leaned against the paneling, marveling at the proposition Charles Langford had made her. She had only to remain in her compartment until the train pulled into Denver Union Station, and an invitation to the holiday dance would be hers. Hers and J.J.'s, although she knew the real challenge would lie in convincing J.J. to attend.

She closed her eyes and swayed in rhythm with the train, imagining herself in J.J.'s arms, gliding across the polished floor of the Denver Country Club, orchestral music filling the perfumed air, and all of the Sacred Thirty-six admiring the gown she would have made for the occasion. She had waited two years for this invitation.

Her eyes snapped open. She could wait awhile longer. The dark-haired girl was in danger now.

Molly flung open the door and hurried to the coach car. At the far end, a small group of miners waited outside the water closet. Other passengers sat upright, eyes ahead, as if on the lookout for the killer in their midst. Molly gripped the backs of the seats and pulled herself along the aisle, looking for the dark-haired girl. She stopped at the vacant seat across from the man in the red plaid coat. Tossed in the seat was a single black cloak, the fabric shiny and thin, a patch neatly stitched to the hood. She felt her heart turn over. The girl was gone.

Molly whirled toward the man across the aisle. "Where is the girl with dark hair?" she demanded.

The man moved his head from side to side as if to bring Molly into clearer focus. "Ain't you the lady that seen her get tossed off the train?" His voice had the scratchy texture of tobacco.

"You're mistaken." Molly held the man's gaze. "The blond girl in the blue dress was thrown from the train."

"Beggin' your pardon"—the man shook his head—"but the pretty one with the long yellow hair got off at Como." Shouts and hard thuds came from the front of the coach. Molly glanced around. Two miners were pounding on the water closet door. Turning away from the commotion, she said, "What makes you believe the blond woman disembarked at Como?"

"I got her grip down from the rack. Took it out to the platform myself." A wistful smile played at the corners of the man's mouth. "She was a pretty thing. I seen her back at the Leadville depot. Don't mind sayin' I was lookin' forward to gettin' acquainted. Too bad she was only goin' as far as Como."

Molly tried to swallow back the alarm rising inside her. Obviously the man had concocted a story meant to exonerate himself: she had seen the girl flying over the ledge when the train was twenty miles beyond Como. And where was the dark-haired girl? Had he also tossed her from the train?

The shouts and pounding were louder, angrier. Looking around, Molly saw that the conductor had joined the group. She started toward him. "Mr. Stout," she called. "A girl is missing—"

"Please, Mrs. Brown." The conductor waved a hand in the air. "One emergency at a time." He turned and rapped on the door. "Open up!" he shouted. "There's folks need the facilities."

Molly stared at the closed door. So that was where the dark-haired girl had gone to. She was hiding from a killer. Molly pushed through the crowd of miners and, ignoring the look of astonishment on the conductor's face, knocked hard on the door. "This is Mrs. J.J. Brown," she called. "I know what happened to your friend. No one is going to harm you. You can come out now."

The only sounds were those of the miners drawing in sharp breaths, the wheels rattling beneath the floor. Slowly the door slid open. The girl leaned against the frame, dark curls pressed around a pale face, both hands clasped under her chin. Her knuckles rose in little white peaks.

One of the miners sneered. "About time."

Molly placed an arm around the girl's thin shoulders and drew her forward. As she guided her past the men, Molly called back: "Mr. Stout, please join us in my compartment."

Laura Binkham sat at the far end of the plush seat, huddled against the window. Molly sat beside her, legs tucked sideways to make room for the conductor, who leaned back against the compartment door, arms folded across his broad chest. The murdered girl—"A good girl, she was," Laura said—was Effie Rogers. "She never meant to go wrong, but after she was let go . . ." Laura sniffled and dabbed at her eyes with the handkerchief Molly had handed her.

"Let go?" Molly prodded.

"From the grand house where Effie was the second-floor girl. Times got hard after the silver crash. Lots of fancy people couldn't keep help like me and Effie anymore."

Molly pictured the fine mansions in Leadville, the army of former domestics searching for other employment after the silver market had crashed. Even she and J.J. had hit upon hard times, until J.J. had struck gold.

The girl went on: "I was the lucky one. My mistress kept me on at half wages. Leastwise I had a roof over my head. Not like Effie. She caught on at a shop on Harrison Avenue, but the wages wasn't enough to keep her. What choice did she have?" The girl pressed her lips together against the answer; light from the overhead lantern glinted in her dark eyes.

"Effie began entertaining gentlemen friends, is that it?" Molly was beginning to understand: One of the friends was the man in the red plaid coat—a man Effie had most likely rejected.

The conductor shifted from one foot to the other; his uniform made a scratchy sound against the door. "I hardly think any of this matters, Mrs. Brown."

"Please go on," Molly said to the girl.

"I told Effie, you gotta get hold of your gentleman."

"Gentleman?" The man in the red plaid coat was certainly not a gentleman.

" 'Cause he's the one that . . ." Laura threw an embarrassed glance toward the conductor, then lowered her eyes. "When Effie was employed in his grand home . . ." Her voice faltered. "I told her, he's gotta help you out, your gentleman. He's gotta take care of you."

The picture was beginning to change, like tiny glass pieces in a kaleidoscope forming and re-forming. Molly had misjudged the man in the red plaid coat. She wondered which of Leadville's millionaires had imposed himself on the second-floor girl.

"So Effie sent a telegram to Denver," the girl was saying.

"Denver? You said Effie worked in Leadville."

Laura nodded. "That's right. She come up there after she was let go."

"Did she tell you the gentleman's name?" Molly asked.

"Oh, no. Effie was very protective of his reputation. She always called him 'my gentleman.' And sure enough, he telegraphed her back. Said to meet him at the Vendome Hotel."

"The Vendome?" Molly felt the muscles in her chest contract. The compartment felt warm and close; it was difficult to breathe.

"That's right," Laura said. "Only he never showed up."

"I must return to my duties." The conductor withdrew a gold watch from his vest, snapped open the cover, and peered at the face. "We will pull into Pine Grove in exactly nine minutes."

"One moment, Mr. Stout." Molly patted the girl's hand. "Please continue."

"Well, the gentleman come to the shop and give Effie

some money and a one-way ticket on the Denver Express. He says she was not to worry. He was gonna make things right with her in Denver. But she told me he was acting nervous, not like his old self. I think she was scared. So she asked me to come to Denver with her. You know, just till she knew everything was gonna be fine. My mistress give me two days off, and Effie used the gentleman's money to get me a round-trip ticket. Soon's the train pulled into Como, she pretended to get off, just like the gentleman told her. When it was all clear, she got back on and—"

"And went to Charles Langford's compartment," Molly said.

"I must protest." The conductor's tone was sharp with astonishment. "Surely, Mrs. Brown, you cannot believe this"—he waved toward the girl huddled beside the window—"this domestic's story has anything to do with a fine gentleman like Mr. Langford."

Molly got to her feet. "I suggest we check Mr. Langford's compartment. I believe the murdered girl's cloak and canvas grip are in the overhead, nicely hidden by a chinchilla coat."

The conductor hesitated, then squared his shoulders and threw open the door. Molly brushed past and led the way down the corridor. She knocked sharply on the first door.

After a moment the door swung open, and Charles Langford peered out, annoyance and concern mingling in his handsome face. His gaze shifted from Molly to the conductor. "Yes? What is it?" he asked.

Molly said, "I believe you have something that belongs to Effie Rogers."

Langford looked at her with unconcealed disdain. "I'm afraid your imagination has outrun my patience, Mrs. Brown," he said finally. He stepped back and started to close the door. The conductor rammed his shoulder against it, holding it open, and Molly slipped inside.

Langford faced the conductor. "If you do not remove this meddlesome woman from my compartment, I shall contact the president of this railroad and have you removed from your position."

"Mrs. Brown believes the dead woman's things are in this compartment," Stout said. "If that is untrue, we shall be on our way with my sincerest apologies."

Molly reached up to the rack and pulled down the chinchilla coat. It fell away in great, heavy folds, enveloping her arms and shoulders, the fur tickling at her nose. Her heart thumped against her ribs. The rack was empty. She looked around the small compartment. Nothing, except Langford's black case. He must have already thrown the cloak and canvas bag overboard.

And then she glimpsed the small rectangle of brown beneath the seat. She dropped to her knees and began tugging at the canvas bag.

"Leave that alone!" Langford shouted. "It is none of your business!"

Out of the corner of her eye, Molly saw the man rear over her, one fist in the air, and the conductor grab his arm. "Now, now, Mr. Langford. We will have no violence."

Molly pulled out the grip, trailing the shabby black cloak across the floor. Then she got to her feet and faced Langford. "Effie threatened to expose your treatment of her, isn't that true? So you came to Leadville with the purpose of murdering her."

Langford turned to the conductor. "I have no idea what this madwoman is raving about."

"Oh, I think you do, Mr. Langford," Stout said, still gripping the other man's arm.

Molly went on: "You couldn't take the chance of meeting Effie at the Vendome after you saw me leaving the lobby, so you decided to entice her to come to Denver and murder her on the train. It was your door that shut just after I saw the poor girl hurled over the ledge. You meant to throw her things overboard, too, but after I started shouting for the conductor, it was too risky for you to attempt to dispose of them. You planned to carry them off the train wrapped in your chinchilla coat. Your plan might have worked, Mr. Langford, if Effie hadn't brought along a companion who knew she did not get off at Como."

Langford pulled his arm free and lurched toward the

opened door, but Molly threw her weight against it, slamming it shut. The conductor wrapped both arms around the other man's chest and wrestled him onto the seat. Standing over him, he said, "You will remain locked in this compartment, Mr. Langford, for the duration of the trip."

"You'll regret this!" Langford shouted, his long legs tangled in the chinchilla coat. "I will see that you never work for another railroad. And this horrible woman will never, never be accepted in society . . ." Suddenly the man doubled over and began sobbing.

Stout ushered Molly into the corridor. From outside came the mournful sounds of brakes screeching and the locomotive whistling as the train jerked into a slower rhythm. Laura was holding on to the window bar muttering over and over, "Poor Effie, tossed off the train."

"He drugged her first, so Effie didn't know what happened." Molly spoke softly. She wondered what would have become of her had she taken the tonic Langford had offered.

Stout inserted a key into the lock and tried the knob. Satisfied, he turned to Molly. "I commend you, Mrs. Brown. The railroad company will honor you."

"Oh, no." Molly held out both hands in protest. "I wouldn't want publicity."

"I quite understand. You are a lady, Mrs. Brown." The conductor smiled and gave her a little bow. Then he began backing toward the gangway as the train eased into a crawl. "We are pulling into Pine Grove," he said. "I must telegraph the police. Be assured that they will meet the train in Denver."

Pale lamplight flooded the platform and washed over the gray stone facade of the Denver Union Station. Steam burst from beneath the cars as Molly stepped from the train, steadied by Stout's helpful hand. She glanced at the crowd milling about: baggage men pulling wagons loaded with suitcases, passengers disembarking from the coach car. Suddenly she saw J.J.'s red head bobbing above the others. He hurried toward her.

"Mol, girl!" She felt herself being lifted off the platform and enclosed in his arms. "Good to have you home again," he said, gently setting her back onto her feet.

"Stand away, stand away!" The shouts came from the station entrance. As the crowd parted, a phalanx of blue-uniformed Denver policemen wielding nightsticks marched to the train and, one by one, swung into the gangway.

"I say, what's going on?" J.J. glanced in the direction of the conductor, starting up the steps after the policemen.

Molly saw Laura huddled nearby, dabbing at her eyes with the handkerchief she'd given her earlier. Walking over, she took the girl's hand and led her back to J.J. "This is Laura," she said. "She'll be staying with us until she returns to Leadville."

J.J. peeled his attention from the blue shadows moving past the window in the first-class compartment, the muffled shouts of protest. "If Molly invited you," he said, still distracted, "then you're most welcome."

The policemen spilled into the gangway and started down the steps, bringing along a tall man with a chinchilla coat thrown over his shoulders, handcuffs gripping his wrists in front. Forming a tight circle, they led the man into the station.

"I say, wasn't that Charles Langford?" J.J. made no effort to conceal his astonishment.

"I hope he hangs," Laura said, her tone vehement.

"No doubt that will be accomplished." Molly saw the way J.J.'s eyebrows rose in puzzlement. Taking hold of his arm, she said, "I have much to tell you, my dear."

He patted her hand. "I take it, Mol, your trip was not dull."

"Oh, J.J.," Molly said, "dull would have been ever so nice."

Miriam Grace Monfredo *is the author of six* Seneca Falls/Glynis Tryon *historical mysteries. The series, set in mid-nineteenth-century America, focuses on the struggle of women and minorities to win their civil rights. The initial book in the series,* Seneca Falls Inheritance, *features the first Women's Rights Convention held in the summer of 1848; the two most recent,* The Stalking Horse *and* Must The Maiden Die, *are set during the years of the American Civil War. In the following story, based on one of history's authentic, unsolved mysteries, Monfredo offers the solution to the disappearance of a Confederate spy who very likely influenced the course of that war.*

A SINGLE SPY

Miriam Grace Monfredo

The storm struck the small Pennsylvania town just after midnight. Lightning jagged over woods and wheat fields, while a long roll of thunder made the young woman, alone in a century-old house, moan in her sleep. She heard the thunder as artillery fire. As the salvo of cannon before Rebels began their doomed charge across pastureland sweeping green below the Union's high ground on Cemetery Ridge. In a matter of hours, thousands would die.

Again came a booming cannonade. The woman fought a tangle of bedsheets, struggling to fully wake because what she heard now must be a series of explosions: Luke's helicopter disintegrating into fragments that fell like hard rain over rice paddies in Vietnam.

Her breath coming in short gasps, the woman sat huddled in the bed with a sheet clutched to her breast, telling herself that the past could not be relived, that dead men did not rise and fight and die again, while a howling wind rattled the casement windows of the house and rain began to beat against the panes. After a minute or two, she forced herself

314

to leave the bed and draw back the drapery on lightning that flashed like strobe lamps. The wind rose to a shriek, the bombardment of light and sound intensifying until an earsplitting crash made the house shake.

The lightning must have struck something nearby. She prayed, while peering downward through the rain, that it hadn't been the garage with her rusting Volkswagen parked inside. The garage, though, looked to be intact. Then, over the wind, came a wail of sirens. And to the north, the sky over Gettysburg was stained bloodred.

At a distance beyond the brick house, mist of the summer dawn drifted across quiet rolling fields. The young woman wiped a hand over her forehead as she stood in her rear yard, staring bleakly at the ruins of an ancient oak. The lightning strike had split its massive trunk, and the wind had ripped it from the ground. Now it lay like a fallen warrior cleaved by broadsword, its lifeline of root, bare and deathly white, dangling above a gaping maw of earth.

She saw something else there. It chilled her, thrusting palely from the raw dirt, but as she began to walk toward it, she heard the rumble of a vehicle pulling into the front drive. Following the metallic clunk of a car door, a man's voice called, "Sara! Sara, are you outside?"

"In the back." She answered with reluctance, but there was no way to avoid him. He was a determined man.

She deliberately moved away from the tree as he came around the corner of the house, the trouser cuffs of his gray sheriff's uniform darkened by the rain-soaked grass. Hair grew shaggy around his neck and clung to the forehead of a lean face, a face younger than hers, although she and he were the same age.

"You all right?" he asked her. "First chance I've had to check on you—"

His words broke off as he glanced toward the tree. "My God, look at that! What a damn shame. That oak must be over a hundred years old—imagine what it must have seen in its time. I always thought it would live forever."

"Nothing lives forever, Josh," she stated in a flat voice, and moved farther from the tree. She wanted to be left alone with the dead.

"And you can't mourn forever, either," he said quietly, reaching up to graze her cheek with his fingers.

Sara, shying from the touch of his hand and the need in his voice, took a step backward. "Did you come for a reason?" she asked him, darting a look at the oak, and suddenly resenting his pine-scented shaving lotion.

He dropped his hand and gave her a long, steady look. "Wanted to make sure you came through the storm all right. Last night's storm," he added.

She caught his meaning, but said only, "I'm fine."

"Lightning struck more than your oak," he went on when she offered no more. "Started a fire up there in the woods by Little Round Top. Rain and the fire department managed to put it out before there was much damage."

Friendly fire. That's what they had told her: Her husband of one year had most likely been killed by friendly fire. She hated the absurd phrase.

"I'm glad to hear it, Josh. Now if you'll excuse me, I have to work." Work at least filled up a day, and she could look no further than each day as it came. There was no future beyond it.

"You can't work," he told her. "There's no power. No phones either. Storm knocked out everything from here to York."

Her electric typewriter would be useless. He knew that. He knew much more than that. They had been children together, high-school and college sweethearts until Luke came. Then, a month ago, they had almost been lovers until Luke came again, his dead eyes watching them in her bed until she'd had to leave it, and Josh.

"Let it go, Sara," he said now, gently. "Can't you just let it go?"

He didn't mean her work. Or maybe he did.

Luke's body had not been recovered. His remains were thought to be in the vicinity of the downed Cobra gunship he'd been piloting to cover a risky medical evacuation. So said the report. Sara had left the high school where she'd taught American history to begin writing letters. She wrote to the men in Luke's platoon, to his commanding officer, to the War Department, the State Department, senators and representatives, President Lyndon Johnson, anyone who might be able to tell her where he had died.

When asked, by those who said they cared, why she needed to know *where,* she couldn't give them a rational answer. Leaving herself open to the usual psychobabble. She was told that her quest had become an obsession, an obsession born of unresolved grief that compelled a search for the unknowable in the unknown past. No, she'd protested again and again; she simply wanted to know where Luke had died. As if the answer would bring him back. But there was no answer, she had been informed again and again; or, if there was, it lay mired in the mud of an abandoned rice field. And then, finally, four days ago, she had come up against the last stone wall: denied a passport visa to North Vietnam.

She watched as Josh disappeared around the house, and waited until the sound of his Ford Galaxy backing out of the drive assured her that he was gone. Then she walked to the uprooted oak and the ghostly remains exhumed by the storm.

Going down on her knees, she raked away dirt with her fingers until she'd completely uncovered the long, pallid bone. When she moved aside larger handfuls of dirt, she found more skeletal parts, and then the skull, partially shattered.

Sara rocked back on her heels, wiping her hands on the knees of her jeans. It was not all that rare, finding human bones in this region of Pennsylvania. During the third summer of the Civil War, thousands of men had been killed in battle on the green fields of Gettysburg; thousands more had died of their wounds within the following days. The Armies of the Potomac and of Northern Virginia had left their dead men and horses to be buried and their wounded to be nursed. It was too overwhelming a mission for one small town to perform. Many bodies, unidentified, were placed in long, shallow trenches. Some were simply put in the earth where they had fallen.

This man, though, had been buried deep beneath a tree standing more than a mile from the battlegrounds. Sara bent forward to rake through the dirt again, looking for brass buttons, copper spurs, metal insignia, or remnants of gold braid that might have survived to tell her something about him; but in the passage of one hundred years the earth had done its work well, and she could find nothing. She wondered, then, if some woman had searched for this man, trying to learn where and how he had died. And had she, too, the woman of long past, been driven to despair by the unknown?

It would be indecent to further expose the remains, Sara decided, if only for the sake of that woman. She bent forward, and while pushing the earth back over the bones in the root-webbed hollow, something sharp scraped her thumb. After brushing away more dirt, she uncovered a small metal box that looked as if it had been coated with tin. She glanced toward the road to make sure there was no one to see it, no one to argue that it belonged to the ages and should be shared by all.

But if it had been Luke buried there, his things should belong only to her. And now the act of lifting the box from the earth gave her some small sense of power where for months she had been denied it.

The lid of the tin box fit so tightly it would not yield, and she had to rummage through the garage for pliers to remove it. When she at last pried it off, she found inside the box a still-intact leather bag. Inside it were rolled sheets of paper, strong paper with rag content that, like carefully stored scrolls of papyrus, had lain protected by the dark of time.

She cautiously unrolled them, fearing they might crumble in the light of day. They held, and with care she spread them over her knees to read the fine, spidery handwriting:

1 July 1863

I, Will Parsons, being born in the year of our Lord eighteen forty six, do swear before God as my witness that what I set forth here is truth. For the sake of my eternal soul, I will put down what has been done this day and will trust no man but only the Lord to judge me.

High overhead, a red-tailed hawk screamed, and distractedly Sara glanced up at the northern sky, where black clouds were fast gathering. More rain. She gingerly lifted the papers, got to her feet, and started for the house.

When buying the property several months before, she had seen the deed and title papers. One Thomas Parsons, occupation schoolteacher, had built the house in 1858, then apparently abandoned it, and it had been some years before another name appeared on the title. What she held here in her hands had been written a century ago. But since the writer had been only seventeen in 1863, and named Will, he could not have been the schoolteacher. His son, perhaps?

Once inside, Sara sat down at the kitchen table beneath a window that overlooked the rear yard and the stricken tree. Rain spattered against the glass as she again smoothed the paper to read.

Five days past, I rode to Chambersburg to collect a debt owed my father. He and my mother had died of fever in the spring, and left little to sustain my two younger sisters. There were rumors of Rebel soldiers advancing from the South, but as my need was urgent I could pay them no mind. Upon reaching my destination, the good man who owed the debt readily repaid it in gold coin. My purpose accomplished, and though it had fallen dark, I then started for home. And soon a fierce rain commenced.

I drove my mule under a tree to wait until the worst of it passed, and moments later found myself surrounded by men in light grayish-blue uniform. They spoke in a strange manner, demanding to know why I was about on such a night. I was forced to dismount, and when the men searched my clothing, they found the gold coin and ordered me to disclose whence it came. I told them true, but they bid me mount again, and led the mule back the way I had just come.

We then reached a camp with many tents, and with small fires sputtering in the dying rain, where I was told once more to dismount and to be seated on the ground. I was sore bewildered, but had done no wrong and did not expect to be accused of such.

Shortly thereafter, a second group of what I now took to be Rebel soldiers arrived at the camp, leading a mare on which sat a wiry, round-shouldered man in civilian garments. When this man had dismounted, the soldiers jostled him none too gently toward a large tent, and all went inside. My captors seemed to heed me not, and after some little time I rose and went toward my tethered mule. Immediately I was seized by two men and urged forward into the tent.

The wiry man sat hunched over a table upon whose surface a map was spread. Beside him stood a man in uniform who resembled a tall and sturdy tree trunk. This man's full brown beard reached well below the collar of his uniform, and he grasped a cigar with which he pointed at the map.

One of the men who held me spoke to him, saying, "General Longstreet, we have apprehended what may be a spy, sir."

The big, bearded man turned to regard me with grave, dark eyes. Then he looked with question at the wiry, hunched man and said, "Harrison, do you know this fellow?"

Harrison shook his head, saying, "He's not with me, General."

"No, I am not a spy," I said to the man Longstreet, more out of concern for my sisters than on my own account. "My name is Will Parsons, and I am only a farmer, on the way to my home, which lies a short distance beyond Gettysburg. My kin await me there. Please do not further detain me, good sir."

He looked long at me with his dark gaze as if to measure the truth of my words, then waved the cigar at the men holding me, after which they bade me sit once more on the ground. I was grateful to be under the tenting and out of the rain, however anxious I might have become.

I then seemed to have been disregarded while the general named Longstreet asked the man Harrison question after question. It fast became evident that this Harrison must himself be a spy, as he told in detail of Union troops in substantial strength marching north by northeast of the Blue Ridge Mountains. This greatly excited the other men present, all save the general, who quietly smoked his fine-smelling cigar and listened in thoughtful fashion.

After a time he said to the soldiers, "Take this man Harrison to see General Lee. I don't like to wake him, but this information cannot wait until morning."

The newspapers had written often of General Lee, who commanded the Rebel army, and thus I became most unsettled. The rumors of invasion must be true.

The soldiers took the spy Harrison out of the tent, and Longstreet followed. I had begun to get to my feet, but he was gone before I could speak. I determined to stay awake until he returned, but weariness overcame me and I slept.

Just before dawn, Longstreet returned to the tent and again studied the map. With apprehension I rose and asked of him, "Sir, if I may speak a word?"

The great shaggy head turned sharply as if he had been unaware of my presence. Again the dark gaze fell upon me, and he said, "You may speak, but it must be quick."

I informed him of my circumstances and again requested his leave to go. "My sisters are alone," I added. "Please allow me to return to them, sir, General Longstreet."

He unaccountably smiled at me. It was a smile of good humor, free of mockery or guile. "How old are you, son?" he asked.

"Seventeen years."

"You are well-spoken for your youth. Your father taught you well. And did he teach you also to be a man of honor?"

"Yes, sir, he did."

"Can you then swear to me that you will not reveal to any man in any manner what you have heard and seen here?"

"I can so swear."

"Do I have your word on it, Will Parsons?"

"You do, sir, General Longstreet."

One of his aides waiting at the tent entrance stated, "General, with all respect, sir, this man is carrying a fair amount of gold coin and—"

"He has explained that to my satisfaction," Longstreet broke in on his soldier. *"We are not here to rob or harm civilians. Give the lad a pass and let him go home."*

Longstreet put his hand on my shoulder and gripped it firmly. "Your word on it," he said.

With that, he picked up the map and strode off into the morning.

Thus I set out to make my way home to what I knew must be my anxious sisters. Would that were all which then came to pass.

For the last few minutes Sara had been conscious of someone banging on her front door. She tried to ignore it, as she had also become keenly aware of the historic significance of what lay before her. When the banging persisted, she shouted to the intruder, "Please come back later! I'm . . . I'm on the phone!"

After a long silence, a gruff male voice responded, "I'm from the telephone company, ma'am. Report says you've got no service."

Hoist by her own petard. "Come back another time," Sara insisted, despite her mild embarrassment.

"Ma'am, I've been sent by the phone company—"

"Damn it! I don't care if you've been sent by God! Another time!"

She waited, impatiently glancing at the papers curled on the tabletop, then jumped from the chair and went to the living room, where from the window she could view the driveway. The last thing she wanted was people tromping around the rear yard, where they could hardly miss the oak and the still partially exposed tomb; although she thought that she'd completely covered the remains.

Relieved to see the phone-company van pulling onto the rain-streaked road, she went back to the kitchen. The gloom outside was dense, and the room had become darker than she'd realized. She flipped a light switch. Nothing. The power was still off.

She had candles. Appropriate for reading a nineteenth-century document, one that should make Civil War historians levitate with joy. She could hardly believe it herself, Will Parson's reference to the mysterious man known to history only as "Harrison."

General James Longstreet had mentioned Harrison briefly in his autobiography, stating that the man had come to him recommended as a good scout by the Confederate secretary of war. Harrison, however, after providing invaluable intelligence about the presence of the Army of the Potomac, on the move and marching north, had inexplicably vanished during the three-day Gettysburg battle.

In the century since, a number of theories—some plausible, some less so—had been put forth to explain Harrison's disappearance, but most historians remained skeptical of them. They couldn't even agree on his given name: some said James, some said Henry. Later, in the autumn of 1863, he was reportedly spotted in Richmond, employed by an acting company. After which Longstreet, by his own account, tried to contact Harrison, but was unsuccessful in locating him.

The man had remained an enigma, one of those shadowy figures who emerge now and then for a moment in time with consequences all out of proportion to the brevity of their appearance. The information that Harrison carried to

Longstreet changed the course not only of Lee's intended invasion of the North, but also, many historians would argue, the course of the Civil War.

Sara stood gazing through the window at the oak shrouded in gray rain. What of the man buried beneath it? She had guessed, when reading Will Parsons's opening declaration—one appearing to be some kind of confession—that it must be him, dead by his own hand; a self-inflicted gunshot that would account for the shattered skull, and after which he'd been buried by others. Now she was not so certain. He struck her as having been a self-respecting, determined young man. Would such a man be likely to take his life? If not, who had been buried there? Surely not the mysterious Harrison, because there was no reason for him to have been anywhere near this house. So who was it?

With a start, Sara realized that she had been so engrossed in Will Parsons's account, and the riddle that was Harrison, that for an unprecedented span of time she had not even thought of Luke. While this seemed something of a betrayal, her guilt felt unexpectedly bearable as she fished candles out of the cluttered kitchen drawer and stood them in a dented pewter candelabra. Then she sat down again to read.

> *I did not arrive home as I had anticipated. On the road into Gettysburg, I came upon a band of mounted men in blue uniforms. They informed me that they belonged to a Union cavalry company. I was then unwillingly escorted up the hill to the cemetery, where, after many long and anxious hours of waiting, a Union officer the men called General Buford rode into the makeshift camp.*
>
> *"Why were you on that road, lad? Coming from the direction of Rebel troops?" asked the man Buford when he had dismounted.*
>
> *Although fair and strong enough of feature, he had a melancholy cast and moved as if in pain. I told him what I had told Longstreet, although my oath given to that man kept me from mention of him.*

"And so, sir, I am merely trying to reach my home," I finished, while Buford regarded me with a keen, quizzical eye.

"Even if this fellow's no Rebel," one of the cavalry soldiers said, *"he may be a Southern sympathizer. Sir, we know this place is alive with Union spies—so why not Rebel ones?"*

Sara stopped squinting at the thin, penned words to look out the window in the direction of Gettysburg. Will Parsons's was truly an astonishing account. It had been only a few years now since theretofore unknown, operational files of the Union army's Bureau of Military Information had been unearthed, bundled with lengths of red tape in the National Archives. In those files had been a record of civilian spies known as the Gettysburg Group. This recent discovery had altered the way historians viewed what had long been considered an almost accidental meeting of the two great armies here in Pennsylvania. But it had been no accident. John Buford's cavalry had been tracking Lee by way of information provided by the Gettysburg spies.

With a sense of wonderment, Sara returned to the startling document before her.

"Well, are you a spy, lad?" General Buford queried me in brusque fashion.

After I declared that I was not, he asked, "How many Confederate corps did you see on that road?"

"I did not count them," I answered in truth.

After being led away, with no knowledge as to whether my replies had been satisfactory, I was made to sit on the slope with my ankles bound. I was given hardtack and a tin cup of coffee and then left beside a stone wall. Some distance away, General Buford sat astride a rail fence, searching the road west through field glasses. On occasion he would swing the glasses south, and the lines around his eyes and mouth would deepen. I surmised he must be looking for the Union troops about which the Rebel spy Harrison had spoken.

The sun slowly dipped below the horizon, and lights had begun to gleam in the town below, when agitated riders galloped into the cemetery camp. One dismounted hurriedly and went at once to Buford.

"General, we followed those Rebs who were in the town. There are Confederate troops, sir, backed all the way up that road. It looks certain that the main body of Lee's army is gathering to move in this direction."

Buford raised the glasses again, and after a time lowered them, nodding slowly. "Lieutenant, find yourself a fresh horse. I need you to take a dispatch south to the infantry, and they're miles behind us. We've got good high ground here, and we'll try to hold it until those troops can get here. But make it clear they need to get here fast!"

After the lieutenant had dashed toward the horses, I heard Buford mutter to himself, "It's damn good ground, and by God, I'll hold it as long as I can." Then he motioned for a lantern to be brought to him, and by its glow he began to write.

When dispatch and courier had departed, Buford went to mount his horse. The rope around my ankles hindered my struggle to rise, but I called, "General Buford, if you please, sir! I ask your leave to go to my home. I am no part of this fight."

"You're part of it, son, whether you like it or not. I don't reckon you're a spy, but you know too much now for me to let you go."

"Sir, my sisters are alone. If there is to be a battle, I need to be with them. I give you my word of honor, General, sir, that I will not speak of anything I have heard here. I willingly swear it on my parents' grave." And I pointed to the tombstones behind him.

Buford did not turn in the saddle, but instead seemed to consider me awhile. Then he shook his head, saying, "Too much at stake here—can't let you go tonight. Maybe in the morning, but you've got to swear not to talk. You have to do that."

"I do so swear."

Buford gave me a short nod and rode off in the direction of the Lutheran Theological Seminary.

I spent an uneasy night, sleeping little, and a fine rain began just at dawn. The Union camp was astir with great excitement on the part of the cavalry soldiers. Their horses remained tethered, however, so I reasoned that there would be no battle for a time.

In this I was profoundly mistaken. Rebel gunfire from the west began almost immediately thereafter.

In the ensuing commotion, I was left to myself. I did not delay in loosing my bonds while determining to find my mule, as it was a good beast and had cost my father dear. Fortune led me to where it was tied, after which I set out with all due haste. I could hear an increase in the rifle fire behind me, and now I could see to the south many colorful flags flying in the long blue lines of approaching Union infantry.

When I reached the main square of Gettysburg, there were few townsfolk in sight. I imagined that prudence kept them in their cellars, but as I now heard a great amount of shouting and rifle fire, I despaired of reaching my own home without further interference.

I was attempting to decide which path would be most sensible to take, when I was seized roughly from behind and pushed some distance down the road and into a wood-frame house. I found myself confronted by a number of agitated citizens, some of whom were known to me.

"From where were you coming, Will Parsons?" asked one man, a shopkeeper stout and hardy.

Another man followed with, "And where were you bound in such haste?"

"I am attempting to reach my home," I answered, wondering if I would again be required to recount my oft-told story.

"I would not have guessed you to be a Rebel sympathizer, Will Parsons," said the stout shopkeeper. "But why else would you have been seen yesterday morn riding from the camp of the enemy—and without drawing fire from Johnny Reb? You had best explain this to our satisfaction."

Alas, my dilemma became all too clear. There was no explanation possible. Not without breaking my word to the Rebel General Longstreet, or to the Union General Buford. And this I could not do.

"Speak up, Will Parsons," demanded the shopkeeper, "or it will go hard with you! We have reports that the whole Rebel army is out there."

"Hold!" said a man I knew to be a lawyer. He turned to me, saying, "I knew your father, Will. A good and honest man. Surely he would turn in his grave if he thought you were in league with the enemy."

"I am not with them," I said as firmly as my quaking spirit would allow. I did not know what else I might say without compromising my honor.

Gunfire crackled nearby as if soldiers were advancing into the town. And now shouting could be heard in the road outside. The faces of the men around me were grim, and I confess that I felt like a lone tree buffeted by winds that blew from every side.

"Very well, Will Parsons," said the lawyer, "we will give you fair opportunity to prove your loyalty. Bring out the prisoner," he said to several others.

These men went into another room, and when they returned they held between them, to my dismay, the Rebel spy Harrison. And, with even more dismay, I guessed what would be asked of me.

"Have you seen this man before, Will Parsons?" the shopkeeper questioned. "Inside the enemy camp which you were seen leaving? We believe him to be a Rebel spy who has done grave harm."

In the faintness of heart that I experienced, my father's visage rose before me. And I then remembered that, in better times, my family had spent many a winter evening before the fire, each taking our turn at reading aloud from William Shakespeare's work, which my father greatly admired. Indeed, hence came my name. I now imagined myself again on that warm, familial stage, *where I had been encouraged to play my part with fervor. I warned myself to caution, however, as I did not think, given the circumstances, that it would be well met if I were to quote here Shakespeare's: "When sorrows come/they come not single spies/but in battalions."*

Thus I wordlessly cocked my head to one side, took chin in hand, and narrowed my eyes at the hapless Harrison as if to study him with diligence. He, no slouch as actor himself, returned my gaze without expression.

"Speak up, Will Parsons! Have you seen this man before, embraced by the enemy?" the shopkeeper repeated.

"His face," I answered, "does perhaps look some familiar. But I cannot say that I have seen him in the enemy camp."

"Look closely! Are you certain you did not see him there?"

"I cannot say. Of that I am certain."

Harrison still regarded me with no expression; but when, at a storm of rifle fire, the other men turned toward the door, his eye closed and opened quickly in an unmistakable wink.

From directly outside came a sharp volley of gunshots. One of the men barked, "To the cellar, fast!" and he and the others raced to a stairway and thumped down it.

Harrison rushed to the door, as did I, and while he pulled it open he said, "You are a fair actor, lad. It is my own calling, you know. Thank you, my friend."

"No thanks are due," said I.

With that, he stepped into the road. I followed with trepidation. The air outside was thick with smoke and acrid with the smell of gunpowder, and many shots were being exchanged. And suddenly a young man—a Rebel soldier by his uniform—fell wounded a short distance away. He succeeded, nonetheless, in raising his revolver and aiming it directly at my head, as if in his pain he imagined I had been the one who shot him. I confess I believed that my time had come.

Then, with nimbleness of step, Harrison moved to stand directly between the soldier and myself, shouting to him, "No! Don't shoot. He is a friend—"

The gun discharged. Harrison staggered backward against me. I caught him as he fell and we both went down in the road, while the wounded soldier crawled away.

I tried to lift Harrison's head, but it was spilling blood, and when I felt for heartbeats, there were none. The soldiers on the road moved on, and I sat there in the dust, holding the dead man who had saved me.

Inside the house several heads now appeared at a window, and one of the men yelled, "Good work, Will Parsons! You must have hit him square. We should not have doubted your father's son."

Sara, finding her vision blurred by tears, brushed at her eyes. She hadn't cried for months. Not since the first word about Luke. And now she couldn't seem to stop. She rose and went to get a Kleenex, then wiped her eyes while looking down at the papers. She knew now, of course, who had been buried beneath the tree. The spy killed by friendly fire.

Picking up the last sheet of paper, she read that, as she had guessed, Will Parsons had brought Harrison's body back on the mule.

And thus my account is nearly at an end.

I placed Harrison's remains deep beneath a stout young oak tree. He had been a Rebel spy, an invader, but how could I call him enemy? This is a fearsome war indeed, that good men like Harrison and Longstreet and Buford must fight one another and die in the land their own fathers' blood had bequeathed them.

I will bury this account with Harrison, so that if he be found here, his kin will know where he lays, and that he died to spare another man from death.

Then I shall gather my sisters and we will leave this place. We have relations in Nebraska and can travel

*there with the gold that brought me to this pass. For
although there will be small danger while the town is in
the midst of battle, the citizens of Gettysburg must at
some time recall that I had carried no gun with which
to shoot Harrison. They are good men, defending their
homes and their families, and they might well think me
a traitor. My conscience does not tell me this, and I
believe that I have done no wrong, but I must leave it
to the Lord to decide.*

Sara read this last line again, and beneath it the firmly
set signature. She wondered if the young man and his sisters had left before the end of the terrible three-day battle.
If so, Will Parsons would not have witnessed the Army of
Northern Virginia's defeat, and with it the end to a threatened invasion of the North. Historians continued to debate
the reasons for the defeat, but most could agree that Harrison's report had prodded Robert E. Lee to the crossroads
of Gettysburg. And that John Buford's hold on the good
high ground had been vital to the Union success.

Outside Sara's kitchen window, the rainy drizzle had
ceased, and now long tendrils of mist wavering upward
gave her the illusion that there rose the ghosts of those lost
in the war. She leaned forward when she suddenly also saw
there, amid spikes of grass poking through the flooded yard
like rice sprouts in a paddy, the indistinct figure of a dark-
haired young woman; she was kneeling in a silvery pool,
dressed in baggy trousers and slight of frame like Sara herself, but with long almond eyes. The woman was carefully
lifting things from the water, things as stark and white as
bone. She turned with them in her arms and seemed to gaze
at Sara, before she began replacing them, burying them
again beneath the watery grasses.

The image faded gradually and not until Sara's weeping
was spent.

At last she rolled the document between her fingers. Will
Parsons's account had brought to her a gift of grace, and
while historians, if they knew, would never forgive her, this
gift was not to be shared. She would bury the tin box and

its contents with Harrison's remains and let them lie in solitary peace.

Wars and their dead cast behind them timeless shadows. But now, on this day, she could plant for the future another stout young oak.

MARGARET COEL

THE EAGLE CATCHER

When tribal chairman Harvey Castle of the Arapahos is found murdered, the evidence points to his own nephew. But Father John O'Malley doesn't believe the young man is a killer. And in his quest for truth, O'Malley gets a rare glimpse into the Arapaho life few outsiders ever see—and a crime fewer could imagine...

❑ 0-425-15463-7/$6.50

THE GHOST WALKER

Father John O'Malley comes across a corpse lying in a ditch beside the highway. When he returns with the police, it is gone. Together, an Arapaho lawyer and Father John must draw upon ancient Arapaho traditions to stop a killer, explain the inexplicable, and put a ghost to rest...

❑ 0-425-15961-2/$5.99

THE DREAM STALKER

Father John O'Malley and Arapaho attorney Vicky Holden return to face a brutal crime of greed, false promises, and shattered dreams...

❑ 0-425-16533-7/$5.99

THE STORY TELLER

When the Arapaho storyteller discovers that a sacred tribal artifact is missing from a local museum, Holden and O'Malley begin a deadly search for the sacred treasure.

❑ 0-425-17025-X/$6.50

Prices slightly higher in Canada

Payable by Visa, MC or AMEX only ($10.00 min.), No cash, checks or COD. Shipping & handling: US/Can. $2.75 for one book, $1.00 for each add'l book; Int'l $5.00 for one book, $1.00 for each add'l. Call (800) 788-6262 or (201) 933-9292, fax (201) 896-8569 or mail your orders to:

Penguin Putnam Inc.   Bill my: ❑ Visa ❑ MasterCard ❑ Amex _____ (expires)
P.O. Box 12289, Dept. B
Newark, NJ 07101-5289   Card# _____
Please allow 4-6 weeks for delivery.
Foreign and Canadian delivery 6-8 weeks.   Signature _____

Bill to:

Name _____

Address _____ City _____

State/ZIP _____ Daytime Phone # _____

Ship to:

Name _____ Book Total $ _____

Address _____ Applicable Sales Tax $ _____

City _____ Postage & Handling $ _____

State/ZIP _____ Total Amount Due $ _____

This offer subject to change without notice.   Ad # 743 (3/00)

New York Times Bestselling Author

ANDREW M. GREELEY

❏ **HAPPY ARE THE OPPRESSED** 0-515-11921-0/$6.99
"Ryan is unforgettable."—*Publishers Weekly*

❏ **HAPPY ARE THOSE WHO MOURN** 0-515-11761-7/$6.99
"A fascinating novelist...with a rare, possibly unmatched point of
view."—*Los Angeles Times*

❏ **HAPPY ARE THE POOR IN SPIRIT** 0-515-11502-9/$6.99
"Greeley is a wizard at spinning a yarn."—Associated Press

❏ **HAPPY ARE THE PEACE MAKERS** 0-515-11075-2/$6.99
"The unflappable Blackie Ryan could definitely become
habit forming!"—*Publishers Weekly*

❏ **WAGES OF SIN** 0-515-11222-4/$6.99
"The mystery keeps you guessing until nearly the last page."
—*USA Weekend*

❏ **HAPPY ARE THE MERCIFUL** 0-515-10726-3/$6.99
"Greeley uncover(s) the passions hidden in men and women."—UPI

❏ **FALL FROM GRACE**   0-515-11404-9/$6.99
"Love, deception, and scandal."—Associated Press

Prices slightly higher in Canada

PPayable by Visa, MC or AMEX only ($10.00 min.), No cash, checks or COD. Shipping & handling:
US/Can. $2.75 for one book, $1.00 for each add'l book; Int'l $5.00 for one book, $1.00 for each
add'l. Call (800) 788-6262 or (201) 933-9292, fax (201) 896-8569 or mail your orders to:

Penguin Putnam Inc. P.O. Box 12289, Dept. B Newark, NJ 07101-5289 Please allow 4-6 weeks for delivery. Foreign and Canadian delivery 6-8 weeks.	Bill my: ❏ Visa ❏ MasterCard ❏ Amex _____ (expires) Card# _____ Signature _____

Bill to:

Name _____

Address _____City _____

State/ZIP _____Daytime Phone # _____

Ship to:

Name _____Book Total $ _____

Address _____Applicable Sales Tax $ _____

City _____Postage & Handling $ _____

State/ZIP _____Total Amount Due $ _____

This offer subject to change without notice.   Ad # 465 (3/00)

In eighteenth century London, Sir John Fielding, the blind magistrate who cofounded London's first police force with the help of Jeremy, his young assistant and ward, crime doesn't stand a chance...

BRUCE ALEXANDER

The Sir John Fielding Mysteries

MURDER ON GRUB STREET
❑ 0-425-15550-1/$6.50

BLIND JUSTICE
❑ 0-425-15007-0/$6.50

WATERY GRAVE
❑ 0-425-16036-X/$6.50

PERSON OR PERSONS UNKNOWN
❑ 0-425-16566-3/$6.50

JACK, KNAVE AND FOOL
❑ 0-425-17120-5/$6.50

Prices slightly higher in Canada

Payable by Visa, MC or AMEX only ($10.00 min.), No cash, checks or COD. Shipping & handling: US/Can. $2.75 for one book, $1.00 for each add'l book; Int'l $5.00 for one book, $1.00 for each add'l. Call (800) 788-6262 or (201) 933-9292, fax (201) 896-8569 or mail your orders to:

Penguin Putnam Inc.   Bill my: ❑ Visa ❑ MasterCard ❑ Amex _____ (expires)
P.O. Box 12289, Dept. B   Card# _____
Newark, NJ 07101-5289   Signature _____
Please allow 4-6 weeks for delivery.
Foreign and Canadian delivery 6-8 weeks.

Bill to:
Name _____
Address _____ City _____
State/ZIP _____ Daytime Phone # _____
Ship to:
Name _____ Book Total $ _____
Address _____ Applicable Sales Tax $ _____
City _____ Postage & Handling $ _____
State/ZIP _____ Total Amount Due $ _____
This offer subject to change without notice.   Ad # 674 (3/00)

Miriam Grace Monfredo

*brings to life one of the most exciting periods
in our nation's history—the mid-1800s—when the passionate struggles
of suffragettes, abolitionists, and other heroes touched the lives of every
American, including a small-town librarian named Glynis Tryon...*

__**BLACKWATER SPIRITS**   0-425-15266-9/$5.99

*Glynis Tryon, no stranger to political controversy, is fighting
the prejudice against the Seneca Iroquois. And the issue
becomes personal when one of Glynis's Iroquois friends is
accused of murder...*

__**NORTH STAR CONSPIRACY**   0-425-14720-7/$6.50

__**SENECA FALLS INHERITANCE**

                                                    0-425-14465-8/$5.99

__**THROUGH A GOLD EAGLE**   0-425-15898-5/$6.50

*When abolitionist John Brown is suspected of moving counter-
feit bills, Glynis is compelled to launch her own campaign for
freedom—to free an innocent man.*

Prices slightly higher in Canada

Payable by Visa, MC or AMEX only ($10.00 min.), No cash, checks or COD. Shipping & handling:
US/Can. $2.75 for one book, $1.00 for each add'l book; Int'l $5.00 for one book, $1.00 for each
add'l. Call (800) 788-6262 or (201) 933-9292, fax (201) 896-8569 or mail your orders to:

Penguin Putnam Inc.   Bill my: ❏ Visa ❏ MasterCard ❏ Amex _____(expires)
P.O. Box 12289, Dept. B
Newark, NJ 07101-5289   Card# _____
Please allow 4-6 weeks for delivery.   Signature _____
Foreign and Canadian delivery 6-8 weeks.

__Bill to:__
Name _____
Address _____City _____
State/ZIP _____Daytime Phone # _____
__Ship to:__
Name _____Book Total $ _____
Address _____Applicable Sales Tax $ _____
City _____Postage & Handling $ _____
State/ZIP _____Total Amount Due $ _____

This offer subject to change without notice.   Ad # 649 (3/00)